# THE DAY WATCH

In Russia, the three volumes of the *Night Watch* trilogy have sold over two million hardcovers between them. *The Night Watch* has been adapted into an internationally successful film, which has been distributed round the world. Sergei Lukyanenko lives in Moscow.

Also by Sergei Lukyanenko

*The Night Watch*
*The Twilight Watch*

# SERGEI LUKYANENKO

# THE DAY WATCH

arrow books

Published by Arrow Books 2008

2 4 6 8 10 9 7 5 3 1

First published in Russian under the title Дневой Дозор by
Издателъство АСТ, 2004

First published in Great Britain in 2007 by
William Heinemann
The Random House Group Limited
20 Vauxhall Bridge Road, London SW1V 2SA

www.rbooks.co.uk

Addresses for companies within The Random House Group Limited can be found at:
www.randomhouse.co.uk/offices.htm

The Random House Group Limited Reg. No. 954009

A CIP catalogue record for this book
is available from the British Library

ISBN 9780099489931

The Random House Group Limited supports The Forest Stewardship Council (FSC), the
leading international forest certification organisation. All our titles that are printed on
Greenpeace approved FSC certified paper carry the FSC logo. Our paper procurement policy
can be found at www.rbooks.co.uk/environment

**Mixed Sources**
Product group from well-managed
forests and other controlled sources
www.fsc.org Cert no. TT-COC-2139
© 1996 Forest Stewardship Council

Typeset by Palimpsest Book Production Limited, Grangemouth, Stirlingshire
Printed and bound in Great Britain by CPI Cox & Wyman, Reading RG1 8EX

The distribution of this text has been banned as injurious to the cause of the Light.

*The Night Watch*


The distribution of this text has been banned as injurious to the cause of the Dark.

*The Day Watch*

The coincidence of any names, titles or events in this book with human reality is entirely accidental and fortuitous.

## Story One

# UNAUTHORISED PERSONNEL PERMITTED

# PROLOGUE

THE ENTRANCE DID not inspire respect. The coded lock was broken and not working, the floor was littered with the trampled butts of cheap cigarettes. Inside the lift the walls were covered with illiterate graffiti, in which the word 'Spartak' figured as often as the usual crude obscenities; the plastic buttons had been burned through with cigarettes and painstakingly plugged with chewing-gum that was now rock-hard.

The door into the apartment on the fourth floor was a good match for the entrance: some hideous old kind of Soviet artificial leather, cheap aluminium numbers barely held up by their crookedly inserted screws.

Natasha hesitated for a moment before she pressed the doorbell. She must be insane to hope for anything from a place like this. If you were so crazy or desperate that you decided to try magic, you could just open the newspaper, switch on the TV or listen to the radio. There were serious spiritualist salons, experienced mediums with internationally recognised diplomas ... It was all still a con, of course. But at least you'd be in pleasant surroundings, with pleasant people, not like this last resort for hopeless losers.

She rang the bell anyway. She didn't want to waste the time she'd spent on the journey.

For a few moments it seemed that the apartment was empty. Then she heard hasty footsteps, the steps of someone in a hurry whose worn slippers are slipping off their feet as they shuffle along. For a brief instant the tiny spy-hole went dark, then the lock grated and the door opened.

'Oh, Natasha, is it? Come in, come in . . .'

She had never liked people who spoke too familiarly from the very first meeting. There ought to be a little more formality at first.

But the woman who had opened the door was already pulling her into the apartment, clutching her unceremoniously by the hand, and with an expression of such sincere hospitality on her ageing, brightly made-up face that Natasha didn't feel strong enough to object.

'My friend told me that you . . .' Natasha began.

'I don't know, I don't know about that, my dear,' said her hostess, waving her hands in the air. 'Oh, don't take your shoes off, I was just going to clean the place up . . . oh, all right then, I'll try to find you a pair of slippers.'

Natasha looked around, concealing her disgust with difficulty.

The hall wasn't so very small, but it was crammed incredibly full. The light bulb hanging from the ceiling was dull, maybe thirty watts at best, but even that couldn't conceal the general squalor. The hallstand was heaped high with clothes, including a musquash winter coat to feed the moths. The lino of the small area of floor that could be seen was an indistinct grey colour. Natasha's hostess must have been planning her cleaning session for a long time.

'Your name's Natasha, isn't it, my daughter? Mine's Dasha.'

Dasha was fifteen or twenty years older than her. At least. She could have been Natasha's mother, but with a mother like that you'd want to hang yourself . . . A pudgy figure, with dirty, dull hair and bright nail varnish peeling from her fingernails, wearing a washed-out house coat and crumbling slippers on her bare feet. Her toenails glittered with nail varnish too. God, how vulgar!

'Are you a seer?' Natasha asked. And in her own mind she cried: 'What a fool I am.'

Dasha nodded. She bent down and extracted a pair of rubber slippers from a tangled heap of footwear. The most idiotic kind of slippers ever invented – with all those rubber prongs sticking out on the inside. A Yogi's dream. Some of them had fallen off long before, but that didn't make the slippers look any more comfortable.

'Put them on!' Dasha suggested joyfully.

As if hypnotised, Natasha took off her sandals and put on the slippers. Goodbye, tights. She was bound to end up with a couple of ladders. Even in her famous Omsa tights with their famous Lycra. Everything in this world was a swindle invented by cunning fools. And for some reason intelligent people always fell for it.

'Yes, I'm a seer,' Dasha declared as she attentively supervised the donning of the slippers. 'I got it from my grandma. And my mum too. They were all seers, they all helped people, it runs in our family . . . Come through into the kitchen, Natasha, I haven't tidied up the rooms yet . . .'

Still cursing herself for being so stupid, Natasha went into the kitchen, which fulfilled all her expectations. A heap of dirty dishes in the sink and a filthy table – as they appeared, a cockroach crawled lazily off the table-top and round under it. A sticky floor. The windows had obviously not been spring-cleaned and the ceiling was fly-spotted.

'Sit down.' Dasha deftly pulled out a stool from under the table and moved it over to the place of honour – between the table and the fridge, a convulsively twitching Saratov.

'Thank you, I'll stand.' Natasha had made her mind up definitely not to sit down. The stool inspired even less confidence than the table or the floor. 'Dasha . . . That's Darya?'

'Yes, Darya.'

'Darya, I really only wanted to find out . . .'

The woman shrugged. She flicked the switch on the electric kettle – probably the only object in the kitchen that didn't look as if it had been retrieved from a rubbish tip. She looked at Natasha.

'Find out? There's nothing to find out. Everything's just as clear as can be.'

For a moment Natasha had an unpleasant, oppressive sensation, as if there wasn't enough light in the kitchen. Everything went grey, the agonised rumbling of the refrigerator and the traffic outside on the avenue fell silent. She wiped the icy perspiration from her forehead. It was the heat. The summer, the heat, the long journey in the metro, the crush in the trolleybus . . . Why hadn't she taken a taxi? She'd sent away the driver with the car – well, she'd been embarrassed to give anyone even a hint of where she was going and why . . . but why hadn't she taken a taxi?

'Your husband's left you, Natashenka,' Darya said affectionately. 'Two weeks ago. Left all of a sudden, packed, threw his things into a suitcase and just upped and left you. Without any quarrels, without any arguments. He left the apartment, left the car. And he went to the other woman, that pretty young bitch with black eyebrows . . . but you're not old yet, my daughter.'

This time Natasha didn't even react to the words 'my daughter'. She was trying desperately to remember what she'd told her friend and what she hadn't. She didn't think she'd mentioned black eyebrows. Although the girl really did have dark skin, and black hair . . . Natasha was again overcome by a wild, blind fury.

'And I know why he left, Natashenka . . . Forgive me for calling you my daughter, you're a strong woman, used to making up your own mind about things, but you're all like my own daughters to me ... You didn't have any children, Natasha. Did you?'

'No,' Natasha whispered.

'But why not, my dear?' the seer asked, shaking her head reproachfully. 'He wants a daughter, right?'

'Yes, a daughter ...'

'Then why didn't you have one?' Darya asked with a shrug. 'I've got five children. Two of them went into the army, the eldest. One daughter's married, she's nursing her baby now, the other's studying. And the youngest, the wild one ...' She waved her hand through the air. 'Sit down, why don't you ...'

Natasha reluctantly lowered herself onto the stool, holding her handbag firmly on her knees. Trying to seize the initiative, she said:

'It's just the way life worked out. Well ... I would have had a child for him, but you can't ruin your career for that.'

'That's true too.' The seer didn't try to argue. She rubbed her face with her hands. 'It's your choice ... Right then, you want to bring him back? But why did he leave? The other woman's already carrying his child ... and she made a real effort too. Listening to him, and sympathising with him, and getting up to all sorts of tricks in bed ...'You had a good man, the kind every woman wants to get. Do you want to bring him back? Even now?'

Natasha pursed her lips.

'Yes.'

The seer sighed.

'We *can* bring him back ... we *can* ...' Her tone of voice had changed subtly, become firm and emphatic. '... only it won't be easy. Just bringing him back isn't all that hard, it's keeping him that's the problem!'

'I want to anyway.'

'All of us, my daughter, have our own magic inside us.' Darya leaned forward across the table. Her eyes seemed to be drilling right through Natasha. 'Simple, ancient female magic. With all your ambitions, you've completely forgotten about it, and that's a mistake. But never mind. I'll help you. Only we'll have to do everything in three stages.'

She knocked gently on the table.

'The first thing . . . I'll give you a love potion. This is not a great sin . . . The potion will bring your man back home. It will bring him back, but it won't keep him there.'

Natasha nodded uncertainly. The idea of dividing the spell into 'three stages' seemed inappropriate somehow – especially coming from this woman in this apartment . . .

'The second thing . . . Your rival's child must never be born. If it is, you won't be able to keep your man. So you'll have to commit a great sin, destroy an innocent child in the womb . . .'

'What do you mean?' Natasha said, shuddering. 'I'm not going to end up in court!'

'I'm not talking about poison, Natashenka. I'll make a pass with my hands' – and the seer did just that with her open palms – 'and then clap them . . . And the job's done, the sin's committed. No courts involved.'

Natasha said nothing.

'Only I won't take that sin on myself,' said Darya, crossing herself hurriedly. 'I'll help you if you like, but then *you'll* have to answer to God!'

Evidently taking silence as consent, she continued:

'The third thing . . . You'll have a child yourself. I'll help with that too. You'll have a beautiful, clever daughter who'll be a support to you and a joy to your husband. Then all your troubles will be over.'

'Are you serious about all this?' Natasha asked in a quiet voice. 'You can really do all this . . . ?'

'I'll tell you how it is,' said Darya, standing up. 'You say "yes", and it will all happen. Your husband will come back tomorrow and the day after tomorrow your rival will miscarry. And I won't take any money from you until you get pregnant. But afterwards I will – and I'll take a lot, I tell you that now, I swear by Christ the Lord.'

Natasha gave a crooked smile.

'And what if I cheat you and don't bring you the money? After everything's already happened . . .'

She stopped short. The seer was looking at her sternly, saying nothing. With an air of gentle sympathy, like a mother looking at a foolish daughter . . .

'You won't cheat me, Natashenka. Just think about it for a moment and you'll realise it's not even worth trying.'

Natasha swallowed hard. She tried to make a joke of it:

'So it's cash on delivery?'

'Ah, my little businesswoman,' Darya said ironically. 'Who's going to love you, so practical and clever? A woman should always have some foolishness in her . . . Ah, yes . . . cash on delivery. Delivery of all three items.'

'How much?'

'Five.'

'You want *five*?' Natasha burst out and broke off. 'I thought it was going to be a lot less than that.'

'If you just want to get your husband back, that will be cheaper. Only then, after a while, he'll go away again. But I'm offering you real help, a certain cure.'

'I want to do it,' Natasha said with a nod. What was happening felt slightly unreal. So that was all there was to it, just a clap of the hands – and the unborn child would disappear? Another clap – and she would bear her beloved idiot husband a child of her own?

'Do you take the sin upon yourself?' the seer asked insistently.

'What sin is there in that?' Natasha retorted, her irritation suddenly breaking through. 'Every woman's committed that sin at least once! And perhaps there isn't anything there anyway!'

The seer pondered, as if listening to something. She nodded her head.

'There is . . . And I think it's definitely a daughter.'

'I'll take it,' said Natasha, still irritated. 'I'll take all the sins on myself, any you like. Do we have a deal?'

The seer looked at her sternly, disapprovingly: 'That's not right, my daughter . . . All the sins. Who knows what sins I might decide to hand over to you? My own, somebody else's . . . and then you would have to answer to God.'

'We'd sort it out somehow.'

Darya sighed:

'Oh, these young people are so foolish. Do you think He wastes his time rummaging about in people's sins? Every sin leaves its own trace, and the judgement fits the trace . . . But all right, don't be afraid. I won't make you answerable for anybody else's sins.'

'I'm not afraid.'

The seer didn't seem to be listening to her any more. She was sitting there as if she was listening alertly to something else. Then she shrugged:

'All right . . . let's get the job done. Give me your hand!'

Natasha held out her right hand uncertainly, keeping a worried eye on her diamond ring. It didn't come off her finger very easily, but . . .

'Oh!'

The seer had pricked her little finger so quickly and deftly that Natasha hadn't felt a thing. She froze, dumbfounded, watching the red drop welling up. As if this was all perfectly routine, Darya dropped the medical needle onto a dirty plate encrusted with old borscht. The needle was flat, with a sharp little point – the kind they use to take blood in laboratories.

'Don't be afraid, everything's sterile, the needles are disposable.'

'What do you think you're doing?' Natasha tried to pull her hand away, but Darya shifted her grip with a surprisingly powerful and precise movement.

'Stop, you idiot! Or I'll have to prick you again!'

She took a small chemist's bottle of dark-brown glass out of her pocket. The label had been washed off, but poorly, the first letters were still visible: 'Tinc . . .'. She deftly twisted out the cork, set the bottle down and shook Natasha's little finger over it. The drop of blood fell into the bottle.

'Some people believe,' the seer said contentedly, 'that the more blood there is in a potion, the stronger it will be. It's not true. The blood in it has to be good quality, but the quantity makes no difference at all . . .'

The medicine woman opened the fridge and took out a fifty-gram bottle of Privet vodka. Natasha remembered her driver calling that kind of vodka 'the reanimator'.

A few drops of the vodka went onto a wisp of cotton wool that was wound round Natasha's little finger. The medicine woman held the bottle out to Natasha.

'Want some?'

Natasha suddenly had a vivid vision of herself waking up the next morning – somewhere at the far end of the city, robbed, raped and not remembering a single thing about what had happened. She shook her head.

'Well, I'll have a drop.' Darya raised the 'reanimator' to her lips and drained the vodka in a single gulp. 'That's a bit easier . . . for working. And you, you've no reason to be afraid of me. I don't make my living by robbing people.'

The last few remaining drops of vodka also went into the little brown bottle. And then, quite unperturbed by Natasha's curious gaze, the seer added salt, sugar, hot water from the kettle and a little powder with a strong smell of vanilla.

'What is that?' asked Natasha.

'Have you got a cold? It's vanilla.'

The medicine woman held the little bottle out to her.

'Take it.'

'Is that all?'

'Yes, that's it. You get your husband to drink it. Can you manage that? You can put it in tea, or even in vodka — but that's not the best way.'

'But where's the . . . magic?'

'The magic?'

Natasha felt like a fool again. Her voice almost broke into a shout as she said:

'This is a drop of my blood, a drop of vodka, sugar, salt and vanilla!'

'And water,' Darya added. She put her hands on her hips and looked at Natasha ironically. 'What did you expect? Dried eye of toad? Oriole's testicles? Or for me to blow my nose into it? What do you want — ingredients or effect?'

Natasha didn't answer, overwhelmed. And Darya continued, no longer trying to conceal her mockery: 'My dear girl, if I'd wanted to impress you, then I would have done. Have no doubt about it. What matters is not what's in the bottle, but who made it. Don't you worry, go home and give it to your husband. Will he be coming round again?'

'Yes . . . in the evening, he phoned to say he'd come and collect a few things . . .' she mumbled.

'Let him collect them, only you give him some tea. Tomorrow he'll bring the things back again. That is, if you let him in, of

course.' Darya laughed. 'All right then . . . There's one more thing
we need to do. Do you take this sin on yourself?'

'I do.' Natasha suddenly realised that she no longer felt entirely
able to laugh at what she had said. There was something here that
wasn't funny. The seer had made her promise far too seriously.
And if her husband did come back tomorrow . . .

'Your word, my deed . . .' Darya slowly drew her hands apart
and began speaking rapidly: 'Red water, others' grief and rotten
seed and evil breed . . . What was is no more, what was not will
not be . . . Return to the void, you are dissolved without trace,
by my will, at my word . . .'

Her voice fell to an incoherent whisper. She continued to move
her lips for a minute. Then she clapped her hands hard.

It must have been a trick of the imagination but Natasha
thought she felt a gust of icy-cold wind blow through the
kitchen. Her heart started pounding, she felt a shiver run down
her spine.

Darya gave her head a shake, looked at Natasha and nodded:

'That's all. Go now, my dear. Go home, my daughter, and wait
for your husband.'

Natasha got up. She asked:

'But what . . . when do I . . . ?'

'When you get pregnant, you'll remember about me yourself.
I'll wait for three months . . . and then if I'm still waiting — don't
blame me . . .'

Natasha nodded. She swallowed hard to keep down the lump
that had risen in her throat. Somehow she now believed utterly
in everything the seer had promised . . . and at the same time, it
was painfully clear to her that in three months' time, if everything
really did work out, she would be reluctant to pay the woman.
She would be tempted to put it all down to coincidence . . . why
should she give this filthy charlatan five thousand dollars?

And yet she realised that she would. She might drag it out until the very last day, but she would bring her the money.

Because she would remember the clap of those unmanicured hands and that wave of cold that had suddenly spread through the kitchen.

'Go now,' the seer repeated with gentle insistence. 'I still have to cook supper and clean up the apartment. Go on, go on . . .'

Natasha went out into the dark hall, took off the slippers with a sigh of relief and put on her shoes. Her tights seemed to have survived the ordeal . . . that was certainly more than she'd dared hope for . . .

She looked back at the seer and tried to find the right words. Should she thank her, ask her about some detail, maybe even make a joke – if she could manage to, of course . . .

But Darya had completely forgotten her. The seer's eyes were wide open and she was staring at the closed door, feebly waving her hands through the air in front of her as she whispered:

'Who . . . who . . . who?'

The next moment the door behind Natasha opened with a sudden crash and the hall was instantly full of people: two men were holding the seer firmly by the arms and another had walked quickly through into the kitchen – without looking around him first: he obviously knew the layout of the apartment very well. A young, black-haired girl had appeared beside Natasha. All the men were dressed in a simple and somehow deliberately inconspicuous manner: T-shirts and the same shorts that ninety per cent of the male population of Moscow was wearing in this incredible heat. Natasha suddenly had the frightening thought that clothes like that were something like the unobtrusive grey suits worn by agents of the special services.

'That's awful,' the girl said, looking at Natasha and shaking her head. 'How disgusting, Natalya Alexeevna.'

Unlike the men, she was dressed in dark jeans and a denim jacket. She had a sparkling pendant on a silver chain round her neck and several massive silver rings on her fingers – fancy, complicated rings with dragons' heads and tigers' heads, intertwined snakes and patterns that looked like the letters of a strange, mysterious alphabet.

'What do you mean?' Natasha asked in a dull voice.

Instead of answering, the girl unzipped Natasha's purse and took out the little bottle. She held it up in front of Natasha's eyes. And then she shook her head again in reproach.

'Got it!' shouted the young man who had gone into the kitchen. 'It's all here, guys.'

One of the men holding the seer by the arms sighed and said in a strangely bored tone:

'Darya Leonidovna Romashova! In the name of the Night Watch, you are under arrest.'

'What watch?' There was an obvious note of puzzlement, as well as panic, in the seer's voice. 'Who are you?'

'You have the right to respond to our questions,' the young man went on. 'Any magical action on your part will be regarded as hostile and punished without any warning. You have the right to request the settlement of your human obligations. You are accused of . . . Garik?'

The young man who had gone into the kitchen came back out. As if she were dreaming, Natasha noticed that he had an intellectual, thoughtful, rather sad kind of face. She had always rather liked men like that . . .

'I suppose it's the usually,' said Garik. 'The illegal practice of black magic. Third- or fourth-degree intervention in the consciousness of other individuals. Murder, tax evasion – but that's not for us, that's for the Dark Ones.'

'You are accused of the illegal practice of black magic, intervention in the consciousness of others and murder,' the man holding Darya repeated. 'You will come with us.'

The seer gave a long, piercing, terrifying scream. Natasha involuntarily glanced at the open door. Of course, it would be naïve to hope that the neighbours would come running to help, but they could call the police, couldn't they?

The strange visitors didn't react to the scream. The girl only frowned and nodded in Natasha's direction.

'What shall we do with her?'

'Confiscate the potion and wipe her memory clean.' Garik looked at Natasha without a hint of sympathy. 'Let her believe there was no one in the apartment when she got here.'

'And that's all?' the girl took a packet of cigarettes out of her pocket and lit one casually.

'Katya, what other choice is there? She's a human being, how can we do anything with her?'

This wasn't even frightening any more. It was a dream, a nightmare . . . and Natasha reacted as if she were dreaming. With a sudden movement she grabbed the precious bottle from the girl's hand and dashed towards the door.

She was flung back as if she had run into an invisible wall. She shrieked as she fell at the seer's feet, the bottle went flying out of her hand and shattered easily against the wall. A tiny patch of sticky, colourless liquid appeared on the lino.

'Tiger Cub, pick up the pieces for the report,' Garik said calmly. Natasha burst into tears.

No, she wasn't afraid, although Garik's tone of voice left no doubt that they really would wipe her memory clean. They'd clap their hands or something like that and wipe it clean. And she would find herself standing out in the street, firmly convinced that the seer's door had never opened.

She cried as she watched her love dribble across the dirty floor.

Someone stuck their head in through the open door to the landing. 'We've got company, guys!' Natasha heard an alarmed voice say, but she didn't even look round. There was no point. She was going to forget it all anyway. It would all be shattered into sharp little fragments and soak away into the dirt.

For ever.

# CHAPTER 1

I NEVER have enough time to get ready in the morning. I can get up at seven, or even at six, but I still always need another five minutes.

Why is it always like that, I wonder?

I was standing in front of the mirror, quickly putting on my lipstick. And as always happens when you're in a hurry, the lipstick was going on unevenly, as if I was a schoolgirl who'd secretly borrowed her mother's lipstick for the first time. It would have been better not to bother at all, and go out without any make-up on. I don't have any complexes about that, I look good enough without it.

'Alya!'

Here we go.

That just has to happen, doesn't it?

'What is it, Mum?' I shouted, fastening my sandals in a hurry.

'Come here, my little one.'

'Mum, I've already got my shoes on!' I shouted, adjusting a twisted strap. 'I'm late.'

'Alya!'

There was no point arguing.

Deliberately clattering my heels, although I wasn't really angry at all, I went through into the kitchen. Mum was sitting in front of the TV the way she always does and drinking yet another cup of tea with yet another cake. What is it she likes so much about those horrible Danish cakes? They're such terrible garbage! Not to mention how bad they are for your figure.

'Little one, are you going to be late again today?' Mum asked, without even turning her head in my direction.

'I don't know.'

'Alisa, I don't think you ought to put up with it. Nine to five is one thing, but keeping you there until one in the morning . . .' Mum shook her head.

'They pay for it,' I said offhandedly.

And then Mum did look at me. And her lips began to tremble.

'So you hold that against me, do you?'

My mother always did have an expressive voice, like an actress's. She should have worked in the theatre.

'Yes, we do live on your wages,' my mum said bitterly. 'The state robbed us and threw us out to die at the side of the road. Thank you, dear daughter, for not forgetting us. Your father and I are very grateful to you. But there's no need to keep reminding us . . .'

'Mum, I didn't mean anything of the kind. You know I don't have a standard working day!'

'Working day!' My mum threw her arms in the air. She had a crumb of cake on her chin. 'Working night, more like! And who knows what you get up to?'

'Mum . . .'

Of course, she didn't really think anything of the kind. Quite the opposite, she was always proudly telling her friends what a fine, upstanding girl I was. It was just that in the morning she felt like arguing. Perhaps she'd been watching the news and she'd heard yet another awful story about our life here in Russia. Perhaps she and Dad had had a row first thing in the morning – that would be why he had left so early.

'And I've no intention of becoming a grandmother at forty!' my mum went on, following no apparent logic. What logic did she need, anyway? She'd been terrified for ages that I would get married and leave home and she'd be left on her own with my father. Or maybe she wouldn't – I'd looked at the reality lines, and it was very likely that my dad would leave her for another woman. He was three years younger than Mum, and unlike her he took care of himself.

'You'll be fifty this year, Mum,' I said. 'Sorry, I'm really in a hurry.'

When I was already in the hall, I heard my mum's voice, full of righteous indignation:

'You never did want to talk to your mother like a normal human being!'

'There was a time when I wanted to,' I muttered to myself as I headed out of the door. 'When I still was a human being I wanted to. But where were you then . . . ?'

And now I knew for sure that Mum was taking comfort in thinking about the row she would have with me in the evening. And she was dreaming of involving Dad in it too. When I thought about that, it instantly put me in a foul mood.

What kind of way to behave is that – deliberately provoking a row with someone you love? But Mum just loves to do it. And she simply doesn't understand that it's her own character that's destroyed my father's love for her.

I'll never do that to anyone.

And I won't let Mum do it either!

There was no one in the hall, but even if there was it wouldn't have stopped me. I turned back to face the door and looked at it in a particular way, with my eyes slightly screwed up . . . so that I could see my shadow.

My real shadow. The one that's cast by the Twilight.

It looks as if the gloom is condensing in front of you. Until it becomes an utterly black, intense darkness, so black it would make a starless night look like day.

And against the background of that darkness you see a trembling, swirling, greyish silhouette, not quite three-dimensional but not flat either. As if it had been cut out of dirty cotton wool. Or maybe it's the other way round – a hole has been cut through the great Dark, leaving a doorway into the Twilight.

I took a step forward into the shadow and it slid upwards, enfolding my body, and the world changed.

Colours almost completely disappeared. Everything was frozen in a dark, grey blur like what appears on a television screen if you turn the colour and contrast all the way down. Sounds slowed down, leaving silence; nothing but a barely audible background rumble, as faint as the murmur of a distant sea.

I was in the Twilight.

I could see Mum's resentment blazing in the apartment. A bitter, lemon-yellow colour, mingling with her self-pity and her acid-green dislike of my dad, who had chosen the wrong time to go to the garage and tinker with his car.

And there was a black vortex slowly taking shape above Mum's head. A curse directed at someone specific, still weak, still on the level of 'I hope that job of yours drives you crazy, you ungrateful creature!' – but it was a mother's curse, and they're especially powerful and tenacious.

Oh no, my dear mother!

Thanks to your efforts Dad had a heart attack at thirty-seven and three years ago I barely managed to save him from another . . . at a cost that I don't even want to remember. And now you've set your sights on me?

I reached out through the Twilight as hard as I could, so hard

I got a stabbing pain under my shoulder blades, and grabbed hold of Mum's mind – it twitched and then froze.

Okay . . . now this is what we'll do . . .

I broke into a sweat, although it's always cool in the Twilight. I wasted energy that would have been useful at work. But a moment later Mum no longer remembered that she'd been speaking to me. And more generally, she was pleased that I was such a hard worker, that I was appreciated and liked at work, that I went out when it was barely light and didn't come back until after midnight.

Sorted.

Probably the effect would only be temporary; after all, I didn't want to delve too deep into Mum's mind. But at least I could count on a couple of months of peace and quiet. And so could my dad; I'm my dad's daughter – I love him much more than I do my mum. It's only kids who can't tell you who they love more, their mum or their dad; adults have no problem answering the question . . .

When I was done, I removed the half-formed black vortex, and it drifted out through the walls, looking for someone else to attach itself to. I took a breath and cast a critical eye round the hall.

It hadn't been cleaned for a long time. The blue moss had crept back over everything again, and it was thickest of all round our door. That was only to be expected; with Mum's hysterical fits there was always something for it to feed on. When I was little I used to think the Light Ones planted the moss to annoy us. Then I was told that the blue moss is native to the Twilight, a parasite that lives on human emotions.

'Ice!' I commanded, flinging out my hand. The cold obediently gathered at my fingertips and ran across the walls like a stiff brush. Frozen needles of moss dropped to the floor, decaying instantly.

Take that!

That will teach you to go feeding on people's petty little thoughts!

That's real power, the power of an Other.

I emerged from the Twilight – in the human world less than two seconds had gone by – and straightened my hair. My forehead was damp, I had to take out my handkerchief and blot the sweat away. And of course, when I looked in my mirror I could see that my mascara was smudged.

I had no time to fuss over how I looked. I just threw on a light veil of attractiveness that would prevent any human being from noticing the faults in my make-up. We call them 'paranjahs', and everybody likes to tease Others who wear them, but we all do anyway. When we're short of time or we need to be absolutely sure of making a good impression, or sometimes just for fun. There's a pretty young witch from Pskov who can't really do anything right except throw on a paranjah, and she's been working as a model for three years. She makes her living from it. The only trouble is that the spell doesn't work in photographs or on video, so she has to keep turning down all the offers she gets to work in advertising . . .

Everything was against me today. The lift didn't come for ages, and the other one's been out of order for a long time now; and on my way out of the lobby I ran into Vitalik, the young guy who lives above us. When he saw me in my paranjah, he just froze with a stupid smile on his face. He's been in love with me since he was thirteen – stupidly, hopelessly, silently in love. To be honest, it's all because of my sloppy work. I was learning the love spell and decided to practise on our neighbours' little boy, since he took every chance he could get to ogle me while I was sitting on the balcony, sunbathing in my bikini. Well . . . I practised. And I missed out the limiting factors. So he fell in love for ever. When he doesn't see me for a long time, it all seems to pass off, but it only takes one sight of me, and it all starts up again. He'll never be happy in love.

'Vitalik, I'm in a hurry,' I said, smiling at him.

But he just stood there, blocking the doorway. Then he decided to pay me a compliment.

'Alisa, you look really beautiful today . . .'

'Thanks.' I gently moved him aside and felt him tremble when my hand touched his shoulder. He'll probably remember that touch for a week . . .

'I've passed my last exam, Alisa!' he said quickly, talking to my back. 'That's it, I'm a student now!'

I turned and took a closer look at him.

Was this boy who still used anti-pimple lotion getting crazy ideas into his head? Was he hoping that now he'd got into college and launched into 'adult life' he could have aspirations?

'Skiving out of the army?' I asked. 'Men today have no balls. They're all wimps. They don't want to do their time and get a bit of experience, and *then* go and study.'

His smile was slowly fading. It was a wonderful sight!

'Ciao, Vitalik,' I said and skipped out into the sweltering heat of summer. But my mood was a bit better now.

These little lovesick pups are always fun to watch. They're boring to flirt with and actually having sex with them is disgusting, but just watching them is pure pleasure. I ought to give him a kiss some time . . .

But anyway, a moment later I'd entirely forgotten my lovesick neighbour. I stuck out my hand. The first car drove straight past – the driver looked at me with greedy longing in his eyes, but his wife was sitting beside him. The next car stopped.

'I'm going into the centre,' I said, leaning down towards the window. 'Manege Square.'

'Get in,' said the driver, reaching across and opening the door. He was an educated-looking man with dark hair, about forty. 'How could I refuse such a good-looking girl a lift?'

I slipped into the front seat of the old Zhiguli 9 and turned the window all the way down. The breeze hit me in the face – that was some relief at least.

'You'd have got there quicker on the metro,' the driver warned me honestly.

'I don't like the metro.'

The driver nodded. I liked him – he wasn't staring too brazenly, even though I'd obviously overdone things with the paranjah, and the car was well cared for. And he had quite beautiful hands. They were strong, and their grip on the wheel was gentle but firm.

What a shame I was in a hurry.

'Are you late for work?' the driver asked. He spoke very politely, but in a manner that was somehow personal and intimate. Maybe I ought to give him my number? I'm a free girl now, I can do what I like.

'Yes.'

'I wonder, what kind of jobs do such beautiful girls do?' It wasn't even an attempt to strike up an acquaintance or a compliment, it was genuine curiosity.

'I don't know about the others, but I work as a witch.'

He laughed.

'It's a job like any other . . .' I took out my cigarettes and my lighter. The driver gave me a fleeting glance of disapproval, so I didn't bother to ask. I just lit up.

'And what are a witch's duties?'

We turned off onto Rusakov Street and the driver accelerated. Maybe I was going to be on time after all?

'It varies,' I replied evasively. 'But basically we oppose the forces of Light.'

The driver seemed to have accepted the rules of the game, although it wasn't really a game at all.

'So you're on the side of the Shadow?'

'The Dark.'

'That's great. I know another witch, my mother-in-law,' the driver said with a laugh. 'But she's already retired, thank God. So why don't you like the forces of Light?'

I stealthily checked out his aura. No, everything was okay, he was a human being.

'They get in our way. Tell me, for instance – what's the most important thing in life for you?'

The driver thought for a second.

'Just life itself. And for nobody to stop me living it.'

'That's right,' I agreed. 'Everyone wants to be free, don't they?'

He nodded.

'Well, we witches fight for freedom too. For everyone's right to do what they want.'

'And what if someone wants to do evil?'

'That's his right.'

'But what if he infringes other people's rights in the process? Say I stab someone and infringe his rights?'

This was funny. We were straight into the classic dispute on the subject 'What is the Light and what is the Dark?' We Dark Ones and those who call themselves the Light Ones – we all brainwash our novices on this subject.

'If someone tries to infringe your rights, then simply stop them from doing it. You have that right.'

'I get it. The law of the jungle. Whoever's stronger is right.'

'Stronger, cleverer, more farsighted. And it's not the law of the jungle. It's just the law of life. Is it ever any different?'

The driver thought about it and shook his head.

'No, it isn't. So I have the right to turn off the road somewhere, throw myself on you and rape you?'

'But are you sure you're stronger than me?'

We'd just stopped at a red light and the driver looked at me closely. He shook his head.

'No . . . I'm not sure. But the reason I don't attack girls isn't because they might fight back!'

He was beginning to get a bit nervous. The conversation seemed like a joke, but he could sense that something wasn't right.

'It's also because they might put you in jail,' I said. 'And that's all.'

'No,' he said firmly.

'Yes,' I said with a smile. 'That's exactly the reason. You're a normal, healthy man, with all the right reactions. But there's a law, so you prefer not to attack girls, but date them first.'

'Witch . . .' the driver muttered with a crooked smile. He stepped hard on the accelerator.

'Witch,' I confirmed. 'Because I tell the truth and don't play the hypocrite. After all, everyone wants to be free to live his or her life. To do what they want. Not everything works out, after all, everyone has their own desires — but everyone has the same aspirations. And it's the clash of these that gives rise to freedom! A harmonious society in which everybody wants to have everything, although they have to come to terms with other people's desires.'

'But what about morality?'

'What morality?'

'Universal human morality.'

'What's that?'

There's nothing better than forcing someone into a dead-end and making him formulate his question properly. People don't usually think about the meaning of their words. It seems to them that words convey truth, that when someone hears the word 'red' he will think of a ripe raspberry, and not a pool of blood, that the word 'love' will bring to mind Shakespeare's sonnets and not the erotic films of *Playboy*. And they find themselves baffled when the word they've spoken doesn't evoke the right response.

'There are basic principles,' said the driver. 'Dogmas. Taboos. The . . . what do they call them . . . Commandments.'

'Well?' I said encouragingly.

'Thou shalt not steal.'

I laughed. And the driver smiled too.

'Thou shalt not covet thy neighbour's wife.' His smile was really broad now.

'And do you manage it?'

'Sometimes.'

'And you even manage not to "covet"? You control your instincts that well?'

'Witch!' the driver said enthusiastically. 'All right, I repent, I repent . . .'

'Don't repent!' I interrupted. 'It's quite normal. It's freedom! Stealing . . . and coveting.'

'Thou shalt not kill!' the driver declared. 'Eh? What do you say to that? A universal commandment!'

'You might as well say "don't boil a young goat in its mother's milk". Do you watch TV and read the newspapers?' I asked.

'Sometimes. But I don't enjoy it.'

'Then why do you call "Thou shalt not kill" a commandment? Thou shalt not kill . . . It was in the news this morning – down south they've taken another three people hostage and they're demanding a ransom. They've already cut a finger off each of them to show they're serious about their demands. And one of the hostages, by the way, is a three-year-old girl. They cut her finger off too.'

The driver's fingers tightened their grip on the wheel and he turned pale.

'Bastards . . .' he hissed. 'Monsters. Sure I heard that. But they're scum, they're inhuman, they have to be to do something like that. I'd strangle them all with my bare hands . . .'

I kept quiet. The driver's aura was blazing bright scarlet. I didn't want him to crash, he was almost out of control. My thrust had been too accurate – he had a little daughter of his own . . .

'String them up from the telegraph poles!' he went on, still raging. 'Burn them with napalm!'

I kept quiet and waited until the driver had gradually calmed down. Then I asked:

'Then what about those universal moral commandments? If they gave you a machine gun now, you'd press the trigger without even hesitating.'

'There aren't any commandments that apply to monsters!' the driver snarled. His calm cultured manner had disappeared without trace now! Energy was streaming out of him in all directions . . . and I soaked it up, quickly replenishing the power that I'd spent earlier that morning.

'Not even terrorists are monsters,' I said. 'They're human beings. And so are you. And there are no commandments for human beings. That's a scientifically proven fact.'

As I drew in the energy that was pouring out of him, the driver calmed down. It wouldn't last long, of course. That evening the pendulum would swing back, and he'd be overcome by rage again. It's like pumping all the water out of a well very quickly – it comes rushing back in again.

'But even so, you're not right,' he replied more calmly. 'Logic does exist, of course, yes . . . But if you compare things with the Middle Ages, then morality has definitely advanced.'

'Don't be ridiculous!' I said, shaking my head. 'How has it advanced? . . . Even in the wars back then they had a strict code of honour. A war then was a real war, and kings fought with their armies, risking their thrones and their heads. And now? A big country wants to put pressure on a little one, so it bombs it for three months and gets rid of its outdated armaments at the same time. Not even the soldiers risk their lives! It's the same as if you drove up onto the pavement and started knocking down pedestrians like skittles.'

'The code of honour was for the aristocrats,' the driver objected sharply. 'The common people died in droves.'

'And is it any different today?' I asked. 'When one oligarch settles scores with another, there's a certain code of honour that's observed! Because both of them have goons to kill for them, compromising information about each other, interests in common, family ties. They're just like the old aristocracy! Kings sitting up to their ears in cabbage. And the common people are trash. A herd of sheep that are good for shearing, but sometimes it's more profitable to slaughter them. Nothing's changed. There never were any commandments, and there aren't any now!'

The driver fell silent.

And after that he didn't say another word all the way. We turned off Kamergerskaya Street onto Tverskaya Street and I told him where to stop. I paid, deliberately giving him more than I should have. It was only then that he spoke again.

'I'll never give a witch a lift again,' he told me with a crooked grin. 'It's too hard on the nerves. I never thought a conversation with a beautiful girl could spoil my mood so badly.'

'I'm sorry,' I said and smiled sweetly.

'Have a good day at . . . work.' He slammed the door and drove off abruptly.

Well, well. I'd never been taken for a prostitute before, but he seemed to think that was what I was. That was the effect of the paranjah . . . and the area of town, of course.

But at least I'd more than made up for the power I'd used earlier. He'd turned out to be a magnificent donor, this intelli-

gent, cultured, strong man. The only time I'd ever done better was
. . . it was with the Prism of Power.

I shuddered at the memory.

It had all been so stupid . . . everything about it had been so
monstrously stupid.

My entire life had gone downhill as a result. I'd lost everything
in a single moment.

*'You fool! You greedy fool!'*

It was a good thing that nobody could see my real face. It probably looked about as pitiful as my stupid young neighbour's.

Anyway, what was done was done. I couldn't turn back the
clock, put things right and win back . . . his affection. It was my
own fault, of course. And I ought to be glad that Zabulon hadn't
handed me over to the Light Ones.

He used to love me. And I loved him . . . it would have been
absurd for a young, inexperienced witch not to fall in love with
the head of the Day Watch when he took a special interest in her
. . .

My fists were clenched so tight that the nails were biting into
the skin. I'd struggled through. I'd survived last summer. The Dark
only knew how, but I'd survived.

And now there was no point in remembering the past and snivelling and trying to catch Zabulon's eye again. He hadn't spoken
to me since the hurricane last year, the one that had hit on the
day when I was captured so shamefully. And he wouldn't speak
to me for a hundred years, I was sure of it.

A car moving slowly along the kerb stopped with a quiet squeal
of tyres. It was a decent car, a Volvo, and it hadn't come from the
tip. A jerk with a shaven head stuck his smug face out of the
window, looked me up and down and broke into a satisfied smile.
Then he hissed.

'How much?'

I was dumbstruck.

'For two hours – how much?' the idiot with the shaved head asked more precisely.

I looked at the number plate – it wasn't from Moscow. So that was it.

'The prostitutes are further down, you twit,' I said amiably. 'Get lost.'

'Anyone would think you didn't screw,' the disappointed idiot said, trying to save face. 'Think it over, I'm feeling generous today.'

'You hold on to your money,' I advised him and clicked my fingers. 'You'll need it to fix your car.'

I turned my back on him and walked towards the building. My palm was aching slightly from the recoil. The 'gremlin' isn't a very complicated spell, but I'd cast it in too much of a hurry. I'd left the Volvo with an incorporeal creature fiddling about under its hood – not even a creature really, but a bundle of energy with an obsessive passion for destroying technology.

If he was lucky, his engine was finished. If he was unlucky, then his fancy bourgeois electronics would blow – the carburettors, the ventilators, all those gearwheels and drivebelts that the car was full of. I'd never taken any interest in the insides of a car except in the most general terms. But I had a very clear idea of the effects of the 'gremlin'.

The disappointed driver drove off without wasting too much time arguing. I wondered if he'd remember what I'd said when his car started going haywire. He was bound to. He'd cry 'She hexed it, the witch!' And he wouldn't even know just how right he was.

The thought amused me, but nevertheless, the day had been hopelessly spoiled.

I was five minutes late for work, and there was that quarrel with my mother, and that idiot in the Volvo . . .

With these thoughts in my head I walked past the magnificent, gleaming shop windows, raised my shadow from the ground in a pure reflex action, without even thinking about it, and entered the building through a door that ordinary people can't see.

The headquarters of the Light Ones, near the Sokol metro station, is disguised as an ordinary office. We have a more respectable location and our camouflage is a lot more fun. This building – seven floors of apartments above shops that are luxurious even by Moscow standards – has three more floors than people think. It was specially built that way as the Day Watch HQ, and the spells that disguise the building's real appearance are incorporated into the very bricks and stone of the walls. The people living in the building, who are mostly perfectly ordinary, probably feel a strange sensation when they take the lift. As if it takes too long to get from the first floor to the second . . .

The lift really does take longer than it should. Because the second floor is really the third, and the real second floor is invisible – it houses our duty offices, armaments room and technical services. Our two other floors are on the top of the building, and no human being knows about them either. But any Other who is powerful enough can look through the Twilight and see the severe black granite of the walls and the arches of the windows that are almost always covered with thick, heavy curtains. Ten years ago they installed air-conditioning, and the clumsy boxes of the split systems appeared on the walls. Before that the internal climate was regulated by magic, but why waste it like that, when electricity is much cheaper?

I once saw a photograph of our building taken through the Twilight by a skilful magician. It's an incredible sight! A crowded street with people walking along it all dressed up, and cars driving along. Shop windows and apartment windows . . . a nice old lady looking out of one window, and a cat sitting in another one, looking disgruntled and gloomy – animals can sense our presence very easily . . . And in parallel with all this – two entrances to the building from Tverskaya Street, with the doors standing open, and in one doorway there's a young vampire from security, polishing his nails with a file. Directly above the shops there's a strip of black stone, with the crimson spots of windows in it . . . And the two top floors seem to weigh down on the building like a heavy stone cap.

If only I could show that photograph to the people who live there. But then, they'd all think the same` thing – a clumsy piece of photomontage. Clumsy, because the building really does look awkward . . . When everything was still all right between Zabulon and me, I asked him why our offices were located so oddly, mixed up with the humans' apartments. The boss laughed and explained that it made it more difficult for the Light Ones to try any kind of attack – innocent people might get killed in the fighting. Everybody knows that the Light Ones don't really worry about people at all. But they have to hedge round what they do with all sorts of hypocritical tricks, and so the seven floors of apartments make a really reliable shield.

The tiny duty office on the ground floor, with the two lifts (the people living in the building don't know about them either) and the fire stairs, seemed to be empty. There was no one behind the desk or in the armchair in front of the television. It took me a moment to spot the two security guards who should have been there according to the staff list: a vampire – I think his name was Kostya – who had only joined the Watch very recently, and the werewolf Vitaly from Kostroma, also a civilian employee, who'd been working for us as long as I could remember. Both the guards were standing quite still, doubled over in the corner. Vitaly was giggling quietly. Just for an instant I had a quite crazy idea about the reason for such strange behaviour.

'Boys, what's that you're doing over there?' I asked sharply. There's no point in being too polite with these vampires and shape-shifters. They're primitive beasts of labour – and as well as that the vampires are non-life, but they still claim to be no worse than magicians and witches.

'Come here, Aliska!' Vitaly said, beckoning to me without turning round. 'This is a real gas.'

But Kostya straightened up sharply and took a step backwards, looking a bit embarrassed.

I walked over.

There was a little grey mouse dashing around Vitaly's feet. It stopped dead still, then jumped up in the air, then began squeaking and beating desperately at the air with its little paws. I didn't understand for a moment, until I tried looking through the Twilight.

So that was it.

There was a huge, glossy cat jumping about beside the mouse. Sometimes it reached its paw out towards the tiny creature, some times it snapped its jaws together. Of course, it was only an illusion, and a primitive one at that, created exclusively for the small rodent.

'We're seeing how long it can hold out!' Vitaly said happily. 'I bet it will die of fright in a minute.'

'I see,' I said, beginning to see red. 'Now I understand. Having fun are we? Did your hunting instincts get the better of you?'

I reached down and picked up the mouse that had frozen dead still in fear. The tiny bundle of fur trembled on my hand. I blew on it gently and whispered the right word. The mouse stopped trembling, then it stretched out on my palm and went to sleep.

'What's it to you?' Vitaly asked in a slightly offended tone. 'Aliska, in your line of work you're supposed to boil these creatures alive in your cauldron!'

'There are a few spells like that,' I admitted. 'And there are some that require the liver of a werewolf killed at midnight.'

The werewolf's eyes glittered brightly with malice, but he didn't say anything. His rank was too low to try arguing with me. I might only be a simple patrol witch, but that made me a cut above a mercenary werewolf.

'All right, then, you guys, tell me the procedure to be followed following the discovery in the premises of rodents, cockroaches, flies, mosquitoes,' I said in a slow, lazy voice.

'Activate the pest control amulet,' Vitaly said reluctantly. 'If any of the creatures should be observed not to be affected by the action of the amulet, then it should be captured, exercising great care, and handed over to the duty magician for checking.'

'You do know it . . . So we're not dealing with a case of forget-fulness here. Have you activated the amulet?' I asked.

The werewolf gave the vampire a sideways glance and then looked away.

'No.'

'I see. Failure to carry out duty instructions. As the senior member of the duty detail, you will be penalised. You will inform the duty officer.'

The werewolf said nothing.

'Repeat what I said, security guard.'

He realised it was stupid to defy me and repeated my words.

'And now get back to serving your watch,' I said and walked to the left, still carrying the sleeping mouse on my open palm.

'*Bon appétit*,' the werewolf muttered after me. Those creatures have no discipline – the animal half of them is just too strong.

'I hope that in a real battle you would be at least half as brave as this little mouse,' I replied as I got into the lift. I caught Kostya's eye – and it seemed to me that the young vampire was embar-rassed, and even glad that the cruel amusement was over.

My appearance in the department with a mouse in my hand caused an uproar.

Anna Lemesheva, the senior witch on our shift, was about to launch into her usual tirade about young people who haven't been taught any discipline – 'Under Stalin for being five minutes late you'd have been packed off to a camp in Kolyma to brew potions' – when she saw the mouse and was struck dumb. Lenka Kireeva squealed and then howled: 'Oh, how lovely'. Zhanna Gromova giggled and asked if I was going to make the 'thief's elixir', which has a boiled mouse as an essential ingredient, and what I was planning to steal afterwards. Olya Melnikova finished painting her nails and congratulated me on a successful hunt.

I put the little creature down on my desk as if I never came to work without a fresh mouse and told everyone how the security guards had been amusing themselves.

Anna shook her head:

'Is that why you were late?'

'Partly,' I said honestly. 'Anna Tikhonovna, I was incredibly unlucky with the traffic. And then there were those nitwits playing their games.'

Anna Lemesheva is an old and experienced witch; it's pointless trying to deceive her by putting on a brave front. She's about a hundred years old, and after all the things she'd seen, the game with the mouse was hardly going to seem cruel. But even so she pursed her lips and declared:

'These werewolves have no respect for the idea of duty. When we were stationed at Revel, fighting the Swedes, we had a saying: "If they send the Watch a werewolf, detail a witch to watch him." What would have happened if an assault group of Light Ones had burst in while both guards were gawping at that rodent? They could have sent the mouse in deliberately. It's disgraceful. I think you should have demanded more serious punishment, Alisa.'

'The lash,' Lenka Kireeva said in a quiet voice. She flicked her head of long red hair. Oh, that hair of Lenka's, anyone would envy it. But the comforting thing is that none of the rest of her is up to the same standard.

'Yes, it was a mistake to end the practice of punishment with the lash,' Anna replied coldly. 'Throw that creature out of the window, Alisa.'

'I feel sorry for it,' I objected. 'It's blockheads like those two who are responsible for the image of Dark Ones that exists in the mass consciousness, a caricature of vicious sadists and monsters . . . Why torment the poor mouse?'

'It does create a certain discharge of energy,' said Olya, screwing the lid onto her nail varnish. 'But it's ve-ry ti-ny . . .'

She shook her hands in the air.

Zhanna snorted derisively.

'A discharge! They used up so much energy creating the illusory cat, they'd have to torture a kilo of mice to make up for it.'

'We could work it out,' Olya suggested. 'We torture this mouse to death and measure the total power emitted . . . only we'd need a pair of scales as well.'

'You're terrible,' Lena said angrily. 'And you're quite right, Alisa! Can I take the mouse?'

'What for?' I asked jealously.

'To give to my daughter. She's six, it's time she had something to care for and look after. That's good for a girl.'

There was an awkward silence. Of course, it's not so unusual. It's rare for an Other to have a child who is also an Other . . . Very rare. It's simpler for vampires – they can initiate their own child, and it's simpler for shape-shifters – their children almost always inherit the ability to change form. But the chances are not so good for us, or for the Light Ones either. Lena hadn't been lucky, even though her husband was a Dark Magician and a former staff member of the Day Watch, who had retired after he was wounded and become a businessman.

'Mice don't live very long,' Olya observed. 'There'll be tears and tantrums.'

'That's all right, it'll live a long time with me,' Lena laughed. 'Ten years at least. Pavel and I will make sure of that.'

'Then take it!' I said, indicating the mouse with a magnanimous gesture. 'I'll come round to visit some time.'

'Did you put it into a deep sleep?' Lena asked, picking the mouse up by the tail.

'It will sleep until the evening for sure.'

'Good.'

She carried the mouse to her desk, shook the floppy disks out of a cardboard box and put the little creature in it.

'Buy a cage,' Olga advised as she admired her nails. 'Or an aquarium. If it escapes it will gnaw everything to pieces and leave filthy droppings everywhere.'

Anna Lemesheva had followed the conversation thoughtfully and then clapped her hands.

'All right, girls. That's enough distraction. The unfortunate creature has been saved and it has found a new home. Things could hardly have been resolved more elegantly. Now let's begin our briefing.'

She's a very strict boss, but not malicious. She doesn't make things hard for anyone for no reason, and she'll let you fool about, or leave early if necessary. But when it comes to work, it's best not to argue with her.

The girls all sat in their places. Our room is small; after all, the building wasn't meant for the present numbers of the Watch. All that could fit were four small tables for us and one big desk, where Anna Lemesheva sat. The room reminded me of a school classroom in some tiny village somewhere, with a class of four pupils and one teacher.

Lemesheva waited until we'd all switched on our computers and accessed the network; then she began in her resonant voice:

'Today's assignment is the usual: patrolling the south-east region of Moscow. You will choose your partners in the guardroom from among the available operatives.'

We always go on duty in pairs, usually one witch and one shape-shifter or vampire. If the level of patrols is stepped up, then instead of ordinary operatives they give us warlocks or some of the junior magicians as partners. But that doesn't happen very often.

'Lenochka, you're patrolling Vykhino and Liublino.'

Lena Kireeva, who had stealthily begun playing patience on her computer, started and prepared to argue. I could understand why. Two huge districts and a long way away too. Nothing would come of it, of course. Anna Lemesheva would insist on having her own way as always, but Kireeva couldn't help feeling indignant.

But just at that moment the phone on Lemesheva's desk rang. We exchanged glances, and even Lena's eyes became serious. It was the direct line from the operations duty officer, it didn't just ring for nothing.

'Yes,' said Lemesheva. 'Yes. Of course. I understand. I accept the detail.'

For a moment her expression became vague – the duty magician was sending her a telepathic briefing on the situation.

That meant it was serious, that there was work to do.

'To your brooms . . .' Lenka whispered quietly. The line, from a children's cartoon, was a traditional saying with us. 'I wonder who they'll send,' she said.

But when Anna Lemesheva put the receiver down, her expression was firm and tough.

'Into the bus, girls. Everyone. Look lively.'

So much for 'to your brooms'.

This meant something very serious. This meant a fight.

# CHAPTER 2

THE MINIBUS was driven by Deniska, a young Dark Magician so incredibly lazy that he preferred working in the garage among the vampires and other small fry. But his laziness didn't mean he couldn't drive, and he knew the few spells that were essential for his job very well indeed. We literally flew along the road as we made our way out of the city centre at a speed that the presidential cortège could only dream of. I felt the surges of power as he examined the reality lines, made the militiamen look the other way or made other drivers steer their cars off to the side. On this occasion he had Edgar sitting beside him, a plump, swarthy, dark-haired magician from Estonia who looked nothing like a person from the Baltic but possessed magical abilities that were almost second grade.

There were nine of us in the vehicle. I could hardly ever remember Anna Lemesheva leaving the Watch building before, but she was sitting in the chair by the door, reciting the briefing in a monotone:

'Darya Leonidovna Romashova. Sixty-three years old, looks considerably younger, probably, constantly nourished by power. Presumably a witch, but could possibly be a Dark Sorceress. Under observation for the last four years as an uninitiated Other.'

At this point Lemesheva permitted herself to swear briefly and obscenely, directing her abuse at the members of the detection department.

'Apparently she refuses all contact. She avoids conversations on mystical subjects, citing her religious piety! What has faith got to do with the abilities of an Other? It's another question who that Christ of theirs was.'

'Anna Tikhonovna, don't blaspheme,' Lenka said quietly but insistently. 'I believe in the Lord God too.'

'I'm sorry, Lena,' Lemesheva said with a nod. 'I didn't mean to offend you. Let's continue . . . Romashova has probably been earning something from small-scale magic. Love potions, hate potions, hexes, removing curses . . .'

'The standard charlatan's stock-in-trade,' I put in. 'No wonder they didn't bother to check her seriously.'

'And what about monitoring her results and finding out if she really did help people?' Lemesheva asked. 'No, I'm going to write a report. If Zabulon thinks that's good work   then fire me. It's time for me to retire.'

Olga cleared her throat in warning.

'I'm prepared to say it to his face!' Lemesheva was obviously worked up. 'Well, I ask you, they suspect a woman is a witch for four years, but they don't bother to check properly. It's a standard procedure – we send an agent and monitor the discharge of power . . . And the Light Ones did it, by the way.'

So that was it. Now I understood and immediately gathered myself. This wasn't going to be just an incident with a crazy witch who had done something she shouldn't have. It was a fight with the Night Watch.

Vitaly growled indistinctly in his seat opposite me, more likely trying to keep his courage up than looking forward to the battle ahead. He'd grown lazy standing watch, this brave mouse-hunter.

I smiled spitefully and the werewolf snarled and bared his teeth slightly. They had already started to grow, and his lower jaw was extending forward.

'Vitaly, spare us the spectacle of transformation in the vehicle,' Lemesheva said sharply. 'In this heat the stink of dog will be quite unbearable!'

The trio of vampires on the back seat all began to laugh. I knew these guys quite well, they had been tried in action and on the whole I didn't find them repellent at all, not like most non-life. Three brothers, born a year apart from each other, strong, well-built young men from an ordinary human family. The eldest had become a vampire first, when he was in a paratroop regiment, and he'd done it deliberately, out of ideological considerations – his commanding officer, who was a vampire, had suggested the young man should become a vampire too. Their unit was in action somewhere in the south at the time, things weren't going too well, and the young man had agreed. Naturally, after that the unit became incredibly effective in battle. Killing a dozen enemies a night, penetrating the enemy's rear line, walking past sentries without being seen – for a vampire, even an inexperienced one, all this is child's play. Afterwards, when he returned to civilian life, the young man had told his younger brothers everything, and they had offered up their own throats.

'Anna Tikhonovna, how many of them are there?' Olga asked. 'The Light Ones?'

'A few. Four ... maybe five. 'But' – Lemesheva ran her stern gaze over all of us – 'you mustn't relax, girls. There's at least one second-grade Light Magician.'

The oldest vampire brother whistled. Facing up to a magician, especially one that powerful, was beyond a vampire's abilities. And if there were two of them ...

'And the female shape-shifter's there,' said Lemesheva, looking at me.

I clenched my teeth. So, Tiger Cub was there. The shape-shifting battle magician as the Light Ones preferred to call her. An old acquaintance of mine ... and a close one. I seemed to feel an ache in my left arm where it had once been pulled out of its joint. And I remembered the wounds on my face – four bloody lines from her claws.

But Zabulon himself had helped me then. He had healed me completely so there was no harm done either to my appearance or to my health. And I used to go into battle boldly and cheerfully, aware of his approving glance and restrained, patient smile.

It's over. That's all behind you now, Aliska. What used to be is gone now. Forget it and don't torment yourself. If they tear your face, you'll have to wear the paranjah all the time, until your turn comes for magical healing, and the queue's six months long, and you'll be lucky if they consider you worthy of complete healing, including cosmetic magic.

'Everybody check your equipment,' Anna Lemesheva ordered.

The girls started bustling about, and I patted my pockets, checking on the tiny packets, little bottles and amulets. A witch's power doesn't lie only in controlling energy through the Twilight. We also employ auxiliary means, which is what really distinguishes us from sorceresses.

'Alisa?'

I looked at Lemesheva.

'Do you have any suggestions?'

That was better. I had to think of the future, not the past.

'The operatives can neutralise Tiger Cub. All four of them.'

'We don't need any help, Aliska,' the oldest vampire brother said good-naturedly. 'We'll manage.'

Lemesheva thought for a moment and nodded.

'All right, the three of you work together. Vitaly, you're with me, my reserve.'

The werewolf smiled happily. What a fool. Anna Lemesheva
would toss him into the fire like a splinter of wood. Right where
it was hottest.

'And the four of us . . .'

'Five,' Lemesheva corrected me.

Aha, so the old crone has decided to get involved herself?

'The five of us form a Circle of Power,' I suggested. 'And we
feed it all to Edgar. Deniska maintains contact with headquarters.'

The minibus bounced over a few potholes and bumps. We were
already driving into the courtyard.

'Yes, that's the only possible way to play it,' Lemesheva agreed.
'All right, everybody! That's the plan.'

I felt slightly excited that my plan had been accepted so
completely. I was still a genuine battle witch after all. Even with
all my personal problems. That was why I took the risk of volun-
teering and trespassing on the senior witch's absolute prerogative
to decide on tactics.

'But I would suggest summoning help in advance. If there are
two second-grade magicians there.'

'All available help has already been summoned,' Lemesheva
snapped. 'And we still have an ace of trumps up our sleeve.'

Vitaly looked at the old witch in surprise and grinned proudly
with his wolf's fangs. An idiot twice over. She didn't mean him.
He was no ace, just a common low card . . . and certainly not a
trump.

'Right, girls, let's get started!'

Our minibus stopped. Anna Lemesheva jumped out spryly and
waved her left hand. A fine, dark dust swirled around her fingers
for an instant and I felt a spell of inattention enfold the yard. Now,
no matter what we did, ordinary people would take no notice of
us.

We all tumbled out of the minibus.

It was just an ordinary courtyard in South Butovo. Oh, what a dump . . . I'd rather live somewhere in Mytishchi or Lytkarino than be formally registered as a Muscovite and live in that terrible place. There seems to be everything there should be: houses and stunted little trees trying to grow in the compressed clay, and wretched little cars standing at the entrances, but . . .

'Get on with it!'

Lemesheva gave me a kick that bounced me three metres from the minibus. I almost went flying into a sandpit, where a boy and a girl about five years old were discussing the mysterious art of building sandcastles.

But even the little children didn't notice me, although they're always more sensitive to the presence of Others.

The vampire brothers went dashing past me like three shadows. They surrounded the minibus, already in the process of transformation: their fangs were growing out between their teeth, and their skin was taking on a pale, sickly tinge. The typical non-life look . . .

'The Circle!' Lemesheva barked. I dashed across to the minibus like a shot and grabbed Olya and Lena by the hand. Oh, but the old witch was strong!

But there was someone standing in the entrance to the apartment block, visible only to our sight as Others — a short, stocky guy . . . precisely that, a guy, you couldn't call him anything else, wearing worn Turkish jeans and a synthetic T-shirt, with a ridiculous cap on his head.

That was really bad.

The guy is called Semyon. And he's a magician of astounding power, even if he isn't always quick to use it. And even more terrifying — he's a magician with a huge amount of experience of field operations.

I felt Semyon's gaze glide over me — firm, resilient and flexible, like a surgical probe. Then he turned and went back into the entrance.

This was really bad!

Then Zhanna grabbed Olga by the hand, Anna Lemesheva completed the Circle – and all my emotions disappeared.

We became a living accumulator, connected to Edgar, who was already walking towards the entrance with a smooth, unhurried stride, at the human level of perception and in the Twilight at the same time.

Edgar walked up the stairs, as his opponent had done. Of course, he didn't overtake him there. And when he reached the door of the apartment on the fourth floor, they were waiting for him. Fused into the Circle of Power, we were all perceiving the world through his senses now.

The door was standing open – at the human level of the world. In the Twilight the doorway was blocked by a solid wall.

There were two magicians on the landing. Semyon and Garik. I couldn't feel any emotion now, but I still had my thoughts. Cold, calm and unhurried. This was the end. Two magicians, each equal or superior to Edgar.

'The entrance is closed,' said Semyon. 'There's a Night Watch operation taking place here.'

Edgar nodded politely.

'I understand. But there's also a Day Watch operation taking place here.'

'What do you want?' Semyon moved aside slightly. Standing behind him in the narrow hallway of the apartment was a tigress. An immense beast with shiny fur, its teeth exposed in a smug smile.

What is Lemesheva counting on? We can't handle this. There's no way!

'We'd like to take the person who belongs to us,' Edgar said with a shrug. 'That's all.'

'The witch has been arrested and charged: magical intervention of the third degree, murder, practising black magic without a licence, concealing the abilities of an Other.'

'You provoked her into taking this action,' Edgar said coolly. 'The Day Watch will conduct its own investigation of events.'

'No.' Semyon leaned against the wall and the blue moss crept convulsively along its surface, trying to get as far away as possible from the magician. 'The matter is settled.'

Garik didn't even say anything. He twirled a small amulet that looked like a cube of ivory in his fingers and glimmers of energy pierced the air. Most likely it was an ordinary magical accumulator.

'I'm going through and I'm taking what belongs to us,' said Edgar.

He's incredibly calm. Maybe he also knows something that I don't?

The Light Magicians didn't say a word. But such a piece of obvious stupidity seemed to have put them on their guard. The witch's fate now depended on who would conduct the investigation. If we could get her, we'd be able to defend her and make her one of us. If the Light Ones got her, then her life was over.

But better her life than all of ours! Two second-grade magicians, a shape-shifter, and another two or three Others in the apartment! They'd crush us!

'I'm going in,' Edgar said calmly and took a step forward. The Twilight around him howled as it was filled with power – the magician had set up a defensive screen.

All I remember after that is the battle.

The Light Ones struck as soon as Edgar took that step. Not with deadly spells, but an ordinary 'press', trying to force our magician off the staircase. Edgar bent over as if he was walking into a wind and the outline of the vortex of power protecting him became clearly visible. The battle was being waged at the level of pure energy. It was primitive and not at all spectacular. Ah, if only Zabulon had been there instead of Edgar! He'd have swept those upstarts aside in a second, forced them to expend all their energy and tossed them aside, drained of all their powers!

But Edgar was putting up a worthy fight. For about five seconds he moved forward using his own power and even forced the press right back to the door of the apartment. Then I felt the cold in my fingertips.

The magician had started to draw on our power.

I immediately sensed the Light Ones tense as they registered the energy channel between us and Edgar. They didn't try to disrupt it, a hasty attempt would only have led to Edgar gathering in their energy as well. They simply increased their pressure, counting on their own superiority. And I had the impression that the magicians concealed inside the apartment started feeding them with power as well.

For a few moments everything hung in the balance. The current of our combined power had immediately increased Edgar's pressure, but the Light Ones had their own reserves. The little cube in Ilya's hand crumbled and scattered across the floor in golden dust and their counterblow pushed Edgar back a metre. Olga began groaning beside me – her basic energy reserves were exhausted, and now she was pumping out the very substance of her power, the deep reserves that can't be replenished so easily. She didn't seem to be in very good shape today.

What was Lemesheva hoping for?

There was a noise from behind the Light Ones. The vampire brothers . . . they must have got in through the balcony.

But the magicians didn't even seem to notice what was happening. Only the tigress went towards the noise, brushing aside the lightweight furniture in her way and tearing the lino with her claws. And a moment later I heard a pitiful howl from one of the brothers.

Three vampires weren't really enough for the shape-shifter.

'Vitaly!' Lemesheva commanded curtly. The mental command slipped through the Twilight and our werewolf raced towards the entrance of the apartment, throwing off his clothes and changing into a wolf on the way. We carried on feeding Edgar with energy and he started moving forward again, even managing to push Ilya back into the apartment. Then a huge wolf appeared from behind Edgar and rushed forward, paying no attention to the magicians.

It was a good idea. But inside the apartment the appearance of the werewolf was met with a bolt of fire. One of the Light Ones who had been kept in reserve had joined in the struggle. And he'd immediately shown that he was serious.

The werewolf's thick brown fur burst into flames; he leapt into the air and fell to the floor, thrashing his paws about and rolling over and over, trying to put the flames out. If he had continued the attack, he would have had a chance to get to the magician before he could prepare a second fireball . . .

But he'd obviously been on watch duty for far too long.

Vitaly kept trying to put out the flames, and new charges kept striking him from out of the darkness. A second, a third, a fourth . . . Blood spurted and burning lumps of flesh went flying through the air. The wolf howled and fell silent — only its back legs were twitching now, with its tail lying between them, blazing like a firework. It was actually rather beautiful.

The amulet hanging at my chest — a small crystal jug with a drop of red liquid sealed inside it — crunched and shattered into tiny fragments. That was bad. It was a signal that my power was running low and it simultaneously released my final reserve. A drop of the blood of a woman who has died giving birth to an

Other is a very powerful source of energy, but even that wouldn't last for long.

'Lena!' Lemesheva commanded.

I felt the wordless command again and Lena left the Circle, moving slowly, like a sleepwalker. My right hand was empty now and the trance receded for a few seconds, before Anna Lemesheva reached out to me. But it was enough time for me to see something standing in the centre of our Circle – a small folding table of black wood, with a narrow blade of burnished steel lying on it. And Lena was already standing by the sandpit, frozen over the playing children as if she were choosing between them . . .

'The girl!' Lemesheva shouted. 'One girl is more use than a dozen boys!'

Now I understood everything. Apart from one thing, that is. How had Anna Lemesheva been granted the right to a human sacrifice, and why had she decided to waste such tremendous power on saving some ordinary witch?

But then Lemesheva grasped my hand and once again I became a mindless part of the Circle of Power.

Edgar was already squeezed back into the corner of the stairwell – they weren't just pushing him back now, they were trying to crush him against the wall. He threw up one hand:

'Stop!'

A terrible pain . . .

The Circle was draining the very last reserves of energy from me. And Olga wasn't giving any more at all, she'd been wrung completely dry and she was standing there with us, twitching as if she were holding a bare power cable; Zhanna was groaning quietly too, her head gradually sinking down onto her chest.

'We have the right to a sacrifice,' Edgar said coolly. 'If you don't let her go . . .'

The Light Ones froze. I saw the way they looked at each other and Garik shook his head.

But Semyon seemed to believe it straight away.

A sacrifice provides a massive discharge of energy. Especially if it's the sacrifice of a child, and especially if it takes place inside a Circle of Power, and especially if it's performed by an experienced witch. Lenka Kireeva was already standing inside the Circle, the knife was already in her hands, and the girl was already lying on the black table.

If we poured the power that would be liberated into Edgar, the Light Ones wouldn't be able to resist it. Of course, they had extreme methods of their own, but did they have the authority to make use of them?

The shape-shifter tigress sprang out into the corridor. She must have been battering the vampire brothers on the balcony and seen what we were preparing to do.

'You can't stand against us,' Edgar said aloofly. 'We'll take what is ours anyway, and a human child will die, and you'll be to blame.'

The Light Ones were dumbfounded. That was hardly surprising: the situation behind this particular conflict didn't seem especially significant in any way. It wasn't a matter of superpowers threatening nuclear strikes against each other if their agents were arrested for spying. Others don't threaten to use first-degree magic in the case of a petty fight between operational agents.

But the Light Ones were still keeping up the pressure on our magician, they were maintaining the press, if only by inertia, and we had no more power left to share with Edgar. Olga had gone rigid and lost consciousness; now she was standing in the ring like a limp wooden puppet. Zhanna was already sinking to her knees, but heroically maintaining a grip with her hands as she gave up the last of her energy. Lena's face contorted in an agonised grimace and she raised the knife above the twitching little girl – she was conscious, otherwise the discharge of energy would have been reduced, but she was restrained by a spell of silence. My body felt as limp as cotton wool, I felt myself beginning to sway. I wish they'd hurry . . . I won't be able to hold out . . .

'Stop!' shouted Semyon. 'We surrender the witch!'

Hold it . . . hold the Circle. I tried to draw energy from the surrounding space, from the little girl who was frightened to death, from the people walking nearby, diligently paying no attention to what was going on.

It was useless, I'd been completely drained. It was Lemesheva . . . that was why she was standing there stronger than everyone else, the lousy . . . we were all going to die here for an old woman no one needed, and she'd be left . . . that vile creature . . .

But the Light Ones had already shoved a scruffy, plump woman in a dirty house coat and torn slippers into Edgar's arms. She had no idea what was happening — she was staring all around and trying to cross herself.

'You'll pay for this,' were Semyon's last words.

Edgar pulled the witch's arm behind her back with a sharp jerk — he had no time for explanations and no strength left for magic. He dragged her down the staircase.

Hold the Circle . . .

A sacrifice is an act of such great power that it is best held in reserve. The right to use it might have been won twenty or thirty years earlier by the cunning use of intrigue and provocation. That was why Kireeva was still standing stony-faced above the little girl, with the knife gleaming in her hand, ready to cut out her heart in a single swift movement, while Deniska monotonously recited the words of the appropriate spells. At any moment we could have received a powerful stream of energy . . . only it was better for us to do without it.

Hold the Circle . . .

My anger was the only thing that saved me. Anger at the entire unsuccessful day, at all the failures of the last year, at Lemesheva, who clearly knew more than she was saying. I don't know where I found that final reserve of power, but I did! And I drove it through the limp bodies of Olga and Zhanna, so that Lemesheva could transmit the thin stream of power to Edgar.

The first to climb back into the minibus were the vampire brothers . . . those useless field agents . . . Then Lenka let the little girl go and she raced off, howling. Deniska stopped intoning spells, picked up the little table and tossed it into the back of the minibus. And it was only then that Lemesheva broke the Circle.

Everything was swimming in front of my eyes. For some reason I started coughing as I tried in vain to free my hand from Olga's rigid fingers.

'Into the bus!' Anna Lemesheva shouted. 'Quickly!'

Edgar appeared – at least he looked fairly cheerful. He pushed the witch into the back of the bus and jumped into the seat beside Deniska. Anna Lemesheva dragged Olga into the bus and I helped Zhanna in – she was in a very bad way, but she was still conscious.

'Who are you? Who are you?' the rescued woman wailed. Lemesheva slapped her hard across the face and the witch shut up.

'Deniska, step on it,' I said. As if he needed to be told . . .

We tore out of the courtyard with a screech of tyres. Edgar was holding his head in his hands and working – correcting the reality lines, clearing the way ahead of us.

'Feeling bad, Aliska?' Lena asked with avid curiosity. I gritted my teeth and shook my head. But Lena complained: 'I'm completely exhausted. I'll have to take time off.'

The rescued witch whined quietly until she caught my hate-filled glance. Immediately she fell silent and tried to move backwards, away from me, but the vampires were sitting there. Battered, bloody and angry – I think they'd been sensible enough to try to keep away from the shape-shifter, but each of them had caught one or two blows from her paws.

'And they burnt Vitalik to ashes,' Deniska said gloomily. 'He was an idiot, of course, but he was our idiot . . . Anna Tikhonovna, are you sure this bitch was worth all this bother?'

'The order came from Zabulon,' Lemesheva replied. 'He probably knows best.'

'He could have helped us then,' I couldn't help remarking. 'This was a job for his powers, not for ours.'

Anna Lemesheva gave me a curious kind of glance.

'I don't think so. That was a wonderful effort, my girl. Quite marvellous. I didn't think you could give so much power.'

I barely managed to stop myself crying like a child. To hide my tears I looked at Olga – she was still unconscious. At least I could take comfort in that – she'd come off far worse than me.

I raised myself with a struggle and slapped Olga on the cheek. No response. I pinched her. She didn't stir.

Everybody was looking at me curiously. Even the quietly swearing vampires stopped licking their wounds and waited.

'Anna Tikhonovna, couldn't you help her?' I asked. 'She was hurt in the line of duty, and according to standing instructions –'

'Alisa, my dear, how can I help her?' Lemesheva asked in an affectionate voice. 'She's dead. Since five minutes ago. She miscalculated and drained herself completely.'

I jerked my hand away. Olga's limp body jerked backwards and forwards in the chair and her chin lolled across her chest.

'What, can't you tell?' Zhanna whispered. 'Aliska, what's wrong with you?'

Telling the living from the dead doesn't even require any spells. It's elementary power work. That subtle substance that some call the soul can be sensed immediately . . . if it's there.

'You gave up too much power!' said Lenka. 'Oh, Alisa, you're completely empty now! For five years – empty. Like Yulia Bryantseva, who drained herself during an operation two years ago, and since then she can't even enter the Twilight!'

'Don't get your hopes up,' was all I said; trying to keep a calm expression on my face. 'According to standing instructions, they have to help me restore myself.'

It sounded pitiful.

'Did they help Bryantseva?' Lena asked.

But Anna Lemesheva sighed and said:

'Alisa, if only everything had been according to standing instructions a year ago, when Zabulon was so fond of you.'

Before I could even think of a reply, Romashova suddenly squealed hysterically:

'Where are you taking me? Where are you taking me?'

That's when I lost it. I jumped up and started lashing out at the solitary witch's face, trying to scratch her as badly as I could. She was so frightened she didn't even try to resist. I pounded her for about three minutes to the approving cries of the vampire brothers, reproaches from Lemesheva and encouragement from Lenka and Zhanna. Only dead Olga couldn't say anything; I kept stumbling over her in the crowded space of the minibus. But I think she would have supported me.

Then I sat down to catch my breath. The old witch was sobbing and feeling her bloodied face.

If only they were chasing us! I'd bite into those Light Ones' throats as hard as any vampire! I'd finish them off without any magic!

But there wasn't anyone chasing us.

Nobody could have called our return triumphant.

The vampires took Olga's body and set off to headquarters with it without saying a word, as if even they understood the full tragedy of the situation. But then why shouldn't they understand? They had exchanged life for non-life, but they could still think and feel, and theoretically they could carry on like that for all eternity. But now Olga was gone for ever.

Deniska drove the minibus away to the car park. Edgar took the rescued witch firmly by the arm and led her towards the Watch building. She didn't resist. We brought up the rear of the procession.

Carrying a body along a crowded street in the centre of Moscow, close to the walls of the Kremlin, is not the most relaxing of occupations, even with the spell of inattention that Lemesheva had pronounced again. People didn't look at us, they just quickened their step and walked round the procession. But the Twilight became agitated.

The fabric of existence is woven too fine here. There's too much blood, too many emotions, the traces of the past are too clearly evident. There are places like that, where the boundary between the human world and the Twilight is almost imperceptible, and the centre of Moscow is one of them.

If I'd been in a fit state, I would have seen the surges of power emerging from the depths of a different reality. Probably even Zabulon couldn't explain exactly what stands behind them. All that we could do was not react, pay no attention to the greedy breathing of the Twilight that had sensed the death of a witch in magical combat.

'Faster!' Lemesheva said, and the vampires quickened their stride. The Twilight must have become seriously agitated.

Only I couldn't tell any longer.

We went in by the door that was invisible to human beings, and Lena had to take me and Zhanna through. Our colleagues were already running towards us. The witch, who had started yelling again, was dragged off to the tenth floor, to the interrogation room. Olga was handed directly to magicians from the department of healing – without the slightest hope of being able to help, but the fact of death had to be registered. One of the healers on duty examined us carefully. He shook his head disapprovingly as he assessed Zhanna's condition and frowned when he looked at the wounded vampires. But when he turned his attention to me, his face simply froze.

'Is it really that bad?' I asked.

'That's putting it mildly,' he said without superfluous sentimentality. 'Alisa, what were you thinking of when you gave out your power?'

'I was acting according to instructions,' I answered, feeling my tears welling up again. 'Edgar would have been killed – he was up against two second-grade magicians!'

The healer nodded:

'Very praiseworthy zeal, Alisa. But the price is very high too.'

Edgar was already hurrying towards the lift, but he stopped and gave me a look of sympathy. Then he came over to me and kissed the palm of my hand. These Baltic types are always making themselves out to be Victorian gentlemen.

'Alisa, my most profound gratitude! I could sense that you were giving everything you had. I was afraid that you would go the same way as Olga.'

He turned to the healer.

'Karl Lvovich, what can be done for this brave girl?'

'I'm afraid nothing can be done,' the healer said with a shrug. 'Alisa was drawing power from her own soul. It's like acute dystrophy, if you see what I mean. When the body doesn't have enough food, it starts digesting itself. It destroys the liver, the muscles, the stomach – anything to maintain the brain until the very last. Our girls found themselves in a similar situation. Zhanna seems to have lost consciousness in time and stopped drawing on her last reserves. Alisa and Olga held out to the end, but Olga's inner resources were not so great and she died. Alisa survived, but her mental reserves have been completely exhausted.'

Edgar gave a sympathetic nod and everyone else listened to the doctor with interest as he continued with his florid rhetoric.

'The special abilities of an Other are similar in some ways to any other energy reaction – take a nuclear reaction, for instance. We maintain our abilities by drawing power from the world around us, from humans and other less complex objects. But in order to begin receiving power, first you have to invest some of your own – such is the cruel law of nature. And Alisa has practically none of that initial power left. Simply pumping in power is no help in this case, just as a piece of heavily salted pork fat or an over-cooked, crispy steak won't save someone who's starving to death. The body can't digest that kind of food – in fact, it will kill, not cure. It's the same thing with Alisa – we could pump energy into her, but she would choke on it.'

'Could you please not talk about me in the third person?' I asked. 'And not in that tone of voice!'

'I'm sorry, my girl.' Karl Lvovich sighed. 'But what I'm saying is the truth.'

Edgar gently released my hand and said:

'Alisa, don't take it too much to heart. Perhaps the boss will think of something. And by the way, talking of steaks . . . I'm starving.'

Lemesheva nodded:

'Let's go to some little bistro.'

'Wait for me, okay?' said Zhanna. 'I'll just have a shower, I'm drenched in sweat . . .'

I didn't even have enough strength left to feel horrified. I stood there like a fool, listening to their conversation, trying to sense anything at all as an Other. To see my real shadow, to summon the Twilight, to feel the emotional background . . .

There was nothing.

And they seemed to have forgotten about me already.

If it had been Zhanna or Lenka in my place, I would have behaved exactly the same way. After all, there's no point in hanging yourself just because someone else got careless, is there? Did anyone ask me to give everything, right down to the limit? No, it was my fault for trying to be a hero!

It was all because of Semyon and Tiger Cub. When I realised who we were up against, I decided to take my revenge. To prove something . . . to someone . . . for some reason . . .

Now what was I going to do? I'd proved it, all right, and I'd been crippled. And far more badly than in the fight with Tiger Cub.

'Just be quick, Zhanna,' said Lemesheva. 'Alisa, are you coming with us?'

I turned towards her, but before I could say anything, someone spoke behind me:

'Nobody's going anywhere.'

Lemesheva's eyes opened wide and I shuddered as I recognised the voice.

Zabulon was standing by the lift.

He was in his human form: skinny and sad-looking, rather preoccupied. Many of our people only know him like that – calm and unhurried, even a little boring.

But I know another Zabulon too. Not the restrained head of the Day Watch, not the mighty warrior in demonic form, not the Dark Magician beyond classification, but a cheerful, inexhaustibly inventive Other. Simply an Other, without any sense of the gulf between us, as if there were no difference in age, experience or power.

That's the way it used to be. Before . . .

'I want everyone in my office,' Zabulon ordered. 'Immediately.'

He disappeared – into the Twilight probably. But before that he rested his glance on me for a brief moment. There was no expression at all in his eyes. No mockery or sympathy or affection.

But he did look at me, and my heart stood still. For the last year Zabulon had seemed not even to notice the unfortunate witch Alisa Donnikova.

'So much for bistros and showers,' Lemesheva said dourly. 'Come on, girls.'

It was an accident that I ended up sitting apart from the Others.

My feet automatically took me to the armchair by the fireplace – the broad leather armchair in which I used to curl up, half sitting, half lying, watching Zabulon at work, looking at the smokeless flame in the hearth, the photographs hanging all round the walls.

And when I realised that I'd unwittingly separated myself from the Others, who had taken appropriate places on the sofas by the wall, it was already too late to move. It would only have looked stupid.

Then I kicked off my sandals, pulled my feet up and made myself comfortable.

Lemesheva glanced at me in astonishment before she began her report. The others didn't even dare look – their eyes were fixed adoringly on the boss. The sycophantic toadies.

Leaning back in his chair behind his huge desk, Zabulon didn't react to me at all either. At least not visibly.

Well, don't look then . . .

I listened to Lemesheva's smooth voice – she gave her report well, speaking briefly and to the point, nothing superfluous was said and nothing important was omitted. And I looked at the photograph hanging above the desk. It was very, very old, taken a hundred and forty years earlier, using the colloidal process – the boss once explained to me in detail the differences between the 'dry' and 'wet' methods. The photograph showed Zabulon in old-fashioned clothes as a student at Oxford, with the tower of Christ Church in the background. It was a genuine original by Lewis Carroll. The boss once remarked that it had been very difficult to persuade the 'dried-up prim and proper poet' to spend some time on one of his own students instead of a little girl. But the photograph had turned out very well, Carroll must have been a real master. Zabulon looks serious, but there's a lively glint of irony in his eyes, and he looks a lot younger too . . . but then, what does a century and a half mean to him?

'Donnikova?'

I looked at Lemesheva and nodded.

'I entirely agree. If the absolutely essential goal of our mission was to free the prisoner, then forming the Circle of Power and threatening to perform the sacrifice was the best approach.'

I paused for a moment and then added sceptically:

'Of course, that's if that stupid idiot was worth all the effort.'

'Alisa!' There was a metallic ring to Lemesheva's voice. 'How dare you debate the chief's orders? Chief, I apologise for Alisa, she's overwrought and not . . . not entirely well.'

'Naturally,' said Zabulon. 'Alisa effectively ensured the success of the entire operation. She sacrificed all her power. It's hardly surprising that she feels like asking questions.'

I raised my head sharply.

Zabulon was quite serious. Not a hint of mockery or irony.

'But –' Lemesheva began.

'Who was just talking about respect for seniority?' Zabulon interrupted her. 'Be quiet.'

Lemesheva was silent.

Zabulon got up from behind the desk and walked over to me without hurrying. I kept my eyes fixed on him, but I didn't get up.

'That stupid fool,' said Zabulon, 'was not worth all the effort. Of course not. But the actual operation against the Night Watch was extremely important. And all of the injuries you suffered in the battle are entirely justified.'

I felt as if I'd been stabbed in the back.

'Thank you, Zabulon,' I replied. 'It will be easier for me to live through all these years, knowing that my efforts were not in vain.'

'All what years, Alisa?' Zabulon asked.

It was strange . . . we hadn't spoken at all for a whole year . . . I hadn't even received any orders from him in person . . . and now when he spoke to me, there was that cold, prickly lump in my chest again.

'The healer said it will be a long time before I can restore my power.'

Zabulon laughed. And suddenly he reached out his hand! And he patted me on the cheek. Affectionately . . . in that old, familiar way . . .

'Never mind what the healer said,' Zabulon declared peaceably. 'The healer has his opinion, and I have mine.'

He took his hand away and I had to struggle to stop my cheek following it . . .

'I think no one will disagree that Alisa Donnikova was substantially responsible for the success of today's operation?'

Aha . . . I'd have liked to see anyone try to object! Lemesheva simply observed cautiously:

'We all made a significant effort.'

'From your condition it's not hard to see who made what kind of effort.'

Zabulon went back to his desk. But he didn't sit down, he just leaned over with his hands on the desktop, looking at me. I think he was studying me closely through the Twilight.

But I couldn't sense it . . .

'Is everyone agreed that the Day Watch should help Alisa?' Zabulon enquired.

A glint of fury appeared in Lemesheva's eyes. The old witch had once been Zabulon's girlfriend herself. That was why she had hated me when I was in favour . . . and why she had become fond of me as soon as the chief had turned his back on me.

'If it's a matter of help,' she began, 'then Karl Lvovich made a good comparison. We are prepared to share our power with Alisa, but that would be like giving a dying person a piece of fatty bacon instead of light broth. But I am willing to try . . .'

Zabulon turned his head and Lemesheva shut up.

'If light broth is what is required, then she shall have light broth,' he said in a very calm voice. 'You can all go.'

The vampire brothers were the first to jump to their feet, then the witches stood up. I started shuffling my feet about, looking for my sandals.

'Alisa, stay, if it's no trouble,' Zabulon said.

The glint in Lemesheva's eyes flared up – and then faded away. She had realised what I was still afraid to believe in.

A few moments later Zabulon and I were left alone. Looking at each other without speaking.

My throat was dry and my tongue wouldn't obey me. No, it couldn't be true . . . I shouldn't even try to deceive myself . . .

'How are you feeling, Alya?' Zabulon asked.

Only my mother ever calls me Alya.

And Zabulon used to call me that . . .

'Like a squeezed lemon,' I said. 'Tell me, am I really such a terrible idiot? Did I exhaust myself doing a job that is no use to anybody?'

'You did very well, Alya,' said Zabulon.

And he smiled.

The same way he used to smile. Exactly the same way.

'But now I . . .'

I stopped, because Zabulon took a step towards me – and I didn't need words any more. I couldn't even get up out of the chair: I put my arms round his legs and hugged him, pressed myself against him – and burst into tears.

'Today you laid the foundation for one of our finest operations,' said Zabulon. His hand was ruffling my hair, but even so at that moment he seemed to be somewhere very far away. Of course, a great magician like him could never afford to relax: he carried responsibility for the entire Day Watch of Moscow and the surrounding region, for the fates of the ordinary Dark Ones living their calm and peaceful lives; he had to fight the intrigues of the Light Ones and pay attention to people's needs . . . 'Alisa, after your stupid trick with the Prism of Power, I decided you weren't really worthy of my attention.'

'Zabulon, I was a conceited fool,' I whispered, swallowing my tears. 'Forgive me. I let you down.'

'Today you made up for everything.'

Zabulon lifted me up out of the armchair in a single swift movement. I stood on tiptoe, otherwise I would have been left dangling in his arms, and I remembered how astonished I had been the first time by the incredible strength of his skinny body. Even when he was in his human form.

'Alisa, I'm pleased with you,' he said and smiled. 'And don't worry about having drained your power. We have certain special reserves.'

'Like the right to perform a sacrifice?' I asked, trying to smile.

'Yes.' Zabulon nodded. 'You're going on holiday, starting today. And you'll come back better than ever.'

My lips started trembling treacherously. What was happening to me? I was wailing like a hysterical child, my mascara must have run all over my face, I didn't have an ounce of power left.

'I want you,' I whispered. 'Zabulon, I've been so lonely . . .'

He gently took my arms away.

'Afterwards, Alya. When you come back. Otherwise it would be . . .' Zabulon smiled. '. . . an abuse of my position for personal ends.'

'Nobody would dare say that to you!'

Zabulon looked into my eyes for a long time.

'There are some who would, Alya. Last year was a very difficult one for the Watch; there are many who would like to see me humiliated.'

'Then don't do this,' I said quickly. 'Don't take the risk. I'll restore my own power bit by bit . . .'

'No, it's the right thing to do. Don't you worry, my little girl.'

My heart skipped a beat at the sound of his voice. At that calm, confident power.

'Why would you take such a risk for me?' I whispered, not expecting any answer, but Zabulon did answer:

'Because love is also a power. A great power, and it should not be disdained.'

# CHAPTER 3

LIFE IS a strange business.

A day earlier I had left my apartment, a young, healthy witch full of power – but unhappy.

Half a day earlier I had been standing in the Watch offices, crippled, with no hope or belief in the future.

How everything had changed!

'Would you like some more wine, Alisa?' Pavel, my escort, asked, looking quizzically into my eyes.

'A little,' I said, looking out of the window.

The plane had already begun its descent into Simferopol airport. The old Tupolev jet creaked as it slowly heeled over, and the passengers' faces were anxious and tense. But Pavel and I sat quite calmly – Zabulon himself had checked to make sure the flight was safe.

Pavel handed me a crystal wine glass. Of course, the glass wasn't the stewardess's standard issue, and neither was the South African Sauternes. The young shape-shifter seemed to be taking his mission very seriously. He was flying south for a holiday with some friends of his, but at the last minute he'd been taken off the flight to Kherson and instructed to accompany me to Simferopol. The rumours that my relationship with Zabulon had been renewed had clearly already reached him.

'Why don't we drink to the chief, Alisa?' Pavel asked. He was trying so hard to ingratiate himself that it was beginning to annoy me.

'All right,' I agreed. We clinked glasses and drank. The stewardess walked past us, checking for the last time that all the seat belts were fastened, but she didn't even look at us. The spell of inattention that Pavel had cast was doing its job. Even this wretched shape-shifter could do more than I could now.

'You must admit,' Pavel said after he'd taken a sip of wine, 'that the way our chief treats the staff is pretty good!'

I nodded.

'And the Light Ones,' he said, putting all the contempt he could muster into those two words, 'they're much greater individualists than we are.'

'Don't overdo it,' I said. 'That's not really true.'

'Oh come on, Alisa!' The wine had made him talkative. 'Do you remember how we stood in the cordon a year ago? Just before the hurricane?'

That cordon was probably the only place I remembered having seen him before. The shape-shifters do all the crude work and our paths seldom cross. Only during combat operations and on those rare occasions when the entire Watch is brought together.

'I remember.'

'Well then, that . . . Gorodetsky. That lousy servant of the Light!'

'He's a very powerful magician,' I objected. 'Very powerful.'

'Oh, sure! He grabbed all that power, squeezed all of it out of ordinary people, and then what? What did he use it for?'

'For his own remoralisation.'

I closed my eyes, remembering how it had looked.

A fountain of light shooting up into the sky. The streams of energy that Anton had gathered from those people. He had risked everything on a single throw of the dice, even risked using borrowed power, and for a brief instant he had acquired power comparable to or even surpassing that of Zabulon and Gesar.

And he had expended all that tremendous power on himself.

Remoralisation. The search for the ethically optimum solution. The Light Ones' most terrible problem was how to avoid causing harm, how to avoid taking a step that would result in inflicting evil on human beings.

'That makes him a super-egotist!' Pavel said with relish. 'He could have defended his girlfriend, couldn't he? And he could have fought us, couldn't he? And how – with that power! But what did he do? He used everything he collected on himself. He didn't even try to stop the hurricane . . . but he could have done, he could have!'

'Who knows what any other course of action would have led to?' I asked.

'But he acted just like any of us. Like a genuine Dark One!'

'If that were true, he'd be in the Day Watch.'

'And he will be,' Pavel said confidently. 'Where else can he go? He couldn't bear to give away all that power, so he used it on himself. And afterwards he made excuses – it was all so that he could make the correct decision . . . And what was his decision? Not to interfere! That was all – not to interfere! That's our way, the Dark way.'

'I'm not going to argue with you, Pavlusha,' I said.

The plane shuddered as the undercarriage was lowered.

At first glance the shape-shifter seemed to be right. But I could remember Zabulon's face during the days after the hurricane. The expression in his eyes was very gloomy – I'd learned to tell the difference. It was as if he'd realised too late that he'd been tricked.

Pavel carried on discussing the subtleties of the struggle between the two Watches, their different approaches, their long-term operational planning. What a strategist . . . he should have been at HQ, not roaming the streets.

I suddenly realised how tired he'd made me feel during our two-hour flight. But at first glance he'd made quite a pleasant impression.

'Pavlusha, what do you transform into?' I asked.

The shape-shifter started breathing heavily through his nose and answered reluctantly:

'A lizard.'

'Oho!' I looked at him again with more interest. Shape-shifters like that were a genuine rarity, he was no ordinary werewolf, like the late Vitalik. 'That's serious! But why don't I see you on operations more often?'

'I . . .' Pavel stopped and frowned. He took out a handkerchief and dabbed his sweaty forehead. 'You, see, the thing is . . .'

His embarrassment was wonderful to watch, he was like an erring schoolgirl on a visit to the gynaecologist.

'I transform into a herbivorous lizard,' he finally blurted out. 'Not the most useful kind in a fight, unfortunately. The jaws are strong, but the teeth are flat, for grinding. And I'm too slow. But I can break an arm or a leg . . . or chew off a finger.'

I couldn't help laughing. I said sympathetically:

'Well, never mind. We need personnel like that too! The important thing is for you to look impressive, to instil fear and confusion.'

'I look impressive all right,' said Pavel, glancing sideways at me suspiciously. 'Only my scales are too colourful, like a painted Khokhloma toy, it's hard to disguise myself.'

I managed to keep a straight face.

'Never mind, I think that's interesting. When people have to be frightened, especially little children, colourful scales are just the thing.'

'That's the kind of work I usually do,' Pavel admitted.

A sharp jolt cut short our conversation as the plane touched down on the runway. The passengers burst into applause, somewhat prematurely. I gazed avidly out of the window for a few seconds, looking at the greenery, the airport terminal, a plane taxiing to take off.

I simply couldn't believe it.

I'd escaped from stuffy, oppressive Moscow, I had the holiday I'd been waiting for for so long . . . and my special rights . . . and when I got back − Zabulon would be waiting for me again . . .

Pavel saw me as far as the trolleybus stop. It's the most amusing trolleybus route I know, all the way from one town to another, from Simferopol to Yalta. But strangely enough, it's actually a convenient way to travel.

Everything here was different, quite different. It seemed hot − but it wasn't the asphalt-and-concrete city heat of Moscow. And even though the sea was a long way away, I could sense it. And the luxuriant greenery, and the whole atmosphere of a huge resort at the height of the season.

It felt good . . . it really did feel good. I just wanted to get a shower as soon as possible, get a good night's sleep, tidy myself up.

'You're not going to Yalta, are you?' Pavel asked.

'Not exactly to Yalta,' I said. I looked gloomily at the long queue. Even the children were all keyed up, ready to grab a seat in the trolleybus. I had no things with me at all − just my handbag and the sports bag over my shoulder, and I could have stood quite easily − but only if I managed to get on the trolleybus without a ticket.

And I didn't feel like standing.

If it came down to it, I had a thick wad of cash for my travel

allowance, holiday allowance and medical allowance – Zabulon
had managed to get me almost two thousand dollars. That was
certainly plenty for two weeks. Especially in Ukraine.

'All right, Pavlusha,' I said and kissed him on the cheek. The
shape-shifter blushed. 'I'll get there, no need to see me off.'

'Are you sure?' he asked. 'I was instructed to give you every
possible help.'

Oh, my little protector . . . A herbivorous lizard, a cow with
scales . . .

'I'm sure. You need to get some rest too.'

'I'm going bicycling with friends,' he informed me for some
reason. 'They're really nice guys, Ukrainian werewolves and even
a young magician. Maybe we could call in to see you?'

'I'd like that.'

The shape-shifter walked back towards the airport, clearly
intending to board another flight. And I set off along the thin line
of taxis and private cars offering lifts. It was already getting dark,
and there were only a few left.

'Where to, lovely lady?' a fat man with a moustache called. He
was standing beside his little Zhiguli and smoking. I shook my
head – I'd never travelled between towns in a Zhiguli . . . I ignored
the Volga as well, and the tiny Oka too – goodness only knew
what that driver was hoping for.

But that brand new Nissan Patrol would suit me very well.

I leaned in over the wound-down window. There were two
dark-haired young guys sitting in the car. The one in the driving
seat was smoking and the other was drinking beer from a bottle.

'Are you guys free?'

Two pairs of eyes stared at me, summing me up. I didn't look
too creditworthy – that was necessary for my cover.

'Maybe,' the driver said. 'If we can agree a price.'

'We can,' I said. 'To the "Artek" camp. Fifty.'

'Are you a young pioneer?' the driver laughed. 'For fifty we'll give you a ride round town.'

The witty type. He was so young he shouldn't have been able to remember what a 'young pioneer' was. And he was excessively ambitious . . . fifty roubles – that was almost ten dollars.

'You didn't ask the most important thing,' I said. 'Fifty what?'

'Well, fifty what?' the driver's friend repeated obligingly.

'Bucks.'

The young guys' expressions immediately changed.

'Fifty bucks, we go fast, without any other passengers and we don't turn the music up loud,' I added. 'Deal?'

'Yes,' the driver decided. He began looking around. 'What about your things?'

'I've got them all here.' I got into the back seat and dropped my bag down beside me. 'Let's go.'

My tone of voice seemed to have had the right effect. A minute later we were already swinging out onto the road. I relaxed and leaned back a bit more comfortably. This was it. Holiday. I needed to rest . . . eat peaches . . . gather my strength.

And afterwards Moscow and Zabulon would be waiting for me . . .

Just at that moment my mobile rang in my bag. I got it out without opening my eyes and took the call.

'Alisa. How was the flight?'

I felt a warm glow in my chest. One surprise after another! Even during our best times Zabulon hadn't felt the need to take any interest in such petty details. Or was this just because I was unwell and feeling down?

'It was excellent, thanks. They said there were problems with the weather, but—'

'I know about that. The guys in the Simferopol Day Watch gave us a hand with the weather. That's not what I meant, Alisa. Are you in a car now?'

'Yes.'

'Your forecast for this trip is bad.'

I pricked up my ears.

'The road?'

'No. Apparently your driver.'

In front of me the young guys' cropped heads were like blank stone. I looked at them for a second, furious at my helplessness. I couldn't even feel their emotions, let alone read their thoughts.

'I'll handle it.'

'Have you let your escort go?'

'Yes. Don't worry, sweetheart. I'll handle it.'

'Are you sure, Alisa?' There was genuine concern in Zabulon's voice. And that had the same effect on me as dope on an athlete.

'Of course. Try looking further ahead in the forecast!'

Zabulon was silent for a moment. Then he said:

'Yes, it straightens out . . . But keep in touch. I'll come if it's necessary.'

'If they do anything to me, just skin them alive, sweetheart,' I said.

'I'll do more than that, I'll make them eat their own skins,' Zabulon agreed. It was no empty threat, of course, but a real promise. 'Well, have a good holiday, darling.'

I switched off the mobile and slipped into a doze. The Nissan drove on smoothly and we were soon out on the main road. The young guys occasionally lit a cigarette and I could smell tobacco – fortunately not the worst kind. Then the sound of the engine became more laboured – we were climbing the mountain pass. I opened my eyes and glanced through the open window at the starry sky. How big the stars were in the Crimea. How close.

Then I fell asleep for real. I even began dreaming – a sweet, languorous dream, I was swimming in the sea at night and there was someone beside me, and sometimes in the darkness I could almost make out the lines of his face, and I could feel the gentle touch of his hands . . .

When I realised that the touch was real, I instantly woke up and opened my eyes.

The engine was silent and the car was parked a little distance off the highway. I think it was on an emergency side road for poor souls whose brakes have failed.

My driver's brakes and his friend's had definitely failed. I could see it in their eyes.

When I woke up the driver's friend took his hand away from my face. He even gave a crooked smile as he said:

'We're here, sister.'

'It doesn't look like Artek, brother,' I replied.

'It's the Angarsky pass. The motor's overheated,' said the driver, licking his lips. 'We have to wait. You can get out for a breath of fresh air.'

If he was still trying to make lame excuses, he was obviously far more nervous than the other guy, who screwed up his courage and said:

'You can have a piss . . .'

'Thanks, I don't need one.' I carried on sitting there, watching the pair of them curiously, wondering what they'd try. Would they try to drag me out of the car? Or try to rape me where I was?

And afterwards?

It would be too dangerous to let me go. They'd probably throw me off a cliff. And probably into the sea – the murderer's best friend throughout the ages. The land preserves clues for a long time, but the sea has a short memory.

'We were starting to wonder,' the driver declared, 'if you really have the money . . . young pioneer.'

'Since I hired you,' I said, emphasising the word 'hired', 'it means I have.'

'Show us,' the driver demanded.

Oh, how stupid you are . . . you little people . . .

I took the wad of dollars out of my purse, peeled off a fifty and held it out, as if I hadn't noticed the greedy eyes devouring the money. Well, now I was certainly done for.

But they still seemed to need some kind of justification. If only for themselves.

'It's counterfeit!' the driver squealed, carefully hiding the fifty in his pocket. 'You bitch, you were trying to . . .'

I looked at them imperturbably as I listened to him swearing obscenely. I felt something inside me tense up, but even so, I didn't have the normal Other powers that would have let me turn these two runts into obedient puppets.

'Hoping your friend can help, are you?' the driver's friend asked. 'Is that it? Going to skin us alive, is he? We'll skin him, you bitch!'

I laughed as I imagined the million and one amusing things Zabulon would have done to these pups. Just for saying that.

The driver grabbed hold of my arm. His young face was basically rather handsome – I wouldn't have minded having a resort romance with an attractive young man like that – but now it was contorted by a mixture of anger, fear and lust.

'You're going to pay in kind, you bitch.'

Ugh. In kind. And with all my things, and a brief flight through the air down an almost vertical incline . . .

No, I didn't want my acquaintance with the warm water of the Black Sea to start that way.

The other young guy reached out towards me, clearly intending to rip my blouse. The bastard, it cost two hundred and fifty bucks!

His hands had almost reached me when I pressed the barrel of my pistol against his forehead.

There was a brief pause.

'My, what tough kids you are,' I purred. 'All right, get your hands off, and get out of the car.'

The pistol had really stunned them. Maybe because I'd come out of the airport, so there was no way they could have expected me to be carrying a gun. Or maybe because their little pup's instincts told them it would be a pleasure for me to blow their brains out.

They jumped out of the car and I followed them. They hesitated for a few seconds and then tried to make a run for it. But that didn't suit me now.

I put the first bullet into the ankle of the driver's friend. His legs were less important, he didn't have to work the pedals. It was a trivial glancing scrape, more like a skin burn than a bullet wound, but it was more than enough. The friend fell to the ground with a howl and the driver stopped dead in his tracks with his hands in the air. I wondered who they thought I was. A Federal Security Service agent on holiday?

'I understand your greed perfectly,' I said. 'The economy's in ruins, people aren't getting paid . . . And the lust too. After all, you still have a young sexual hyper-drive seething inside you. So do I, as it happens!'

Even the wounded one stopped making a noise. They listened to me without saying a word – as night came on the road had emptied and there was just one set of headlights approaching in the distance. It was an enchanting, still night, with the sky covered in stars – a warm Crimean night; and down at the bottom of the cliff, the sea was murmuring.

'You're both very good-looking boys,' I said. 'The only trouble is, I'm not in the mood for sex now. You've behaved too badly. But –' I raised one finger and they stared at it as if they were hypnotised – 'we can find a way round that.'

Judging from the expressions on their faces, they were

expecting the worst. But they needn't have. I'm not a murderer, after all.

'Since there are two of you, and you're clearly good friends,' I explained, 'it won't be any problem for you to pleasure each other. And after that we'll go on to the camp, calmly, with no more adventures.'

'Why, you –' The driver took a step towards me, but the pistol barrel aimed at his crotch had the desired effect.

'There is another possibility,' I agreed. 'I could relieve you of certain unnecessary body parts. And I bet you three to one I can do it with the first shot.'

'You . . .' hissed the wounded one. 'For us they'll—'

'They wouldn't give a bent kopeck for you,' I told him. 'Get your trousers down and get on with it.'

I didn't have the power that allows any Other to break a human being's will. But my voice probably still carried the old conviction.

They obeyed me. Or they tried to obey me.

We sometimes watch gay porn in our department – it's very amusing. And the vampires and magicians often show lesbian films in the duty room.

In the films the actors always go to it with enthusiastic skill, but these two halfwits were obviously upset by this sudden turn of events, and they lacked the necessary experience. So I just basically admired the night view of the sea and kept an eye on the boys to make sure they weren't slacking.

'Never mind,' I comforted them when I thought they'd been humiliated enough. 'Like the man said – the first time doesn't count. You can practise a bit more in your spare time. Get in the car!'

'What for?' the driver asked when he'd finished spitting. He probably thought I wanted to shoot them in their fancy car and push them over the cliff into the sea.

'Well, you agreed to take me to Artek, didn't you?' I said in an astonished voice. 'And you've already got the money.'

We drove the rest of the way without any more adventures. Except that halfway there the driver started howling that he couldn't live with himself, he had nothing left to live for and he was going to turn the wheel and drive off the cliff.

'Go on, go on!' I encouraged him. 'With a bullet in the back of your head you won't even feel the landing!'

That shut him up.

I kept the pistol in my hands all the way to the gates of the Artek camp.

After I opened the door, I leaned back and said:

'Ah, there's just one more thing, guys . . .'

They looked at me with hate in their eyes. All that power I could have drained off if only I'd been in good shape!

'Better not even to try to find me again. Or this night will seem like paradise. Get it?'

No answer.

'Silence signifies agreement,' I said decisively, putting the little Astra Cub back in my purse. The ideal weapon for a frail woman . . . although Pavel had had to carry it through customs.

I walked towards the gates and the Nissan roared off back the way we'd come. I hoped the failed rapists and robbers would have enough sense not to attempt any kind of revenge.

But then, in a couple of days' time I wouldn't be concerned about local petty bandits any more.

And so I arrived at the Artek camp, where I was supposed to restore my health, at two in the morning.

'To sup light broth' as Karl Lvovich had said as he signed the necessary forms.

Every exemplary Soviet young pioneer was supposed to do three things: visit Lenin in his mausoleum, go on holiday to Artek and tie some little Child of October's tie. After that he could proceed to the next stage of his development – the Komsomol.

In the course of my brief childhood career as a young pioneer, I had only managed the first point. This was my chance to make up for one of the things I'd missed.

I don't know how it was in Soviet times, but now the exemplary children's camp had a serious look to it. The perimeter fence was in perfect shape, and there were guards at the entrance. I couldn't actually see any weapons . . . not at first glance . . . but the tough young guys in militia uniform looked serious enough without them. There was a kid of about fourteen or fifteen there too, looking completely out of place beside these guardians of order. Was he perhaps a hangover from the old days, when the bugles were sounded and the drums beaten as the neat ranks of young pioneers walked to the beach for their water therapy following the strict camp schedule?

To be honest, I'd been expecting a lot of bureaucratic red tape. Or at least considerable surprise. But it seemed like it wasn't the first time young pioneer leaders (although now my job had the simpler title of teacher) had arrived at Artek at two o'clock in the morning in a foreign car. One of the guards took a quick look at my papers – they were genuine, checked and approved at all the appropriate offices, certified with signatures and stamps – and then he called the kid over.

'Makar, take Alisa to the duty camp leader.'

'Uhuh,' the kid mumbled, looking me over with interest. He was clearly a good kid, with no complexes. When he saw a beautiful young woman he wasn't afraid to show he was interested. He'd go a long way . . .

After we left the guards' hut, we walked past a long row of boards with lists of daily activities, announcements of various events and children's wall newspapers . . . what a long time it was since I'd seen wall newspapers! Then we set off down a badly lit path, and I found myself trying to spot the traditional Soviet plaster statues of boy buglers and girls clutching oars along it, but there weren't any.

'Are you a new leader?' the boy asked.

'Yes.'

'Makar.' He held out his hand in a dignified manner.

'Alisa.' I shook hands with him, barely managing to restrain a smile.

The difference between our ages was about ten years, or maybe twelve. But even the names showed how everything had changed in that time. Where were all the girls named after Lewis Carroll's Alice now? They'd gone the way of the plaster buglers, the young pioneer banners, the lost illusions and the failed dreams. Marched off in tidy columns to the strains of a cheerful, rousing song . . . The little girl who had made every boy in the country fall in love with her when she played Alice in the old film was now quietly working as a biologist and merely smiled when she was reminded of her old romantic image.

There were other names now. Makar, Ivan, Egor, Masha . . . It was an immutable law of nature – the worse things become in a country, the more it's trampled into the mud, the stronger the yearning for the old roots. For the old names, the old ways, the old rituals. But these Makars and Ivans were no worse. They were probably better, in fact. More serious, more singleminded, not shackled by any ideology or false show of unity. They were much closer to us Dark Ones than all those Alisas, Seryozhas and Slavas.

But I still felt a bit slighted somehow, maybe because we hadn't been like that. Or maybe it was just because they *were* like that.

'Are you just going to be temporary here?' the boy asked, as serious as ever.

'Yes. My friend's ill, I'm going to replace her. But I'll try to come back again next year.'

Makar nodded.

'Do, this is a good place here. I'm going to come next year too. I'll be fifteen then.'

Maybe I imagined it, but I thought I saw a brief sparkle in the little imp's eyes.

'And after you're fifteen?'

He shook his head and replied with obvious regret.

'You can only come until you're sixteen. But anyway, at sixteen I'm going to go to Cambridge to study.'

I almost choked in surprise.

'That's pretty expensive, Makar.'

'I know. It was all planned five years ago, don't worry.'

He had to be the son of one of those New Russians. They had everything planned in advance.

'Well, that's certainly thorough. Are you going to stay there?'

'No, what for? I'll get a decent education and come back to Russia.'

A very serious child. No doubt about it, these human beings sometimes threw up amusing types. It was a pity I couldn't test him for Other abilities right now . . . we could use kids like that.

I followed my guide as he turned off the pathway with its square flagstones onto a narrow track.

'This is a shortcut,' the boy explained. 'Don't worry, I know my way around here . . .'

I followed him in silence – it was pretty dark, and I was relying on just my human abilities, but his white shirt was easy to follow.

'There, you see that light?' Makar asked, turning back to look at me. 'You go straight towards that, I'm off now . . .'

It seemed like the boy just wanted to play a trick on me . . . it was three hundred metres to the Light through the dense growth of the park. He would have been able to boast to his friends about how he led the new teacher into the bushes and left her there.

But Makar had no sooner taken a step off to the side than he caught his foot on something and fell with a cry of surprise. I didn't even feel like gloating – it was so funny.

'Didn't you say you knew your way around here?' I couldn't resist asking.

He didn't even answer, just breathed heavily through his nose as he rubbed his bruised and bleeding knee. I squatted down beside him and looked into his eyes:

'You wanted to play a trick on me, didn't you?'

The kid glanced at me and quickly turned his eyes away. He muttered:

'I'm sorry . . .'

'Do you play tricks like that on everyone?' I asked.

'No . . .'

'So why was I accorded such an honour?'

It was a moment before he answered.

'You looked like . . . you were very sure of yourself.'

'I should think so,' I agreed simply. 'I had some adventures on my way here. I was almost killed on the way, word of honour! But I got through it. So how am I supposed to look?'

'I'm sorry.'

All his seriousness and self-assurance had completely deserted him. As I squatted beside him I said:

'Show me your knee.'

He took his hand away.

Power. I know what it is. I could almost feel it, the power pouring out of the boy: generated by the pain, the resentment, the shame – it was pure power . . . I could almost take it – like any Dark Other, whose strength is people's weakness.

Almost.

But it wasn't what I actually needed. Makar sat there gritting his teeth and not making a sound. He wouldn't give way, and he held the power inside himself. It was too much for me right now.

I took a torch as slim as a pen out of my purse and switched it on.

'It's nothing. Do you want me to put a plaster on it?'

'No, don't. It will be okay like that.'

'Up to you.' I stood up and shone the torch around. Yes, it would have been difficult trying to find my way to that lighted window in the distance . . . 'What now, Makar? Are you going to run away? Or are you going to show me the way after all?'

He got up without saying anything and set off, and I followed him. When we reached the building, which turned out not to be small at all – it was a two-storey mansion house with columns – Makar asked:

'Are you going to tell the duty teacher?'

'About what?' I laughed. 'Nothing happened, did it? We just had a quiet stroll along the path . . .'

He stood there sniffing loudly for a second, then repeated his apology, only this time far more sincerely:

'I'm sorry. That was a stupid trick I tried to pull.'

'Take care of that knee,' I advised him. 'Don't forget to wash it and dab it with iodine.'

# CHAPTER 4

I COULD hear water splashing on the other side of the wall – the duty camp leader had excused himself and gone out to wash after I woke him up. He'd been dozing peacefully to the hissing of a trashy Chinese tape recorder. I don't understand how anyone can possibly sleep to the sound of Vysotsky's songs, but I suppose that heap of junk wasn't fit for playing anything else.

> There'll be poems and maths,
> Honours and debts, unequal battle . . .
> Today all the little tin soldiers
> Are lined up here on the old map.
> He should have kept them back in the barracks,
> But this is war, like any other war,
> And warriors in both armies fall
> In equal numbers on each side.

'I'm done, sorry about that,' the duty leader said as he came out of the tiny shower room, still wiping his face with a standard-issue cotton waffle-cloth towel. 'I was exhausted.'

I nodded understandingly. The tape recorder carried on playing, obligingly making Vysotsky's voice even hoarser than ever:

> Perhaps it's the gaps in their upbringing
> Or the weakness of their education?
> But neither one of the two sides
> Can win this long campaign.
> All these accursed problems of conscience:
> How not to do wrong in your own eyes?
> Here and there, the tin soldiers on both sides,
> How do we decide who ought to win . . . ?

The duty leader frowned and turned the volume down so low I couldn't make out the words any longer. He held out his hand.

'Pyotr.'

'Alisa.'

His grip was as firm as if he was shaking hands with a man; it immediately gave me a sense of distance: 'A strictly professional relationship . . .'

Well, that was fine. I didn't feel particularly inspired by this short, skinny man who looked like an adolescent himself. Naturally, I was intending to take a lover over my holiday, but someone a bit younger and better-looking would suit me more. Pyotr must have been at least thirty-five, and even without any Other abilities I could read him like an open book. An exemplary family man – in the sense that he was almost never unfaithful to his wife, and didn't drink or smoke much and devoted the appropriate amount of time to his children, or rather, his only child. A responsible man who loved his work, he could be trusted with a crowd of snot-nosed kids or teenage hooligans without any worries: he would wipe away the kids' snot, have a heart-to-heart talk with the hooligans, take away their bottle of vodka, lecture them on the harmfulness of smoking and pile on the work, the play and the morality.

In other words, the perfect embodiment of the Light Ones' dream, not a living human being at all.

'I'm very pleased to meet you,' I said. 'I've dreamed about working at Artek for so long. It's a shame it has to be under these circumstances.'

Pyotr sighed.

'Yes, it's a sad business. We're all very upset for poor Nastenka . . . Are you a friend of hers?'

'No,' I said and shook my head. 'I was two years below her at college, to be honest I can't really remember her face.'

Pyotr nodded and began looking through my papers. I wasn't worried about meeting Nastya, she would probably remember my face – Zabulon is always very thorough about details. If there wasn't a single Other anywhere in Artek, then someone would have come from Yalta or Simferopol, stood close to Nastya for a moment or two . . . and now she would remember me.

'Have you worked as a pioneer leader before?'

'Yes, but . . . not in Artek, of course.'

'That's doesn't matter,' Pyotr said with a shrug. 'There's a staff of 2,300 here, that's the only difference.'

The tone in which he pronounced these words seemed almost to contradict their meaning. He was proud of Artek, as proud as if he'd founded the camp himself; as if he'd personally fought off the fascists with a machine gun in his hands, built all the buildings and planted the trees.

I smiled in a way that said: 'I don't believe that, but I won't say anything out of politeness.'

'Nastya works in the Azure section,' Pyotr said. 'I'll take you there, it's already time for Nastya to get up anyway. Our bus goes to Simferopol at five . . . How did you get here, Alisa?'

'There were no problems,' I said. 'I came by car.'

Pyotr frowned.

'They ripped you off, I suppose?'

'No, it was okay,' I lied.

'In any case it's a bit risky,' Pyotr added. 'A beautiful young woman alone in a car at night with a stranger.'

'There were two of them,' I said, 'and they were absorbed in each other.'

Pyotr didn't understand. He sighed and said:

'It's not for me to tell you how to behave, Alisa, you're an adult with a mind of your own. But never forget that anything can happen! Artek is a kingdom of childhood, a realm of love, friendship and justice. It's the one small thing that we have managed to preserve! But outside the camp . . . there are all sorts of people.'

'Yes, of course there are,' I said repentantly. It was amazing how sincerely he pronounced those words, full of inspired pathos! And how genuinely he believed in them.

'Well, all right.' Pyotr stood up and picked up my bag with an easy movement. 'Let's go, Alisa.'

'I can manage on my own, just show me the way.'

'Alisa!' he said with a reproachful shake of his head. 'You'll lose your way. The grounds here cover two hundred and fifty-eight hectares! Come on, let's go.'

'Yes, even Makar got a bit lost,' I agreed.

Pyotr was already in the doorway, but he swung round sharply:

'Makar? The fifteen-year-old boy? Was he at the gate again?'

I nodded, slightly confused.

'I see,' Pyotr said dryly.

We walked out into the warm summer night. It was already getting light. Pyotr took a torch out of his pocket, but he didn't switch it on. We set off along a path that led down, towards the seashore.

'That Makar's a real problem,' Pyotr remarked as we walked along.

'Why's that?'

'He doesn't need much sleep . . . that's the trouble.' Pyotr laughed gloomily. 'He's always running off to the guards at the gate, or to the sea, or even somewhere outside the grounds.'

'I thought he was on some kind of duty at the gate . . . A young pioneer post,' I surmised.

'Alisa!'

Pyotr was wonderful at making objections like that. He could express a whole gamut of emotions just by pronouncing a name.

'Children ought to be asleep at night! Not standing guard duty . . . at the camp gates, at the eternal flame or anywhere else . . . And all normal children do sleep at night, they wear themselves out horsing around before they go to bed and they sleep. They can have so much fun here during the day.'

Gravel began crunching under his feet as we turned off the paved pathway. I took off my sandals and walked on barefoot. It was a good feeling – the hard, smooth little stones under my feet . . .

'If I wanted, I could give the guards a dressing–down,' said Pyotr, thinking out loud. 'Make them send the kid away. But what then? I can't tie him to his bed all night. It's better if he stays with adults, where he can be seen, than swimming alone in the sea at night.'

'But why does he do that?'

'He says he only needs three hours' sleep a night,' said Pyotr, with a note of regret and pity in his voice. He was obviously one of those people who are more interesting to talk to on the phone or when it's dark – his face was boring, without much variety of expression, but the range of intonation in his voice! 'And from the way he dashes around all day long, it must be true. But that's not the real problem . . .'

'Then what is?' I asked, realising that he was expecting a question.

'He doesn't want to miss a moment of this summer, of Artek, of his childhood.' Pyotr's tone was thoughtful now. 'His first and last time at Artek, and what else has life ever given him?'

'The first and last time? But the boy told me . . .'

'He's from a children's home,' Pyotr explained. 'And he's already too old. It's not likely he'll be able to come here again. Nowadays, of course, a child can come to Artek any number of times, but only for money, and the charity sessions.'

I actually dropped a step behind him.

'From a children's home? But he was so convincing.'

'They're all very convincing,' Pyotr replied calmly. 'He probably said something really impressive, didn't he? His parents are in business, he comes to Artek three times a year and this autumn he's going to Hawaii . . . They want to believe it all, so they fantasise. The little ones do it all the time, the older ones not so often. But I expect he took a liking to you.'

'I wouldn't have said so.'

'At that age they still can't express it when they like someone,' Pyotr informed me very seriously. 'Love and hate are easy to confuse in any case, and for a child . . . And you know, Alisa . . . just one comment . . .'

'Yes?'

'You're a very beautiful girl, this is a children's camp after all, but with a quite a few older boys. I'm not asking you not to wear make-up and all that, but . . . Try not to wear that mini-skirt. It really is too short.'

'It's not the skirt that's short,' I replied innocently. 'It's my legs that are long.'

Pyotr glanced sideways at me and shook his head reproachfully.

'Sorry, I was joking,' I said quickly. 'Of course I won't wear it.

I've got jeans, shorts and even a long skirt. And my swimming costume is very modest!'

We walked on in silence.

I don't know what Pyotr was thinking about. Maybe he was wondering if I was suitable for educational work. Maybe he was feeling sorry for the boy in his care. Maybe he was pondering the imperfection of the world. That would have been like him.

But I smiled, remembering how smartly the kid had fooled me.

He ought to be our future brother-in-arms.

A future Dark One.

But even if he wasn't an Other and he was fated to live a boring human life, people like him were still our foundation and support.

It wasn't even a matter of the trick he'd played, of course. The Light Ones like to joke too. It was what drove the kid to play pranks like that – to lead a stranger into the middle of a park at night and abandon her, to thrust out his skinny chest proudly and pretend to be a kid with no problems from a great family ... All of that was *ours*.

Loneliness, dejection, the contempt or pity of people around you – these are unpleasant feelings. But they are precisely the things that produce genuine Dark Ones. People or Others who are marked out by a sense of their own dignity, endowed with pride and a longing for freedom.

What kind of person would result from a child of well-off parents, one who really did spend every summer by the sea and studied in a good school, who made serious plans for the future and had been taught his manners? Despite the widespread opinion to the contrary, he wasn't very likely to turn out close to us. And he wouldn't necessarily go over to the Light Ones either. He'd just bob backwards and forwards his whole life like a lump of shit in a drain – petty wrongdoings, minor good deeds, a wife he loves and a mistress he loves, waiting to take his boss's place and promote one of his friends ... Greyness. Nothing. Not even our enemy, but not our ally either. I have to admit that a genuine Light One inspires respect. He may oppose us, his goals may be unattainable and his methods may be absurd, but he is a worthy opponent. Like Semyon or Anton from the Night Watch ...

So-called good people are equally distant from us and the Light Ones.

But solitary wolf cubs like Makar are our foundation and support.

He would grow up knowing for certain that he would have to struggle. That he was on his own against everyone else, that it was pointless to expect any sympathy or help, and equally pointless to waste his own energy on pity and compassion. He wouldn't get any ideas about being a benefactor to the entire world, but he wouldn't play mean, petty tricks on other people either, he would train his own willpower and character. He wouldn't go under. If the kid possessed the natural abilities of an Other, the extremely rare and unpredictable ability to enter the Twilight, which is all that distinguishes us from ordinary people, then he would come to us. But if he remained a human being, he would unknowingly still assist the Day Watch.

Like many others.

'This way, Alisa.'

We walked up to a small building. A veranda and open windows, a faint light at one of them.

'This is a summer house,' Pyotr told me. 'The Azure section has four main dachas and eight summer houses. You know, I think in summer it's a lot more fun living here.'

He seemed to be apologising for the fact that I and my young charges would be living in the summer accommodation. I couldn't resist asking:

'And what about in winter?'

'Nobody lives here in the winter,' Pyotr said sternly. 'Even though our winters are so warm, the conditions would be inadequate for children to stay here.'

He made the transition to official bureaucratic language very easily too. It was as if he was giving a lecture intending to reassure someone's mother – 'the temperature is pleasant, the living conditions are comfortable, the catering provides a balanced diet.'

We stepped onto the terrace, and I felt a slight stirring of excitement.

I thought . . . I thought I could already feel it.

Nastya turned out to be small and dark-skinned, with features that had something of the Tatar about them. A pretty girl, except that now her face was too sad and tense.

'Hello, Alya.' She nodded to me as if I were an old friend. And in a certain sense, I was – they had obviously given her a false memory. 'Look what's happened now . . .'

I stopped looking round at the room – there was nothing special about it anyway. An ordinary little camp leader's room: a bed, a cupboard, a table and a chair. The little Morozko fridge and the cheap black-and-white television looked like luxury items here.

But then, I'm not fussy . . .

'Nastya, everything will be all right,' I promised her with false sympathy. The girl nodded wearily, the way she must have been doing all day long.

'It's good you were able to fly down so quickly.' She picked up the bag that was already packed, but Pyotr immediately took it. 'Have you worked at Artek before?'

'No.'

Nastya frowned. Maybe whoever implanted the false memory had got something confused, but she had no time to worry about that now.

'I'll be in time for the morning flight, Petya,' she said. 'Is the bus going to Simferopol?'

'In an hour,' Pyotr said with a nod.

The former camp leader turned her attention to me again:

'I've already said goodbye to the girls,' she told me. 'So no one will be surprised. Tell them I love them all very much and I'll definitely . . . I'll try to come back.'

For an instant tears glinted in her eyes – evidently at the thought of one of the possible reasons for a rapid return.

'Nastya,' I said, putting my arm round her shoulders. 'Everything's going to be all right, your mum will get better.'

Nastya's little face crumpled into a grimace of pain.

'She's never been ill!' The words seemed to burst out of her. 'Never.'

Pyotr delicately cleared his throat. Nastya lowered her eyes and stopped talking.

Of course, there had been various different ways I could have been sent to work at the Artek camp. But Zabulon always prefers the simplest possible methods. Nastya's mother had suddenly suffered a massive heart attack, so now she was flying back to Moscow, and another student had been sent from the university to replace her. It was elementary.

Most likely Nastya's mother would have suffered a heart attack anyway: maybe a year later, maybe five. Zabulon always calculates the balance of power very thoroughly. To provoke a heart attack in someone who is perfectly healthy is a fourth-grade intervention that automatically gives the Light Ones the right to respond with magic of the same level.

Nastya's mother would almost certainly live. Zabulon is not given to senseless cruelty. Why kill the woman when the necessary effect can be produced simply by a serious illness?

And so I could have comforted my predecessor. Except that I would have had to tell her too much.

'Here's the notebook I wrote a few things in.' Nastya held out a slim school exercise book with a brightly coloured cover showing a popular singer grinning moronically on stage. 'Just a few details, but it might come in useful. A few of the girls need a special approach.'

I nodded. Then Nastya suddenly waved her hand through the air and said:

'I don't need to tell you all this. You'll manage just fine.'

But she still spent another fifteen minutes introducing me to the subtle details of the camp regime and asked me to pay special attention to some girls who were flirting with the boys too precociously. She advised me not to demand silence after lights out: 'Fifteen minutes is long enough for them to talk themselves out, half an hour at the most.'

Nastya only stopped talking when Pyotr pointed to his watch, without speaking. She kissed me on the cheek, then picked up a small bag and cardboard box – maybe she was taking some fruit to her sick mother?

'All the best, Alisa.'

And at last I was left alone.

There was a pile of clean bed-linen lying on the bed. The electric light bulb glowed feebly under its simple glass shade. Pyotr and Nastya's steps and their simple conversation quickly faded away.

I was left alone.

But not absolutely alone. On the other side of two thin walls, just five steps along the corridor, eighteen little girls aged ten or eleven were sleeping.

I suddenly started trembling. It was a rapid, nervous trembling, as if I were an apprentice again, trying for the first time to extract someone else's power. Nabokov's Humbert Humbert would probably have trembled the same way in my place.

But then, compared to what I was going to do now, his passion for nymphets was nothing but childish naughtiness.

I switched off the light and tiptoed out into the corridor. How I missed my Other powers!

I would just have to make do with the human powers I had left.

The corridor was long and the floorboards squeaked. The threadbare carpet runner was no help, my steps could easily be heard. I could only hope that at this early hour the girls were still sleeping and dreaming.

Simple, straightforward, uncomplicated children's dreams.

I opened the door and went into the dormitory. For some reason I'd been expecting some kind of state institution, halfway between a children's home and a hospital – iron bedsteads, the dull glow of a night lamp, depressing curtains and children sleeping as if they were standing to attention.

But in fact it was all very nice. The only light came from the lantern on the pillar outside. The shadows swayed gently, a fresh sea breeze blew in at the open windows and I could smell the scent of wild flowers. A television screen glowed dully in the corner and the walls were covered with drawings in coloured pencil and watercolours that looked bright and cheerful even in the semi-darkness.

The little girls were sleeping, sprawled out across their beds or tucked right up under the blankets, with all their things neatly arranged on their bedside lockers or scattered untidily on the headboards of the beds and the backs of the chairs – swimming costumes that were still wet, skirts, little pairs of jeans and socks. A good psychologist could have walked through that dormitory at night and come up with a full character portrait of each of those girls.

But I didn't need one.

I walked slowly between the beds, adjusting blankets that had slipped off, lifting up arms and legs that had dropped down to touch the floor. The girls were sleeping soundly. Soundly and with no dreams . . .

I only got lucky with the seventh girl. She was about eleven years old, plump with light hair. An ordinary little girl whimpering quietly in her sleep.

Because she was having a bad dream . . .

I knelt down beside her bed, reached out my hand and touched her forehead. Gently, with just the tips of my fingers.

I felt power.

As I was now without any Other powers, I couldn't have read an ordinary dream. But sensing the opportunity to nourish yourself is a different matter. It all takes place at the level of instinctive animal reaction, like an infant's sucking reflex.

And I saw it . . .

It was a bad dream. The girl was dreaming that she was going home, that their session at camp wasn't over yet, but she was being taken away because her mother had fallen ill, and her gloomy, frowning father was dragging her towards the bus and she hadn't even had time to say goodbye to her friends, she hadn't had any time for a last dip in the sea, or to take some little stones that were very important . . . and she was struggling and asking her father to wait, but he was just getting more and more angry . . . and saying something about disgraceful behaviour, about how girls her age shouldn't have to be beaten, but since she was behaving like this, she could forget about his promise not to punish her with his belt any more . . .

It was a really bad dream. Nastya's departure had affected the little girl very badly.

And anybody would have tried to help the child at that moment.

A human being would have stroked her hair and said something affectionate in a gentle voice, maybe sung a lullaby . . . In short, tried to interrupt the dream.

A Light Other would have used his power to turn the dream inside out, so that the father would laugh and say the little girl's mother was well again and go running to the sea with her. He would have replaced the cruel but realistic dream with a sweet lie.

But I'm a Dark Other.

And I did what I could. I drank her power. Sucked it into myself – the gloomy father, and the sick mother, and the little friends lost for ever, and the sea stones left behind, and the shameful beating . . .

The little girl gave a quiet squeak, like a mouse caught under something heavy. And then she began breathing calmly and regularly.

There's not a lot of power in children's dreams. It's not like the ritual killing that we had threatened the Light Ones with, which provides a truly monstrous discharge of energy. These were dreams, just dreams . . .

Light nourishing broth for an ailing witch.

I got up off my knees, feeling slightly dizzy. No, I hadn't recovered my lost powers yet. It would take a dozen dreams like that to fill the yawning gap.

But those dreams would happen. And I would do my best to encourage them.

None of the other little girls were dreaming. Well, one was, but her dream was no use to me, a silly little girl's dream about the freckle-faced boy who had given her yet another of those stupid stones with a hole in them: what they called 'chicken gods' – I suppose chickens must have their own gods.

I stood beside this girl's bed – she was probably the most physically advanced of them all, she even had the first beginnings of breasts. I touched her forehead several times, trying to find at least something, but there was nothing. Sea, sun and sand, water splashing and that freckle-faced boy. Not a drop of anger, envy or sadness. A Light Magician could have drawn power from her by drinking in her dream and then gone away satisfied. But I was wasting my time here.

Never mind, there would be another evening and another night. And my plump donor's dream would come back to her – I had drawn out all of her fear, but not its causes. Her nightmare would return, and I would help her again. The important thing was not to try too hard, not to push the girl into a genuine nervous break-down: I had no right to do that. That would smack of serious magical intervention, and if the Light Ones had even a single observer in the camp, or even – who knows what tricks the Dark might play – if there was an Other there from the Inquisition, then I would be in serious trouble.

And I wasn't about to let Zabulon down again.

Never.

It was amazing that he had forgiven me for what had happened the previous summer. But he wouldn't forgive me a second time.

At ten o'clock in the morning I went to breakfast with my charges.

Nastya had been right – I was managing just fine.

At first, when the girls had just woken up, they had been a bit cautious. How could they not have been, when the leader they had already come to love had gone away in the middle of the night to see her sick mother, and another young woman had come into the dormitory instead of her – a stranger, an unknown quantity, someone quite unlike Nastya? I had immediately felt the unfriendly, wary gaze of eighteen pairs of eyes on me – they were all together and I was isolated.

The situation was saved by the fact that the girls were still little and I am beautiful.

If they had been boys of the same age, my appearance wouldn't have made the slightest difference. Ten-year-old boys are far more interested in the ugliest of puppies than the most beautiful of girls. And if my charges had been two or three years older, my appearance would only have irritated them.

But for ten-year-old girls a beautiful woman is an object of admiration. They are already beginning to develop the desire to flirt and to please, but they still don't understand that not everybody can grow up beautiful. I know, I was the same myself, and I used to gape wide-eyed at my tutor, the witch Irina Alexandrovna.

So I soon established contact with the girls.

I sat on Olechka's bed, because the notes in the exercise book suggested that she was the quietest and most timid of them. I talked to the girls about Nastya, about how bad it is when your mother is unwell and told them they mustn't be angry with Nastya . . . she had really wanted to stay with them, but your mother is the most important person in your life.

When I finished, Olechka began snivelling and pressed herself against me. And the eyes of all the Others were looking moist and weepy too.

Then I told them about my dad and his heart attack, and I said that nowadays they knew how to cure people's hearts, and Nastya's mother was going to be perfectly all right too. I helped the dark-skinned little Cossack girl Gulnara to weave her plaits – she had magnificent hair, but as Nastya had noted, she was a bit slow. I argued with Tanya from St Petersburg about what was the most interesting way to come to Artek, by train or by plane, and, of course, I finally admitted that she was right – it was much more fun on the train. I promised Anya from Rostov that by the evening she would be swimming and not just floundering about in the shallow water. We discussed the solar eclipse that was expected in three days' time and regretted that it would be just a tiny bit less than total in the Crimea.

We arrived at breakfast as a united and cheerful group. Only Olga, who was 'not Olechka, but always Olga', and her friend Ludmila were still sulky. But that was not surprising, they had obviously been Nastya's favourites.

Never mind, in another three days' time they would come to love me too.

And our surroundings were genuinely lovely.

August in the Crimea is just fantastic. The sea was glittering at the bottom of the slope, the air was saturated with the scent of salty water and flowers. The girls squealed and ran about all over the place, bumping into each other. The marching rhymes in the old pioneer camps were obviously invented for a good reason – you can't do much squealing if your mouth's busy trying to sing.

But I don't know any marching rhymes, and I don't know how to march in line anyway.

I'm a Dark One.

In the dining hall I simply followed my little charges' lead – they knew where we were supposed to sit. We were surrounded by five hundred children creating a huge din who somehow managed to eat at the same time. I sat there quietly with my little band of girls, trying to assess the situation. After all, I had to spend an entire month here.

There were twenty-five leaders who had come to breakfast with their brigades. My facile pride in how skilfully I was managing my charges rapidly evaporated. These young men and women were more like the boys' and girls' older brothers and sisters. Sometimes they were stern, sometimes they were affectionate, their word was law and they were also loved.

Where did they find people like that?

My mood began to deteriorate. I prodded feebly at the 'liver pancakes' that we had been given for breakfast with our buckwheat and cocoa and thought wearily about the unenviable plight of a spy in enemy territory. I was surrounded by too many expressions of delight, too many smiles and innocent pranks. This was a pasture for Light Ones to tend their charges and raise human children in the spirit of love and goodness, not a feeding ground for a Dark One like me.

Sheer hypocrisy on every side. As false as gilded and varnished iron!

Of course, I consoled myself, if I could have looked around with the eyes of an Other, many things might have changed, and among all these nice people I might find villains, perverts, individuals who were malicious or indifferent.

But I couldn't be sure. It could well be that I wouldn't find any. That they were all sincere – to the extent that that is possible. That they sincerely loved the children, the camp and each other with a love that was pure. That this place really was a reservation for idiots, the kind of place the Light Ones dreamed of turning the whole world into.

But that would mean there was at least some basis for the way the Light Ones acted.

'Hello.'

I looked round at the boy walking past. Aha, my old acquaintance . . . or, rather, my first acquaintance in Artek.

'Good morning, Makar.' I squinted at his skinned knee. 'So where's the iodine?'

'It's nothing. It'll heal on its own,' the boy muttered. He gave me a slightly alarmed look – evidently he was trying to figure out if I'd found out anything about him already or not.

'Better run, or you won't have time to eat anything.' I smiled. 'Maybe you only need three hours' sleep, but food's a different matter. The food here's institutional too, but it's good.'

He strode off quickly along the line of tables. Now he knew that I was in the know – about his nocturnal wanderings and his genuine social status. If I'd been in better shape I could have drawn in a lot of power.

'Alisa, how do you know him?' Olechka whispered loudly.

I put on a mysterious face.

'I know everything about everybody.'

'Why?' Olechka asked curiously.

'Because I'm a witch!' I told her in a hollow, ghostly voice.

The little girl laughed happily.

Oh yes, it's very funny . . . especially because it's the absolute truth. I patted her on the head and pointed to her full plate with my eyes.

I still had to go through the official part of proceedings – the introduction to the head of the Azure section. And then – the beach and the sea that my little girls were already twittering about.

And to be quite honest, I realised I was looking forward to it just as much as the night ahead. I might be a Dark One but, contrary to common ignorant opinion, even vampires love the sea and the sunshine.

The year before, at the end of summer, I'd managed to get away to Jurmaala. I don't know why I went there – I must have wanted to be somewhere uncomfortable. If so, I was lucky: August turned out rainy, cold and miserable. The stiff Latvian waiters immediately started speaking Russian as soon as they'd added up the price of my order, the service in the hotel was primitive and Soviet-style, despite its pretentious four-star rating. I wandered all around Jurmaala, sat for ages in a little beer hall in Majori, strolled on the wet sand of the deserted beach, and in the evenings I escaped to Riga. There were two attempts to rob me, and one to rape me. I enjoyed myself as best I could . . . I had my Other powers then and no human being in the world could cause me any harm. My heart was weary and empty, but I had all the power I needed and more.

And then I suddenly felt sick of it all. All at once, one day. Maybe it was because of the two Night Watch agents who detained me in Dzintari for ages while they tried to frame me for some unsolved crime involving third-grade magic. They were irreproachably polite and absolutely adamant. That was probably what the Latvian Red Riflemen were like, and then the 'forest brothers' after them. The Latvians are a very thorough, consistent people – once they take a job on, they see it right through to the end.

I managed to refute the charges – they were genuinely groundless in any case. But the following morning I took a plane to Moscow. Without having swum in the sea even once all summer.

But now it was payback time.

Everything was going fine, everything was normal. I met the woman in charge of the Azure section – a very nice woman, brisk and pleasantly businesslike, who spoke briefly and to the point, quite pleasantly. I felt we had parted company entirely satisfied with each other.

Maybe it was because today I'd put on my thin summer jeans, and not the provocative mini-skirt?

At last I had done a bit of sunbathing and been in the sea. The beach at Artek was wonderful, except that there was too much howling from the kids. But that was an inevitable evil, no matter how I looked at things. My little girls turned themselves over in the sun in a highly professional manner, trying to get an even tan. Almost half of them had suntan lotion and after-tan lotion, which they shared generously with each other, so there was no prospect of problems in the evening with burnt shoulders and backs.

If only I didn't still have to keep an eye on the girls . . . I imagined myself swimming out a kilometre or two, or even three, throwing my arms out and floating on the water . . . looking up into the cloudless sky, swaying on the gentle waves, not thinking about anything or hearing anything . . .

But no. I had to watch them. I had to teach Anya to swim and prevent Verochka, with her grade-one swimming diploma, from trying to swim off too far. I had to herd the girls into the shade – they might have suntan lotion, but rules were still rules. Basically, along with the wonderful sea I had been given another eighteen capricious, noisy, fidgety little presents. The only thing that kept me smiling was the thought of the night ahead, when the time would come for me to get even with the most bothersome ones – I'd already decided it would be Verochka, Olga and Ludmila! That night I wasn't going to gather chance scraps of power. I was going to sow the seeds that would sprout in their dreams.

And then I saw Igor.

No, I didn't know what he was called then. I simply looked around as I was lying on the warm sand and noticed a well-built young man the same age as myself. He was messing about in the water with his little squirts – a gang of ten- or eleven-year-old boys. Throwing them into the water, offering them his shoulders as a diving board – in short, having a really good time. He wasn't tanned at all, but that seemed to suit him somehow – in the middle of the crowd of swarthy children's bodies he stood out like . . . like a white elephant moving condescendingly through a crowd of dark-skinned Indians.

A handsome young man.

I felt a sweet ache somewhere below my stomach. We haven't really moved all that far away from people. I understood well enough that there's an immense gulf between Others and human beings, that this young guy was not my equal and we couldn't have any lasting kind of relationship, but even so . . .

I just like men like that: with strong muscles, light-brown hair and intelligent faces. There's nothing to be done about it.

And what would be the point of doing anything?

I'd been intending to find myself a friend for the summer anyway . . .

'Olechka, do you know what that camp leader's called?' I asked the little girl pressing herself against me. Olechka clearly felt fond of me because I'd singled her out from the crowd just a little, and now she was staying close to me, trying to build on her success. People are funny, especially children. They all want care and attention.

Olechka looked and shook her head.

'That's brigade number four, only they used to have a different leader before.'

A look of alarm appeared in the girl's eyes – as if she was afraid that I would be disappointed with her for not knowing the answer. Perhaps she really was afraid . . .

'Do you want me to find out?' Olechka asked. 'I know some boys in that brigade.'

'All right,' I said with a nod.

The little girl jumped up, scattering sand around her, and ran towards the water. I turned away, hiding a smile.

So now I already had my first informer. A nervous, skinny little girl desperately seeking my attention.

'He's called Igor,' Natasha suddenly said out of the blue: she was sitting beside me. This was the same girl who had been dreaming about a boy the night before. She didn't sunbathe like a child either – she sat up on the sand with her legs stretched out and her head thrown back, with her hands propping her up from behind. She must have seen the pose in some fashion magazine or a film. Or perhaps she'd simply realised that in that position her new little breasts stood out clearly under her swimming costume. She would go a long way . . .

'Thank you, Natasha,' I said. 'I thought I'd met him somewhere before.'

The girl squinted at me and smiled. She said dreamily:

'And he's handsome . . .'

Whatever are young people coming to these days!

'But he's too old, right?' I said, trying to tease her.

'No, he's still not too bad,' the girl declared.

And then she totally amazed me by declaring:

'He's reliable, though, isn't he?'

'Why do you think so?'

Natasha pondered for a moment and replied lazily:

'I don't know. I just think so. My mum says the most important thing in a man is reliability. They don't have to be handsome, let alone intelligent.'

'That depends on what you have in mind.' I wasn't going to be bested by an eleven-year-old smarty-pants.

'Yes,' Natasha agreed readily. 'There have to be handsome ones too. But I wasn't talking about that sort of nonsense.'

How delightful! I thought that if this girl turned out to be an Other, I would definitely take her on as an apprentice. There wasn't much of a chance, of course, but just maybe . . .

A moment later, shedding all her precocious wisdom in an instant, Natasha jumped up and went dashing off along the beach after some kid who had splashed water on her. I wondered if the concept of reliability included daily dousings on the beach.

I looked at the young guy again. He'd already stopped messing about in the water and was driving his charges out onto the sand.

What a striking figure! And the form of his skull was very regular. Maybe it's funny, but apart from a good figure there are two things I like in men – a beautifully shaped head and well-tended toes. Maybe it's some kind of fetish?

I couldn't see his toes, of course. But so far I liked everything else I'd seen.

My little spy came back to report. Wet, excited and happy. She plumped down on the sand beside me and started whispering, nervously winding a lock of hair round her finger:

'His name's Igor Dmitrievich. He's good fun and he only came yesterday. He plays songs on the guitar and tells interesting stories. The leader of the fourth brigade went away, his wife had a little boy, he thought it was going to be a month later, but it happened now!'

'Well, wasn't that lucky,' I said, thinking mostly of my own interests. Bearing in mind that I had no powers at all and I couldn't make the young guy fall in love with me, a coincidence like that was very useful. He'd just arrived, he hadn't had a chance to form any romantic attachments. He surely wasn't planning to spend his entire session just practising his educational skills, was he? He was there for the taking . . .

Olechka giggled happily and added in a very quiet voice:

'And he's not married either.'

What on earth can you do with them?

'Thank you, Olechka.' I smiled. 'Shall we go in for a swim?'

'Uhuh.'

I picked up the little girl, who squealed with delight, and ran into the water. It was clear that in the evening the favourite topic of conversation would be the new camp leader and my interest in him.

But that was okay.

In a couple of days I'd be able to make them forget anything I thought they ought to.


The day rushed by like a film played at high speed.

The comparison was all the more appropriate because I'd arrived in Artek during the sixth session, when a children's film festival was traditionally held there. Two days later there was going to be a grand opening, and film directors and actors were already giving talks in some of the camps. I didn't have the slightest desire to watch any old or new children's films, but the festival promised to give me a short break from keeping an eye on the girls. And I already felt like taking a break – I was as exhausted as after a long, tense spell of duty on the streets of Moscow.

After the afternoon snack, which consisted of apple juice and rolls with the romantic name 'Azure', I couldn't hold out any longer and phoned Zabulon. His satellite phone worked anywhere in the world, but there was no answer, which could only mean one thing – the boss was not in our world, but somewhere in the Twilight.

Well, he was a very busy man.

And sometimes his business wasn't very pleasant. Travelling through the lower levels of the Twilight, where all parallels with the human world completely disappeared, was quite an ordeal. I'd never been down there myself, it required absolutely immense powers. Except, that is, for that one time, after my stupid stunt, when I was caught gathering energy from people illegally.

I can hardly remember anything about what happened. Zabulon rendered me unconscious, at one and the same time punishing me for my misdemeanour and protecting me against the deep levels of the Twilight. But sometimes I do recall something. As if there was one moment of clear awareness in the blank greyness.

It's like a dream or a delirious vision. Maybe I *was* delirious? Zabulon, in the form of a demon, carrying me thrown across his shoulder. His scaly hand squeezing my legs and my head dangling above the ground, above that shimmering, rainbow-coloured sand. I look up and I see a glowing sky. A sky made entirely of blinding light. With big, black stars scattered across it.

And between me and the sky there are two arches rising up to an immense height. Dull grey, as if they are made out of mist . . .

there's nothing frightening about them, but for some reason I am struck with terror.

And the rustling – a dry, menacing rustling sound on all sides, as if the grains of sand are trembling and rubbing against each other, or there is a cloud of insects hovering somewhere outside my field of vision.

I was probably delirious after all.

Maybe now, when everything had been put right between us, I could risk asking Zabulon what was down there in the depths of the Twilight?

But the day rolled on, and now it was rapidly approaching evening. I got Olga and Ludmila to make up after they quarrelled, we went to the beach again and Anya swam a few metres for the first time without any help. She beat the palms of her hands against the surface of the water, with her eyes staring wildly, but she still swam . . .

This was hard labour, not a holiday. This was all for the Light Ones, they'd be only too happy to spend all their time on educational work. My only consolation was that night was approaching. The sun was already getting low in the sky and even the indefatigable children were beginning to get tired.

After fish, pancakes and potatoes for supper – I wondered where they put it all – I was all ready for action. Now I only had to amuse the girls for another two hours until their second supper (anyone would think all the kids who had come were severely undernourished), and then it would be time to sleep.

It probably showed in my face.

Galina, the leader of the seventh brigade, came up to me. I'd got to know her that afternoon, more in order to keep up my cover than out of any real interest. She was an ordinary human girl, a standard product of the Light Ones' tedious moralising – kind, calm and reasonable. She had a tougher job than me – her brigade was made up of girls who were twelve to thirteen years old, and that meant they were constantly falling in love, getting hysterical and crying into their pillows. But even so Galina was positively on fire with the desire to help me.

'Tired?' she asked in a low voice, smiling as she looked at my girls.

I just nodded.

'The first session's always like that,' said Galina. 'Last year, after I'd worked here for a month, I swore I'd never come back again. And then I realised I couldn't live without Artek any longer.'

'Like a drug,' I prompted her.

'Yes.' Galina didn't even notice my irony. 'Everything here's in colour, if you know what I mean. And the colours are all so pure and bright. Haven't you felt that yet?'

I managed a forced smile.

Galina took hold of my hand and, glancing mysteriously at the girls, she whispered:

'Do you know what? The fourth brigade are going to build a bonfire now. They've invited us to the bonfire, and I'm inviting you! You'll get two hours' rest, your girls will be amused without you having to do anything.'

'Is it all right?' I asked quickly, although I didn't have the slightest desire to refuse. Not only because it was a chance to be free of work for two hours, but also because of the attractive camp leader Igor.

'Of course it is!' said Galina, looking at me in surprise. 'Igor comes to Artek every year, he's one of our best leaders. You ought to get to know him too. He's a nice guy, isn't he?'

Her voice had a warm ring to it. It wasn't surprising. I'm not the only one who likes the combination of firm muscles and an intelligent face.

'We'll come,' I agreed. 'Right now.'

# CHAPTER 5

I FOUND myself changing my clothes with unfamiliar haste. Where was I going in such a hurry? What for? Just to get to know a guy with a cute face and pumped-up muscles? In two or three days' time any man would be mine for the taking, I'd be spoilt for choice. I'm no succubus, I'm an ordinary witch, but I could already enchant a man if I liked him when I was a child and had barely learned to control power. I only had to wait a little bit longer, and then . . .

But no, I couldn't wait! I put on my best underwear, far too good for a pioneer camp leader, it should have been shown off by a model on a catwalk. And the slim silver chain with the diamond pendant, even though no one would realise they were real diamonds and not cheap artificial stones. A drop of Climat perfume behind my ears, a drop on my wrist, a drop on my pubis . . . was I really serious about trying to seduce him today?

Yes, I was! Really serious!

And I even understood why.

I was used to relying on my abilities as an Other. Whether they were appropriate or not, even when I could get what I wanted by making ordinary conversation or simply asking. It would have been strange if it hadn't become a habit. But since I'd been temporarily deprived of my supernatural powers, why not see how I got on without them?

Could I do anything without magic or not?

Even something as elementary as seducing a man that I liked?

After all, I was young, beautiful and skilful . . . there was the sea, a campfire on a summer evening . . . the pesky children would all have gone to bed . . . surely I could manage it without any magic?

If not, then what was I worth?

I'd promised not to wear the mini-skirt, but the shorts that I took out of my bag were even more provocative. I turned round in front of the mirror, examining myself. Not bad. A more revealing blouse would have been better, but there was no point in asking for trouble. This was a young pioneer camp, after all, not a normal resort.

I was so absorbed in all my preparations that I even missed the knock on the door. I only turned round when it creaked open and Olechka peeped into my room and started gabbling:

'Alisa, we're all ready . . . oh!'

She stared at me with admiration. With such genuine admiration that I didn't even rebuke her for entering the room without permission.

'Alisa, how beautiful you are!'

I smiled proudly. It was nothing really, a word of praise from a dowdy little girl who painstakingly decorated her skinny little arms with silly bead trinkets and hung a stone with a hole in it on a string round her thin neck, but even so it was pleasant . . . Those stones with holes in them again, I was sick to death of them.

'What do you think,' I asked, 'could someone fall in love with me?'

Olechka beamed happily. She dashed up to me, put her arms round me, pressed her face into my stomach and said passionately:

'He's bound to fall in love with you! As soon as he sees you he will!'

'It will be our little secret!' I said in a whisper. 'All right?'

Olechka began nodding rapidly.

'Run to the girls now, I'll be out in a moment,' I said. Olechka gave me one last admiring glance and skipped out of the room.

Okay. Now just a little bit of make-up. When you're in a hurry, everything always goes awry, but . . .

I touched up my lips quickly — with my softest, least-bright lipstick — and my eyebrows with waterproof mascara: for some reason I was sure it had to be waterproof. And that was it. Enough.

I wasn't going to a concert. Just a little pioneer brigade campfire.

Every one of the summer houses had a campfire site. It was obviously one of the Artek traditions. The impression was spoiled a bit by the fact that the wood for the campfire looked a bit too 'official' — it was all neatly cut blocks. I could just imagine the camp leaders turning up at the supply office and writing out a request: 'firewood for the holding of a brigade bonfire to last two hours . . .'

But this was no joke. I would probably have to organise something of the kind too. Write out a request, bring the wood — or would workmen deliver it? Never mind, I'd find out later.

Everything was ready, the wood had been heaped up, the boys of the fourth brigade and the girls of the seventh were sitting round it. And space had considerately been left for my charges too.

How very thoughtful.

Igor was sitting beside the huge campfire with his boys swarming all over him. He was quietly strumming the strings of a guitar, and I almost groaned out loud when I realised that songs by the Russian 'bards' were an integral element of parties like this. What an unfortunate instrument the guitar is! An instrument of such great nobility, a genuine monarch of music – reduced to a pitiful lump of wood with six strings, constantly abused by people with no ear and no voice.

But I would have to put up with it.

It would just be a shame if such an attractive human specimen turned out to be one more singer without any voice or any talent.

Oh, and what if he even sang his own songs?

That's a real nightmare, when someone who writes bad verse learns three chords, decides that one negative quantity multiplied by another will give a positive result, and becomes a 'singer-songwriter'. I've seen so many of them. When they start to sing, their eyes glaze over, their voices are filled with mysterious, romantic, manly courage, and it's absolutely impossible to stop them. Like wood grouse in the mating season! The only alternative is pop songs in the garbled renditions which are the best they can manage. Numbers by Victor Tsoi and Kino or Alisa, or whatever it is that young people like today.

Anyway, whatever it was, I wasn't going to like it!

When he saw us there, Igor got up to greet us and all my forebodings immediately evaporated. Yes, he was a really handsome man!

'Hello.' He spoke as if we were already close. 'We haven't started, we were waiting for all of you.'

'Thank you.' I could feel myself losing control. My little girls were already sitting down, elbowing the boys aside – they were a little bit wary of the older girls – and I was still standing there like a fool, attracting knowing glances.

'You're a great swimmer,' Igor said with a smile.

Aha!

So he had found time to look around on the beach after all.

'Thank you,' I said again. What was wrong with me? I was petri-fied, like some naïve, inexperienced girl, I didn't even need to pretend.

My anger at myself immediately gave me strength. I sat down on the grass between Olechka and Natasha. My own private little guard, the spy and the adviser. But they had no interest in me right now, they were too excited by the prospect of the campfire.

'Okay, Alyoshka, begin!' Igor said in a jolly voice and threw a box of matches to a thickset boy with blond hair. The boy caught it deftly, then crawled up to the campfire on all fours and sat down with his legs crossed. It was like the preparations for some sacred ritual.

The boy took a match out of the box with meticulous preci-sion, cupped his hands like an inveterate smoker and struck it. He leaned over towards the fire. It didn't look as if there was any paper there to start the blaze, just pine needles and small chips of wood. Everybody held their breath.

In other words, it was a ridiculous performance.

But even so, I was curious to see if the little pyromaniac would manage to light the campfire with one match or not.

He did. The first tongue of flame flickered in the gathering gloom. It was greeted with universal howling and squealing, as if the campfire were surrounded by a tribe of primordial humans who were freezing in bitterly cold weather.

'Well done!' Igor reached out and shook the boy's hand and ruffled his hair with a smile. 'You'll be our campfire monitor.'

Alyoshka's face expressed immense pride.

Five minutes later the campfire was already blazing and the chil-dren had settled down a bit. All around they were chattering, laughing and whispering, running away from the fire and then back again, throwing on little branches and pine cones, trying to roast pieces of sausage threaded onto twigs. In short, the rejoicing was unconfined. Igor sat in state in the middle of the children, punctuating the conversation with phrases that sent everyone into peals of laughter, or tasting the half-burnt food, or calling back children who were getting too close to the fire. The life and soul . . . Galina was besieged by her charges too. I was the only one sitting there like a total fool in the middle of the happy crowd, giving irrelevant answers to the girls' questions, laughing belatedly when they did and turning my eyes away the moment Igor looked in my direction.

Fool! What a fool I am! The last thing I need is to fall in love for real with a human being.

I failed to look away in time yet again and Igor smiled at me. He reached out and picked up a guitar off the grass. The silence spread out from him in a wave – the children nudged each other, stopped talking and prepared to listen with a strange, affected sort of attention.

I suddenly wished desperately that he would sing some kind of stupid nonsense. Maybe some old-time young pioneer song about potatoes roasted in the fire, the sea, the pioneer camp, firm friendship and the kids' readiness to enjoy themselves and to study. Anything that would dispel this idiotic enchantment, anything to stop me inventing all sorts of nonsense and seeing imaginary virtues in that handsome physical shell!

When Igor started to play, I realised I was done for. He could play. The melody wasn't all that complicated, but it was beautiful, and he didn't hit any wrong notes.

And then he began to sing:

Two boys saw a heavenly angel
Come flying into their attic.
Without telling anyone, the boys
Went rushing up the fire escape . . .
Two boys climbed in through the window,
It was dusty, deserted and dark,
But just four steps away from the corner
A pair of white wings lay on the floor . . .
Yes, boys, oh yes!
Angels are not for ever,
But stealing is a sin,
There aren't enough wings for everyone . . .
They want to soar up into the sky,
They only have to put on the wings . . .
But they didn't dare, they had been taught well,
They knew what was right, what was wrong.

This wasn't a song for children. Of course, they listened to it quite attentively, but at that moment you could have sung them a maths textbook set to guitar music – anything would have been good enough. A campfire in the evening, with your favourite camp leader and his guitar – in a situation like that children will like anything.

But I realised Igor was singing for me. Even if he was looking into the flames all the time, even if the song wasn't about love, even if we'd barely spoken two words to each other. It was as if he had sensed my expectations – and decided to refute them. Maybe that was what it was, I thought – many people possess strong powers of intuition, even if they're not Others.

Two boys grew up and they followed
Different paths through the maze of life.

One was a bandit and one was a cop,
And both of them regretted it . . .
Yes boys, oh yes!
Angels are not for ever.
But stealing is a sin,
There aren't enough wings for everyone . . .

He looked at me and smiled. His fingers ran quietly across the strings again and he repeated quietly:

'There aren't enough wings for everyone . . .'

The kids started making a racket.

They actually seemed to like the song, though I couldn't imagine what they could have understood in it. Maybe they were amused by the phrase about 'right and wrong', or maybe in their little minds they imagined a real adventure – climbing into an attic that an angel had flown into . . . But I thought the song fitted the Others – Dark Ones and Light Ones.

It was a good song. Just not quite right about one thing. The boy who would later join our side would have put on the wings. Or at least tried them on.

Because for us the idea of 'right and wrong' doesn't exist.

'That's a good song. But it's very serious,' said Galina. 'Did you write it?'

Igor laughed and shook his head:

'No, afraid not. It's by Yulii Burkin. Not a very well-known singer, unfortunately.'

'Igor, could you play . . . one of our songs?' Galina was flirting with him for all she was worth. The stupid fool . . .

'Sure!' Igor agreed.

He strummed the strings, striking up a jolly rhythm and started singing simple-minded nonsense about 'the very, very best camp of songs and friends in all the world'.

That was what they wanted. From the second couplet everybody started joining in, because it was easy to guess what the next word would be. When they sang about the sea, and how you had to go running into it with your camp leader, because he loved 'the splashing water and the sand' too, they all howled together in inspired voices. Everybody was pleased, even Galina and her girls. At one point Igor sang about 'a stone with a hole inside it' that was found on the seashore . . . as if anyone could imagine a stone with a hole outside it. I noticed that lots of the kids reached for the stones dangling round their necks.

Well, well. Faithful devotees of the chicken god! Maybe someone in Artek had a special job – producing stones with holes in them? Some drunk who never shaved, sitting in a workshop somewhere, drilling holes in stones all day long and scattering them on the beach in the evening to delight all the kids.

If not, an opportunity had clearly been missed!

Igor appeared to be enjoying himself as much as the kids He sang the song enthusiastically, except that . . . all the enthusiasm was for the children. Igor was amusing them. But he really felt nothing for the song one way or the other.

I relaxed.

At the very least he liked the look of me.

And I liked the look of him too.

Igor sang another couple of songs. Then Galina took over the guitar and coerced it into playing – the instrument resisted as hard as it could, flatly refusing to produce any normal sounds, but Galina still sang 'Let's all hold hands, my friends' and yet another young pioneer song. Even the boy from the fourth brigade who was barely strong enough to hold down the metal strings played better than she did.

Then Igor clapped his hands.

'All right! Now we'll put the fire out and go for supper!'

They brought two buckets of water from somewhere and he began dousing the glowing embers.

I stood there for a while, following his sparse, precise movements. Igor looked as if he'd spent his entire life putting out campfires. Probably he did everything like that – playing the guitar, and putting out fires, and working on his computer, and caressing a woman. Precisely, conscientiously. Reliably. Satisfaction guaranteed.

Hot white steam billowed up from the hot embers. The children scattered in all directions. Then suddenly, still dousing the fire, Igor asked:

'Do you like swimming at night, Alisa?'

I shivered.

'Yes.'

'So do I. By one o'clock, the children will have settled down and I'll go to the beach for a swim, where we were this morning. Come along if you like.'

For just a moment I lost my head. It was a feeling I'd completely forgotten! Instead of me hitting on a man, he was hitting on me.

Igor splashed the remains of the water onto the campfire and looked at me. He smiled.

'I'd be really glad if you could come. Only ... don't get the wrong idea.'

'I think I've got the right idea,' I replied.

'Will you come?'

I really wanted to say no. Just to provoke him. But it would have been stupid, after all, to give up my own pleasure for the sake of one little gibe.

'Probably,' I said.

'I'll be waiting,' Igor replied calmly. 'Shall we go? A glass of ryazhenka before bed is very good for tired camp leaders. It guarantees sound, healthy sleep.'

His smile was wonderful.

In Artek 'lights out' comes at half past ten.

The bugles sounded solemnly in the loudspeakers and a gentle woman's voice wished everyone goodnight. I was standing in front of the mirror, looking at my reflection and trying to figure out what was happening to me?

Had I fallen in love?

No, that was impossible. I loved Zabulon. I loved the greatest Dark Magician in Moscow. One of the few individuals who really controlled the fate of the world. And what was an ordinary human being, compared to him? Even if he was attractive, even if he had a fine figure, even with that idiotic reliability that simply oozed out of him with every move he made. He was an ordinary male of the human species. With the ordinary little thoughts of human males. Pretty good for a holiday romance, but nothing more than that.

I couldn't really fall in love with him!

The mobile in my bag rang and I started. Mum? Unlikely, she was terribly careful with money and never rang me on my mobile.

I took it out and accepted the call.

'Hello, Alisa.'

Zabulon's voice sounded tired. Affectionate and tired, as if he'd barely been able to find the strength to make the call, but really felt he had to.

'Hello,' I whispered.

'You're feeling anxious, I can sense it. What's happened to you, my little girl?'

There's no way to hide anything from him. Zabulon knows everything . . . at least, everything he wants to know.

'I'm thinking about taking a friend for the month,' I sighed into the phone.

'Well, what of it?' Zabulon sounded puzzled. 'Alisa, I'm not jealous of your dog, and I'm not going to be jealous of some little man who amuses you either.'

'I haven't got a dog,' I said miserably.

Zabulon laughed, and all my stupid thoughts just seemed to evaporate.

'All right then! I'm not bothered if you have a dog or you don't. I'm not bothered if you have a human lover. Calm down, my little one. Relax. Recover your strength. Amuse yourself any way you like. Debauch the whole of Artek, including all the young pioneers and the old plumbers if you like. My little fool . . .'

'I'm behaving like a human being, aren't I?' I suddenly felt ashamed.

'It's nothing to worry about. It won't last long, Alisa. Build up your strength . . . only . . .' Zabulon paused for a moment. 'Never mind. It's nothing.'

'No, tell me!' I tensed up again.

'I have faith in your common sense,' Zabulon said and hesitated. 'Alisa, just don't get carried away, all right? Your holiday is strictly governed by the terms of the old Treaty between the Watches. You don't have the right to take a lot of power. Only small amounts. Don't turn into some crude energy vampire, you're on holiday, not out hunting. If you overstep the mark, we'll lose this resort for ever.'

'I understand,' I said.

How long was that blunder with the Prism of Power going to keep coming back to haunt me?

I didn't start pouring out promises or swearing by the Dark and my own Power. Promises mean nothing, the Dark doesn't bother itself with petty details, and I had no power right then. I simply promised myself that I wouldn't overstep the defined boundaries for anything, I wouldn't let down Zabulon and the entire Day Watch.

'Then have a good holiday, my little girl.' I thought I caught a hint of sadness in Zabulon's voice. 'Have a good holiday.'

'Couldn't you come? Just for a short while?' I asked hopelessly.

'No. I'm very busy, Alisa. I'm afraid we won't be able to talk for the next three or four days. But don't you worry. What good is a tedious old miscreant obsessed with global problems as a partner for a young witch on holiday?'

He laughed.

We generally tried not to say things like that on the phone, especially on mobiles, because they listen to all of them and record everything. It all sounded like a flippant conversation . . . But what if some ordinary little human being picked up the thread and started following it? Then we would have to waste time and energy on him.

'I love you,' I whispered. 'Thank you.'

'Good luck, my little one,' Zabulon said affectionately 'I kiss you.'

I switched off the phone and smiled to myself.

Well then, everything was all right. So where had that stupid feeling of alarm come from? And where had I got the crazy idea that I was in love with Igor? Love was something different, love was pure delight, a fountain of emotions, sensual pleasures and enjoying spending time together. But what I was feeling, this strange, timid alarm, was only the consequence of my illness. It just felt odd to associate with a man without having any idea of how to control him. I couldn't threaten him with a pistol, like those half-witted bandits.

'Alisa?' Olechka's curious little face had appeared in the doorway. 'Are you coming in to see us for a minute?'

The girl was barefoot, in just her pants and top. She'd already gone to bed, but she had got impatient.

'I'll be right there,' I said. 'Shall I tell you all a story?'

Olechka lit up:

'Uhuh.'

'A happy one or a scary one?'

The girl wrinkled up her little forehead. But, of course, curiosity won out.

'A scary one.'

All children like scary stories.

'Run back to bed now,' I said. 'I'll be right there.'

Ten minutes later I was sitting on Olechka's bed in the dormitory, telling the girls a story in a low voice:

'And in the morning the girl woke up and went over to the mirror and looked – and all her teeth were red! She tried cleaning them with toothpaste, and washing them with soap, but they were still as red as ever. She couldn't say a single word to her parents, in case they noticed. It was a good thing her younger brother was ill and her parents took no notice of her at all. That's the way it always is, the little ones get all the attention and nobody even looks at you, not even if all your teeth are red . . .'

Scary children's stories are so wonderful! Especially if you tell them at night, with a mysterious half-light coming in through the window, to a pack of silly little girls.

'I've guessed it already,' Natasha said in a bored voice. Such a serious girl, you couldn't impress her with scary stories. The others started hissing at her indignantly and she shut up. I carried on, feeling Olechka's heart pounding as she pressed herself against me. There would be a good harvest for me there . . .

'On the third night the girl tied her right plait to her bed with a piece of string,' I went on in a mysterious whisper. 'And at midnight she woke up because the string was stretched tight and it was pulling on her hair and hurting. And the girl saw that she was standing over her little brother's bed and her teeth were chattering! Chattering!'

Larisa gave a quiet squeal. Not because she was frightened, but because it was the right thing to do. And of course one of the girls began happily chattering her teeth together.

'Then the girl went into the kitchen and took out the hammer and the pincers that her father kept in the cupboard, and before morning came she secretly pulled out all her own teeth. It hurt very badly, but she managed it, because she was a brave girl and she had strong hands. And the next morning her little brother got better. And the girl's teeth grew back better than ever, because the first ones were her milk teeth!'

I lowered my voice to a whisper and said solemnly:

'Only they were still pink anyway!'

One of the girls who had been waiting for a happy ending gasped in fright. And I concluded solemnly:

'And the parents still loved her little brother more than her anyway. Because he was really very ill that time and they were really worried about him.'

And that was all. I wondered how many of the girls had younger brothers. The birth rate in Russia is low, but if the first child is a girl, people usually try for a second.

My mother had wanted to do that. When she was already too old, past thirty, what a fool . . . But I was already an Other, even at the young age of twelve. And I dealt with the unexpected problem. Though probably I shouldn't have bothered. If I did have a brother, what would have been so bad about that? Even if he was only a half-brother . . . and only I would have known that for sure, even my mum had her doubts . . . and especially since he could have turned out to be an Other, not just a brother but an ally . . . But what's done can't be undone.

'And now – to sleep!' I ordered the girls in a cheerful voice.

Of course, they started asking me to tell them another story. But I refused. It was half past eleven already, and I still had to get to the beach . . . the girls' voices were already ragged and sleepy. When I left, Gulnara tried to tell a scary story of her own, but all the pauses and hesitations suggested that she would fall asleep halfway through it.

I went back to my room, stretched out on the bed and started waiting.

I wondered what Igor was doing right then.

Was he entertaining his kids too?

Or was he drinking vodka with some other camp leaders?

Or was he screwing one of them?

Or had he forgotten he was intending to go swimming that night and sleeping peacefully in his bed?

I shook my head. No. Anything but the last option.

He was reliable. Almost . . . almost like Zabulon. What an absurd comparison: there weren't many, even among the Dark Others, who could call Zabulon 'reliable'. But I could. I had a perfect right to do it. Love is a great power, and such a strange power.

What if Igor turned out to be a potential Other?

I squeezed my eyes tight shut in simultaneous sweet anticipation and panic. What would I do then? Then it wouldn't be amusement with an ordinary man that Zabulon had approved, but a genuine love triangle.

What was wrong with me?

There couldn't be any triangle. Not even if Igor did turn out to be an uninitiated Other. He'd go running off with his tail between his legs and forget he ever had an affair with Zabulon's girl.

And I would forget it too.

The time dragged by unbearably slowly. The hands on my watch crept along hesitantly, as if they weren't even sure that time was passing. I had been going to wait for half an hour, but I gave in after twenty minutes. I didn't have the strength to hold out any longer.

I got up and walked quietly through into the girls' dormitory . . .

There was silence. The calm, pleasant silence of a large children's dormitory with just a few sounds – breathing, snuffling, lips smacking sleepily.

'Girls!' I called quietly.

No answer.

I set off along the row of beds, gently touching shoulders, arms, hair . . . Nothing . . . nothing . . . nothing . . .

Here was something.

It was Olechka.

I knelt down beside her bed and lowered my hand onto her sweaty forehead. I heard her dream and felt the flow of power.

The dream was confused and incoherent, it had nothing to do with my bedtime story. Olechka was dreaming that she was climbing to the top of a tower – an old tower that was leaning slightly and had a half-ruined stone balustrade with huge gaping holes in it. Down below at the foot of the tower there was either a medieval town or an ancient monastery. And the strange thing was that although the tower was in semi-darkness, down below the sun was shining. And there were people wandering about between the decrepit buildings – happy and cheerful, dressed in light summer clothes, holding cameras and colourful magazines. They were enjoying themselves so much, it couldn't possibly occur to them to look upwards at the sky and see the little girl walking towards a gap in the balustrade as if she was under a spell.

I needed to hang on just a little bit longer. Wait until Olechka started falling – she was bound to fall, that was where the dream was leading her. I don't know what happened to me, but I suddenly gathered my strength and sucked in her dream. Every last morsel of it.

The dark tower above the cheerful crowd, and the gaping holes in the balustrade, and the cold indifference and the fearsome, alluring height. Everything that could give me power.

Olechka held her breath for a moment. I even felt afraid that she might fall into a coma − it's rare, but it sometimes happens to people when you draw power from them too suddenly.

But she started breathing again.

I got up off my knees. I'd even broken into a sweat myself. I could feel that a bundle of energy had fallen into the empty gap left by my usual power. No, it still hadn't filled it, not by a long way . . . and I'd acted hastily, for some reason . . .

But I was recovering.

Again − the gentle touches, the soft hair, the lips parted in sleep, the relaxed fingers . . .

Nothing here . . . nothing here . . . but there was something here.

It was Natasha.

And her dream had been prompted by me.

Natasha was standing in a bathroom. Naked and covered in soapy lather. She was holding a boy about five or six years old and hammering his head against the tiled wall, saying over and over again: 'Are you going to peep again? Are you going to peep?'

The boy was dangling in her hands like a rag doll. His eyes were wide open in terror, but he didn't say anything. He seemed to be far more afraid of being punished by his parents than hurt by his sister.

But Natasha wasn't feeling too good either. Her soul was filled with a mixture of furious anger at her insufferable brother, fear that she would hit his head against the wall too hard, shame, even though until only very recently she and her brother had taken baths together, and guilt . . . because she'd deliberately left the door unlocked in the expectation that her brother would try to peep in, driven by the natural urge of children to violate all prohibitions.

This was really something. Passions like that in someone who wasn't even twelve yet.

Natasha gave a deep sigh, and in her dream she hit her brother's head especially hard against the wall, so that it started to bleed. I couldn't see where the blood came from, but it suddenly covered his entire head.

I sucked in her dream.

Completely. The fury, the fear, the shame, the guilt and the budding sensuality, still vague and ill-defined.

But the dream didn't end.

Natasha had just released her grip when she grabbed her brother again by the shoulders and, with the cold calculating movement of an executioner, forced his head into the water in the bath, which instantly turned pink. Even the clumps of foam on the surface of the water turned pink. The boy began twitching helplessly, struggling to pull his head out of the water.

I froze in surprise. A murder committed in a dream gives almost the same discharge of power as a real one. Now I'd be able to fill the gap in my soul in a single moment!

All I had to do was draw Natasha's newly awakened fear out of her, and . . .

But I didn't do anything. I stood there, leaning down over the bed, watching another person's dream as if it was a horror film that was showing on TV instead of the children's cartoons.

Natasha suddenly jerked her brother's head out of the water and he gulped in air greedily. There was no blood on him any longer, he just had a small bruise under one eye. Dreams have their own laws.

'You tell them you fell in the bath yourself and banged your head, all right?' Natasha hissed. The boy nodded in fright. Natasha quickly pushed him out of the bathroom and closed the door – then slowly got into the foamy water. The nice, bright-pink water . . .

I waited for another second or two and then drank in the remains of the dream. Triumph, excitement, tranquillity.

And the gaping wound in my soul was immediately half-filled.

I should have let Natasha kill her brother. I only needed to take away her fear, and she would have drowned her little brother like a kitten.

I was covered in perspiration. My hands were shaking. Who could ever have expected nightmares like that from such a rational little miss know-it-all?

All right. Slow and steady does it.

I moved on.

By half past twelve that night I had absorbed another three dreams. They weren't so satisfying, but they provided fine surges of power. This was a good place for a holiday, if the girls accumulated that much energy.

I had almost completely restored the strength that I'd lost. The lion's share, of course, had come from Natasha. I even had the feeling that if I could just suck in one more dream, then I would be completely restored and become a normal Other. But nobody had any more dreams that were any use to me. There was one that simply repelled me: Gulnara was dreaming that she was taking care of her old grandfather. Dashing around the kitchen, pouring his tea, constantly asking him solicitous questions. Oh, how I hate that awful eastern culture . . . Turkish delight laced with arsenic.

If it wasn't for Igor . . .

I would only have to wait half an hour, or an hour, and one of my eighteen donors would have a frightening dream.

But . . .

I didn't hesitate for long.

I would collect all the power I needed, absolutely everything, the following night. But today I could relax and try out the role of an ordinary woman.

I closed the door firmly and slipped out into the summer night. The camp was sleeping. There were lamps lit here and there on the pathways and an almost full moon hung in the sky.

Nights like this are great for the werewolves. They're at the peak of their powers, they can transform easily and at will, they're full of high spirits, the thirst for life and the urge to hunt, to tear living flesh to pieces, to stalk and pounce on their prey. Of course, the vampires and the shape-shifters are the very lowest caste of the Dark Ones. And most of them are simply stupid and primitive. But . . . on nights like this I envied them just a little. I envied them the primitive power that comes from the deepest animal depths of their nature. The ability to transform into an animal — and get rid of all those stupid human feelings.

I started to laugh and set off along the path at a run, flinging my arms out and throwing my head back to look up at the sky. I might not have the powers of an Other yet, but my blood was seething with fresh power, and I didn't stumble even once or hesitate for a moment in my choice of direction. It was like just before my initiation, when 'mother's old friend' Irina Andreevna had arrived at our apartment unexpectedly. I could sense that my parents were behaving strangely, awkwardly, and every now and then Irina Andreevna would look at me in a strange way, as if she was evaluating me, with a gentle, condescending smile. And then my parents suddenly decided to go out somewhere in a great hurry, leaving me alone for the entire evening with the 'old friend'. And my future mentor told me everything. She said this was the first time she had ever seen my parents, that she had simply put a spell on them. She told me about the Others, and about the Twilight that gives them miraculous powers and said that the first time I entered the Twilight would determine who I would be, a Light One or a Dark One . . . She said I was a future Other. That I had been noticed by a certain 'very, very powerful magician'. Later I wondered if it could have been Zabulon himself, but I couldn't bring myself to ask.

Back then I hesitated for a long time. I was a little fool. I didn't like the words 'Dark Ones'. In fairy tales and films the Dark Ones were always bad. They had power over the entire world, ruled countries and commanded armies, but at the same time they ate all sorts of disgusting things, spoke in horrible, repellent voices and betrayed everyone whenever they got the chance. And on top of all that – in the end they always lost.

Irina Andreevna laughed for a long time when I told her all that. And she admitted that all the fairy tales were invented by the Light Ones. The Dark Ones didn't usually bother with that kind of nonsense. She said what the Dark Ones really wanted was freedom and independence, they didn't strive for power, they didn't impose their own foolish desires on others. She demonstrated some of her abilities to me – and I learned that my mum had been unfaithful to my dad for a long time already, and my dad wasn't anything like as brave as I thought, and that my best friend Vika told people all sorts of nasty things about me.

I really knew about my mum already, even at the age of ten. Only I tried not to think about her and uncle Vitya. I was really hurt for my dad. But when I heard about Vika, I got really furious. And I realised that I wanted to get even with her. It seems funny to me now, but when I was ten, to learn that my friend had told our classmate Romka my most terrible secret – that I used to wet the bed until the second year . . . that was really horrible! I'd been wondering why he smirked in that disgusting way when I gave him a card and some coloured pens for Army Day on the twenty-third of February.

Irina helped me to enter the Twilight for the first time. She said while I was there I would decide for myself who I would be. The Twilight would see straight through my soul and make the most appropriate choice.

After that my friend Vika started getting bad marks all the time and swearing at all the teachers, even the head, then they took her out of our school. I heard she spent a long time in a children's psychiatric hospital being treated for a rare condition, Gilles de la Tourette syndrome. The handsome Romka pissed his pants in the middle of the end-of-term Russian dictation and had to live with the nickname 'Pisser' for two years afterwards, until he and his parents moved to a different area.

Uncle Vitya drowned while he was swimming in the shallow pond at our dacha, but that wasn't until three years later. That's quite difficult for a child, after all. And it still makes me feel sick to remember the way I managed to get hold of a lock of his hair

I didn't regret my choice in the least.

There are some who think that we Dark Ones are evil. But that's not true at all. We're simply just. Proud, independent and just.

And we decide things for ourselves.


The beach at night is filled with wistful enchantment. Like a park in autumn, or a concert hall after a première. The tired crowd goes away for a while to gather its strength for new insanities: the sea licks its wounds and throws the melon rinds, sodden chocolate wrappers, corn cobs and other human rubbish up onto the beach; the cool, wet sand covers over the tracks of the seagulls and the crows.

I heard Igor when I was still approaching the beach. First his guitar and then his voice.

As he sang, I suddenly realised with piercing clarity that nothing was going to happen. There was a group of people sitting over there on the sand, enjoying themselves with a bottle or two and some bread rolls stolen from the supper table. And the most that I could hope for, stupid fool that I was, was an invitation to spend the rest of the night in his room.

But even so I walked towards the sound. Just to make sure.

> You say there's no such thing as love,
> There's nothing but the carrot and the stick,
> But I say flowers bloom
> Because they don't believe in death.
> You tell me that you never want
> To be a slave to anyone at all.
> I say that means the slave will be
> Whoever you have by your side.

I never liked that song. I don't like Nautilus Pompilius in general, their songs sound almost as if they were ours, but there's something subtly different about them. No wonder the Light Ones are so fond of them.

But I particularly disliked that song.

I was only two or three steps away from Igor when I realised that he was there on the beach alone. Igor noticed me too – he raised his head and smiled, still singing:

> Maybe I am wrong,
> Maybe you are right.
> But I have seen with my own eyes
> The grass reaching for the sky.
> Why should we argue all night long
> And lie sleepless till the dawn?

Maybe I am wrong,
Maybe you are right.
What good is arguing to us,
The day will come and then
You'll see for yourself
If there's a bottom to the sky
And why
The grass reaches up to it . . .

I sat down beside him on a large fluffy towel spread out on the sand and waited patiently for the song to end. When Igor finally put down his guitar, I asked him:

'Playing for the waves and the sand?'

'For the stars and the wind,' he corrected me. 'I thought it would be hard for you to find me in the dark. And I didn't like the idea of bringing a cassette player.'

'Why not?'

He shrugged.

'Surely you can feel it? This is a time for live sound.'

Igor was right. Maybe I didn't like his choice of song, but I was all for the idea of live sound . . .

I looked him over without saying anything — or rather, I tried to look him over in the darkness. He was barefoot, dressed in nothing but his shorts. His hair had a wet gleam to it — he must have been in the sea already. He reminded me of someone at that moment . . . someone from one of the old fairy tales, either a jolly troubadour or a prince dressed up as a troubadour.

'The water's warm,' Igor said. 'Shall we go in?'

That was when I realised I'd been in too much of a hurry to get to the beach.

'Igor . . . you'll laugh at me . . . I can't go swimming. I forgot my costume.'

He thought for a moment and then asked very calmly:

'Are you shy? Or are you afraid I'll think you did it deliberately?'

'I'm not afraid, but I don't want you to think that.'

'I don't think that at all,' Igor said and stood up. 'I'll go into
the water and you come and join me.'

He took off his shorts right at the water's edge, started to run
and dived almost immediately. I didn't hesitate for long. I hadn't
even thought about seducing Igor in such a primitive way, I really
had forgotten my costume and left it in my room. But there was
no way I was going to feel shy, especially of an ordinary human
being.

The water was warm and the waves caressed me like a lover's
hands. I swam after Igor and the shoreline receded and blurred
until only the lighted lamps marked Artek out in the night. We
swam far beyond the buoy, probably a kilometre from the shore.
I caught up with Igor, and then we were swimming beside each
other in silence, not saying a word. Not competing with each
other, moving in the same rhythm.

Finally he stopped, looked at me and said.

'That's enough.'

'Are you tired?' I asked, a little surprised. It had seemed to me
that he could go on swimming for ever . . . and I – well, I could
have swum across the Black Sea and landed in Turkey.

'No, I'm not tired. But the night is deceptive, Alisa. This is the
maximum distance I could pull you to the shore if anything
happened.'

I remembered what Natasha had said about him being 'reliable'. Looking into his face I realised it wasn't bravado and he
wasn't joking. He really was in control of the situation at every
moment. And he was ready to save me.

You funny little human being. In the morning or tomorrow

night I'll gather a little more power – and then I'll be able to do whatever I like with you. And it won't be you who'll save me if anything happens, I'll save you – you big, strong, confident, reliable man . . . But right now you're sure of yourself, sure of your ability to protect and save, like a little child walking along a dark street with his mother and telling her: 'Don't be afraid, Mum, I'm here.'

Maybe it is the Light Ones' style, but even so, I like it somehow.

I swam slowly up to Igor. Right up to him. I put my arms round him and whispered:

'Save me.'

The water was warm, but his body was hotter than the water. He was as naked as I was. We kissed, sometimes going under the water, then surfacing with a rush and gulping in the air and searching for each other's lips again.

'I want to go back to the beach,' I whispered. We started swimming, sometimes touching each other, sometimes stopping to exchange another long kiss. I had the taste of salt and his lips on my lips, my body seemed to be on fire, the blood was pounding in my temples. You could drown like that . . . from the excitement, from the impatience, from the longing to be closer.

About five metres from the beach, where the water was already shallow, Igor picked me up in his arms as easily as if I weighed nothing at all, carried me to our clothes and put me down. I felt the towel under my back and the stars swayed over my head.

'Come on,' I whispered, spreading my legs. Like a depraved little girl, like a seasoned slut . . . and this was me, a witch of the Moscow Day Watch who was loved by Zabulon himself.

But right now that didn't bother me at all.

There was only the night, the stars, Igor.

He lowered himself towards me, his right hand slid under my back and caught me between the shoulder blades, his left hand slid across my breasts and for just a moment he looked into my eyes — as if he felt doubtful, hesitating, as if he wasn't feeling the same burning desire for intimacy that I was. I arched up involuntarily to meet his body, felt for his aroused member with my hips, swayed — and it was only then that he entered me.

How I wanted him . . .

It was like nothing else in the world. Not like sex with Zabulon, who always took on the form of a demon for this. With Zabulon I had always experienced a wild, painful pleasure, but it had always had a feeling of humiliation in it, sweet and arousing, but still humiliation. Not like sex with ordinary men, whether they were inexperienced young men full of strength, muscle-bound hunks or experienced, ageing womanisers. I'd tried everything, I knew it all and I could make an evening with any man interesting in its own way.

But this was different.

It was as if we really did become one, as if my desires were immediately transmitted to him and his to me. I could feel him trembling inside my body and I knew that he could come at any moment, but he was putting that moment off and I was balanced there on that same agonisingly sweet, timeless boundary of pleasure.

It was as if he had known me for years and could read me like an open book. His hands responded to the desires of my body before I could even feel them myself, his fingers knew where to be gentle and where to be rough, his lips slid over my face without stopping, his thrusts became more and more powerful, carrying me up into the dark sky on a swing-boat of delight and I whispered something without knowing what I was saying.

And then the world stopped and I groaned, clutching at his shoulders and scratching, moving after him, not wanting to let him go. The pleasure was as brief as a flash of lightning, and as blindingly bright. But he didn't stop, and I was buoyed up again, balancing on that wave of sweetness – and at the precise moment when his eyes opened wide and his body went tense, I came again. But this time in a different way, the pleasure wasn't as piercing, it was long and pulsating – as if it was following the rhythm of his spurting into my body.

I couldn't even groan any more. We lay beside each other – I was on the towel and Igor was on the sand – touching each other, caressing each other, as if our hands had a life of their own. I pressed my cheek against his chest, catching the salty smell of the sea and the sour smell of sweat; his body shuddered under my hand. And I didn't even realise when I started kissing him, moving lower and lower and burying my face in the rough hair, caressing him with my lips and my tongue, feeling the excitement mounting in him again. Igor lay there without moving, just touching my shoulders with his hands and that was right, that was what he should do, because now I wanted to give him pleasure. And when he came again with a quiet groan, unable to stop himself, I felt as happy as if he had been caressing me.

Everything was just the way it should be.

Everything was like nothing that had ever happened before.

No orgy, not even the most exciting, had ever given me so much pleasure. I had never felt such happiness, not with one man or two or three, never felt this feeling before . . . this feeling of . . . completeness? Yes, that was it, completeness. I simply didn't need anyone else.

'I love you,' I whispered. 'Igor . . . I love you.'

He could have answered that he loved me too – and he would have spoiled everything, or almost everything. But he only said:

'I know.'

When Igor got up and took something out from under the heap of clothes on the sand, I could hardly even believe my eyes at first.

A bottle and a glass. A crystal glass. Just one.

Igor smiled, the cork went flying into the air and the foaming champagne poured into the glass. I took a mouthful. Brut, and cold too.

'Now am I good or bad?' he asked.

'Bad,' I said, holding out the glass to him. 'For hiding a precious treasure like that!'

Igor smiled and drank the wine. Then he said thoughtfully:

'You know, I think I'm getting that feeling again—'

He started and stopped speaking, straightening up abruptly. I jumped up – just in time to see an indistinct shadow slip away into the night from behind a beach umbrella not far away.

'That's not good,' Igor whispered.

'Who was it?' I asked. The realisation that someone had been watching us didn't increase my excitement as it usually did. Completeness. Total completeness. Even the sip of champagne was just a pleasant extra now, not really necessary. And I certainly didn't need any outsiders.

'I don't know . . . it looked like one of the children.' Igor was clearly upset. 'That's really bad . . . how stupid.'

'It's no disaster,' I said, putting my arms round his shoulders. 'The little ones are already asleep, and it's good for the older ones . . . it's part of their education too.'

He smiled, but he was obviously concerned. That's people for you . . . always making a big deal out of nothing.

'Let's go to your room,' I suggested.

'Okay,' said Igor with a sharp nod. He looked at me. 'But remember, in that case you won't get any sleep today.'

'I was just going to warn you about that,' I said. And it was true.

# CHAPTER 6

WHEN I was a fully functional Other, I could easily go without sleep for five or six days. But even now I wasn't feeling sleepy at all. Quite the opposite, I could feel my blood simply seething with energy.

I got back to our summer house half an hour before reveille and looked in on the girls – some of them were tossing and turning as they woke up. But everything was all right. No one had run off to go swimming and drowned, no one had been kidnapped by evil terrorists, no one had got it into her head to go looking for their brigade leader in the middle of the night.

I went into my room with a smile of stupid satisfaction. I got undressed slowly and lazily, standing in front of the mirror, then ran my hands sensuously over my thighs and stretched like a satisfied cat.

An insane night. A magical night. I must have done just about all the wild things that a woman can do when she's in love with a man. Even things I hadn't liked before had suddenly become tantalising pleasures that night.

Surely I couldn't really have fallen in love with a human being? It wasn't possible . . .

Not with an ordinary man, even if he did understand me better than anyone else in the world.

It just wasn't possible.

'Dark, let him be an Other,' I whispered. 'Great Dark, I implore you . . .'

It's a dangerous game to bother the primordial Power with such petty requests. Although . . . I don't believe the Dark is able to hear a simple witch. But I expect Zabulon can shout loud enough for it to hear him.

Zabulon.

I sat on the bed and covered my face with my hands.

Only two days ago nothing would have brought me more joy than being loved by him. But now?

Of course, he himself had suggested that I should amuse myself. And of course, he couldn't give a damn for banal human dogmas, especially those that made up the credo of the Light Ones. Unfaithfulness meant nothing to him. And as for jealousy . . . he wouldn't even say a word against it if Igor and I—

Stop! Where is this taking me?

'Alisa, you're lost your wits,' I whispered.

Was I really still so much like ordinary people? Could I really think – what a terrible thing to say – of getting married? To a human being? Of cooking him borscht, washing his socks, bearing his children and raising them?

It was just like the old saying: The Watch by day, disgrace by night . . .

But yes, I could . . .

I shook my head, imagining how the other girls would react. No, there was nothing unusual about the actual fact. Most witches are married and, as a rule, to human beings. But . . .

It was one thing to cast a spell on some wealthy and influen-tial man, an oligarch, or even a deputy of the State Duma or some big-time Moscow gangster. But a simple young guy, a student, without money or contacts? I imagined the kind of jokes that would be thrown at me . . . and with good reason, that was the most terrible thing.

But it wasn't the sex that was driving me insane.

What was it that was happening to me?

It was as if I'd been enchanted by an incubus.

I shuddered at the monstrous thought. What if Igor was an ordinary incubus? A colleague . . . one of the primitive Dark Ones?

No. It was impossible.

An incubus would have sensed that I was an Other. A Dark Other, even if I had been temporarily deprived of power. And he would never have turned his power on a witch, knowing the price he would have to pay. I'd grind him into dust if my power returned and I discovered love had been imposed on me.

Love? So it was love then?

'Oh, Alisa,' I whispered. 'What a fool you are.'

Well, all right, so I am a fool.

I took a clean pair of pants out of my bag and went into the shower.

I dashed about like someone possessed all day long, until the evening. Everything went badly, but that didn't bother me in the slightest. I even had a bit of a quarrel with the camp commandant when I was trying to get good places for my girls at the film festival. But I got them, and I think I left her with an improved opinion of me! Then they gave out the pieces of dark glass that had been brought from somewhere in Nikolaev for us to watch the next day's solar eclipse. Five pieces of glass were given out to every brigade, but I managed to get hold of six. I hadn't even expected anyone in Ukraine to think of making them, but since they had . . .

After that came the beach, but of course didn't it just happen that today the boys' brigades had gone off on some stupid trip. Even the sea brought me no joy. But at a certain moment I looked at Natasha, understood her sad glance and realised the comedy of the situation. I wasn't the only fool, there were two of us: the girl, pining for her boy and barely even daring to fantasise about kisses, and me, who had done things the night before that you wouldn't even find in that alley with the porn videos at Gorbushka market. Opposite extremes coming together.

'Are you missing him?' I asked in a quiet voice. Just for a moment it seemed Natasha was going to get furious and she looked at me indignantly; then suddenly she sighed:

'Uhuh . . . are you missing yours too?'

I nodded without speaking. The girl hesitated for a second and asked:

'Were you with him until morning?'

I didn't lie to her, especially since there was no one else there. I just asked:

'Did you follow me?'

'I felt scared in the night,' the girl said quietly. 'I woke up. I was having such horrible dreams . . . I came to you, but you weren't in your room.'

'Until the morning,' I confessed. 'I like him very much, Natasha.'

'Were you making love?' she asked in a businesslike tone of voice.

I wagged my finger at her:

'Natasha!'

She wasn't embarrassed at all. On the contrary, she lowered her voice and told me, as if I were her bosom friend:

'I can't get anywhere with mine. I told him that if he tried to kiss me, I'd punch him in the eye, and he said: "As if I wanted to!" Why are boys so stupid?'

'He'll kiss you,' I promised her. And I thought to myself: 'I'll do my best to make sure he does.'

After all, what could possibly be simpler? The next day I would have my powers back, and the boy with ginger hair and freckles would follow Natasha around, gazing at her with eyes filled with genuine love. Why shouldn't I give my best donor a little happiness?

'What were you dreaming about?' I asked.

'Something horrible,' the girl answered briefly. 'I can't honestly remember. But it was something really, really horrible.'

'About your younger brother?' I asked.

Natasha wrinkled up her forehead. Then she replied:

'I don't remember. But how did you know I have a younger brother?'

I smiled mysteriously and stretched out on the sand. Everything was all right. The dream had been extracted completely.

That evening I realised I just couldn't stand it any longer.

I found Galina and asked her to keep an eye on my girls for a couple of hours.

There was a strange look in her eyes. No, it wasn't hurt, although she'd obviously understood everything, and she'd had designs on Igor herself. And it wasn't anger. It was more like the sad look of a dog who's been punished unjustly.

'Of course, Alisa,' she said.

That's the trouble with these so-called good people. Spit in their faces, thwart their desires, trample on them — and they put up with it.

But then, of course, it is also very convenient.

I set off towards the fourth brigade's small house. Along the way I frightened two little boys in the bushes — they were smoking shards of glass on a little fire of disposable plastic cups. Actually, to say I frightened them is putting it rather strongly. The kids frowned and tensed up, but they didn't stop what they were doing.

'Tomorrow they'll give everyone special pieces of glass,' I said amicably. 'But you'll cut yourselves with those.'

'There aren't enough of the special ones,' one of the kids objected reasonably. 'We'll smoke some for ourselves, the cups make great smoke.'

'And we'll stick plasters round the edges,' the second one added. 'And they'll be just fine!'

I smiled, nodded to them and went on. I liked the kids' attitude. Proud and independent. The right attitude.

I was already getting close to the summer house and I could hear the sounds of a guitar, when I saw Makar.

The kid was standing by a tree, as if he wasn't really hiding, but so that he couldn't be seen from the direction of the house. Just standing there looking at Igor, who was sitting in the middle of his boys. When Makar heard my steps, he turned round sharply, started . . . and lowered his eyes.

'It's not good to spy on people, Makar.'

He stood there, chewing on his lip. I wondered what he'd been planning to do. Play some nasty trick on Igor? Challenge him to a duel? Or had he just clenched his fists in helpless fury as he looked at the grown man who'd been making love to the woman he liked the evening before? You stupid, stupid boy, you ought to be looking at girls your own age, not at enchanting grown-up witches with long legs.

'You'll have it all, Makar,' I said softly. 'Girls, and a night beside the sea, and . . .'

He raised his head and looked at me derisively, even rather condescendingly. 'No I won't,' his eyes seemed to say. 'There won't be any sea, there won't be any beautiful naked woman by the edge of the foaming waves. It will all be quite different – cheap wine in a tiny room in some dirty hostel; a girl who could be anybody's after her second glass; a sweaty body turned flabby before its time and a whisper hoarse from smoking: "Where do you think you're sticking that thing, you greenhorn!"'

I knew that, as an experienced and cynical witch. And he knew it, this chance visitor to Artek, this short-term guest in 'the realm of friendship and love'. And there was no point in us pretending with each other.

'I'm sorry, Makar,' I said and patted him affectionately on the cheek. 'But I really like him very much. You grow up strong and clever, and you'll have every . . .'

He turned and ran away, an almost grown-up boy who didn't want to waste even a minute of his brief happy summer, who didn't sleep at nights and invented a different, happy life for himself.

But what could I do? The Day Watch has no need for human servants. There are enough werewolves, vampires and other small-fry. I would check Makar, of course. He would make a magnificent Dark One. But the chances were very, very slim that the boy had the natural gifts of an Other.

My girls were probably just perfectly ordinary people too.

And the chances were just as slim that Igor had the gifts of an Other.

Maybe that was for the best? If he was human, then we could be together. Zabulon couldn't give a damn about a trivial detail like his girl having a human husband. But he would never tolerate a husband who was an Other.

I looked down thoughtfully at my feet as I walked out of the trees towards the little house. Igor was sitting on the terrace, tuning his guitar. There were only two of his boys there with him – the 'campfire monitor' Alyoshka and a plump, sickly-looking child I didn't think had been at the campfire.

Igor looked at me and smiled. The boys spoke, greeting me, but we didn't say anything to each other – we read everything in each other's eyes. The memory of that night, and the promise of the next one . . . and the ones after that.

But there was a hint of confusion and anguish in Igor's eyes too. As if there was something making him feel very sad. My darling . . . if only you knew how great my sadness is . . . and how difficult it is for me to smile.

I don't care if you don't have the gifts of an Other, Igor. I don't care if my colleagues laugh at me. I'll put up with it. And you'll never know anything about Zabulon. Or about the Watch either. And you'll be amazed at your own success, at the way your career develops, your magnificent health – I'll give you all that!

Igor strummed his guitar-strings, gave his boys an affectionate look and started to sing:

I'm afraid of babies, I'm afraid of the dead,
I feel my own face with my fingers.
And I turn cold with horror inside –
Am I really the same as all these people?
These people who live above me,
These people who live below me,
Who snore on the other side of the wall,
Who live beneath the ground . . .
What wouldn't I give for a pair of wings,
What wouldn't I give for a third eye,
For a hand with fourteen fingers on it!
I need a different gas to breathe!
Their tears are salty, their laughter is harsh,
They never have enough for everyone.
They love seeing their faces in fresh newspapers,
But next day the papers are flushed away.

These people who give birth to children,
These people who suffer from pain,
These people who shoot at people,
But can't eat their food without salt.
What wouldn't they give for a pair of wings,
What wouldn't they give for a third eye,
For a hand with fourteen fingers on it –
They need a different gas to breathe.

Something cold and sticky stirred inside me. A terrible, dreary, hopeless feeling. That was our song. This was like *our* song . . . far too much like a song for the Others.

I could feel the emotions of the boys sitting beside him, I was almost a normal Other now, I felt as if I'd be able to summon the Twilight at any moment. It was like when we were having sex the night before – that gathering momentum on a swing, that balancing on a razor's edge, that waiting for the explosion, the chasm beneath my feet. There were streams of power flowing all around   still too coarse for me, not the light broth of children's nightmares, just the fat-cheeked boy's depression because he was missing his parents: he had some problem with his heart, he didn't play much with the other boys, he followed Igor around more or less the same way as Olechka stuck to me.

It wasn't light broth.

But it was still almost exactly what I needed.

I can't wait any longer!

I swayed forward, reached out and took hold of the boy's shoulder, drawing in his blank sadness, and the sudden surge of energy almost made me throw up, but then the world turned cool and grey, my shadow fell across the worn floorboards of the veranda like a black chasm, and I fell into it, into the Twilight, just in time to see . . .

. . . to see Igor drawing in power from the boy Alyosha, who was pressing against him – a thin lilac stream of power: the expectation of pranks and adventures, delights and discoveries, joys and frights – the entire bouquet of feelings and emotions of a healthy, happy child, content with the world and with himself . . .

A Light bouquet.

Light power.

The dark unto the Dark Ones.

The light unto the Light Ones.

I stood up, still half in the real world, half in the Twilight, to face Igor, who was also standing up, to face the lover that I loved, a Light Magician of the Moscow Night Watch.

To face my enemy.

I heard him shout:

'No!'

And I heard my own voice shout:

'Don't!'

The very first thought that came into my head proved to be wrong. No, Igor hadn't been working against me, playing out some insidious plan of the Night Watch. He had lost his power – exactly as I had. He hadn't seen my aura, he couldn't have had any idea that he was looking at a witch.

He had fallen in love with me. With his eyes closed. Exactly as I had with him.

The world is grey and dreary, it is the cold world of the Twilight that makes us what we are, power-hungry, but also helps us to find that power. No sounds, no colours. The leaves frozen still on the trees, the frozen figures of the two boys, the guitar suspended in mid-air – Igor had let go of it as he entered the Twilight. Thousands of icy little needles pricked my skin, drawing out of me the energy I had only just acquired, drawing me down into the Twilight for ever . . . but I was an Other again and I could draw power from the world around me. I reached forward and scraped out everything Dark that there was in the fat boy. I no longer had any problems absorbing power. I no longer had to focus on what I was doing and how. It was all easy and familiar.

And Igor did the same thing with Alyoshka. Maybe a bit less skilfully – the Light Ones only rarely harvest power from others directly, they're shackled by their own stupid limitations, but he drank in all of the boy's joy, and I felt an unnatural joy for my beloved, for my enemy, for a Light Other who had just acquired power.

'Alisa . . .'

'Igor . . .'

He was suffering. It was far harder for him than for me. The Light Ones spend all their lives chasing illusions, they're filled with false hopes and don't know how to survive a heavy blow, but he was handling it . . . and I was handling it too . . . I was . . . I was . . .

'How absurd,' he whispered and shook his head sharply – a strange gesture in this gloomy haze, in the Twilight. 'You . . . you're a witch . . .'

I felt him reach out to my mind – not deep into it, just to the very surface, simply trying to make sure . . . or hoping to be proved wrong . . . and I didn't try to resist. I just reached out in reply.

And I laughed – at the unbearable pain.

South Butovo.

Edgar standing against the Light Magicians.

We were feeding Edgar with power, and the Light Ones were being fed by the magicians in their second line.

Including Igor.

I recognised his aura, remembered his power profile. Things like that are never forgotten.

And he recognised me.

Of course, I didn't know him by sight and I'd never heard his name. But why should an ordinary patrol witch know all one thousand agents of the Moscow Night Watch? All those magicians, wizards, enchanters, shape-shifters. When we needed to know, they gave us a specific briefing. The way they had for Anton Gorodetsky, when we'd followed him on Zabulon's secret instructions a year and a half earlier and managed to catch him committing an illegal intervention. And there were some you just couldn't help remembering, like Tiger Cub, for instance.

But I'd never known about Igor.

A third-grade Light Magician. Probably a bit more powerful than me, although it was hard to compare the powers of a natural magician and a witch.

My beloved, my lover, my enemy.

My fate.

'What made you do it?' Igor asked. 'Alisa . . . why did you do it?'

'What do you mean why?' I almost cried out, but I stopped myself because I realised he wouldn't believe me. He would never believe that what had happened was mere coincidence − just a stupid and tragic accident − that there hadn't been any evil intent in what had happened, that a cruel twist of fate had brought us together in the moment of our weakness, when we could not recognise each other, could not sense our enemy . . . at the very moment when all we could do and all we wanted to do was to love.

How can we say 'why' anything in this world happens? Why am I a Dark One? Why is he a Light One? After all, both of these are mixed together in all of us − at the beginning.

Igor could have been my friend and colleague, a Dark One.

And I . . . probably . . . could have become a Light One. And then I wouldn't have been taught by a wise witch, but a wise enchantress, and I wouldn't have paid my enemies back in kind, but sentimentally set them on 'the true road' . . . by turning the other cheek . . . and I would have delighted in every pompous piece of their stupid nonsense.

I only realised that I was crying when the world started spinning around me. You must never cry in the Twilight – everybody knows that. The more emotion we allow ourselves to show, the more eagerly the Twilight drains our power.

And to lose your powers in the Twilight means to stay in it for ever.

I tried to draw power from my donor, the fat boy, but he was already drained; I reached towards Alyoshka, but he was absolutely neutral, squeezed dry by Igor. I couldn't draw energy from Igor and I didn't want to anyway, and everyone else was too far away, and the world was spinning . . . how stupid . . .

My knees struck the ground and I even had the foolish thought that I would stain my skirt, although no dirt from the Twilight ever stays with us in the real world.

An instant later Igor hurled a charge of energy at me.

No, not to finish me off. To save me.

It was alien, Light power. But passed through him and then given to me.

And power is always power.

I stood up, breathing heavily, as exhausted as during that night of our senseless, impossible love. Igor had helped me to hold out in the Twilight, but he didn't reach out his hand.

He was crying now. He was in a bad way too.

'How could you do it?' he whispered.

'It was an accident, Igor.' I took a step towards him and held out my arms, as if I could hope for something. 'Igor, it was an accident!'

He jumped away from me as if I was a leper, with the light, elegant movement of a magician who is used to working in the Twilight.

Fighting in the Twilight. Killing in the Twilight.

'Accidents like that don't happen,' he said, spitting the words out. 'You're – you're filthy scum – you witch – You . . .'

He froze as he absorbed the remaining traces of my magic.

'You take power from children!'

I couldn't stop myself from answering:

'And you, what are you doing here, Light One?' My tongue almost refused to obey me, it was impossible, unthinkable to call him that, but he really was a Light One, and the abuse had become a simple statement of fact. 'What are you doing here if not grazing on little human children?'

'Light cannot be removed.' He shook his head. 'What is taken returns a hundredfold. You take Dark, and the Dark grows. I take Light and it comes again.'

'Tell that to the boy Alyosha, who'll be miserable the whole evening!' I shouted. 'Make him feel better by saying his joy will return!'

'I shall have other things to do, witch! Saving the children you have driven into the Dark!'

'Console them,' I said indifferently. Everything in the world seemed to be covered with a crust of ice. 'That's your job . . . my darling.'

What am I doing?

He'll only be convinced that I knew everything in advance, that the Day Watch planned a cunning operation, that he has been cruelly mocked and deceived, that everything that has happened between us was only a cunning pretence.

'Witch,' Igor said contemptuously. 'You will leave this place. Do you understand?'

I very nearly answered him: 'Gladly!' After all, what joy was there left for me in this summer, this sea, this abundance of power? I could restore myself little by little, the important part of the work was already done.

'You can leave,' I said. 'I have permission for a holiday and the use of human energy. You can ask your own organisation. But do you have permission . . . darling?'

What are you doing, you fool? What are you doing, my love? What am I doing?

What am I doing? I am a Dark One. I am a witch. I am beyond human morality and I have no intention of playing petty childish games with those primitive organisms known as 'people'. I came here to rest, and that's what I'm doing! And you, what are you doing? If you really do love me? And you do, I know. I can see it right now, and you can see it too . . . if you want to.

Because love stands above Dark and Light.

Because love is not sex or a shared faith, or 'the joint maintenance of a household and the upbringing of children'.

Because love is also power.

And Light and Dark, people and Others, morality and law, the Ten Commandments and the Great Treaty have damn all to do with it.

And I love you anyway, you bastard, you skunk, you Light son of a bitch, you good-hearted blockhead, you reliable cretin! I love you anyway! Even though only three days ago we stood against each other and dreamed of only one thing – destroying the enemy. Even though we are separated by an abyss that nobody can ever bridge!

Don't you understand, I love you!

And everything I say is only to protect myself, my words are my tears, but you don't see them, you don't want to see them.

Oh, come to me, it doesn't matter where – in the Twilight,

where no one can see us, or in front of the astonished boys, take me in your arms and we will cry together, and there'll be no need for words, and I'll clear out and go back to Zabulon in Moscow, back to Lemesheva's smug supervision. Or do you want me to leave the Day Watch? Do you? I wouldn't stop being a Dark One, that's not in my power, and I don't want to do it, but I will withdraw from the endless war between Dark and Light, I will simply live and not even take anything from the ordinary, little people, even if you don't want to be with me, I don't even ask that, only leave me the memory of our love for each other.

Simply come to me.

No, do not reply to my words.

I am a Dark One.

I cannot be any different.

I love only myself in this world.

But now you are a part of me. The greatest part. The most important part. And if I have to − I will kill part of myself, and that means I will kill all of myself.

But don't do this.

You are a Light One.

You sacrifice your entire lives, you protect people and stand up for each other. Oh, try to look at me in the same way, even if I am a witch, even if I am your enemy. You know that sometimes you can . . . understand. The way Anton Gorodetsky understood, when he gathered such immense power for one purpose − and never made use of it. I can only admire Anton as a worthy enemy, but I love you, I love you, I love you. Oh, why won't you understand what I'm saying and take a step towards me, you scum that I love, my darling rat, my only enemy, my beloved idiot.

'Idiot,' I shouted.

And Igor's face contorted in such monstrous torment that I understood everything.

Light and Dark.

Good and Evil.

They're nothing but words.

Only we speak different languages and we just can't understand each other – even if we're trying to say the same thing.

'Leave, or I'll destroy you.'

And with those words he left the Twilight. His body became blurred and indistinct and immediately reappeared in the human world, beside the two boys on holiday at Artek. And I hurried after him, tearing myself out of my shadow – if only it were as simple as that to escape from myself, from my nature, from my fate.

I was even in time to see what Igor did as he emerged from the Twilight: he caught the guitar that had almost touched the floor, threw a paranjah – I don't know what the Light Ones call it – over his face that was contorted in pain, and brought the boys out of their trance. He must have put them into a stupor when he entered the Twilight. So that they wouldn't be frightened by the camp leaders' sudden disappearance.

What was that you said, little Natasha?

Reliable?

Yes, he's reliable.

'It's time for you to go, Alisa,' Igor said. 'What do we say, boys?'

Only I could see his real face now. Full of grief, nothing but grief.

'Goodbye,' said the fat boy.

'Ciao,' said Alyoshka.

My legs felt like cotton-wool. I tore myself away from the railings of the veranda that I was leaning on, and took a step.

'Goodbye now,' said Igor.

It was dark.

It was good that it was dark.

I didn't have to waste any energy on a paranjah. I didn't have to pretend to be happy. I just had to be careful with my voice. The weak light coming from the window didn't matter.

'And then they divided into Light Ones and Dark Ones,' I said. 'And the Light Ones believed that they shouldn't allow others to tear their lives to pieces. That the most important thing was to give, even if those who took were not worthy of it. But the Dark Ones believed that they should simply live. That everyone deserves what he has taken from life, and nothing more.'

They didn't say anything, my stupid little girls, these human children − I hadn't found a single Other among them, Dark or Light. Not a single enchantress, or witch, or even vampire.

'Good night, girls,' I said. 'Sweet dreams, or even better − no dreams at all.'

'Good night, Alisa.'

So many voices. I was rather surprised. It wasn't even a fairy story, it was a fable that every Other knew, Dark Ones and Light Ones. But they hadn't gone to sleep, they had listened.

I was already halfway out of the door when Natasha's voice asked:

'When the eclipse happens − will it be frightening?'

'No,' I said. 'It's not frightening at all. Just a little bit sad.'

In my room I picked up my mobile yet again and dialled Zabulon's number.

'The number you have dialled is temporarily unavailable.'

Where can you be, Zabulon, if your famous Iridium isn't receiving my call? Where are you, where?

I don't love you, Zabulon. And I probably never did love you. I think I've only just realised what love is. But you do love me! We were together and we were happy, you gave me this whole world and . . . please answer! You're my boss, you're my teacher, you're my lover, so tell me − what should I do now? When I'm left face to face with my enemy . . . and my beloved? Run? Fight? Die? What should I do, Zabulon?

I entered the Twilight.

The shadows of the children's dreams flickered all around me. A banquet . . . those streams of energy. Light and Dark. Fears and sorrows, misery and resentment. I could see right through the whole Azure section. There was the boy Dimka feeling offended in his sleep because his friends hadn't offered him some of their lemonade. There was the tireless little girl Irochka, who was nicknamed the Energiser, whining quietly into her pillow because someone had stolen her inflatable ring for swimming. And there was my faithful energy donor Natasha – she'd lost her little brother in the strange, dark back alleys of a dream and now she was running, crying as she tried to find him.

I don't want to gather power. I don't want to prepare for battle. I don't want anything.

'Zabulon!' I shouted into the shimmering grey gloom. 'I call to you! Zabulon . . .'

No answer.

It was easier for Aunt Polly to get an answer from Tom Sawyer with his hand stuck in the jar of jam than for me to get through to Zabulon.

'Zabulon . . .' I repeated.

This isn't the way I imagined this night . . . nothing like it.

Igor . . . Igor . . .

What are you doing now? Gathering power? Consulting with the all-wise Gesar? Or are you sitting staring dully into the mirror . . . like me?

Mirror, mirror, can you tell my fortune?

I'm not very good at fortune-telling, but sometimes I have managed to see the future.

No.

I don't want to.

I know there's nothing good there.

They reached the beach when the eclipse had already begun.

My girls were squealing and grabbing the pieces of dark glass from each other. They couldn't understand why I didn't ask for a piece. Oh girls, girls, what difference does the blinding light of the sun make to me? I can look the sun full in the face and not blink.

The boys of the fourth brigade were jumping around Igor, hurrying him on. They couldn't understand why their beloved camp leader wasn't going faster. They couldn't understand why he'd led them to the beach by such a long, roundabout route.

But I understood.

Through the Twilight I could see the faint flashes of power being gathered.

What are you doing, Igor . . . my beloved enemy?

At each step the smile faded on one more face. Now a ten-year-old fidgety nuisance is no longer feeling happy about making up with his friend. Now an eleven-year-old fidget has forgotten about the black shell he found on the seashore. Now the serious man of fifteen years has stopped thinking about the date he was promised this evening.

Igor had been walking through Artek in the same way that Anton Gorodetsky had once walked through the streets of Moscow.

And I, who was his primordial enemy, wanted to cry out: 'What are you doing?'

Anton didn't outwit Zabulon because he gathered more power than everybody else. Zabulon was still more powerful.

Anton knew how to use it properly.

Will you?

I don't want you to win. I love only myself. But what am I to do if you have become the greater part of me? Transfixed my life like a bolt of lightning?

Igor was collecting everything. Every last drop of Light energy around him. He was breaking all the laws and agreements and staking everything on a single throw of the dice – including his own life. And not just because he was burning with desire to protect the little human children from the evil witch.

He didn't want to live either. But, unlike me, he was prepared to live for others. If that was the way it had to be.

The last one he drew power from was Makar.

I'd been feeling the boy looking at me for a long time. With the miserable, longing gaze of a boy in love with a grown-up woman. Miserable, and filled with the sadness of farewell.

It wasn't the kind of sadness that we Dark Ones can use. It was a bright sadness.

Igor drank it all up.

He had transgressed all the boundaries. And I couldn't even respond in the same way – I was bound by the promise I had given to Zabulon, bound by my old misdemeanour.

And also by the insane hope that he would do the right thing. That my enemy would win his victory, but I wouldn't lose either.

Up in the sky the bright disc of the sun was slowly dying. The children were already fed up with staring at it through their pieces of glass, they were wallowing in the sea under the strange spectral light that reminded the two Others on the beach of the Twilight.

I turned to Igor and caught his eye.

'Leave,' his lips whispered silently. 'Leave, or I will kill you.'

'Kill me,' I answered silently.

I am a Dark One.

I will not leave.

What is he going to do, this enemy of mine? Attack me? Despite my legal right to be here? Call in the Yalta division of the Night Watch? He must already have consulted with them . . . and he knows there are no charges that can be brought against me.

Igor took a step closer.

'By the Light and the Dark, I challenge you,' his lips whispered.

I shuddered.

I hadn't been expecting this. Not this.

'Beyond Light and Dark, you and I, one against one, to the end.'

He had challenged me to a duel.

It's an old custom that came into being with the Great Treaty between the Light Ones and the Dark Ones. A custom that is hardly ever used. Because the victor has to answer to the Inquisition. Because a duel only takes place when there is no legitimate basis for conflict, when the Watches have no legal competence to intervene, when emotions speak louder than reason.

'And may the Light be my witness.'

Nobody else could have seen the tiny petal of white fire that flared up for an instant on Igor's open palm. He himself started when he saw it. The higher powers rarely respond to appeals from simple Watch agents.

'Igor, I love you.'

His face quivered as if I had struck it. He didn't believe me. He couldn't believe me.

'Do you accept my challenge, witch?'

Yes, I can refuse. Go back to Moscow, humiliated but secure, with the stigma of having refused a challenge . . . Every lousy werewolf would spit as I walked past.

Or I could try to kill Igor. Gather so much power that I could stand up to him.

'May the Dark be my witness,' I said, opening my hand. And a tiny scrap of Dark quivered on my palm.

'Choose,' said Igor.

I shook my head. I wasn't going to choose the place, the time or the type of duel.

Why can't you understand me? Why?

'Then the choice is mine. Now. In the sea. The press.'

His eyes are dark. An eclipse isn't frightening – it's only something cutting off the Light.

The sea was unnaturally warm. Maybe because the air had turned cold, as if it was already evening. All that was left of the sun was a narrow crescent at the top of the disc – now even a human being could look at it without blinking.

I swam through the warm water without looking back at the shore, where no one had noticed the two camp leaders slip into the sea without paying any attention to the jellyfish that hurried out of their way.

I remembered the first time I ever went to the sea. I was still very little, I still didn't know that I didn't belong to the human race, that fate had decided I would be an Other. I was staying at Alushta with my dad, and he was teaching me to swim. I remembered the feeling of delight when the water first submitted to my will.

And I remember how strong the waves were in the sea. Very strong. Or was it just that all waves looked huge to me then? My dad was holding me in his arms, he was jumping up and down in the waves, making me laugh, it was such fun . . . and I shouted that I could swim across the sea, and my dad said of course I could.

You'll be really hurt, Dad.

And it won't be easy for Mum, either.

The shore, full of delighted children and contented adults, had been left far behind. I didn't even feel the start of the 'press'. It just got harder to swim. The water just stopped supporting me. There was suddenly a weight on my shoulders.

A very simple spell. Nothing fancy. Power against power.

Dad, I really did believe I could swim across the sea.

I extended a defensive canopy above myself and it took the invisible weight off my shoulders. And once again I whispered:

'Zabulon, I appeal to you.'

The strength that I had managed to gather was rapidly melting away. Igor struck again and again, battering my defences mercilessly.

'Yes, Alisa.'

He has responded after all! He has answered me! Just in time, as always!

'Zabulon, I'm in trouble!'

'I knew already. I'm very sorry.'

I didn't realise immediately what those words 'I knew' meant. And that impersonal tone, and the feeling that there was no power on its way. He always used to share his power with me, even when I didn't really need it that badly.

'Zabulon, am I going to die?'

'I'm afraid so.'

My defensive canopy was dissolving, and I still couldn't make sense of what was happening.

He could intervene! Even from a distance! A small part of his strength would be enough for me to resist the pressure and fight out a draw.

'Zabulon, you said that love is a great power!'

'Have you not been convinced of that? Goodbye, my little girl.'

It was only then that I understood everything.

Just as my strength melted away and I felt the invisible pressure on my shoulders again, forcing me down into the warm, twilit depths.

'Igor!' I shouted, but the splashing of the water drowned out my voice.

He was swimming about fifty metres away, not even looking in my direction. He was crying, but the sea has no place for tears.

And I was being dragged down, down into the Dark abyss.

How could it have happened . . . how?

I tried to gather power from the beach. But there was almost no Dark there for me to take. That sweet delight and those cries of joy were no use to me.

Only a hundred metres behind us the young teenager who had fallen so hopelessly in love with me was vainly trying to float on the waves and relax the leg that was contorted by cramps. Somehow he must have noticed us going into the water and swum after us, this proud boy called Makar, who had already realised that he couldn't swim back to the shore now.

Love is a great power . . . How stupid you all are, you boys, when you fall in love.

There's Makar, floundering about as his panic grows. I can take his fear and prolong my own agony for a minute or two.

And there's Igor, swimming in the sea: not seeing anything, not hearing anything, not sensing anything around him, not thinking about anything except that I have killed his love. The stupid Light Magician doesn't know that there are no winners in duels, especially when the duel has been carefully planned by Zabulon.

'Igor,' I whispered as I sank, feeling the pressure force me down, down to the dark, dark seabed.

Forgive me, Dad . . . I can't swim across this sea . . .

# Story Two

# A STRANGER
# AMONG OTHERS

# PROLOGUE

HE COULD already make out the lights of the station glimmering up ahead, but inside the gloomy, neglected park beside the Zarya factory the darkness remained as dense and chill as ever. The thin crust of ice over the snow crunched under his feet – it would probably thaw out again before midday. Train whistles in the distance, incomprehensible announcements over the station's public address system and the crunching noise of his own feet – these were the only sounds anyone who happened to be out for a walk could have heard if he wandered into the park at that time of night.

But no one had set foot in here at night – or even during the evening – for a long time now. Not even people out walking massive dogs with huge teeth. Because the dogs could not save them from what they might meet in the darkness of night, among the oaks that had grown tall here over the last forty years.

The solitary traveller with a bulky bag over his shoulder was clearly late for a train and so he decided to take a short cut and go through the park. Along the path, with his feet sometimes crunching on the thin ice, sometimes on the gravel. The stars gazed down in amazement at this bold spirit. The round disc of the moon, as yellow as a pool of Advocaat, shone its :ght through the jagged, naked branches. The fantastic forms of t e lunar seas were like the shadows of human fears.

The traveller noticed the gleam of a pair of eyes v en he was still thirty metres from the last of the trees. He was being watched from the gaunt, skeletal bushes that stretched along both sides of the path. There was the vague, dark form of something over there, in the scrubby thickets; perhaps not even something, but someone, because this dense patch of darkness was alive. Or at leas it could move.

A dull growl – nothing like a roar, more like a low, hollow squawk – was the only sound that accompanied the lightning-swift attack. A wide mouthful of sharp teeth glinted in the moon-light.

The moon had readied itself for fresh blood. For a fresh victim.

But the attacker suddenly stopped dead in his tracks, as if he had run into an invisible barrier, stood there for a moment, and then collapsed onto the path with a ludicrous squeal.

The traveller paused for a second.

'What are you doing, you blockhead?' he hissed at his attacker. 'Do you want me to call for the Night Watch?'

The patch of darkness at the traveller's feet growled resentfully.

'It's lucky for you that I'm late,' said the traveller, adjusting the bag across his shoulder. 'What bloody nonsense is this, Others attacking Others . . . ?' He strode on rapidly across the last few metres of the park and hurried towards the station without looking back.

His attacker crawled off the path, under the trees, and there he transformed into a young man of about twenty, quite naked. The young man was tall, with broad shoulders. The crust of ice crackled under his bare feet, but he didn't seem to feel the cold.

'Damn!' he whispered fiercely and then shivered for the first time. 'Who the hell was that?'

He was still hungry, still feeling savage, but this strange victim who had escaped had completely robbed him of any desire to carry on hunting. He was frightened now, although only a few minutes earlier he had been certain that everyone should be afraid of him — a werewolf out on the hunt. The heady, intoxicating hunt for human flesh. And the hunt was unlicensed — which made the sensation of risk and his own daring even keener.

Two things in particular had entirely blunted the hunter's enthusiasm. First, the words 'Night Watch' — after all, he didn't have a licence. And second, the fact that he had failed to recognise his intended victim as an Other. An Other like him.

Not long ago the werewolf and any Others that he knew would have said that was simply impossible.

Still in the form of a naked human being, the werewolf hurried through the low bushes to where he had left his clothes. Now he would have to hide for many, many days, instead of prowling through the park at night hoping to chance upon a victim. He would have to stay hidden away, waiting for sanctions from the Night Watch. Or maybe even from his own side.

His only hope was that this solitary traveller who had not been afraid to cut across the park in the dark, this strange Other — or someone pretending to be an Other — really had been hurrying to catch a train. That he would catch it and leave the city. And then he wouldn't be able to contact the Night Watch.

Others also know how to hope.

# CHAPTER 1

I ONLY calmed down completely when I was able to relax and listen to the regular, hammering rhythm of the wheels. Although even then, not entirely. How could I possibly feel calm? But at least I had recovered the ability to think coherently.

When that creature in the park broke through the bushes and threw itself at me I hadn't been afraid. Not at all. But now I had no idea how I had found the right words to say. Afterwards I must have surprised plenty of people with the way I staggered across the square in front of the station, past the tight ranks of taxis parked for the night. It's not easy to walk with a steady stride when your knees are buckling under you.

What the hell was all this? 'The Night Watch' . . . What on earth had I meant by saying that? And that beast with the teeth had immediately started whining and crept back into the bushes . . .

I took another mouthful of beer and tried once again to make sense of what had happened.

So, first I left the house.

Stop.

I put the bottle down on the little table, feeling confused. I must have looked very stupid at that moment, but there was no one to look at me – I was the only person in the compartment.

Stop.

I suddenly realised I couldn't remember my own house at all.

I couldn't remember a single thing about my past life. My memories began there, in that chilly winter park, just a few seconds before the attack. And everything before that was hidden in a mysterious darkness. Or rather, not even darkness, but a strange, grey shroud – sticky and viscous, almost completely impenetrable. A dense, grey, swirling half-light.

I didn't understand a thing.

I cast a confused and frightened glance round the compartment. It was a perfectly ordinary compartment. A little table, four bunks, brown plastic and maroon imitation leather. With lights occasionally slipping past in the night outside the window. My bag lying on the other bunk.

My bag!

I realised I didn't have the slightest idea what was in my bag. It had to be my stuff. And stuff can tell you a lot. Or remind you. For instance, it might remind me why I was going to Moscow. For some reason I felt certain the bag could help reawaken my failed memory. I must have read about that somewhere or heard about it from someone.

Then I suddenly had a better idea and reached in under my sweater, because I realised my passport was in my shirt pocket. If I could start with my name, then maybe I really would remember everything else.

As I looked at the yellowish page with its dark pattern of fanciful curlicues, I had mixed feelings. I looked at the photograph. At the face that I had probably been used to identifying with my own unique personality for about thirty years – or was this the very first day?

The face was familiar to the minutest detail. From the scar on the cheekbone to the premature hint of grey in the hair. But never mind the face. That wasn't what interested me just at that moment. The name.

Vitaly Sergeevich Rogoza. Date of birth, September 28, 1965. Place of birth, the city of Nikolaev.

Turning over the page, I read the same information in Ukrainian and also ascertained that my sex was male and the passport had been issued by an organisation with the exceptionally clumsy acronym DO PMC ADIA – the District Office of the People's Municipal Council of the Administration of the Department of Internal Affairs of Ukraine. The 'Family status' page was an unsullied, virginal blank. I heaved a sigh of relief, or perhaps disappointment.

Then came the eternal burden and curse borne by every ex-Soviet citizen: my residence permit and address. Apartment 28, 28 Tchaikovsky Street, Nikolaev.

Well, well, there was the number 28 again, twice in a row.

And then the associations really began to click – I remembered that my house stood on the corner of Tchaikovksy Street and Young Guard Street, next to School No. 28 (that number yet again). I remembered everything quite clearly and distinctly, right down to the charred poplar below my window – the victim of chemical experiments conducted by the young kid who lived on the floor above me, who had poured all sorts of rubbish out of the window onto the long-suffering tree. I remembered a drunken party in the next house five years ago, when someone had casually told the neighbour from downstairs what she could do with herself when she complained about the noise, and she'd turned out to be Armenian, the wife of some local bigwig, and how later a whole mob of those dark Armenians had come bursting in and started battering our faces to pulp and I'd had to clamber out through the little window in the end room, because the main window wouldn't open, and climb down the drainpipe. When they noticed that one of the miserable drunks had disappeared from the blockaded apartment, the Armenians stopped flailing their fists about and some kind of agreement was eventually reached with them. And I also remembered my bitter disappointment when I asked for help from some local mates of mine who I'd often drunk beer with at the kiosks in the area, and not a single one of them came.

I tore myself away from these surprisingly vivid memories.

So I did have a past after all. Or were these merely the forms of memories, with nothing real behind them?

I had to try to figure it out.

From the passport I also gathered the entirely useless piece of information that I had 'exercised the right to privatise without payment the following volume of living space' – the volume was not indicated – 'subject to the standard maximum of 24.3 square metres'.

And that was all.

I thoughtfully put the document back in the same pocket and looked hard at the bag. What will you help me remember, my black-and-green travelling companion with the foreign inscription FUJI on your bulging side?

Well, let's hope you'll help me remember at least something.

The zip opened with a quiet whoosh. I threw back the flap of cloth that covered the contents and looked inside. The polythene bag on top contained a toothbrush, a tube of Blend-a-Med toothpaste, a couple of cheap disposable razors and a small, fragrant black bottle of eau-de-cologne.

I put them on the bunk.

In the next plastic bag I discovered a warm wool sweater, obviously knitted by hand, not on a machine. I put that aside too.

I spent two or three minutes rummaging through the other bags – clean underwear, T-shirts, socks, a warm checked shirt.

Aha, here was something that wasn't clothes.

A little mobile phone in a leather case, with an extendable aerial. My memory instantly reacted: 'When I get to Moscow, I'll have to buy a card.'

The charger was there too.

And finally, at the very bottom, one more plastic bag. Filled with blocks of something.

When I opened it, I was astounded. This ordinary plastic bag, the logo half worn away so that it was completely unrecognisable, contained wads of money, stacked in two layers. American dollars. Ten wads of hundred-dollar notes. That was a hundred thousand.

My hand automatically reached for the door and clicked the latch shut.

Je-sus, where had I got this from? And how was I going to get such a huge amount of money across the border? But then, I could probably stick a hundred-dollar bill under every customs officer's nose and they'd leave me alone.

The discovery provoked almost no associations, apart from the memory of how expensive hotels are in Moscow.

Still in a mild state of shock, I put everything back in the bag, zipped it shut and pushed it under the bunk. I felt glad there was a second, unopened, bottle of beer standing beside the one I'd already started.

I don't know why, but the alcohol had a distinctly soporific effect on me. I was expecting to spend a long time lying there, listening to the hammering of the wheels, screwing up my eyes when the bright light suddenly broke in for a few moments, and racking my brains painfully.

Nothing of the sort happened. Before I'd even finished the

second bottle of beer, I slumped onto the bunk, still in all my clothes, and crashed out on top of the blanket.

Maybe I'd got too close to something taboo in my memories? But how would I know?

I woke up to cold winter sunshine flooding in through the window. The train wasn't moving. I could hear indifferent official voices in the corridor: 'Good morning, Russian customs. Are you carrying any arms, narcotics or hard currency?' The replies sounded less indifferent, but most of them were unintelligible.

Then there was a knock at the door. I reached out and opened it.

The customs officer turned out to be a burly, red-faced guy with eyes that were already turning puffy. For some reason, when he spoke to me, he abandoned the standard routine and simply asked me, without the officialese:

'What have you got? Get your bag out.'

He inspected the compartment carefully. He got up onto the ladder and glanced into the luggage rack just below the ceiling. And then finally he focused his attention on the bag lying all alone in the middle of the bottom bunk.

I lowered the other bunk and sat down. Still saying nothing.

'Open the bag, please,' the customs officer demanded.

'Can they smell money, or something?' I thought sullenly and obediently unzipped the bag.

One by one the plastic bags ended up on the bunk. When he reached the bag with the money, the customs officer brightened up noticeably and reached out in a reflex response to slam the door of the compartment.

'Well, well, well . . .'

I had already prepared myself for a hypocritical tirade about permits and even to have to read a paragraph out of a book – like every written law, perfectly understandable words strung together so that they made absolutely no sense at all. To listen, read and then ask hopelessly: 'How much?'

But instead, I mentally reached my hand out towards the customs officer's head, touched his mind and whispered:

'Go now . . . Go on. Everything's okay here.'

The officer's eyes instantly became as stupid and senseless as the customs regulations.

'Yes . . . have a good journey . . .'

He swung round stiffly, clicked the lock open and staggered out into the corridor without another word. An obedient wooden puppet with a skilful puppet-master pulling his strings.

But since when had I been a skilful puppet-master?

The train moved off about ten minutes later and all that time I was trying to make sense of what was happening. I didn't know what I was doing, but I was doing exactly what was needed. First that creature in the park beside the factory, and now this customs officer whose mind had instantly gone blank.

And why on earth was I on my way to Moscow? What was I going to do when I got off the train? Where was I going to go?

Somehow I was already beginning to feel certain that everything would become clear at the right moment. But only at the right moment, not before.

Unfortunately, I wasn't a hundred per cent certain yet.

I slept for most of the day. Maybe it was my body reacting to all the unexpected answers and new skills. Just how had I managed to see off the customs officer? I'd reached out to him, felt his dull crimson aura with the shimmering greenish overlay of dollar signs . . . And I'd been able to adjust his intentions.

I didn't think ordinary people could do that. But what was I, if I wasn't an ordinary human being?

Oh, yes. I was an Other. I'd told the werewolf in the park that. And I'd only just that moment realised it was a werewolf that had attacked me in the park. I remembered his aura, that bright yellow and crimson flame of Desire and Hunger.

It was as though I was gradually clambering up a stairway out of the blackness. Out of a blank chasm. The werewolf had been the first step, the customs officer the second. I wondered just how long the stairway was. And what would I find up there, at the top?

So far I had more questions than answers.

When I finally woke again we had already passed Tula. The compartment was still empty, but now I realised that was because it was the way I wanted it. And I realised that I usually got what I wanted in this world.

The platform at Kursk Station in Moscow drifted slowly past the window. I was standing in the compartment, already dressed and packed, waiting for the train to stop. The female announcer's muffled voice informed everyone that train number sixty-two had arrived at some platform or other.

I was in Moscow, but I still didn't know what I was doing.

As usual, the most impatient passengers had already managed to block the corridor. But I could wait, I was in no hurry. After all, I'd be waiting anyway, until my slowly reviving memory prompted me or prodded me, like a mule driver with a stubborn, lazy mule.

The train gave a final jerk and came to a halt. There was a metallic clang in the corridor, the queue of people started and came to life, spilling out of the carriage one by one. There were the usual exclamations of concern and greeting, and passengers trying to squeeze back through into compartments to fetch things they hadn't been able to take out the first time . . .

But the confused bustling around the carriage was soon over. The passengers had got out and received their allocation of kisses and hugs from the people meeting them. Or not, if there was no one there to meet them. There were still a few, craning their necks as they gazed around the platform, already shivering in the piercing Moscow wind. But the only people left in the carriage were waiting to pick up the usual parcels of food and so on that relatives had sent in the care of the conductor.

I picked up my bag and walked towards the door, still with no idea of what I was going to do next.

Probably I ought to change some money, I thought. I didn't have a single Russian kopeck. Only our 'independent' Ukrainian currency. But unfortunately it wasn't currency here. Just before we reached Moscow I'd prudently slit open one of the wads in the plastic bag and distributed some of the bills around my various pockets.

I always did hate billfolds.

What was that thought? Always . . . My 'always' had only begun last night.

With an instinctive shudder at the cold embrace of winter, I strode off along the platform towards the tunnel. Surely there had to be someone changing money at the station?

Rummaging about in my unreliable memory, I managed to establish two things: first, I didn't remember the last time I'd been in Moscow but, second, I had a general idea of how the station looked from the inside, where to look for the bureau de change and how to reach the metro.

The tunnel, the large waiting hall in the basement, the short escalator, the ticket hall. My immediate goal was over there on the second floor, beside another escalator.

But this currency exchange looked as though it had been firmly closed for a very long time. No chink of light, no board showing current exchange rates.

Okay. Then I had to head for the exit and turn left, towards the ramp that sloped down to the Chkalovskaya metro station. The place I needed would be near there.

A white retail unit, a staircase up to the second floor, empty little booths flooded with light, a turn ... The security guard glanced up at me quickly and then relaxed when he recognised I was new in town.

'Go on, there's no one inside,' he told me magnanimously.

I carried my bag into a tiny little room, featureless apart from a rubbish bin in the corner and, of course, a small window with one of those little retractable drawers that always reminded me of an endlessly hungry mouth.

'Hey,' I reminded myself, 'don't forget just how recent your "always" is.'

But even so – if I was thinking like a man who really had lived thirty-five years, surely there must be some reason for that?

Anyway, we could get to that later.

The hungry mouth instantly consumed five one-hundred-dollar bills and my passport. I couldn't see who was concealed behind the blank partition, and I wasn't really bothered to get a look. All I noticed were the fingers with pearly nail-varnish, which meant it was a woman. The mouth reluctantly slid open and belched out a sizeable heap of one-hundred-rouble notes along with several smaller denominations. Even a few coins. Without counting the money, I put most of it into my shirt pocket, under my sweater, keeping just the smaller bills and the coins for my trousers. I put my passport in my other breast pocket and threw the receipt, a small rectangle of green paper, into the rubbish bin.

Right, now I was someone. Even in this insane city, which was just about the most expensive on the planet. But no ... that wasn't actually right. It had to be almost a year since Moscow had relinquished that dubious title.

Outside, winter greeted me again with its ice-laden breath. The wind was full of fine hard crumbs, like grains of semolina, a kind of miniature hail.

I strolled back along the front of the station and then down to where I wanted to be – the metro circle line.

It felt like I was beginning to remember where I needed to get to. Well, I could enjoy making some progress, even if I didn't enjoy the uncertainty. And I could hope that whatever business had brought me to Moscow was good. Because somehow I didn't feel I had the power to serve Evil.

Only native Muscovites take taxis home from the railway stations. If their finances permit, of course. Any provincial, even if he has the kind of money I had, takes the metro. There's something hypnotic about this system of tunnels, with its labyrinth of connections, about the rumbling of the trains as they go hurtling past and the rush of air that subsides and then starts up again, about the constant movement. Down here unspent energy seethes and swirls around under the vaults of the station halls: energy free for the taking, more than I could possibly use.

And there is protection. I think it's connected somehow with the depth of the earth above your head . . . and all the past years that are buried in that earth. Not even years – centuries.

The doors of the train parted and I stepped in. An unpleasant, insistent buzzing from the loudspeakers, and then a finely modulated male voice announced: 'Please mind the closing doors. The next station is Komsomolskaya.'

I was on the circle line, anti-clockwise. And I was definitely not getting off at Komsomolskaya. But after that . . . After Komsomolskaya apparently I would get out. That would be Peace Prospect. And, of course, it would be worth walking up the platform at Komsomolskaya to get closer to the front of the train. Then I'd be nearer the exit for my connection.

That meant I was changing onto the brown line. And probably going north, because otherwise I'd have gone round the circle line in the opposite direction and changed at Oktyabrskaya.

The carriage shook as it moved, and since I had nothing better to do, I studied the dozens of ads. There was a long-haired man squatting down but on tiptoe, advertising women's tights; someone using a felt-tip pen had taken the opportunity to give the hairy poser a huge dick. The next poster suggested that I should chase a brightly painted jeep round the city, but I failed to get the point of that. A prize, probably. Miracle tablets for almost every ailment – all in a single bottle – estate agents, the most yoghurty yoghurt of all yoghurts, genuine Borzhomi mineral water with a picture of a ram on the bottle . . . And here was Komsomolskaya.

I was fed up with the adverts, so I dropped my bag by the door and went to look at the plan of the metro system. I don't know why, but my attention was immediately drawn by the little red circle with the letters 'AEEA' above it – the 'All-Union Exhibition of Economic Achievements'.

That was where I was going. No doubt about it. To a massive horseshoe-shaped building. The Cosmos hotel.

No one can deny that life feels easier when you know where you're going. I heaved a sigh of relief, returned to my bag and even smiled at my dull reflection in the glass of the door. The door also bore traces of the mindless hyperactivity of the city's pithecanthropoids – the inscription 'Do not lean against the doors' had been reduced to 'Do lean again do'.

The unknown author of this pointless statement wasn't even a pithecanthropus; he was more likely a monkey, a dirty, smug little monkey. Dirty and stupid, precisely because he was too much like a human being.

I was glad that I was an Other, and not a human being.

Here was Peace Prospect; stairs, turn right, an escalator, and there's the train just arriving. Rizhskaya, Alexeevskaya, AEEA. Leave the carriage and turn right – I'd always known that.

A long, long escalator, on which for some reason I have no

thoughts about anything at all. Those annoying ads again. A pedestrian underpass. And there's the hotel. A horseshoe-shaped monstrosity of French architecture. The hotel has changed, though, and quite noticeably. They've added illuminated hoardings and bright lights; and then there's the casino, with the prize foreign car displayed on a pedestal. Street girls standing around smoking, despite the hard frost. And the doorman inside, whose hands instantly swallow up a hundred-rouble bill.

It wasn't really late yet, so the lobby was still busy. Someone was talking on a mobile, rapping out phrases in Arabic loud enough for everyone to hear, and music was coming from several directions at once.

'A de luxe suite for one,' I said casually. 'And please, no phone calls offering me girls. I've come to work.'

Money is a great thing. A suite was found instantly — did I want dinner in my room? — and I was promised that no one would call me, although I didn't really believe that. They suggested I should register straight away, because I had a Ukrainian passport. I registered. But then, instead of quietly making for the lift to which I was solicitously directed, I set out towards an unremarkable little door in the darkest and emptiest corner of the lobby.

There were no plaques at all on this door.

The receptionist watched me go with genuine respect. I think everyone else had stopped noticing me at all.

Behind the door I discovered a grubby little office — probably the only space in the hotel that hadn't been Europeanised. It was straight out of the barbarous Soviet seventies.

A standard issue desk — not really shabby, but it had seen plenty of service — a standard issue chair and an ancient Polish Aster telephone in the middle of the desk. Perched on the chair was a puny little guy wearing a militia sergeant's uniform. He looked at me inquiringly.

The sergeant was an Other. And he was a Light One – I realised that right away.

A Light One . . . Hmm. Then what was I? I didn't think I was a Light One. No, definitely not a Light One.

Well then, that decided that.

'Hello,' I said to him. 'I'd like to register in Moscow.'

The militiaman addressed me through clenched teeth, with both surprise and irritation in his voice:

'The receptionist handles registration. When you check in. You have to check in to register.'

He rustled the newspaper that he had been studying, pencil in hand, before I arrived – I suppose he was marking interesting small ads from the endless pages of them.

'I've done the ordinary registration already,' I explained. I need the *other* registration. But I haven't introduced myself: Vitaly Rogoza, Other.'

The militiaman immediately straightened up and looked at me differently. He looked perplexed now. He didn't seem able to recognise me as an Other. So I helped him out.

'A Dark One,' he muttered after a while, with a feeling of relief, or so it seemed to me. He introduced himself too: 'Zakhar Zelinsky, Other. Night Watch. Let's go through.'

I could clearly hear in his tone the old complaint about 'all these foreigners flooding into our Moscow'. Others could never help dragging human clichés and stereotypes into their own attitudes. This Light One was definitely annoyed by the arrival of yet another provincial and the need to get up off his arse, tear his eyes away from the newspaper, drag himself to his computer and go through all the hassle of a registration.

There was another door in the middle of the wall, one that a human being could never have seen. But there was no need to open it – we walked through the wall, surrounded by the grey

Twilight that had instantly filled the space around us. Our move-ments were soft and slow, and even the flickering of the light bulb on the ceiling was visible.

The second room was far more presentable than the first. The sergeant immediately sat down at a comfortable little desk with a computer and offered me a seat on a plump sofa.

'Are you staying in Moscow for long?'

'I don't know yet. I think for at least a month.'

'Your permanent residence registration, please.'

He could have seen it for himself, using his sight as an Other, but apparently the rules meant he had to use a more direct method.

My jacket was already unbuttoned, so I just pulled up my sweater, shirt and T-shirt. There on my chest was the bluish mark of permanent registration in Ukraine. The sergeant read it with a pass of his open hand and began slowly tapping at the keyboard of his PC. He took a while to check the data, then tapped away on the keyboard again. He opened a massive safe locked with more than just keys, took something out, ran through the neces-sary procedures and concluded by flinging a small bundle of bluish light at me. For an instant my entire upper body was flooded with fire, and a moment later I had two seals decorating my chest. The second was my temporary Moscow registration.

'Your registration is temporary, but it has no fixed period,' the sergeant explained with no great enthusiasm. 'Since our database indicates that you are an entirely law-abiding Dark Other, we can go easy on you and issue an unlimited registration. I hope the Night Watch won't have any reason to change its opinion about you. The seal will self-destruct as soon as you spend twenty-four hours outside the Moscow city limits. If you have to leave for more than twenty-four hours, I'm afraid you'll have to register again.'

'I understand,' I said. 'Thank you, can I go?'

'Yes, you can go . . . Dark One.'

The sergeant said nothing for a few moments, then he locked the safe (with more than just keys), left the computer as it was and gestured with his hand towards the door.

Back in the grubby little room, he asked me uncertainly:

'Pardon me for asking, but who are you? Not a vampire, not a shape-shifter, not an incubus, not a warlock, I can tell all that. But not a magician either, I think. I don't quite understand.'

The sergeant himself was a Light Magician, about fourth grade. That wasn't very high, but it wasn't exactly nothing either.

Yes, indeed — who was I?

'That's a difficult question,' I replied evasively. 'More a magician than anything else, I think. Goodbye.'

I picked up my bag and went back out into the lobby.

Five minutes later I was already making myself at home in my suite.

I'd been right not to believe the receptionist — the first call to offer me entertainment caught me while I was shaving. Morosely but politely I asked them not to call again. The second time my tone was less polite, and the third time I simply poured so much sticky, viscous power into the innocent phone that the person at the other end choked and stopped in mid-word. But at least they didn't call again.

'I'm learning,' I thought. 'But am I really a magician or not?'

To be honest, I hadn't really been surprised by what the Light sergeant had said. Vampires, shape-shifters, incubuses . . . they all exist. They certainly do. But only for their own kind, for the Others. For ordinary people, they don't exist. But for Others, ordinary people are the very source of existence. Their roots and their nourishment. For both Light Ones and Dark Ones, no matter what nonsense the Light Ones might trumpet on every street corner. They also draw their energy from the lives of human beings. And as for their goals . . . We both have the same goals. It's just that we and the Light Ones both try to overtake our competitors and reach our goals first.

I was distracted from all these revelations by a knock at the door – they had brought my dinner. After I'd fed the waiter a hundred-rouble bill (where did I get this lordly habit of handing out such incredibly generous tips?), I tried to concentrate again, but I'd obviously lost the wavelength. A pity.

But in any case, I had climbed up one more step. At least now I knew there were two different kinds of Others. Light Ones and Dark Ones. I was a Dark One. I wasn't very fond of Light Ones, but I couldn't say that I hated them. After all, they were Others too, even if their principles were rather different from ours.

And I'd begun to understand a bit more about what lay behind my threat to the werewolf in the park, behind the vague but imposing title 'Night Watch'. What it signified was the observation of Dark Ones at night – precisely at night, because the Dark Ones' time was the night. Naturally, there was a Day Watch as well. They were my kind, but I had to be careful with them too, because if I did something wrong it wouldn't exactly earn me a pat on the back. And this whole system was in a rather fragile state of equilibrium, since both sides were constantly seeking means and methods to finally rout their opponents and acquire undivided control over the world of human beings.

That was all I had so far. And from the height of this step I couldn't make out anything more in the encircling twilight.

I heard the Call just as I was finishing my dinner.

Neither too quiet, nor too loud, neither pleading nor imperious. The person it was intended for heard it too. And couldn't resist.

It wasn't intended for me. So it was strange that I could hear it.

That meant I had to do something.

Something implacable inside me was already giving orders. Put your jacket on. Put the bag in the cupboard. Lock the windows and the doors. And not just with the locks and latches, you dolt.

Drawing in power from anywhere I could reach, I made sure that ordinary people wouldn't take any interest in my room. Others had no business being here anyway.

The dead-drunk Syrian in the next room suddenly sobered up. One floor down the Czech who had been in agony with his stomach finally puked and collapsed in relief with his arms round the toilet bowl. In the room across the corridor an elderly businessman from the Urals slapped his wife on the cheek for the first time in his life, putting an end to an old, lingering quarrel – an hour later the couple would celebrate their reconciliation in the restaurant on the second floor. If there was a Light One around then, I'd already set the table for him.

But all this didn't really interest me. I was following the Call. The Call that wasn't intended for me.

Evening was smoothly turning into night. The avenue was full of noise, the wind howled in the trolleybus wires. For some reason the sounds of nature drowned out the voices of civilisation – maybe because I was listening so intently?

To the right, along the avenue. Definitely.

I pulled my cap down tighter on my head and set off along the pavement.

When I had almost reached a long building with shop windows along its ground floor displaying absurd phoney samovars, the Call stopped. But I already knew where to go.

Over there, by the next building, there was the dark tunnel of a narrow alley. And right now it was filled with truly intense darkness.

As if to spite me, the wind grew stronger, lashing at my face and pressing me back like a rugby player, and I had to lean forward in order to move at all.

There was the alley. It looked like I was too late. An indistinct silhouette froze for a moment against the vague patch of light that was the other end of the alley; all I could make out was a pale face that was obviously not human and the dull gleam of two eyes. And I think I saw teeth.

That was all. Someone had been here and disappeared, but there was someone else still here, and they wouldn't be going anywhere.

I leaned down over the motionless body and took a close look. A girl, still very young, about sixteen. With a strange mixture of bliss and torment in her glazed eyes. A fluffy knitted scarf and a matching hat lay beside her. Her jacket was unbuttoned, exposing her neck. And there were four puncture marks clearly visible in it.

Somehow I wasn't surprised that I was able to see in almost total darkness.

I squatted down beside the girl. Whoever had drunk her blood – not a lot of it, no more than a quarter of a litre – had also drunk her life. Sucked all her energy right out of her. A lousy way to go.

And then people burst into the alley at both ends simultaneously, or rather, not people – Others.

'Stop there! Night Watch! Leave the Twilight!'

I straightened up, not realising immediately what they wanted from me, and received a hard blow – but not from a fist or a foot. It was something white, as white as a surgeon's coat. It didn't really hurt, but it annoyed me. One of the Watchmen was pointing a thick rod at me. There was a red stone on the end of it, and he looked as if he was getting ready to hit me again.

And then I was suddenly thrown one more step up the stairway. Not just one, but two at least.

I left the Twilight. Now I understood what was happening when everything around me slowed down and I could suddenly see in pitch darkness. It was the world of the Others. And I'd been ordered – not asked, but ordered – to return to the world of human beings.

So I did, obeying without objection. Because it was the right thing to do.

'Identify yourself!' they demanded. I couldn't see who they were, because they were shining a torch in my face. I could have made out their faces, but just at that moment I knew that wasn't the right thing to do.

'Vitaly Rogoza, Other.'

'Andrei Tiunnikov, Other, Night Watch agent,' said the one who had struck me with his battle wand, clearly taking some pleasure in introducing himself.

Now I could tell that I hadn't been hit with full power, it had just been a warning shot. But if they wanted, they could strike a lot harder, the charge in the wand was strong enough.

'Well now, Dark One. What do we have here? A fresh corpse, and you standing beside it. Are you going to explain? Or maybe you have a licence? Well?'

'Andriukha, hold your horses,' someone called sharply to him from out of the darkness.

But Andriukha took no notice and just gestured in annoyance. 'Wait!'

He spoke to me again:

'Well, then? Why don't you talk, Dark One? Nothing to say?'

I wasn't saying anything.

Andriukha Tiunnikov was a magician. A Light Magician, naturally, and barely up to the fifth grade.

I'd been that strong yesterday.

He obviously hadn't charged the amulet himself – I could sense the work of a much more experienced magician. And I thought the two young guys behind his back looked rather more powerful too.

At the other end the alley was blocked off by a girl, standing on her own. She was young and not very tall, but she was the most experienced and dangerous member of the group. She was a shape-shifting battle magician. Something like a Light were-wolf.

'Well, come on, Dark One!' Andriukha insisted. 'Still got nothing to say? I see. Show me your registration! And someone let the Day Watch know we have a Dark poacher here.'

'You're a fool, Andriukha,' I said derisively. 'So pleased with yourself because you've caught a Dark poacher! Why don't you try taking a look at the victim? Who do you think did for her?'

Andriukha broke off and looked down at the dead girl. He seemed to be getting the picture.

'A va-vampire,' he muttered.

'And who am I?'

'You're a ma-magician.' Andriukha was so confused, he'd begun to stammer.

I turned to the girl, because I'd decided she was the one I ought to talk to.

'When I got here it was all over. I saw the vampire, but he'd already left the alley, he took off into the yard. The girl was already dead, she's been completely drained, but only a mouthful of her blood has been taken. I'm new in town, just off the train two hours ago, I'm staying at the Cosmos hotel.'

And I couldn't resist adding:

'Not the first time vampires have used this alley for poaching, is it?'

Now I could see the traces of the past there, on the ground and on the walls. Now that I'd jumped up several steps at once.

'Only last time you were luckier, Light Ones. But I must say you did a lousy job cleaning up, the signs are still visible now.'

'Don't get any idea we're grateful to you,' the girl answered darkly through clenched teeth. 'And let me take a look at your registration anyway.'

'By all means.' I meekly showed them the seal. 'I trust I'm not needed any longer? I wouldn't like to get in the way of your superlative detectives in their search for the poacher.'

'We'll find you tomorrow,' the girl told me dryly. 'If we need you.'

'Please do!' I said with a grin. Then I moved one of the Watchmen aside and walked out onto the avenue.

I cast off the guise of an ordinary Dark One about a hundred steps further on.

# CHAPTER 2

FOR THE next two days and nights absolutely nothing interesting happened. I wandered round Moscow, making impulse purchases and practising my new abilities, trying not to make them too obvious. I switched on my mobile, without having the slightest idea why – I had nowhere to ring and there was no one to ring me. I bought a minidisc player and spent a couple of hours compiling a disc for it out of the catalogue, looking for both old and new songs that triggered some response in my stubborn memory. I gradually got used to the changes in Moscow, which behind the tinsel glitter of its bright, cheerful neon had remained just as dirty and scruffy as ever. The hotel staff all greeted me, and they seemed to have organised a rota for the right to serve me – I was still living like a man who didn't even acknowledge the existence of any note worth less than a hundred roubles. But oddly enough, I was still careful to pick up the correct change in shops. Even the little nickel-plated coins that are no good for anything except perhaps as souvenirs for foreigners.

During those two days I only came across Others on three occasions: once in the metro, entirely by chance; once at night, when I ran into a drunken witch trying unsuccessfully to fly up to a third-floor balcony because she'd lost her keys and didn't have enough power left to go through the Twilight. I gave the witch a hand. And once during the day I was taken for an uninitiated Other by a rather powerful Light Magician – I even remembered his name: Gorodetsky. He'd just happened to go into a shop for the same reason I had, to put together a new mini-disc for his player. The magician was surprised when he saw my official seals and left me in peace. He was even about to leave, out of disgust, I think, but they'd just finished burning my disc, so I was the one who left.

I was left wondering why he hated Dark Ones so much.

But then, everybody hates us. Well, almost everybody. And they just don't want to believe that what we feel about them is mostly indifference – just so long as the Light Ones don't get in our way. Though they do, all the time. But I suppose we get in their way too.

No one from the Night Watch bothered me, I don't think they even made an attempt to find me and question me. They must have realised that a Dark Magician has no need to drink human blood. Of course, I could have done it, and given myself a chronic digestive disorder – if I hadn't been sick in disgust. I was totally absorbed by waiting for the next step up, but that seemed to require an extreme, unambiguous situation, when something inside me forced me to make use of magic. Not just little things, like getting rid of the fat-faced bus ticket inspectors with their shaved heads, or creating a mantle of calm for the impatient people queing for metro cards when I couldn't be bothered to wait – no, all that was quite literally yesterday's level as far as I was concerned. In order to learn something new and expose another layer of my concealed memory, in order to take possession of my slumbering knowledge, I needed more serious shocks.

I had to wait for them, but not for very long.

Like many other Dark Ones, I turned out to be an inveterate night owl. Since I was living among ordinary people, I couldn't completely ignore the day, but I didn't feel like resisting the call of the night either. I rose late, about midday or even later, and I only returned to the hotel at dawn.

My fourth night in Moscow was already streaked with the first pale hints of sunrise; the blackness had already admitted the first shades of dark grey when I ran smack into the next upward step. I was strolling along a deserted Izmailovsky Boulevard when I suddenly sensed a powerful magical discharge somewhere in among the buildings in the distance.

When I say 'discharge', I don't mean that uncontrolled energy had simply escaped. No. The energy was discharged and then immediately absorbed, otherwise the result would have been a banal explosion. Others transform themselves, and the world, and energy. But in the final analysis the balance of the energy emitted and absorbed always amounts to zero, otherwise . . .

Otherwise the world simply couldn't exist. And we couldn't exist in it.

I felt something urging me on. Go!

So I had to.

I walked for about twenty minutes, confidently turning corners at crossroads and taking shortcuts through courtyards. When I was almost there I sensed Others – they were approaching rapidly from two different directions; and at the same time I heard the sound of several cars. Then almost immediately I picked out the building and the apartment I needed out of the featureless palisade of high-rises. That was where the event had taken place that had caught the attention of the Other me, still hidden somewhere inside my ordinary being.

A standard five-storey Khrushchev-period building on Thirteenth Park Street. Rubbish bins standing along the end wall, though no sign of the kiosks I was so used to seeing in the south.

There were three cars at the entrance: a Zhiguli, a humble, very shabby station wagon and a pampered BMW. There were actually plenty of other cars around, but they were obviously parked for the night, while these had just arrived in a hurry and been dumped.

The fifth floor. At the entrance to the stairwell (the metal door was standing wide open) I sensed powerful magical blocks, and they made me draw my shadow up from the ground and enter the Twilight.

I think the Twilight draws power out of Others. If they don't know how to resist it, of course. Nobody told me what to do, I just started doing it instinctively, as if I'd always known how. Maybe I always had, and I just remembered when I needed to.

The blue moss that inhabits the first level of the Twilight had spread in luxurious abundance over the walls and the stairs, even the banisters. The people living on this staircase must be highly emotional if it was flourishing so well.

Here was the apartment I wanted. Even more powerful blocks, and the door locked even in the Twilight.

And at that point I was hurled up another two steps. Overcoming a momentary weakness, I raised my own shadow from the floor again and went in deeper.

I could immediately tell that this was a place where not many came. There was no building. There was almost nothing at all except a dense, dark-grey mist and the moons that I could vaguely make out through it. All three of them. There ought to have been a bitter wind – the wind doesn't recognise any distinction between the ordinary world and the Twilight – but at this level time flowed so slowly that I could hardly feel it at all.

I began slowly falling, sinking into this mist, but I *held myself up*. Apparently I knew how to do that. A particular effort – hard to describe and more instinctive than conscious – and I moved forward. Another effort, and I glanced back into the previous level of the Twilight.

Everything was happening in glutinous slow motion, as if the world had sunk into a layer of transparent grey tar, and at first sounds seemed like deep, distant peals of thunder, but I managed to adjust to their slowness. I must have set my rate of perception to the same pace, attuned myself to this new reality, and from that moment on everything began to remind me again of the ordinary world – the world of human beings.

A narrow hallway, as they all are in those buildings. Two doors on the left – the bathroom and the kitchen. One room further along on the left and one on the right. The room on the right was empty. In the room on the left there were five Others and a body lying on a dishevelled bed. The body of a guy of about thirty: he had several jagged wounds in the area of his crotch and stomach that immediately put paid to any idea that he could be saved. The wounds were covered by a crumpled, bloody bed-sheet.

There were three Light Others and two Dark Ones. The Light Ones were a skinny young guy with a rather asymmetrical face and the two new acquaintances of mine – the music-lover Gorodetsky and the girl shape-shifter. The Dark Ones were a chubby magician with a keen, intense expression and a gloomy guy who looked to me like an unsuccessful parody of a lizard – he was wearing clothes, but his hands and face were green and scaly.

The Others were arguing.

'It's the second incident this week, Shagron. And another murder. I'm sorry, but it's beginning to look like you've thrown the Treaty out the window.'

The Light One I didn't know was talking.

The Dark One glanced involuntarily at the corpse.

'We can't keep track of everybody, you know that perfectly

well,' he blurted out, but I didn't hear any trace of guilt or regret in his voice.

'But you said you would warn all the Dark Ones about Clean Week. Your chief made an official commitment.'

'We did warn them.'

'Well, thank you!' The Light One clapped his hands in theatrical applause. 'The result is impressive. I repeat: we, the agents of the Night Watch, officially request your co-operation. Call your chief out!'

'The chief isn't in Moscow right now,' the magician replied morosely. 'And, by the way, your boss knows that perfectly well, so he needn't have bothered to authorise you to request our co-operation.'

'Does that mean,' Gorodetsky asked with the hint of threat in his voice, 'that you are refusing to co-operate?'

The Dark Magician shook his head rather more quickly than he need have.

'What do you mean, refusing? No. We're not refusing. I just don't understand what we can do to help.'

That seemed to fill the Light Ones with righteous fury. The magician I didn't know spoke again.

'What you can do? Some shape-shifting tart rips the balls off a client – an uninitiated Other, by the way – and gets clean away! Who knows all your countless low-life best – you or us?'

'Sometimes I think you do,' the Dark Magician retorted glancing at the girl. 'If you remember the conversation in the Seventh Heaven when they caught the Inquisitor and him . . .' He nodded at Gorodetsky and paused, as if he was thinking about something.

'Most likely the shape-shifter's not registered. And most likely the client got a bit too boisterous and er . . . er . . . Well, put it this way: he probably wanted something that was unacceptable even to a tart. And this is the result.'

'Shagron, you can't offload this onto the human cops, because she killed him when she was in her Twilight form. Like it or not, the Watches are involved! So tell me straight, are you going to investigate or are you forcing us to deal with it? And don't even hope that you can just drag things out. We want Saturday's vampire and this whore up in front of a tribunal, and before next weekend. Do you understand?' The skinny youngster was leaning on Shagron, insisting on his rights, and he was obviously enjoying doing it, as an Other who didn't often get involved in showdowns. And he did seem to be justified in putting on the pressure.

'These bloody horny cats,' the scaly one suddenly muttered. 'Brainless bitches.'

'Shut up,' the Light girl told him coldly. 'You overgrown gecko.'

Ah, yes, she was a cat too, even though she was a Light One.

'Cool it, Tiger Cub,' Gorodetsky said to her. Then he turned to the Dark Magician again. 'Do you understand our demands?'

At this point I returned to the first level of the Twilight. To describe what followed as a dumb show would be a gross understatement.

'You!' the girl gasped. 'You again!'

'Buenos noches, lady and gentlemen. My apologies, I saw the Light, so I just dropped in.'

'Anton, Tolik,' Tiger Cub said in a ringing voice, trembling slightly in agitation and pointing a finger at me like a child. 'Andriuhka found him standing over the vampire's victim on Saturday! This Dark One from Ukraine!'

All five of them stared at me.

'I hope,' I said ironically, 'that I don't resemble a shape-shifting tart any more than I do a crazy vampire?'

'Who are you?' the Dark Magician, the one they called Shagron, asked in a hostile voice.

'A magician, dear colleague. A Dark Magician. From out of town.'

When he tried to probe me, I could tell that if I hadn't yet climbed the next step, then I was right there in front of it. He didn't get anywhere. And meanwhile I noticed that Shagron's defences were not entirely his own – I could sense a strong framework that had been put together by a top-class magician. Probably the famous chief who wasn't in Moscow at the moment.

'A second murder, and here you are again,' Tolik drawled suspiciously, also making an attempt to probe me – quite unsuccessfully, as I noted with some satisfaction. 'I don't like it. Perhaps you would care to explain?'

Tolik certainly looked annoyed, but now he was going by the rules, and that suited me just fine. He was obviously the senior of the three Light Ones, busily thinking over the possible courses of action. There seemed to be plenty of options.

'Yes, I would,' I agreed readily. 'I was just walking not far from here. I sensed something bad going on. And I came to see if I could do anything to help.'

'Do you work for the Watch back home in Ukraine,' the scaly one asked unexpectedly.

'No.'

'Then how can you help?'

'Who knows?' I said with a shrug.

Of course, the scaly one's tongue was long and forked. People's imaginations really are pretty limited. You'd think the Twilight image of a Dark One would offer plenty of scope for fantasy – unlike that of the Light Ones, which is just a standard outfit: a luminescent glow and white robes. The more sentimental, mostly women, wear white garlands as well. But even so, almost all Dark Ones go for the boring old cliché of a scaly demon with horns and a forked tongue.

'Of course, you have nothing at all to do with these murders?' the girl said with poorly concealed sarcasm.

'Naturally.'

'I don't trust him,' said the girl and turned away. 'Anton, you have to probe him.'

'We will,' Anton replied without thinking. 'When we get back I'll personally request all the data on him.'

I laughed ironically.

'All right. If you don't want any help, I don't mind. I'm not going to force myself on you. I'll be going then.'

I started towards the door.

'Hey, Dark One,' Tolik said to my back. 'I'd advise you not to leave Moscow. That's an official injunction from the Night Watch.'

'I'll bear that in mind,' I promised. 'In any case, I wasn't planning to leave.'

'I'll go with you,' Tolik said to Anton and Tiger Cub. 'I have something to say to you.'

Anton thought gloomily that he must have done a bad job cleaning up again – for some reason this strange Dark One's words had really stung him. Tiger Cub had mimicked the stranger's way of speaking very precisely, right down to his intonation, and when Anton saw the Dark One, he was convinced yet again that Tiger Cub had the makings of a skilful actor. Or rather, actress. Who could tell what she might have been if she hadn't been an Other?

Shagron and his partner had driven off in their fancy BMW a long time ago. Tolik reached out his hand and Anton obediently gave him the keys of the office Zhiguli. Tiger Cub got into the back without speaking. Anton sat beside Tolik, who drove rapidly out onto Sirenevy Boulevard and headed east.

'Who is he, this Dark One?' Anton asked to break the silence.

He was in a foul mood. Another body – and this time an uninitiated Other!

'He's a very powerful magician,' Tolik said abruptly. 'More powerful than me. I tried to probe him and I failed – he closed up instantly.'

'Closed up?' Tiger Cub said excitedly from the back. 'You mean he came without a shield?'

'That's just the point,' Tolik exclaimed gloomily. 'When he came in, he looked exactly like an ordinary magician, maybe third or fourth grade. Like me and Anton.'

Anton didn't say anything – strictly speaking, Tolik was incorrect, but essentially he was right. Gesar had called Anton a second-grade magician, but Anton's powers had only risen to that level on a few occasions. It would be more honest to admit that for the time being he was still third grade.

'But as soon as I tried to probe him,' Tolik went on, 'that was it. A blank wall. He's definitely more powerful than me. Anton, did you try to probe him?'

'No.'

'Looks like he's first grade,' Tolik said with a sigh. 'If it comes to it, we'll have to call in Ilya.'

'I'm afraid we might even have to call in Olga and Sveta and the boss,' Anton remarked. Nobody responded. Nobody liked the idea of asking the higher magicians for help.

Tiger Cub squirmed about, making herself more comfortable on the seat:

'There's no way he's not connected with these murders. I can understand the first time – he arrived in Moscow, went out for a walk and accidentally stumbled across a poacher. But this time? What was he doing on Pervomaiskaya Street?'

'But did he definitely arrive on Saturday?' Tolik asked.

'Definitely,' Tiger Cub assured him. 'I didn't like the look of him, you know? I even found the train he was on and scanned the conductress for memories. He almost never came out of his compartment, but he was on the train all right.'

'And do we have anything on him?'

Anton thought he caught a hint of hopefulness in Tolik's question.

'Compromising information, you mean? Not a thing. Not a single violation. He doesn't need any licences, he's not a vampire or a shape-shifter. And he was only initiated fairly recently, just seven years ago . . . Like me.'

Tolik nodded thoughtfully.

'There aren't many Others in Nikolaev. So the Watches are small as well, only twenty or thirty agents . . . Okay, when we get back, I'll dig a bit deeper,' Anton promised. 'Did you lock up your station wagon?'

'What's going to happen to it?' Tolik asked with a shrug. 'We'll have to phone the boss after all. Or will we be able to handle this on our own?'

He was obviously feeling uncomfortable. Tolik had been in charge of the IT department for more than a year now, since Anton had moved to operational work. But no member of the Night Watch has the right to let his qualifications slip – and the time had come round for Tolik's regular month of field duty. And on his very first day there was an unpleasant incident like this.

'We'll probably have to tell him,' Anton decided.

'Then there's no point in putting it off.' Tolik sighed.

Tiger Cub eagerly held out her mobile. But before Tolik could even touch it the phone started chirping the tune of 'Midnight in Moscow'.

Anton was about to take the phone, but he held back. You never know . . . It was obviously one of their own calling, but he couldn't sense the tense, nervous energy of a work-related call. Maybe it was simply some member of the Watch calling Tiger Cub? Everybody had a personal life, even members of the Watch.

Tiger Cub took the call. Most of the time she just listened, and once she said: 'I don't know'.

'It's Garik,' she explained in a voice filled with quiet alarm. 'Andriukha's disappeared.'

'Tiunnikov?'

'Yes. Garik thought he was with us.'

'The last time I saw him was this afternoon,' Tolik told her. 'He was planning to go and catch up on his sleep.'

'His phone's not answering. Garik can't sense him either – and he's Andriukha's mentor.'

Anton turned towards Tiger Cub:

'After Saturday he was like a man possessed. What did that Dark One say to him in the alley?'

Tiger Cub shrugged:

'Nothing special, I've told you a hundred times already. He called him a detective. But Andriukha really had screwed up – it was obvious straight away that the Dark One was no vampire. I explained that to him myself.'

'He doesn't have to be a vampire,' Tolik declared in a bored, didactic voice. 'This Dark One could quite easily be behind the whole bloody mess. It goes without saying that his organisational talents are clearly above average!'

'One of Zabulon's pawns,' Anton mused. 'Yes, it's possible. Perfectly possible.'

'Aim a bit higher. Not a pawn, not even a knight or a rook. A bishop. A serious piece. Maybe even a queen.'

'Tolik, don't exaggerate. Without Zabulon there's no way the Dark Ones can match us. And Zabulon's not in Moscow.'

'That's what the Dark Ones say. But who knows what the truth is . . .'

'Zabulon hasn't shown his face much at all recently,' Anton put in.

'That's just it. He's been keeping quiet, planning an operation . . . The lousy thing is that I can't imagine what its objectives are. What do we have so far? Two suspicious killings, with absolutely no idea of how they're connected.'

'If they are connected at all,' said Anton, but even he didn't seem to believe it.

'No, say what you like, but they're connected,' Tolik insisted stubbornly. 'I can sense it. And the connection is that magician from out of town.'

'Why bother thinking about it?' Tiger Cub asked. 'Since Svetlana appeared we've had a substantial advantage. The Dark Ones have yielded one position after another – remember how the boss put pressure on Zabulon at the last round of negotiations? And Zabulon gave way – what other choice did he really have? It looks as if the Dark Ones have launched an operation to restore the balance. But the timing's terrible – just before Clean Week.'

'For the Dark Ones that's the best possible time,' Anton growled. 'They know we won't start anything serious without a good reason. But so far there doesn't seem to be any reason.'

'Be careful what you say,' Tolik told him in a pained voice.

The Zhiguli flew on along Leningradsky Prospect, overtaking the advancing dawn.

They drove the rest of the way to the office without saying another word. Either no one wanted to predict the worst, or they all felt they were in for something serious.

Garik was standing at the entrance, shifting nervously from one foot to the other. And Ilya was there beside him, short of sleep and squinting out from behind his spectacles.

'Right,' Tolik said cheerlessly. 'Brace yourselves.'

Ilya and Garik quickly got into the car, squeezing Tiger Cub from both sides, and Anton immediately realised why they'd got in like that and what the pale, furious and therefore very restrained Garik would say next.

'The Cosmos hotel. Andriukha's dead, guys.'

Tolik slammed the accelerator to the floor, but even the most powerful car isn't fast enough to overtake death. Tiger Cub jerked feebly, squeezed tight between her friends, and then froze.

'How did it happen?' Anton asked dully.

'That Dark One – Vitaly Rogoza – just phoned. He said he'd found the body of an Other in his room.'

'I'll personally bite his throat out,' Tiger Cub vowed hoarsely. 'And don't you try to stop me!'

'I phoned Bear just in case,' Ilya said in a very neutral tone. 'I think he's already at the Cosmos.'

Anton had the idea that his colleagues had understood every thing in advance and come to terms with the fact that a fight was inevitable. He stroked the pistol in the holster under his armpit – the weapon that had never once been any real use to him.

I had a nagging feeling that the events of the night were still far from over. I felt I was just beginning to be able to foresee the immediate future. Not in detail, far from it in fact – more as a tangled ball of threads of probability. But I had begun to sense where the thickest strands were leading.

Alarm, trouble, disaster, danger – that was what the night had in store for me. At first I thought I would wait for the Dark Ones downstairs, beside their BMW outside the entrance, but then I realised I shouldn't do that. I shouldn't enlighten them as to . . . well, as to my total ignorance. Let them think that I really was playing a game. The head of the Day Watch was out of town, and the Others didn't seem to be any competition for me.

But just who was I? Wasn't I aiming too high? Was Moscow so

short of powerful magicians? Even if they didn't work in the Watches? I couldn't keep being led on up the steps for ever, could I? – There are no infinite stairways. Some way would be found to keep me in check – the Moscow magicians had plenty of experience, many of them an entire century's worth. And I didn't really know what I could do and what I couldn't. I was still an unknown quantity. And how did I know my power wouldn't evaporate just as miraculously as it had appeared?

So you take your time, Vitalik, don't try to force things. Better think about what bad things this fading night could bring you. And better not drag things out, lengthen that stride.

I walked quickly as far as Sholkovskoe Chaussee, darted into an underpass and then started hitching a lift on the opposite side of the road.

What I like about Moscow is that even in the dead of night or early in the morning, all you have to do is raise your hand and a car will immediately pull in at the kerb. In Nikolaev you can stand there for half an hour and no one will even think of stopping. But here everything is decided by money. Everyone needs it.

'The Exhibition of Economic Achievements, fifty roubles.' The standard rate.

I got into the sporty Volkswagen and set off towards problems that I could almost feel already.

When I reached the hotel, I immediately sensed that my room's defences had been compromised. The defences had worked just as they were intended to do, and that was my main problem. Without looking at anyone, I went up to the sixth floor, walked to my suite, put the key in the lock and froze for a moment, looking at the door.

Okay, whatever was about to happen, I had to go through it.

He was lying in the middle of the lounge with his arms flung out to the sides. There was an expression of childish surprise and resentment on his face, as if he'd opened a wrapper and instead of the sweet he'd been hoping for he'd found an angry hornet that had instantly sunk its sting into his carelessly exposed finger.

He had stumbled into my Shahab's Ring. Not complex magic, but very powerful. And, naturally, he hadn't known the word that was needed. He was the unfortunate young detective, Andriukha Tiunnikov, a Light One from the Night Watch, who had been trying to prove that I'd murdered the girl on Saturday.

If he'd been more experienced, he would never have stuck his nose into the area enclosed by the Ring. I hadn't even set it round the whole room – only the safe with the bag in it.

This was the very last thing I needed – the Light Ones regarded the deaths of ordinary people as poaching, but the killing of an Other was a different matter altogether. It already looked like a tribunal.

But I had simply closed off my own territory, closed it off in a way that Others understood. This is mine! Keep out! No entry!

Only he hadn't kept out. And he'd met his end in the Twilight . . . The stupid kid. Had he been trying to impress his bosses?

I had to own up. Otherwise they'd ask in a way I couldn't refuse to answer.

I reached for the phone – not my mobile, but the ordinary phone that was standing on the table. The number obligingly surfaced from my memory.

'Night Watch? Vitaly Rogoza, Other, Dark. If I'm not mistaken, I have your employee Andrei Tiunnikov here. He's dead. You'd better come. Hotel Cosmos, suite six twelve.'

Strangely enough, the Light Ones weren't the first to arrive. The moment the first Others reached my floor – there were two of them – I felt as if I were suddenly flooded with energy from someone. The pair were Dark Magicians and they were both brimful of a Dark power that reminded me in some ways of the Twilight, except that it was even denser and darker. A long tongue of Twilight ran straight down through the floors of the hotel, gradually growing thinner as it approached the ground and seeming to run on beyond it, to somewhere deeper, somewhere underground.

There was a knock at the door, emphatically correct.

'Yes, yes,' I replied, without getting up out of my armchair. 'It's open, come in!'

They came in. My acquaintance from the apartment on Pervomaiskaya Street, Shagron. And another one, also a magician, as far as I could tell. A bit overweight, like Shagron, with dark hair. And powerful. More powerful than his partner. But even so, against my expectations, it was Shagron who started talking. It seemed as though it was the accepted thing among members of the Watches for the most powerful member of a team to keep quiet – Anton had preferred to listen too.

'Good morning, colleague.'

'What's good about it? You must be joking, colleague.'

I deliberately pronounced the word 'colleague' in the same tone as Shagron. But he wasn't so easily provoked, and that was where he had the advantage over me. In experience. All I had to rely on were cheap wisecracks like that, plus moments of sudden illumin-ation and the mysterious stairway that obligingly offered me one step after another and then arranged a kick up the arse at the appropriate moment.

'I'm not joking, colleague, simply greeting you. It's a pity you didn't wait for us back there . . . you know where I mean. I'd been counting on having a word with you.'

'I didn't want to get in your way,' I confessed, and it was more than half true. A standard response from an Other – Dark or Light.

'I was counting on help. Help from a brother-in-arms. But you chose to disappear.'

That 'I' was strictly a Dark way of speaking. In Shagron's place, any Light One would definitely have said 'We', and been perfectly sincere. And he'd have meant exactly what Shagron had meant, no less sincerely, of course.

'Okay. Let me introduce you. This is Edgar, our colleague from Estonia, who's recently became a member of the Moscow Watch. What have you got here?'

'What I've got here is yet another body,' I confessed. 'A Light Other. A Watch member. But then you already know all about it, don't you, colleague Edgar?'

'There's not much time? The Light Ones will be here any minute? Is that what you wanted to say?' Edgar asked, abandoning diplomacy and addressing me familiarly. I realised there was no point in arguing with this dark-haired Estonian.

'Last Saturday evening, when I'd just arrived, this Light One was in charge of the operation investigating a poaching vampire.'

'A vampiress,' Edgar corrected me with a frown. 'And then?'

'By sheer chance I just happened to be there beside the victim. They found me beside the corpse and recognised me as a Dark One. Clearly out of inexperience – I can't see any other reason – Tiunnikov accused me of what the vampire – that is, the vampiress – had done. I put him in his place, and I admit I did it quite sharply, but he'd asked for it. And that's really the whole story. When I left my room today, I left some protective spells. And when I came in, there he was. He was already beyond my help.'

The last sentence simply came out on its own, I hadn't been planning to say it. I felt I was beginning to talk nonsense again.

'This snot-nosed kid was in charge of the operation?' Shagron asked incredulously. 'When there were Light Ones with far more experience – the Tigress, the magicians . . .'

'Tiunnikov was in training, that's perfectly normal,' Edgar barked at his partner and then suddenly glanced at me. 'But you set up a Shahab's Ring so strong that it killed the Light Ones' trainee on the spot?'

The question was almost rhetorical. Apparently I'd cast a simple spell, but put too much power into it. Maybe . . .

I sensed the approach of the Light Ones at the same time as Edgar, just as they were nearing the hotel. A few seconds later Shagron picked them up too.

'What did you tell them?' Edgar asked, obviously in a hurry. 'But keep it short.'

I sensed that he had covered us with a cowl of invisibility, and quite a powerful one too. Before I said a word, I added some power of my own to the cowl, drawn partly from somewhere inside myself, from my own mind, and partly from outside. It happened quite spontaneously, but I read the dumb astonishment in Edgar's eyes.

'I phoned and said there was a dead Light One in my room. And told them his name. That's all.'

Edgar gave a barely perceptible nod and glanced significantly at Shagron, who gave the slightest of shrugs.

We waited for the knock at the door – a far less polite one this time – in silence.

The Light Ones didn't wait to be invited. They just walked straight in.

There were five of them. Tolik, Anton and the girl shape-shifter could barely have had enough time to get from Pervomaiskaya Street to their office. Two more had come with them – a cultured-looking young guy wearing glasses with eighty-dollar frames and another with a suntanned face, as if it wasn't winter in Moscow.

These last two and Tolik carefully examined, probed and scanned every centimetre of my suite. The walls here had probably never seen such intense magical activity.

Anton and the girl didn't interfere, but I could clearly sense their aversion. Not even hatred – the Light Ones don't really even know how to hate properly. More like a desire to pin me into a corner, to have me condemned and punished. Or simply to hit me with so much power that I'd be driven into the Twilight for ever.

And I also sensed there was at least one more Light One somewhere outside the room. Probably somewhere else on the same floor, or by the lifts. He was obviously covering the Others' backs, and he had shielded himself really well for the job. I only spotted him, you might say, by accident. But I don't think that Shagron and Edgar had any idea he was there.

I frowned. The Light Ones had the numerical advantage – there were twice as many of them. And the two of them that I was seeing for the first time were very powerful magicians, almost certainly first grade. In any case, the two of them together would be stronger than Shagron and Edgar. And Anton was no pushover either – he could give Shagron a good fight, or even Edgar. Plus the girl – she was a warrior. And that unknown one somewhere nearby. The balance of forces was not good at all. They'd grind us to dust, grind us as fine as powdered vanilla.

Meanwhile the Light Ones had finished their scanning. The one in glasses came up to me and enquired with emphatic indifference:

'Tell me, did you really need to use a protective spell of such power?'

'Well, why do you think I would have used so much power?'

The one in glasses and the other one I didn't know exchanged a quick glance.

'We demand to see your things.'

'Stop, stop,' Edgar put in hastily. 'On what grounds, exactly?'

The one in glasses smiled bleakly – only with his lips:

'The Night Watch has reason to suspect that a forbidden artefact of immense power has been smuggled into Moscow. You must know that such actions contravene the terms of the Treaty.'

My Dark colleagues looked at me doubtfully. They were apparently expecting some unambiguous response. But what was it? On this occasion my internal magical helpline chose not to prompt me. But on the other hand, I knew perfectly well that there weren't any forbidden artefacts in my bag. And so I gestured magnanimously and said:

'Let them look! All night long if they want.'

'I protest,' Edgar said quietly, and without much hope, it seemed. 'You don't have your chief's authority.'

'The protest is rejected,' the one in glasses parried inflexibly. 'I'm the boss here. Show us your things, Dark One.'

I didn't have to be asked twice. I neutralised the remains of the magical defences with a single gesture and opened the door of the safe, where my bag was lying on its own, apart from a pair of clothes brushes. The logo seemed to gaze out at us reproachfully: 'Fuji'. I imagined a bored, squeaky voice pronouncing it 'phooey . . .'

I took the bag and tipped its contents out onto the bed. The Light Ones didn't take much interest in my things, but the sight of the final plastic bag put them on their guard — the second unknown magician even grasped the amulet in the pocket of his jacket.

When I shook the money out onto the bedcover, everybody looked at me. Both my own side and the Light Ones. As if I was some kind of psycho. An absolutely hopeless case.

'There,' I said. 'That's all I have. A hundred thousand. Actually, a bit less now.'

The magician in glasses stepped towards the bed and rummaged disdainfully through my things, glancing into the plastic bags. But I realised that what he really wanted was tactile contact.

He wasn't even satisfied with remote scanning.

Good grief, what did they suspect me of? Probably some cretin really had tried to bring something forbidden into Moscow, and since I'd overdone it a bit protecting my miserable heap of bucks, now they suspected me of everything. That was really funny. And it was getting funnier all the time.

The one in glasses spent about a minute sniffing at my baggage. Then he gave up.

'All right. There's nothing here. We're declaring this suite off-limits. You'll have to change rooms.'

The girl shape-shifter started and gave him a puzzled look. He spread his hands and I understood the gesture. There was nothing to charge me with. No grounds at all. The shape-shifter tensed, but the other magician put his hand on her shoulder, as if he was warning her not to do anything rash.

'Ye-es?' Edgar drawled insinuatingly, and something Estonian finally came through in that 'Ye-es' of his. 'Change rooms? In that case we request official permission for a seventh-degree intervention. In order to avoid unnecessary questions from the hotel management.'

The Light Ones were annoyed by that – but then, they were already all annoyed in any case.

'Why? We can influence the staff without any psychic correction.'

'But you have a habit of declaring any influence a violation,' Edgar explained in a very innocent voice.

'I will per—' Ilya drawled slowly and then broke off. 'No. I won't permit it. Anton, you go with them and do it all yourself. Try to make sure they move him as far away from here as possible, so that . . . Anyway, just do it.'

Edgar sighed in disappointment.

'Okay, if you say no, then it's no. But tell me, dear fellow, do you have any more questions for our colleague?'

Edgar's tone was so prim and polite that I was afraid the Light Ones might decide he was mocking them. But they clearly knew Edgar pretty well. And maybe this caustic, biting politeness was normal behaviour between the two Watches.

'No, we can't detain him any longer. But let us remind you that until our investigations are concluded, he is forbidden to leave Moscow, in connection with these three cases.'

'I remember,' I put in, as innocently as I could.

'In that case, permit us to take our leave. Colleague Vitaly, pack your things.'

I shoved all my bits and pieces into the first plastic bags that came to hand, put the plastic bags into the large bag, picked up my jacket from where I had dropped it on the armchair and stood up. Edgar pointed to the door in invitation.

We went out into the corridor and took the lift down to the lobby, where Edgar suddenly turned to the Light One with us.

'Anton, our colleague is not going to stay in this hotel any longer. We're taking him with us. If you need him, you can enquire at the Day Watch office.'

The Light One seemed to have been taken by surprise; he glanced uncertainly at the hotel administrator sleeping behind his counter, then nodded indecisively. And we set off towards the exit.

I didn't put my jacket on, because I'd already spotted the familiar BMW parked outside the door of the hotel — I'd only been able to see it because I was an Other.

It was warm and cosy inside the car. And roomy too — my knees didn't press against the back of the front seat. I made myself comfortable and asked:

'And where am I going to stay now?'

'At the Day Watch office, colleague. Or, rather, in the office hotel. You should have gone there in the first place.'

'If only I'd known where to go,' I muttered.

THE DAY WATCH    *219*

The BMW went darting off, turned smartly out of the car park towards the entrance, raced under the barrier almost before it had time to rise high enough and eased into the sparse flow of traffic on Peace Prospect.

Shagron might not be the most powerful of magicians, but he could drive extraordinarily well. Peace Prospect flashed past and came to an end, followed by the arc of the Garden Ring Road. And all I saw of Tverskaya Street was an endless row of shop windows with tinted glass. But then, it wasn't really endless after all.

We got out of the car very close to the Kremlin. The magicians left their BMW at the kerb, without even bothering to lock it. I decided to take a look at it through the Twilight, simply out of curiosity and a desire to take a look at the protective spells. So that I wouldn't overdo things again.

I was astounded. Not by the car, but by the building, which had looked so ordinary in the ordinary world.

In the Twilight the building had grown by three whole floors. And one of them was inserted between the ordinary first and second floors, while the other two were on top, making the already substantial building even larger. The Twilight floors were made of polished black granite. Almost all the windows were curtained and dark, but the first weak rays of sunlight were already glinting on the white boxes of the modern air-conditioning.

I forgot about the protective spells immediately.

There was a small entrance leading straight out onto Tverskaya Street; behind the glass door I could sense, rather than see, the silhouette of an Other.

'Well, well, well!' I said. My voice sounded hollow, like all sound in the Twilight. My colleagues all turned their heads as if by command.

'What? Haven't you seen it before?'

'No.'

'It impresses everybody the first time. Come on, you'll have plenty of time to admire it.'

We went up a few steps and found ourselves in a tiny duty office. The vague figure behind the door had materialised into a skinny, miserable-looking young guy – I think he was a shapeshifter. He was laughing delightedly as he read Victor Pelevin's story 'The Werewolf Problem in Central Russia'.

But the moment Edgar entered the duty office, the young guy was transformed. His eyes flashed and the book dropped onto the desk.

'Hi, Oleg,' Edgar greeted him in a Baltic accent that had suddenly appeared out of nowhere.

Shagron simply nodded.

I decided to say hello too:

'Good morning.'

'This is a colleague of ours from Ukraine,' Edgar said, introducing me. 'When he wants, let him through into the guest area without any checks.'

'Understood,' Oleg confirmed. 'Shall I enter him in the database?'

'Yes.'

Oleg glanced into my eyes and bared his teeth in a friendly grin, read my registration mark with some effort, sat down at the desk and took a notebook PC out of one of the drawers.

'And where's your partner?' Edgar asked.

Oleg's face took on a guilty expression.

'He went out for cigarettes . . . Just for a moment.'

'Let's go,' Edgar said with a sigh, taking me by the sleeve and drawing me towards the lifts. Shagron had already pressed the call button.

We seemed to be in the lift for a long time. Certainly longer than I'd been expecting. But then I remembered the additional floors and everything fell into place.

'The guest area is on the ninth floor,' Edgar explained. 'Basically it's just like a hotel, only it's free. I don't think there's anyone staying there at the moment.'

The lift doors parted soundlessly and we found ourselves in a square foyer, decorated with a rational combination of luxury and economical practicality. Leather sofas and armchairs, a live palm tree in a tub, engravings on the walls, a carpet on the parquet floor. A counter like the ones in hotels, but there was no sign of any table and chair for an attendant. Just a locked secretaire, with an elegant metal key in the lock.

Edgar opened the secretaire to reveal neat rows of horizontal wooden pegs, a key hanging on each one. And beside the pegs there were numbers.

But I was being too hasty – there were no keys on two of the pegs: numbers two and four.

'Take your pick. If the key's here, it means the apartment's free.'

He said 'apartment', and not 'suite', as if the fact that this accommodation for Others was free distinguished it from anonymous hotel suites and put it in the category of places that could be called home.

I took number eight. From the right-hand end of the second row.

'You can look the place over later,' Edgar told me. 'Leave your things and come straight back.'

I nodded, wondering what my Dark colleagues were planning. No doubt a polite but thorough interrogation.

That was okay. I'd survive. They were my kind, after all.

The apartment really was an apartment, with a kitchen, a separate toilet and three spacious rooms – and a huge hall. A typical Stalin-era apartment refurbished to 'European' standards. The ceilings were three and a half metres high, if not four.

I hung my jacket on the coat rack and dropped my bag in the middle of the hall. Then I went out into the corridor and pulled the door shut.

I could faintly hear music coming from apartment number four: a minute earlier, as I was walking past, it had been something light and foreign. But now the song had changed. The words were almost drowned out by the harsh rhythm and the hard rock accompaniment — I guessed at them rather than heard them:

> Cast down by the power of fate,
> You are humiliated and crushed.
> It's time to forget who you were,
> And remember who you've become!
> Cast into the depths, where it doesn't matter
> Why fame used to court you before —
> Rogues set a brand of fire on you,
> And your soul is empty.
> People in the depths prowl through the darkness,
> Ready to eat each other up.
> Anything to prolong this wild life,
> And snatch something for themselves . . .
> Angry like them, angry and pitiful,
> You rush round and round in the same herd,
> With them you crawl for food at knifepoint,
> Like a slave or a prophet.

I don't know why, but I froze outside the door. These were more than just words. I absorbed them through my skin, with my entire body. I had forgotten who I used to be, but how could I remember who I'd become? And hadn't I entered a new circle now, running with a herd that I still didn't know?

Oh, if I could listen only to silence.
Not lies, or flattery, not the midday or the darkness.
Be like snow melting in the sun,
And love, knowing no betrayal,
Then you would die of anguish and anger!

No, I clearly wouldn't get any chance to listen to silence in the immediate future. Too many others had taken an interest in me. Light Ones and Dark Ones . . .

Meanwhile the singer's voice had grown stronger and taken on a triumphant, challenging note:

Hey, you inhabitants of the skies!
Which of you has not plumbed the depths?
Without passing through hell,
You can never build heaven!
Hey, you inhabitants of the depths!
The thunder is laughing at you.
To be on equal terms with them –
There is only one way up!
There is only one way up . . .

So that was it. The way up. And you couldn't get to heaven unless you'd already done your time rattling around in hell. Except that heaven and hell were different for everyone – but then that was what Kipelov was really singing about anyway.

Strange. I'd heard the song before, and the singer's name had stuck in my memory, I'd even included it on the mini-disc I put together for my player. But now it sounded completely new, it had suddenly slashed across my mind like an invisible shard of broken glass.

'Colleague! Please hurry!' Edgar called to me.

Regretfully I stepped away from the door.

'I'll have to listen to it later. Buy the whole album and listen to it.'

The singer's voice faded away behind me:

> But if the Light flares up in your brain
> And dislodges all the submission,
> The old days will come alive in your soul,
> And a new sin will be committed.
> Blood on your hands, blood on the stones,
> And over the bodies and the pitiful backs
> Of those willing to die as slaves,
> You strive upward once again.

It somehow seemed to me that Kipelov knew only too well what he was singing about. About blood. About the lower depths. About the sky. This long-haired idol of the Russian heavy metal set could easily turn out to be an Other. I for one wouldn't be surprised if he did.

I went up to the next floor with Edgar and Shagron, and we found ourselves in a genuine office space, with a large open-plan area divided into little compartments separated by screens, individual offices on one side and an open area overlooking Tverskaya Street through a huge window of lightly tinted glass. I noticed that the Dark Ones used hardly any desktop PCs: at least, the three Watch staff members who were there – they must have been either very late owls or very early larks – were all sitting with their noses stuck in the screens of their laptops.

'Hellemar!' Edgar called, and one of the three – a werewolf, like the guard on duty downstairs – reluctantly tore himself away from some game on the screen.

'Yes, chief?'

'I want an urgent news update! All movements of reagents or artefacts of great power. Lost, disappeared, smuggled. Anything that's happened recently.'

'What's happened?' the werewolf Hellemar asked. 'Is there something serious going on?'

'The Light Ones have information that someone's trying to smuggle an artefact into Moscow. Move it, Hellemar!'

Hellemar turned to the other players:

'Hey, you dickheads! Get to work!'

The dickheads instantly dropped what they'd been doing, and seconds later I could hear the quiet tapping of keyboards while on the screens the endless corridors filled with monsters had been replaced by the bright windows of Netscape.

Edgar took me into an office separated off from the large open-plan area by a glass wall and blinds. Shagron went off somewhere for a moment, but he soon came back with a jar of Tchibo and a carton of Finnish glacier water. He poured the water into an electric kettle and switched it on. In a moment the kettle started murmuring industriously.

'I hope you have sugar here,' Shagron muttered.

'I'll find some.' Edgar lowered himself into one armchair and offered me the other: 'Have a seat, colleague. You don't mind if I simply call you Vitaly, do you?'

'Of course not. Feel free.'

'Excellent. Well, then, Vitaly, I'll do the talking, and you correct me if I get something wrong. Okay?'

'Sure,' I said readily. Because I had almost no idea what weird stories might surface from my subconscious for me to tell these intent agents of the Day Watch.

'Am I right in thinking that you have no information about the artefact?'

'You are,' I confirmed.

'A pity,' Edgar said with genuine disappointment. 'It would have greatly simplified matters.'

As a matter of fact, not only didn't I have any information about the artefact, I didn't have any information at all about any arte-facts that Edgar might be interested in. This was a field where experienced Others were like connoisseurs, but I still know less about it than a pig does about oranges.

'Then let's move on. You arrived in Moscow from Ukraine, if I understand correctly?'

'Yes. From Nikolaev.'

'For what purpose?'

I pondered for about half a minute. Nobody tried to hurry me.

'It's hard to say,' I confessed honestly. 'Clearly without any particular purpose. I just got fed up of sitting at home doing nothing.'

'You were only initiated very recently, am I right?'

'Yes.'

'Did you just have an urge to see a bit of the world?'

'Probably.'

'Then why Moscow, and not the Bahamas, for instance?'

I shrugged. But really – why? Surely not just because I didn't have a passport for foreign travel yet?

'I don't know. The Bahamas are a place to go in summer.'

'It's summer now in the tropics. And there are plenty of places to go to.'

True. I hadn't thought of that.

'All the same, I don't know,' I answered. 'Later, maybe.'

I had the feeling that Edgar wanted to ask about something else, but at this point Hellemar entered the office without knocking. His eyes were as wide as Jerry's when he suddenly sees Tom just behind him.

'Chief! Berne, Fáfnir's Talon! It's been stolen from the Inquisition's vault! The whole continent's been in uproar for over two hours now!'

Shagron couldn't restrain himself – he leapt to his feet. Edgar held back, but his eyes glinted and even without entering the Twilight I could see the orange streaks that sprang up in his aura. But he quickly gathered himself again.

'Is this open information?'

'No. It's restricted. The Inquisition hasn't made any official state-ment yet.'

'Your source?'

The werewolf hesitated.

'The source is unofficial. But reliable.'

'Hellemar,' Edgar said with a hint of emphasis, 'your source?'

'One of our men in the Prague information agency,' Hellemar confessed. 'An Other. Dark. I caught him in a private chat room.'

'I see, I see.'

I wanted very much to ask questions, but naturally all I could do for the time being was stare stupidly and keep quiet as I absorbed the important but, unfortunately, incomprehensible things they were saying.

'And how do the Light Ones know about this?' Shagron asked, puzzled.

'Who can tell?' said Edgar, twitching his eyebrows in a bizarre manner. 'They have a wide network of informers . . .'

'Status "Aleph",' Edgar said abruptly to Hellemar. 'Call everyone in.'

About half an hour later the floor was crowded. Of course, they were all Others. And all Dark.

But I still didn't understand a thing.

When Anton got back to suite six twelve, Ilya was sitting in an armchair and massaging his temples, and Garik was striding nervously to and fro across the carpet between the window and the sofa. Tolik and Tiger Cub were sitting on the sofa, and Bear was hovering in the doorway of the bedroom.

'. . . he sensed me, by the way,' Bear was saying gloomily. 'Your "cloud" didn't help.'

'The Estonian?'

'No, the Estonian didn't sense me. And neither did Shagron, of course. But the other one did, almost straight away.'

'But that's crazy, guys. He can't be more powerful than the Estonian, can he?' said Garik.

'But why can't he?' Ilya asked without raising his head. 'A couple of hours ago I thought I knew all four of the Moscow Dark Ones I couldn't handle one on one. But now I'm not sure of anything.'

Anton slumped back against the fridge: the question on his tongue was still unspoken – the conversation was more interesting than he'd thought it would be.

And then Tiger Cub beat him to it:

'Ilya! Why don't you fill us in? About the artefact.'

Ilya stood up abruptly:

'Briefly, Fáfnir's Talon has been removed from the Inquisition's vault in Berne. Two . . .' he glanced at his watch '. . . no, three hours ago now. The Swiss department is in a panic. The Inquisition is fuming and thundering, but so far it hasn't issued an official communiqué. The details are unknown, all we do know is that the Talon is at the seasonal peak of its power. In the Dark phase, of course. Simple calculations indicate that releasing even part of the power accumulated by the Talon in Central Russia is likely to result in powerful discharges, up to and including a localised Inferno breakthrough. And that's how things currently stand.'

'And Zabulon's not in Moscow,' Tolik drawled with slow emphasis.

'You mean the Dark Ones are behind this?'

'Well, we aren't, are we?' Ilya asked and his shoulders twitched as if he suddenly felt cold.

'Does Gesar know about this?'

'Of course. He was the one who told me. He ordered me not to worry, but just keep on working away.'

Ilya sat down again.

'I don't even know what to think,' he said in a voice that was somehow both tough and helpless. 'To be quite honest, when I heard about a Shahab's Ring killing a Light One, I suspected the Talon was already here. There's no point in setting up a Ring with such monstrous power – it's just a sheer, unnecessary waste. I'd understand if it was to protect the Talon, but for a lousy few thousand dollars . . . it's simply idiotic.'

'A Dark One wouldn't have left the Talon in his room without someone to guard it,' Garik put in.

'Of course not. That would be stupid.'

'Yes, it would,' Ilya agreed. 'But we had to check.'

'And what can we do now?' Tiger Cub asked morosely. 'Now Andriukha's dead, and we can't even punish his killer?'

'Katya,' Ilya said, looking at her sympathetically, 'it's sad, but that's the way it is. And now we've got a problem that makes Andrei's death seem almost unimportant. The analysts have been following the approximate balance between the global power nexuses since four o'clock this morning. If the Talon is moved, the balance is bound to be disrupted.'

'And have they come up with anything?'

'Yes. About an hour ago it became clear that the Talon is either already in Moscow or due to appear here any time now.'

'Hang on,' Tolik put in again, 'so the recurrences of poaching and unmotivated aggression by Dark Ones are down to the influence of the Talon?'

'Probably.'

'But the first incident took place on Saturday!' Tiger Cub protested in surprise.

Ilya massaged his temples again; it was obvious that he was very tired.

'The Talon is a very powerful artefact, Tiger Cub. The lines of probability extend far into the future. And the Dark Ones are more powerfully influenced by Dark artefacts than we are. So the small fry have already started running wild.'

'If it's so powerful, how come the Inquisition has mislaid it?'

'I don't know,' Ilya retorted, 'I wasn't there. But I'm quite sure of one thing: if it's possible to do something, sooner or later someone's going to do it.'

'Our people are coming,' Garik remarked, changing the subject.

He was right, someone from the service section had arrived. Obviously Andrei Tiunnikov's body had to be removed.

'And what about this Dark One?' Anton asked at last. 'Do you think he's connected with the thieves?'

'Not necessarily.' Ilya watched sadly as Tiunnikov's body was zipped into a black polythene bag. 'He could be distracting us. Or he might not even be aware of what he's doing. That's what it actually looks like most of all. The Talon is controlling him, or the person who now has it. And the Dark One has definitely become more powerful since our run-in with him last Saturday.'

'Then shouldn't we be following him?' Tolik suggested. 'If he's connected with the Talon, isn't he bound to lead us to the thieves?'

'If he is connected, he'll lead us to them.'

'And if he doesn't?'

Ilya just sighed.

'Then we'll have more surprises and emergencies. And that Dark One will be there all the time, just at the edge of our field of vision. He's bound to be.'

'Wait,' Garik said tensely. 'What if he's intended for the Talon?'

'That's what I'm afraid of.'

Anton shook his head sharply. After the events of eighteen months before, for a while he had thought he could regard himself as an experienced and hardened Watchman. But now he felt like a beginner among virtuosos again. And he didn't like having to admit it.

The phone rang – the local hotel phone. It felt odd to hear the ring of an ordinary phone after the trilling of all the mobiles.

'Hello?' Tolik picked up the receiver, listened for a moment and turned to Ilya. 'For you. It's Semyon.'

Ilya took the receiver and put it to his ear, then ran a piercing gaze over them all.

'Let's get going, guys. The boss is already in the office.'

Anton realised, with a vague feeling of weariness, that now he would see Svetlana again. And again he would feel the gulf between them widening with every second.

I didn't stay at the Day Watch office for long after things livened up. I was dozing off where I sat, so I was sent off to catch up on my sleep. I didn't object; I'd been on my feet for more than twenty-four hours and I couldn't keep my eyes open.

As I fell into sleep I could faintly hear Kipelov's singing coming from somewhere:

Hey, you inhabitants of the skies!
Which of you hasn't plumbed the depths?

# CHAPTER 3

I WOKE up when I realised I was being called. Called in the same way that vampires call their prey. Still not fully awake, I got up and fumbled for my clothes on the chair.

The Call was sweet and alluring, it enveloped me, caressing and urging me, it was impossible, absolutely impossible, to resist. Sometimes it sounded like music, sometimes like singing, sometimes like whispering, and in every form it was perfect, a reflection of my own soul.

And then, like a sudden blow just below the knees, came the jerk up onto the next step.

The Call instantly lost its power over me, although it hadn't stopped. I dropped the trousers I was holding and shook my head quickly.

Oh, that hurt.

The sweet hypnotic syrup slowly drained out of me. Drained out and disappeared beneath the floor. Spent Light energy, faded power.

I suddenly understood very clearly why vampires' victims smile as they present their necks to be bitten. When the Call sounds, they're happy. This is the sweet moment they have been waiting for all their lives, and compared with this, life is as empty and grey as the world of the Twilight.

The Call is a kind of gift. A release. Only it was still too soon for me to be set free.

I had no idea why, but my new ability this time was immunity to the Call. I could hear it and understand it, but I remained entirely in control of myself. And of course, I screened my mind from the caller, so that he wouldn't suspect his victim had been transformed from a sleepwalker into a hunter.

'A hunter?' I asked myself curiously. 'Hmm . . .'

So I was going hunting. Well now, that was interesting.

The Call continued.

'Well, well,' I thought. 'This is the headquarters of the Day Watch. Everything here is saturated with magic. The defences here are quite incredible. But the Call is still effective . . . was effective?'

The Light Ones had invested a lot of effort in this trick. And in concealing it. It was their good luck that the chief of the Day Watch was out of Moscow – the Light Ones would never have been able to trick him, no matter how hard they tried.

Meanwhile I calmly got dressed, thinking sadly that my dream of visiting a restaurant and grabbing a bowl of hot, spicy soup and a plate of something like duck in cherry sauce had to be put off again indefinitely. I set two or three weak protective spells and left my suite . . . I mean, my apartment. If they called them apartments here, I might as well too. My minidisc player was on my belt; I pressed the earphones into my ears and pulled my cap down tight onto my head.

'Why not set it to random?' I thought. 'Play a little game with fate.'

And again fate chose me a song from the Kipelov and Mavrin album. A different one this time.

> There is silence above me,
> A sky full of rain,
> The rain goes straight through me,
> But there's no more pain.
> While stars whispered coldly,
> We burned our final bridge.
> And everything has tumbled into the abyss
> I shall be free
> From evil and good,
> My soul's been walking the razor's edge.

Mm . . . well. A rather gloomy prediction. Just when was it that I burned my final bridge? Or maybe that was what I'd just left the apartment to do? Instead of going up to the next floor and asking what had happened to some extremely powerful Talon or other. But I was being urged to follow the Call by that same certain something that had been lying hidden somewhere deep inside me.

> I'm free! Like a bird in the heavens.
> I'm free! I've forgotten the meaning of fear.
> I'm free! I am the wild wind's equal.
> I'm free! In the real world, not in a dream.

Kipelov's voice was no less enchanting than the Call. It had a hypnotic resonance, as convincing as truth itself. And I suddenly realised I was listening to a Dark anthem. A hymn to their ideal of rebellious souls acknowledging no boundaries or rules:

> There is silence above me,
> The sky full of fire,
> The light goes straight through me,

But I'm free once again,
Free from love,
Free from hate and from rumour,
From a fate foretold in advance
And from the shackles of earth,
From evil and from good.
My soul no longer holds a place for you.

Freedom. The only thing that genuinely interests us. Freedom from everything. Even from dominating the world, and it's sad that the Light Ones simply can't understand that or believe it; they just carry on with their interminable intrigues, and in order to maintain the status quo, we have no choice but to obstruct them.

The lift slid smoothly downward, past the Twilight floors and the ordinary ones. I'm free . . .

If Kipelov was an Other, he had to be Dark. No one else could sing about freedom like that. And only the Dark Ones would hear the song's deeper, true meaning!

The two taciturn warlocks on watch below let me out without any trouble – Edgar had done me a favour in having the image of my registration seal entered in the operational database. I walked out onto Tverskaya Street, into the thickening dusk of another Moscow evening, and set out towards the Call, but free from it. And from everything in the world.

Who wanted me so badly? There are no vampires among the Light Ones – no ordinary vampires, that is. All Others are energy vampires, they can all draw power from people. From their fears, from their joys, from their sufferings. The only fundamental difference between us and the Twilight moss is that we're able to think and move about. And we don't use the accumulated power simply for nourishment.

The Call led me along Tverskaya Street, away from the Kremlin, towards the Belorussian railway station. I walked along, alone in the evening crowds, as if I'd been singled out, chosen. And I had been chosen – by the Call. No one saw me, no one noticed me. No one was interested in me – not the girls warming themselves in the cars, not their pimps, not the toughs in their foreign cars sitting at the kerb. Nobody.

Turn right. Onto Strastnoi Boulevard.

The Call was getting stronger. I could feel it – that meant the encounter would be soon.

Droves of cars raced through the driving, sticky snow, the fine snowflakes dancing erratically in the beams of their headlights.

Cold and dusk. Moscow in winter.

The snow settled evenly on the boulevard pavements, on the benches that were empty at this time of year, on the bushes, and on the railings between the road and the pedestrian park.

They tried to get me halfway towards Karetny Ryad.

The spell of isolation seemed to fall from the sky – ordinary people simply lost interest in what was about to happen on the boulevard, the cars carried on rushing past, minding their own business, the few pedestrians nearby faltered for a moment and then wandered off, even those who had been moving towards me.

The Light Ones slipped out of the Twilight one after another. Four of them. Two magicians and two shape-shifters, already in battle form. A massive polar bear as white as snow and a tigress with bright orange stripes.

I was almost flattened when all the magicians struck together, from both sides. But they had underestimated their quarry – the blow had been calculated for the old me, the one that would have submitted to the Call.

I had already become someone else.

Mentally drawing my hands apart, I stopped the walls that were about to come together and imprison me. I stopped them, drew in power and pressed them back. Not very hard.

I don't know what a tsunami looks like, I've never seen one. But it was the first thing that came to mind when I examined the result.

The Light Magicians' walls, which had appeared so monolithic and irresistible only a second earlier, crumpled as though they were made of rice-paper. Both magicians were thrown back, swept onto the snow and dragged about ten metres across the ground; only the park railings stopped them falling under the wheels of the cars. A cloud of powdery snow flew up into the air.

The Light Ones probably then realised that they couldn't take me only with magic. So the shape-shifters came hurtling at me in their animal forms.

I hurriedly drew more power from wherever I could; there was a dull thud on the road, followed by the sound of broken glass, then another thud, followed by the ear-splitting screech of car horns.

I'd taken the bear's impact on a 'concave shield' and sent him tumbling away along the boulevard. At first I simply dodged the tigress.

I'd taken a dislike to her from the very beginning.

I don't know where shape-shifting magicians get the mass for transformation. In her human form this girl couldn't have weighed more than forty-five or fifty kilos. But now she was at least a hundred and fifty kilos of muscle, sinew, claws and teeth. A real killing machine.

The Light Ones like that.

'Hey!' I shouted. 'Wait. Maybe we can talk?'

The magicians were back on their feet, and they made another attempt to snare me, but it didn't take much of an effort to tie the greedy, trembling threads of energy into knots and fling them back at their owners. I hit both targets again, but this time no one was sent skidding off – I had simply returned their own energy. The bear stood to one side, shifting his weight menacingly from one foot to the other. He was hunching himself up, as if he was about to stand on his hind legs.

'I wouldn't advise it,' I told him, and struck at the attacking tigress.

Not too hard. I didn't want to kill her.

'Just what is the bloody problem?' I shouted angrily. 'Or is this just the way things are done in Moscow?'

Calling the Night Watch would have been stupid – my attackers were on the Watch themselves. Then maybe I should get help from the Day Watch? Especially since it was so close; their office was round the corner and I could be there in no time. But would it do me any good?

The magicians weren't about to give up; one was holding a fully charged flaming wand and the other had some kind of restraining amulet that looked pretty powerful too.

It took all of two seconds to deal with the amulet – I had to tear apart the net it cast over me with an ordinary 'triple dagger' – but the power that went into that very simple spell would have been enough to reduce the entire Moscow city centre to ashes. And then the second Light Magician hit me with the Fire of Bethlehem, but that only made me angry and, I suspect, even stronger.

I froze his wand. Simply turned it into an icicle and put a spell of rejection on it. Fragments of ice spurted from the Light One's hands like some bizarre, cold firework display, and the liberated energy soared up into the sky.

I couldn't really just dump it on the people around us, could I? I'd already done enough damage with those collisions at the nearby crossroads.

The bear stayed put. Apparently he'd realised that, despite their numerical superiority, the balance of power was far from equal. But the tigress just wouldn't stop. She came for me with all the aggression of a crazed female animal when an enemy gets too close to her young. Her eyes blazed with unconcealed hatred, as yellow as the flames on church candles.

The tigress was taking revenge. Taking revenge on me, a Dark One, for all her old grudges and losses. For Andrei, who had been killed by me. And for who knows what else . . . And she wouldn't stop for anything.

I don't want to say she had nothing to avenge – the Watches have always fought, and I'm not in the habit of mincing words. But I didn't intend to die.

I'm free. Free to punish anyone who gets in my way and refuses to resolve things peacefully. Wasn't that what the song had been trying to tell me?

I struck out. With the Transylvanian Mist.

The tigress's body was twisted and stretched, and even above the roar of engines and the piercing beeping of horns I heard the snap of bones quite clearly. The spell crumpled the shape-shifter the same way a child crumples a plasticine figure. The broken ribs tore through the skin and their bloody ends thrust into the snow. The head was squashed into a flat, striped pancake. In an instant the beautiful beast was transformed into a tangled mess of bloody flesh.

With a final, calculated blow, I consigned the tigress's soul to the Twilight.

Once I'd begun, I had no right to stop.

The Light Ones froze. Even the bear stopped stamping his feet.

'And what now?' I thought wearily.

Maybe I would have had to kill them all, but thank heaven – or hell – it didn't come to that.

'Day Watch!' I heard a familiar voice say. 'An attack on a Dark One has been registered. Leave the Twilight!'

Edgar's voice was stern, without a trace of his Baltic accent.

But he needn't have said that about the Twilight. Those who were alive hadn't been fighting in the Twilight, and the tigress had nowhere to come back to.

'The Day Watch demands that a tribunal be convened immediately,' Edgar said ominously. 'And in the meantime be so good as to summon the chief of the Night Watch.'

'Why, he'll scatter you all like kittens,' one of the Light Magicians said angrily.

'No, he won't,' Edgar snapped and pointed at me. 'Not with him here. Or haven't you got the point yet?'

I barely caught the movement as someone shuffled power in space. And then a dark-skinned, sharp-featured man appeared, wearing a brightly-coloured eastern robe; he looked totally absurd in the middle of the snowy boulevard.

'I'm already here,' he barked, mournfully surveying the scene of the recent battle.

'Gesar!' Edgar said in a more spirited voice. 'Good day. In our chief's absence you will have to explain yourself to me.'

'To you?' said Gesar, glancing sideways at the Estonian. 'You're not worthy.'

'Then to him,' said Edgar, shrugging his shoulders and shuddering as if he felt cold. 'Or is he not worthy either?'

'No, I'll explain myself to him,' said Gesar coolly, turning towards me. His gaze was as bottomless as eternity. 'Get out of Moscow,' he said, almost entirely without emotion. 'Right now. Catch a train or ride a broomstick, but just clear out. You've already killed twice.'

'As I see it,' I remarked as amicably as I could, 'certain other individuals have attempted to kill me. And all I did was defend myself.'

Gesar turned his back to me – he didn't want to listen. He didn't want to speak to a Dark One who had dispatched one of his finest warriors into the Twilight for ever.

'Let's get out of here,' he said to his people.

'Hey, hey!' Edgar protested angrily. 'They're criminals, they're not going anywhere, in the name of the Treaty I forbid it!'

Gesar turned back towards the Estonian:

'Yes they are. And you can't do anything about it. They're under my protection.'

I was seriously expecting to be hoisted up onto the next step. Because my current powers were enough for me to realise I couldn't go head to head with Gesar yet. He'd crush me. Not without an effort – after all, I'd already come a long way up the invisible stairway. My powers were pretty strong. But he'd still crush me.

But nothing happened. Probably the time hadn't yet come for me to fight Gesar.

Edgar gave me a plaintive glance – apparently he'd been hoping for more from me.

The Light Ones slipped away into the Twilight, taking with them the remains of their dead sister-in-arms, and then they dived deeper, to the second level. It was over.

'I really can't stop him,' I admitted apologetically. 'Sorry, Edgar.'

'A pity,' the Estonian said, basely forming the words.

They took me to the Day Watch office in the trusty BMW – for the first time in Moscow I was feeling tired.

But still as free as before.

I paid a price for using so much power – I can barely remember how they drove me back, urged me towards the lift, led me to the office, sat me in an armchair and stuck a cup of coffee in my hand. I had a painful ache in my overworked muscles, an ache in my entire being, which just a short while ago had been commanding the powers of the Twilight. I'd beaten them off with convincing skill – it would be a long time before the Light Ones forgot this battle. And my attackers hadn't been young novices either – I reckoned that both Light Ones had been first-grade magicians at least.

'Give the analysts a kick up the backside,' Edgar ordered one of his subordinates. 'I want to find out what's going on finally.'

I glanced at him, and Edgar realised I was coming round.

'Talk to me!' he said.

'A Call!' I said hoarsely and started to cough. I tried to take a sip of coffee, burned myself and hissed in pain. 'A Call,' I said when I could talk again. 'They caught me while I was sleeping.'

'A Call?' Shagron echoed in surprise. He was sitting in an armchair like mine at the next desk. 'The Light Ones haven't used one for about thirty years.'

'They caught you with a Call in the Day Watch building?' Edgar asked suspiciously. 'That's really something! And you mean no one else noticed anything?'

'No. It was a very subtle Call, aimed with masterly precision and camouflaged as natural background noise from the residential floors.'

'And you submitted to it?'

'Of course not.' I made another attempt to take a sip of coffee, this time successfully. 'But I decided to investigate what the Light Ones were up to.'

'And you didn't tell anyone?' Edgar was balancing halfway between disbelief and annoyance. 'That was a crazy risk.'

'If I'd gone trailing after the Call with backup, they'd have sensed it in a moment,' I explained. 'No, I had to go alone and without cover. So I did. They tried to grab me on Strastnoi Boulevard and I had to fight them off. I knocked the tigress down two or three times and tried to persuade her to stop, and it was only after that I hit her really hard.'

Edgar stared at me without blinking.

'You're a dark horse, Vitaly,' he said.

'Yes, Dark,' I confirmed happily. 'They don't come any Darker.'

'Are you a magician beyond classification?' he asked.

'Alas, no,' I said, spreading my hands – but slowly, so as not to spill the coffee. 'Otherwise I wouldn't have let Gesar go.'

Edgar drummed his fingers on the desk, glancing sideways impatiently at the door.

'What are those analysts up to?' he muttered.

The door opened and a brisk middle-aged woman, a witch, appeared in the doorway, along with two men, both magicians.

'Hello, Anna Tikhonovna,' Shagron greeted her hastily. He ought to have been more powerful than the witch, but he seemed to be afraid of her. And he was right, of course. A witch's power is somewhat different from a magician's. And a witch can easily screw things up even for a very powerful magician.

Edgar just nodded.

'Is this him?' one of the magicians asked, looking at me.

'Yes, Yura.'

Yura was an old and powerful magician, I realised that straight away. I also realised that Yura wasn't his real name. Magicians like that keep their real names hidden so incredibly deep, there's no way you can ever uncover them.

And that's as it should be. If you're really following the path of freedom.

'Have a seat, Anna Tikhonovna,' said Shagron, giving up his armchair and going across to join the magicians, who had occupied the broad windowledge.

'Edgar,' said the witch. 'The Light Ones went for broke. They haven't pulled anything this wild since forty-nine. They must have really serious reason to violate the Treaty!'

Edgar shrugged and explained curtly:

'Fáfnir's Talon.'

'But we haven't got it,' the witch declared emphatically,

looking round significantly at everyone there. 'Or have we? Shagron?'

Shagron quickly shook his head. It looked to me as if he'd had a few run-ins with the witch and not come out of them well. She was a pretty powerful witch.

'Kolya?'

The second magician who had come in replied in a calm voice: 'No, and it's by no means clear that we want it.'

'I'm not asking you,' the witch barked at Edgar and Yura. And then for the first time she glanced at me.

'Anna Tikhonovna,' I said with feeling. 'I only learned that the Talon exists today, and I've been asleep for most of the time since then.'

'Why are you in Moscow?' she asked sternly.

'I don't know that myself. Something urged me, told me to come, and so I did. And I was barely off the train before I got caught up in that business with the vampire. Off the boat and into the party, as they say.'

'If I understand anything about any of this,' the magician Yura put in, 'then this is predestination. That would explain everything – the increased powers, the missing Talon, and the way the Light Ones acted. They're simply trying to eliminate him, or at least isolate him, before he can get his hands on the Talon. Because afterwards it will be too late.'

'But why didn't they bring in their enchantress?' Edgar asked, beginning to draw out his vowels slightly again. It seemed his accent only appeared at moments of agitation, when he was concentrating on something apart from what he was saying.

'And even Gesar only intervened at the critical moment,' Shagron remarked. 'And then all he did was cover their retreat.'

'Who knows?' The witch cast another piercing glance at me. 'Maybe they simply can't keep up with him?'

'My name's Vitaly,' I told her. 'Pleased to meet you.'

After all, who likes to hear himself referred to as 'him' all the time?

The others simply seemed to ignore what I'd said.

Yura looked into my eyes and instantly probed me. I didn't bother to screen myself – but why not?

'Good first grade,' he declared. 'With some gaps, though. Only yesterday I would have been delighted by the appearance of a magician like this among us.'

'But today it upsets you, does it?' the witch snorted.

'Today I'm not drawing any conclusions. The Light Ones have cut loose, and we've been left on our own, without Zabulon. Gesar, plus that enchantress, plus Olga, even if she doesn't have her full powers, and then Igor, Ilya, Garik, Semyon . . . We can't match them.'

'But we have the Talon and this . . . Vitaly,' the witch countered. 'And then Zabulon has a habit of appearing right at the crucial moment.'

'We don't have the Talon,' Yura remarked. 'And what guarantee is there that we will have? In any case, Kolya's absolutely right: what would we do with the Talon? Of course, I understand, it possesses ancient, mighty power. But if we don't think carefully before we let it loose . . . We can't afford to mess this up.'

'Well, we'll try hard not to,' the witch said condescendingly. 'Edgar, what have the analysts got?'

As if in response, there was a knock at the door and Hellemar, the lord of the laptops, appeared.

'Got it!' he said triumphantly. 'Vnukovo airport! Flight fifteen zero zero from Odessa. It was delayed twice by bad weather and has only just taken off. It will land in an hour and twenty minutes. The Talon's on board.'

'Right,' said Edgar, leaping to his feet. 'Set up field HQ at the airport. Monitor the weather. Cut off the Light Ones. And they can go whistle for an observer.'

'Chief,' Hellemar said with a sour expression, 'the Light Ones have already set up their field HQ at Vnukovo fifteen minutes ago. Better bear that in mind.'

'We will,' the witch promised. 'Now let's get moving.'

Everyone got to their feet; someone grabbed the phone, someone grabbed the charged amulets out of the safe, someone else started to issue loud orders to the staff.

And I just wearily put my empty coffee cup on the desk.

'Do they at least feed people in your HQ?' I said to nobody in particular. 'I've been running on empty for twenty-four hours now.'

'You'll survive,' I was told sharply. 'Get downstairs and don't even think of trying any more one-man heroics.'

But strangely enough, at that moment I didn't feel the slightest desire for any more heroics.

We reached Vnukovo incredibly quickly. The driver of our comfortable minibus was a lippy young guy the Others called Deniska. He was a magician, but he handled a steering wheel even better than Shagron. First we drove round the embankments, then along Ordynka Street and Lenin Prospect, into the South-West district, round the ring road. Everything flashed by so fast I barely had time to see anything. Shagron and Edgar had gone off somewhere, Yura and Kolya had disappeared too. I was left with Anna Tikhonovna and a trio of young witches; every now and then I caught them looking at me curiously. Anna Tikhonovna must have told them to leave me alone, because none of them made any attempt to talk to me. A fat werewolf floundered about heavily in the baggage compartment behind us and growled huskily whenever Deniska threw the minibus into a tight curve as he overtook someone. The tyres squealed, the drive-shaft groaned and the engine hummed like an industrious bumble-bee in May.

We were the first to reach the airport. Deniska drove up to the service entrance and two other vehicles came hurtling up almost immediately – Shagron's BMW and another minibus carrying the technicians. The Watch members set to work with fantastic co-ordination: they immediately cast information spells that made us empty space to human beings, and a line of technicians carrying laptops set off for the entrance. Someone had already chosen a site for the HQ – a spacious office with a sign on the door saying 'Accounts'. The human employees had been herded into the next room – either an office or a boardroom – and put into a blissful trance. I would have chosen the boardroom for the HQ, but Hellemar said there were more telephone lines in the accounts office.

Yura appeared and I wondered irrelevantly why Edgar was carrying out the duties of senior deputy while the chief was away, even though he was only borderline second grade. Yura seemed more powerful to me. But the affairs of the Day Watch were none of my business, so I just hunkered down in a corner and tried to figure out if I could make a dash to the restaurant for ten minutes. The young technicians were already stroking away at the touchpads of their laptops.

'The flight's making its approach, ETA is twenty minutes plus or minus five.'

'Have you located the Light Ones?' Anna Tikhonovna asked.

'Yes. In the overnight transit rooms, beside the lounge. That's in the next building.'

'What are they doing?'

'Looks like they're tinkering with the weather,' someone said.

'What's the point? To stop the plane landing?'

'They won't do anything that might kill the passengers,' Anna Tikhonovna snorted.

It seemed to me the simplest thing would have been to bring

the plane down, and that would have put an end to the whole business. But Light Ones are Light Ones. Even in a situation like this they worry about ordinary human beings. And then, who knew if a plane crash would even damage the artefact from Berne? Maybe it wouldn't touch it. Power is power, after all.

'Who's a weather specialist here?' Anna Tikhonovna enquired.

'Me!' two witches chorused.

'Right then, feel out what's going on here.'

The witches began feeling things out – that is, scanning the immediate area for weather spells. I could sense dense arrays of sensitive energy impulses that were intangible and invisible, even to many Others. It wasn't that the Others couldn't have traced them – most of them simply didn't know how. Weather magic has always been a speciality of witches and a few magicians, and like any other specialised field, it has its subtleties.

'They're intensifying the cloud cover,' one of the witches announced. 'We need power.'

One of the reserve magicians immediately took an amulet and groped for one of the witches' hands. They concentrated for a while, and finally all three of them held hands, closed their eyes and sank into something like a light trance.

'Everybody, help them if you can,' Anna Tikhonovna ordered.

I was in no state to help them yet. At least, the energy I could have put into the effort was insignificant compared to the power of the amulet. I'd pretty well drained myself back there on Strastnoi Boulevard.

The Watch continued with its work. The headquarters was really buzzing – nobody seemed to be running, nobody seemed to be agitated, but the air was alive with tension. I even began feeling a bit uncomfortable – I was the only one in the whole headquarters sitting there doing nothing. And something told me I still wouldn't be able to do anything for quite a while.

So I sneaked out. I stood up and slid into the Twilight. And then I moved deeper, to the second level.

Falling to the ground from the second floor took me about three minutes, even though I hurried it along as much as I could. It was strange, I'd expected the Twilight to drain me completely but, on the contrary, I felt invigorated, as if I'd just taken a shower and downed a shot of vodka. Amazing.

And by the way, that shot sounded like a good idea.

When I surfaced from the Twilight, I headed for the next building – a long glass-and-concrete slab, quite unlike the administrative building, which was crowned by a tall spire – a relic of the architectural pomposity of the Soviet fifties.

I'd left my jacket at the field headquarters, so I had to sprint for the door. The wind was carrying fine pellets of snow, and I wondered how the plane from Odessa was going to land. Darkness and driving snow – it was a night you wouldn't put a dog out in. And then the Light Ones would be doing their best to spoil things. But if the plane didn't land, where would it go? Would they redirect it to another Moscow airport? Maybe Bykovo or Domodedovo?

That was an idea, I ought to tell Edgar or Anna Tikhonovna they should send Watch members, just in case.

And then again, they could divert the plane to Kaluga or Tula. If the weather was better there. Which it very well could be – after all, here in Butovo the Light weather magicians were obviously giving it their best shot.

After I'd been outside, the terminal building felt warm and cosy. I went straight up to the second floor, to the bar where Boryansky and I once drank beer while we were waiting for a plane and ate nuts while we listened to a song that had followed us everywhere on that trip: '. . . the summer has flown by, it's all behind us now . . .'

It took me a moment to realise that this was a memory – and I hardly had any memories left. What murky depths of my mind had it surfaced from? I couldn't tell.

I tried to think exactly who Boryansky was, but I couldn't even remember his face. And as for where we'd been flying to, and what for . . . For some reason the only memory that kept coming back was that then, in those archaic Soviet times, he had an outsized bidet in his apartment. Of course, it didn't work . . . and anyway, what would a Soviet citizen want with a bidet?

But the bar was still exactly the same as I remembered it. A bar, high stools, gleaming beer taps. And a TV in the corner. But the video it was showing was quite different. A young guy with suspiciously red eyes and a girl in a scarlet dress. He was kissing her hand. And the action after that was like a good thriller – complete with slashing wolf's jaws and all the rest. The moment I really enjoyed was when the young guy, who for some reason was now dressed in the girl's scarlet dress, came into a ballroom and then split apart into several wolves. And I liked the final shot, when the girl's red eyes glinted as she surveyed her guests.

Hmm. Well, whoever made that didn't know too much about shape-shifting Others. Just as the unfailingly hip Pelevin didn't know much about real gluttonous, dirty werewolves. But the video was well done, you couldn't deny that. The werewolves must all have chipped in to pay the producer and influenced the musicians – and what they'd got was a slick, romantic video about themselves. The Russian vampires had done the same thing only just recently.

I remembered the name of the group – Rammstein – for future reference, so that I'd be able to find the song and listen to it more carefully.

I ordered a beer and a couple of hamburgers and then sat at one side near the television, with my back to the room. My stomach already thought my throat had been cut, and I was determined to do something about that.

I sensed the Light Ones when I'd just started my second hamburger, literally felt them with my back. And I immediately screened myself off – I knew how to do that already, and I knew for certain that they hadn't sensed me.

I was a powerful Other, after all, even if I was inexperienced. And these two were still apprentices at best. A weak magician of about twenty or twenty-two and a novice soothsayer. I figured I could see the future a lot more clearly than the soothsayer – the whole gamut of possibilities – and I could predict more precisely which of them were more probable too.

The two Light Ones were talking in low voices: both of them were concealed by a skilful spell of inattention – a fairly exotic variety, in fact. It had been cast by someone who was very powerful indeed.

I listened.

'. . . already here. The boss says things could get rough,' the magician said quietly.

'They'll stick us in the security cordon anyway,' the soothsayer objected wearily. 'Especially after Tiger Cub and Andrei.'

'Oleg, we'll need all our power, you understand. All of it. Every last drop. The Dark Ones mustn't get their hands on the Talon – that would be the end of everything. The end of the Light.'

'Ah, come on,' the soothsayer objected sceptically. 'How can it be the end?'

The magician corrected himself:

'Well, the end of our superiority. We wouldn't be able to put the Dark Ones under any pressure for the foreseeable future.'

'But is it really possible to do that anyway?' There was a note of very healthy, frank scepticism in the soothsayer's words. 'The Light Ones and the Dark Ones have existed alongside each other for thousands of years. They've been fighting for thousands of years. Look at how long the Watches have been competing with each other. And then there's the Inquisition, it doesn't allow any violations of the balance of power . . .'

The Light Ones broke off their conversation for a moment, walked to the front of the queue at the bar and gently clouded everyone's minds, including the barman's:

'Twenty hamburgers and a carton of juice,' the magician said and then turned back to his companion.

I pretended my mind was clouded too. Others are basically pretty happy-go-lucky. Especially young ones. The feeling of their own superiority over ordinary people is fairly intoxicating, and it takes years before they can understand that sometimes being human is much simpler and better than being an Other.

'Anyway, there's going to be a fight. Anton told me the Dark Ones have got some sorcerer from out of town, and he laid out Farid and Danila with an easy sucker punch. And he killed Tiger Cub. The bastard.'

'She had no business attacking a peaceable Dark One,' I thought, feeling annoyed. 'I wasn't chasing her, she was the one who was after me.'

But the Light Ones were wrong about the sucker punch. I'd paid a heavy price for that fight.

A moment later I realised that something was happening. As if on command, the Light Ones turned their faces towards the airfield and immediately withdrew into the Twilight. A second later, so did I.

Outside the building, one of the Dark Ones was standing on a snow-covered runway with his wand held out in front of him. A long tongue of flame licked at the frozen concrete. Once, twice. The magician was drying out the runway before the plane from Odessa landed. But Light Ones were hurrying towards him from the terminal building, sinking into the snowdrifts as they ran.

The magician launched a few more tongues of flame and then shifted deeper into the Twilight.

It looked to me like Kolya.

My two Light chatterboxes hastily tipped their food supplies into white-and-green plastic bags and set off at a fast trot, trampling over the ever-hungry blue moss.

It had an easy life here. All those people, all those emotions . . . A single passenger who was late for a plane was enough to feed this entire ravenous carpet for a day.

I hopped off my stool too, leaving my unfinished beer on the bar. I could barely make out what was happening through the wall of the terminal building – all I could see were the vague shadows of Others with the coloured patches of auras above their heads and viscid bursts of discharged power. At the same time, I could still see the inside of the terminal hall and the people sitting in plastic chairs, patiently waiting for their flights.

Low, rumbling sounds threaded themselves through the Twilight – it was a woman's voice announcing that 'flight fifteen zero zero from Odessa has landed'. I went hurtling down the stairs, manoeuvring between the people who were hardly even moving.

Down. Ahead. And now to the right.

I leapt over the turnstile and found myself facing the exit to the airfield.

There was a full-scale battle going on out there – I could sense the discharges of energy on my skin. All that amulet power, all the magicians' skill – and it could all have been used for other purposes, instead of fighting each other. The Light Ones were so rigidly dedicated to their righteous struggle! It hadn't even entered their heads simply to reach an agreement with us – they'd rushed straight into the attack.

I could sense that the Dark Ones were having a tough time of it. It looked as though the chief of the Night Watch, Gesar, had got involved. And there were at least a further two very powerful magicians out there now, beside the plane that was taxiing to its stand.

And then four figures burst in through the wall of the terminal. They were all Others, of course. All tall, with broad shoulders, blond hair and blue eyes. As if they'd been specially selected – a matching set of twentieth- or twenty-first-century Vikings. All wearing identical warm winter parkas and carrying identical bags. They weren't wearing hats and their hair looked dishevelled, but something told me it wasn't the wind that was responsible for that.

I couldn't understand at first why they had remained in human form. But then I looked at them in the human world and laughed in surprise when I got the idea: an Other's image in the Twilight – his subconscious dream – can take all sorts of forms . . .

They walked quickly across the hall, almost running, towards me and the exit. Towards the bright patch of light in front of the terminal that was the airport car park.

Walking past me.

But just as they drew level, a dark-blue flower, the size of a heavy Ural construction truck, sprang up to the right of them. Everyone in the Twilight was thrown to the ground.

As I lay there on my back, I raised my head and saw a blue veil shimmering in mid-air, looking like a gigantic *Aurelia* jellyfish. But I could sense that something was about to happen behind that transparent curtain.

And I was right – a portal opened up in the blue haze. Right there in the baggage hall, behind that hazy blue curtain. My eyes were stung by a blinding white glow and it was suddenly abnormally bright in the Twilight, even though there were still no shadows. That was a really weird sight – unbearably bright light and not a hint of a shadow.

There were two Light Ones. The Night Watch boss and an attractive young woman. An enchantress of very considerable power.

'You are in my power,' Gesar declared loudly, making a short, economical pass with his hands. 'Get up!'

He was talking to the Vikings. The Light Ones hadn't noticed me lying there closer to the portal than anyone else.

One of the Vikings said something angry and abrupt in English. Gesar replied. I regretted that I didn't understand a single word. Then the Vikings stood up. And began obediently walking towards the portal. I was getting ready to stand up and had even got onto all fours, but when the third Viking drew level with me, the fourth abruptly withdrew deeper into the Twilight.

Gesar reacted instantly – he cast a Net over the Others and disappeared. The enchantress stayed where she was.

The remaining Vikings were pinned to the ground. And so was I – from being on all fours I was flattened back against the floor, this time face down. Like a squashed frog on a motorway. It felt as if a slab of concrete had been dropped on top of me from a passing truck – I couldn't catch my breath or move a muscle. And damned if there wasn't something pressing unbearably into my chest, a long, slightly curved object.

Lying with my nose pressed to the floor was not at all pleasant; I made an effort and turned my head.

My eyes met those of the Viking lying beside me.

I felt a frost more chilly than any Moscow winter.

'You!'

'I . . .'

'You're an Other!'

'Yes.'

'You serve the Darkness.'

'Probably.'

'Take care of it!'

'What?'

But the Viking had already closed his eyes. The silent dialogue had only lasted a few brief moments.

Take care of what? This bloody thing that was poking me in the ribs?

Just to be sure, the enchantress dropped another concrete slab on us – the Vikings began wheezing painfully and something like a groan was torn from my chest.

And then I thought: 'Ah, what the hell!'

I closed my eyes and focused on searching for power . . . and I sensed an almost inexhaustible source right there – the portal that was still open.

Well, well, how simple everything was, really! It would take no more than a few seconds to restore the power I'd expended on Strastnoi Boulevard. And the fact that it was a Light portal didn't bother me in the least – the nature of power is always the same in any case.

I began drawing in the power of the portal. Taking it slow, so that the Light Enchantress wouldn't immediately realise what was going on.

The first thing I tried was to shift the weight off myself slightly – I managed that okay, and I can't say it was really too difficult. Then I enveloped the thing underneath me in a cocoon and stuck it inside my sweater, still fumbling about on the floor. It seemed to me the enchantress was beginning to feel uneasy.

I was all set to stand up, but then Gesar came back; he was radiating white light, just like any peasant's idea of an angel. He was holding the limp, submissive Viking who had fled by the shoulder with one hand. One step, then another – and the Viking dropped like a rag doll to lie beside his comrades. But what I saw on Gesar's face was not joy, but something else.

'Where's the Talon?'

He glanced briefly at the enchantress, who pulled her head back into her shoulders in alarm – I sensed her scanning all of us at once.

Oh no, my girl! You won't break into my cocoon.

And Gesar won't break into it either. I can tell you that for sure, from the height of the next step up the stairway.

But Gesar wasn't wasting any time. He came straight up to me: 'You again . . .'

I didn't catch any hint of hatred in his voice. Only an infinite weariness.

I stood up and dusted my clothes off for some reason.

'Me.'

'You amaze me,' Gesar confessed, drilling through me with his gaze. 'Amaze me one more time. Give back the Talon.'

'The Talon?' I asked, raising my eyebrows expressively. 'What are you talking about, colleague?'

Gesar gritted his teeth – I distinctly saw the muscles at his temples twitch.

'Cut the comedy, Dark One. You've got the Talon, there's nowhere else it can be. I can't sense it any longer, but that doesn't change matters. Now you're going to give me the Talon and clear out of Moscow for good. That's the second time I've told you – and let me tell you it's the first time I've ever given anybody a second chance to leave in peace. The first time in very, very many years. Am I making myself clear?'

'Nothing could be clearer,' I growled, weighing up my own strength and deciding that it was worth going for it.

Mentally I reached out towards the enchantress, who wasn't prepared, and drew as much power as I could from her before she realised what was happening, then added some from the portal, all as quickly as possible.

Then I opened my own portal. Directly under my own feet. And at the same time I emerged from the Twilight.

The effect would basically have been the same if I'd been standing on a manhole and the cover had suddenly disappeared. I just fell through the floor, as far as Gesar and the Others could see. Fell straight through the floor and disappeared.

I hadn't dared to try drawing power from Gesar – something had told me it wasn't worth tangling with him yet: you can create a cocoon that Gesar can't see into without special preparation, you can steal energy from an enchantress who's very probably going to be a Great Enchantress – that's all pure childish mischief and will only work once. But it's a bit too soon for you, Vitaly Rogoza, Dark Other, to get involved in an open fight with the chief of the Night Watch.

Just say thank you that you got away in one piece.

I said 'thank you' and fell straight into a snowdrift from a height of several metres. It was dark all around. Or almost dark. Just the moon overhead. With a forest stretching out on both sides.

I was in a cutting in the forest, a cutting as straight as Nikolaev's Lenin Prospect and very wide, about fifteen metres across. There was a blank wall of forest on my right and a blank wall of forest on my left, and straight ahead, hanging above the silvery strip of untouched snow, there was the moon. Almost full.

It was beautiful, incredibly beautiful – the moonlit cutting, the night, the snow . . . I could have just lain there and admired it.

But I started to feel cold.

I scrambled out of the snowdrift with a struggle and looked around. The snow still looked untouched. But somewhere in the distance I could hear the distinctive hammering rhythm of the wheels of a commuter train.

Hmm. Some great magician I was. Lord of the Dark portals. I'd opened a portal all right. But I hadn't bothered about where it would come out. And this was the result: here I was all alone in the winter forest in nothing but my sweater, without a jacket or a hat.

Furious with myself, I felt the long, hard object under my sweater, decided not to remove the cocoon yet and set off towards the moon. Across the miraculous virgin snow of the moonlit forest cutting.

I soon realised that walking through snowdrifts was a very dubious pleasure. So I veered towards the forest, having sensibly decided that there ought to be less snow by the trees.

I was proved right twice over. First, there were indeed no snowdrifts at the edge of the forest, and second, I found a narrow path, pretty well trodden. I simply hadn't noticed it before in the shadow.

One of the ancients once said that roads always lead to the people who built them. And in any case, I had no other option. I set off along the path. First I walked, and then I started running to warm myself up.

'I'll run until I get tired,' I decided. 'And then I'll enter the Twilight . . . to warm up.'

I just hoped I'd have enough strength for running and the Twilight.

I ran for about fifteen minutes: there was absolutely no wind, so I actually did manage to get warmer. The cutting went on and on, an unbroken stretch of silvery, glittering snow. It wasn't me who should have been running here; it should have been some knight of old in a doublet with fur on the outside and his enchanted sword at his belt. And his faithful tame wolf running a few steps ahead . . .

Almost as soon as I thought about the wolf, I heard barking from somewhere on my left. Dogs. A wolf's bark is different. And they don't bark in winter.

I stopped and looked. There was a warm orange glow flickering through the trees: and as well as the barking I could hear voices. People's voices.

I didn't waste much time thinking. I walked forward until I reached the path branching off towards the campfire and turned onto it.

Soon two dogs came bounding towards me – a white Karelian laika with a tight coil of a tail, almost invisible against the background of the snow, and a shaggy Newfoundland terrier, as black as pitch. The laika was yelping in a voice that rang like a sleigh-bell and the Newfoundland was barking gruffly: 'Boof! Boof!'

'Petro! Is that you?' someone asked from the campfire.

'No,' I replied regretfully. 'It's not Petro. But can I warm myself a while?'

To be quite honest, the first thing I wanted to do wasn't to warm myself but to find out where I was. So I wouldn't have to go wandering through the forest at random, but could go straight to the suburban railway.

'Come on over here! Don't worry about the dogs, they won't touch you!'

And the dogs didn't touch me. The little laika ran round me cautiously at a constant distance of about four metres, and the Newfoundland simply came skipping up to my feet, sniffed my shoes, snorted and ran back to the campfire.

There were more than ten people sitting by the fire. And hanging on a long chain, thrown over a thick horizontal branch of the nearest pine tree, there was a big pot, with something bubbling promisingly inside it. The people were sitting on two logs, I could see most of them had metal mugs in their hands and somebody was just opening a new bottle of vodka.

'Oh, look at that!' said a young, bearded guy who looked like a geologist as I emerged from the darkness into the light. 'Just a thin sweater!'

'I'm sorry,' I sighed. 'I've got a few slight problems.'

'Sit down!' said someone who had come over to me. They sat

me down almost forcibly and immediately thrust a mug of vodka into my hand.

'Drink that.'

I didn't dare disobey. It burned my throat but a few seconds later I'd already forgotten it was the middle of winter.

'Styopa! Didn't you have a spare jacket somewhere?' the bearded guy asked, still giving the orders.

'Yes,' someone answered from the opposite log, and then ran off briskly to one side, where there were dark tents pitched in the gaps between the trees.

'And I've got a hat,' said a plump girl with plaits like a school-girl's. 'Just a moment . . .'

'Been out in the cold long?' the bearded guy asked me.

'Not very. Only about twenty minutes. Just don't ask how I got here.'

'We won't,' he replied. 'We'll find a place for you to sleep, and a spare sleeping bag too. And tomorrow we're going to Moscow. You can come with us, if you like.'

'Thanks,' I said. 'I'd be glad to.'

'We've got a birthday here,' Styopa explained as he came up to me, holding a bluish-green ski jacket. 'Here, take this.'

'Thanks a lot, guys,' I said sincerely, thanking them mostly not for the hospitality, but for not asking any unnecessary questions.

The jacket was warm. Warmer than it looked.

'And whose birthday is it?' I asked.

One of the girls stopped kissing her latest bearded admirer.

'Mine,' she told me. 'My name's Tamara.'

'Happy birthday,' I said. It sounded a bit flat. I felt genuinely sorry that I had nothing to give her as a present, and I felt ashamed to hand her a hundred-dollar note. It would have been too much like my generous tipping at the hotel.

'What's your name?' the first bearded guy asked me. 'I'm Matvei.'

'Vitaly.' I shook the hand that he held out. 'A birthday party in the forest in the middle of winter – I've never been to one of those before.'

'There's a first time for everything,' Matvei remarked philosophically.

The dogs started barking again and dashed off into the dark night.

'Well, is it Petro this time at last?' the birthday girl asked hopefully.

'Is that you, Petro?' Styopa roared in a surprisingly resonant baritone quite unlike the normal voice he used when speaking to other people.

'Yes,' said a voice in the forest.

'And have you brought the champagne?'

'Yes,' Petro confirmed happily.

'Hoo-ray,' the girls all shouted together. 'Hooray for Petro, our saviour!'

I felt stealthily under my jacket for the case that must conceal the mysterious Fáfnir's Talon. And I thought that I could relax until morning and soak in the relaxed atmosphere of somebody else's celebration. The people round the campfire made a point of not singling me out – they filled my mug with vodka as if I were one of them, then handed me a plate of steaming pilaff. As if the light of their fire attracted underdressed travellers out of the forest every day of the week.

It was a great pity there wasn't a single Other among them. Not even an uninitiated one.

# CHAPTER 4

SEMYON WALKED into Gesar's office, froze for a moment just inside the door and shook his head very slightly.

'He's not in Moscow. Definitely not.'

'That's kind of stupid,' Ignat snorted from his armchair. 'If he's supposed to do something with the Talon in Moscow, then what's the point of opening a portal to somewhere outside the city?'

Gesar glanced sideways at Ignat. There was something mysterious in his glance: the first name for it that came to mind was 'higher knowledge'.

'Maybe not so stupid,' he objected quietly. 'The Dark One had no choice. Either stay in Moscow and lose the Talon, or clear out and take the Talon with him, and then try to break back in again. What's bad about all this is that the Brothers managed to get the Talon to this Dark One from Ukraine, and he managed to trick us.'

Gesar sighed, closed his eyes for a moment and corrected himself:

'No, not us, of course. It was me he tricked. Me.'

Svetlana was huddling miserably in the corner of the sofa by the window. She started sobbing again.

'I'm sorry, Boris Ignatievich . . .'

So far Anton had been sitting as straight as a ram-rod, but now he moved close to her and put his arm round her shoulders without speaking.

'Don't cry, Svetlana. It's not your fault. If I couldn't guess what the Dark One was going to do, then you can't possibly be blamed for anything.'

Gesar's voice was cool, but basically neutral. The chief of the Night Watch really didn't have anything to reproach Svetlana with – what had happened was simply beyond the range of her present knowledge and skills.

'There's just one thing I don't understand,' Olga said abruptly. She was sitting on the pouffe between Gesar's desk and the window, smoking nervously. 'If the Dark One's actions couldn't be read in advance at all, doesn't that mean he was acting on intuition? Without planning or thinking anything through in advance?'

'Yes, it does,' Gesar agreed. 'He prefers to create probabilities, rather than choose from the ones that already exist. It's a pretty bold way of doing things, but it has its dangers. Intuition can be deceptive. And that's how we'll get him.'

There was a brief silence; Semyon walked noiselessly across the office and sat on the sofa, a short distance from Anton and Svetlana.

'Actually, there's something else bothering me,' Gesar said darkly, reaching into his pocket and taking out a packet of Pall Mall. He looked at it in surprise, put it back in his pocket and took out a Cuban cigar in a metal tube, a clipper to cut off its tip and a huge table-top ashtray. But he didn't open the cigar. 'Something quite different.'

'The fact that the Dark One had no trouble using the energy of the portal and some of Svetlana's too?' Semyon asked, guessing immediately. 'But that was to be expected.'

'Why was it?' Gesar asked cautiously.

Semyon shrugged.

'It seems to me that he's more powerful than we think. He simply disguises the fact. In principle Ilya and I, and even Garik, can make use of the Dark Ones' power. Under certain circumstances. And with certain consequences for ourselves.'

'But not so brazenly and not so quickly,' Gesar said with a shake of his head. 'Remember Spain. When Avvakum tried to draw power from the Dark portal. Remember how that ended?'

'I remember,' said Semyon, not disconcerted in the least. 'All that means is that our Dark One is significantly more powerful than Avvakum. And nothing else.'

Gesar looked at Semyon for a few seconds, then shook his head and turned his gaze to Svetlana.

'Sveta,' he said in a voice that was noticeably gentler, 'try once again to remember everything that you felt at the time. But don't hurry. And please, don't get upset. You did everything right, the trouble is it just turned out not to be enough.'

Semyon glanced in surprise at Svetlana, with the expression of someone who has missed the most interesting thing.

'What do you mean, try to remember? Create the image and the job's done,' he advised them.

'The image won't materialise,' Gesar growled. 'That's the whole problem. What does materialise is some kind of gibberish, not an image.'

'And have you tried creating a different one?' Semyon asked eagerly. 'An abstract image, not connected with the Dark One?'

'She has,' Gesar answered for Svetlana. 'Any other image is okay, but this one just doesn't work.'

'Hmm,' Semyon muttered. 'Maybe the impressions are too vivid, too oppressive. Remember how I tried for twenty years to re-create the image of the Inferno vortex over the Reichstag when Hitler was speaking. But I just couldn't get it to look real.'

'We're not talking here about trying to get it to look real,' said Gesar. 'There isn't any picture at all. Just a grey blur, as if Svetlana's trying to remember the Twilight world.'

Anton, who still hadn't uttered a single word, glanced hopefully at Sveta.

'Well, then,' she began. 'At first I didn't notice anything at all. When you left to follow the Brother who made a run for it, Boris Ignatievich, I stayed with the portal. Then I noticed that the Dark Ones on the floor had started moving and I fed some power into your Net. The Dark Ones were pressed flat against the floor again; then you came back. And almost immediately – it was like a fainting fit, everything went black, I felt weak . . . And then there's a blank. I came round on the floor when Anton splashed water in my face. The memories are all I have left. And I can't even remember anything properly.' The enchantress bit her lip, as if she was about to burst into tears. Anton looked at her as if he hoped his look alone would be enough to calm her down.

'I don't have a rational explanation,' Ilya put in. 'There's simply nothing to go on – too little data.'

'There's more than enough data,' Gesar snorted. 'But I don't have an explanation either. Not in the sense of a hundred per cent correct explanation. I have a few suspicions of my own, but they need to be checked out. Olga?'

Olga shrugged.

'If you have nothing to say, I won't even try. Either he's a top-flight magician who's never been registered anywhere by anyone, or someone's messing with our heads. For instance, I still can't understand why Zabulon hasn't got involved. You'd think smuggling in the Talon was an operation of the highest importance. But he hasn't raised a finger to help his rabble.'

'That's true,' Gesar drawled thoughtfully, and finally took the cigar out of its tube, looked at it carefully, breathed in the aroma of its tobacco with obvious pleasure and put it away again. 'The Moscow Day Watch might have nothing at all to do with the operation to smuggle in Fáfnir's Talon. The Regin Brothers could easily have been acting on their own initiative. In that case we have absolutely no claim against Zabulon. His rabble appears to have been acting independently. And not all that effectively, either, otherwise they'd never have allowed us to intercept the Brothers.'

'What good are the Brothers to us, boss?' Ignat said in annoyance, getting up. 'If the Dark One from Ukraine really is predestined for the Talon, then the Dark Ones won the fight at the airport.'

'If the Dark One from Ukraine was predestined for the Talon,' Gesar said in a quiet voice, 'we'd all be settling into spending the rest of eternity in the Twilight. Even I wouldn't have been able to save any of you. Not any of you. Is that clear, Ignat?'

'Is that right?' Semyon asked calmly. 'It's that serious?'

'It's exactly right, Semyon. I have only one hope: the Dark One doesn't even understand his own role in all this yet. That's why he's thrashing about like this. Our only chance is to outguess him and take the Talon. And in principle that would balance out the odds.'

'But how can we outguess him?' Ignat persisted. 'Maybe I should try talking to him, convincing him. I'm good at convincing people. If only we can find him.'

'The Dark One won't be able to just sit around doing nothing with the Talon burning his fingers. He's bound to turn up in Moscow.' Gesar stood up and surveyed his subordinates, then rubbed his cheek in a tired gesture. 'That's it. Get some rest. Everybody get some rest.'

He turned to Anton.

'Anton, stay close to Sveta. Stick like glue. And you shouldn't go home – not to your place or hers. Stay here.'

'All right, Boris Ignatievich,' said Anton. He still had his arm round Sveta's shoulders.

Ten minutes later Anton and Sveta were alone in the comfortable duty staff lounge. Anton held out his minidisc player and the earphones to the exhausted enchantress.

'You know,' he said, 'there's this sort of game I play. There's a lot of music on that disc. All sorts. I put it on random, but somehow it always comes up with the right songs. Why don't you give it a go?'

Svetlana smiled faintly and took the earphones.

'Press here.'

She pressed the button. The player blinked its green eye as it span the disc; the laser slid across the tracks and stopped on one.

> I dream of dogs and of wild beasts,
> I dream that animals with eyes like lamps
> Bit into my wings high in the heavens,
> And I fell clumsily, like a fallen angel . . .

'It's Nautilus Pompilius,' said Svetlana, adjusting the earphones slightly. '"Fallen Angel". It's certainly appropriate.'

'You know,' Anton told her emphatically, 'call me superstitious, but I knew it would be Nautilus. I really love that song.'

'Let's listen to it together,' Svetlana suggested, sitting down on the sofa.

'Okay,' Anton agreed, and mentally thanked the person who invented mini-earphones without a headpiece.

> I don't remember the fall, I only remember
> The impact as I struck the cold stones.
> How could I have flown so high and then
> Tumbled down so cruelly, like a fallen angel?

Right back down into the place that we
Had left behind, hoping for a new life.
Right back down into the place from where
We stared avidly up into the blue heavens.
Right down . . .

They sat for a long time with their arms round each other, each with a tiny Nautilus Pompilius singing in one ear. The three of them shared the feelings of bitterness and happiness – the magician, the enchantress and the fallen angel.

'But when I went into the terminal building,' Shagron said, 'there was nobody there. They'd just closed the portal, over near the entrance, just a little to the right, where the baggage hall is. The Light Ones had already moved their HQ out and I could barely sense them, somewhere near the edge of the airport. Either they were getting into their cars or they'd already driven off.'

'What about the Brothers?' Edgar asked.

'Damned if I know what's happened to them. I think one of them got killed. The Light Ones immobilised the Others and took them away with them.'

'What for?' Deniska asked in surprise, even putting down his coffee. 'Why didn't they finish them off on the spot?'

'Come on, they're Light Ones!' said Yura, amazed by the question. 'The Brothers surrendered, so they arrested them. They'll probably hand them over to the Inquisition . . . The sadists. It would have been better just to kill them.'

'I think he got away after all,' said Nikolai, toying idly with his discharged wand. The power it had contained only recently had melted the snow on the airport runway in a few moments and then dried out the ground. 'Well, Yura, what do you think?'

'I can't sense the Talon. It's not in Moscow.'

'But how could he have got away?' said Anna Tikhonovna. She kept pursing her lips, and it made her look like a strict school marm. 'How could he slip through Gesar's fingers? Somehow I can't believe it.'

'I don't know,' Yura snapped, 'but something happened back there.'

'Maybe he could have used a portal?' Edgar asked cautiously.

'A portal?' Yura snorted. 'Can you use a portal?'

'Not easily,' Edgar admitted. 'I don't have the power.'

'And,' Yura said emphatically, jabbing his finger towards the ceiling in a vague gesture, 'apart from that, after the fight on the boulevard our friend looked like a squeezed lemon.'

'But after the fight in the airport it was the Light Ones' enchantress who looked like a squeezed lemon,' Nikolai remarked innocently. 'And don't anyone try to convince me she gave the power away voluntarily.'

'Yes, that's right,' said Shagron, brightening up. 'When you think about it, the energy picture of what happened at Vnukovo looks pretty much like straightforward vampirism. Everything was kind of purple.'

Yura shook his head sceptically.

'I must admit the Ukrainian didn't strike me as capable of that. In order to snatch power from the Light Enchantress right under Gesar's nose, you'd have to be Zabulon at least. And have the right to a first-degree intervention.'

'What have rights got to do with it?' Anna Tikhonovna exploded. 'During the last twenty-four hours we've registered three gross violations of the Treaty by the Light Ones, including one violent attack using power! The Light Ones have forgotten what rights mean!'

'Anna Tikhonovna,' Edgar said with feeling, 'the Inquisition has given the Light Ones another indulgence. As long as their actions are directed to returning the stolen artefact, the Treaty is suspended. Until Fáfnir's Talon is handed over to the Inquisition, the Night Watch has the right to do whatever it likes. In effect, we're at war. Like in forty-nine — you should remember that.'

The silence in the room was like outer space.

'And you didn't say anything?' Anna Tikhonovna asked reproachfully.

'What's the point of making our young people nervous? I'm sorry, Deniska. We're already at a disadvantage as it is. First — the chief isn't here, and second — we've just had two pretty unsuccessful years. How many times have we been forced to give way to the Light Ones during those two years? Five, ten?'

'So we're trying to avoid defeatist attitudes, are we?' Yura enquired acidly. 'Keeping things quiet? Protecting young people from pernicious influences? Well, well.'

'What's the point of just saying "well, well"?' Edgar snarled. 'Why don't you try suggesting where we go from here?'

'The chief left you in charge,' Yura said indifferently. 'So you do the thinking.'

'You and Kolya refused, that's why he appointed me,' said Edgar, turning glum and sulky. 'Some fighters you are.'

'Hey, boys, just shut it, will you!' said Anna Tikhonovna, turning scarlet with indignation. 'This isn't the right time! Even my witches work together better than this!'

'Okay, let's forget it,' said Yura with a wave of his hand. 'You're asking me what we do now? Nothing. The Ukrainian can't go too far out of Moscow. I think he has the Talon with him. If he hasn't done anything yet, it means the time still hasn't come. We wait until he comes back. He has to come back — the Talon has to be in Moscow within the next two days. Otherwise the probability peak will have passed, and it will just be a powerful artefact, nothing more.'

Nikolai nodded approvingly.

Edgar looked closely at them, first at one magician, then the other.

'Then we wait,' he sighed. And he added: 'Yes. Our Ukrainian friend has turned out to be cunning, all right. More cunning than Gesar.'

'Ne kazhi gop,' Kolya advised him. 'That's Ukrainian for "don't count your chickens".'

'Anna Tikhonovna,' Shagron asked rather ingratiatingly. 'Tell the girls to make some coffee. After all this, I feel like I can hardly move.'

'You're a lazybones, Shagron,' said Anna Tikhonovna with a shake of her head. 'But all right, I'll be nice to you, since you distinguished yourself. You'll be an example for the Others.'

Shagron grinned happily.

To my surprise, it was warm in the tent all night long. Of course, we slept without getting undressed – I just took off my jacket and my shoes and climbed into the sleeping bag I was offered. The tent belonged to the bearded Matvei, and it could have held three or even four people if necessary. But there were just the two of us. The next tent was about twenty metres away. As soon as everyone had wandered away from the campfire, I could hear the birthday girl moaning sweetly in it, wrapped in someone's tight embrace – so we weren't the only ones who were warm. It was strange. As a southerner, I'd always thought it was cold and miserable in the forest in winter.

I'd been wrong. Maybe it was cold and miserable in the forest, but man can bring his own warmth and comfort with him wherever he goes. Of course, nature has to suffer a little as a result, but that's a different matter. A different matter altogether.

Matvei woke up first. He crawled out of his sleeping bag,

stopped at the opening for a minute as he fiddled with his stylish mountain boots (far superior to my clumsy, thick-soled shoes), unlaced the flap and went outside. A breath of frost immediately licked at my face. And at the same time I felt against my chest the long object that the Vikings had passed on to me at the airport. I hadn't taken a proper look at it since then — there hadn't been any opportunity.

And I also realised that overnight the cocoon, which hadn't been fed any further energy, had melted away. I could feel a breath of power from the object. Or rather, not power, but POWER. If there had been even one Other there, he couldn't have helped but sense the Talon.

I pulled the long, curved object — a case? — out from under my sweater. It looked like a scabbard for a dagger, but it opened like a bivalve seashell. That is, of course, if there are any shells like that in the sea — thirty or thirty-five centimetres long, and narrow.

The case was locked in the Twilight, so no ordinary person could possibly have opened it. Screwing up my eyes, I moved closer to the entrance of the tent and threw the flap partly back so that there was more light.

Inside, lying on dark-red velvet, there really was a blackish-blue talon from some huge beast. It looked as sharp as a Circassian dagger — on its curved inner surface. It had a long groove that looked as though it was for draining blood stretching along its entire length. The wide end looked as if it had been roughly broken off, as if the talon had been hacked away from the foot very crudely, without ceremony. And I supposed it probably had been.

But then, what kind of beast could have had talons like this? It would have to be some legendary dragon. What else could it be? But did dragons ever really exist? I rummaged through my memory, trying to find an answer to this question, and shook my head doubtfully. Witches and vampires were one thing – they were just Others – but dragons . . .

The snow squeaked under Matvei's feet as he walked back from the stream. With a sigh, I slipped into the Twilight for a moment, closed the case and stuck it back under my sweater.

'Awake already?' Matvei asked as he came closer.

'Uhuh.'

'You weren't cold, then?'

'No. It's incredible. I thought in the middle of winter, in the forest, I was bound to feel cold. But it was warm.'

'You southerners are funny people,' Matvei laughed. 'You think this is a real frost? In Siberia they have real frosts. You know what they say? A Siberian isn't someone who doesn't feel the cold, he's someone who's warmly dressed.'

I laughed. It was well put. I ought to remember that.

Matvei smiled into his beard too.

'There's a stream over there. You can have a wash.'

'Uhuh.' I clambered out of the tent and walked to the frozen stream. At the point where the path reached the low bank, someone had broken a neat hole in the ice: overnight the hole had frozen over with a thin, almost transparent layer of ice, but Matvei had broken it open again. The water was cold, but not cold enough to make even my warmth-loving soul afraid of splashing a few handfuls onto my face. The water invigorated me, and I immediately felt I wanted to do something, run somewhere.

Or perhaps it wasn't the water at all. The day before I'd almost completely drained myself, the airport. And I'd felt exactly the way you'd expect. I'd grabbed some power from the portal and a little from the enchantress, and then expended almost all of it again. But overnight I'd apparently been drawing power from the Talon.

Its power was the right kind, Dark power. I hadn't really liked using the Light Ones' power – it was alien, hard to control. But the Talon's power was like mother's milk to an infant. It even seemed to breathe in a mysterious way that was almost painfully familiar.

I felt as if I could overturn mountains.

'When are you planning to break camp?' I asked when I got back to the tent. Or rather, not to the tent, but the campfire. Matvei was chopping firewood. The two dogs were circling round him, gazing hungrily up at the pot hanging over the fire.

'When everyone wakes up, we'll warm up the pilaff, take another shot of vodka to warm ourselves up and then we'll move on. Why? Are you in a hurry?'

'I probably ought to get going soon,' I said vaguely.

'Well, if you're in a hurry, go. Keep the jacket. I'll give you Styopa's address, you can take it round sometime.'

If only you knew who you're helping, human.

'Matvei,' I said in a low voice. 'I seriously doubt that I'll have a chance to go looking for Styopa. Thanks, but I won't freeze.'

'Don't be silly,' said Matvei, straightening up and holding the axe out in his hand. 'If you don't give it back, you don't. Your health's more important.'

I tried to make my smile look wise and sad.

'Matvei, it's a good thing there's nobody else here. You know, I'm not actually human.'

Matvei's eyes immediately glazed over in boredom. He'd probably decided I was some kind of crazy psychic charlatan. Well, I'd just have to prove it to him.

Both dogs instantly lost their joyful bounce, started to whine and huddled down at Matvei's feet. I raised my barely visible morning shadow from the snow and slipped into the Twilight.

Matvei's reaction was funny to watch – he was so startled he dropped his axe. It landed on the Newfoundland's paw and the poor dog yelped deafeningly.

Matvei couldn't see me. But he wasn't supposed to see me.

I pulled off the jacket; Matvei wouldn't be able to see it either, until I threw it out of the Twilight. I felt for some money in my shirt pocket and stuck two hundred-dollar bills in the pocket of the jacket. Then I tossed it at Matvei.

Matvei shuddered and caught the jacket awkwardly when, as far as he could tell, it suddenly appeared out of thin air. He glanced around and, to be quite honest, he looked rather pitiful, but I could tell that without this kind of demonstration there was no way I could ever convince him.

I didn't want to take anything belonging to anyone else away with me, not even a lousy jacket. If people ask no questions and help a stranger who comes wandering up to their campfire out of the forest, you shouldn't take anything from them if you can avoid it. The jacket was comfortable and obviously not cheap. I didn't want it. I'm a Dark One. I don't need other people's things.

I emerged from the Twilight behind Matvei's back. He carried on staring wildly into empty space.

'Here I am,' I said, and Matvei swung round abruptly. His eyes were completely crazy now.

'A-a-a-a,' he murmured and fell silent.

'Thanks, I really will get by without the jacket.'

Matvei nodded. He obviously didn't feel like objecting any more. I think he was seriously concerned that he'd spent the night in a tent with some kind of monster who could disappear in front of his eyes. And who knew what he might be capable of beyond that?

'Just tell me one thing: how do I get out of here?'

'That way,' said Matvei, waving his hand in the direction of the path I'd followed to get there. 'The trains are already running.'

'And is there a main road over there? I'd rather hitch.'

'There's a main road. Right behind the railway.'

'Excellent,' I said, pleased. 'Okay, be seeing you! Thanks again.

Give the birthday girl my congratulations . . . and I tell you what, give her this.'

It was remarkable how easily I managed the simple but unfamiliar spell. I put my hand behind my back, touched a frozen twig, broke it off . . . and held out a living rose, only just cut from the bush. There were drops of dew glistening on the small green leaves and the petals were flame-red. A fresh rose looks very beautiful in a snowy forest.

'A-a-a,' Matvei mumbled as he automatically took the rose. I wondered if he'd give it to the birthday girl or just bury it in a snowdrift to avoid the hassle of long, awkward explanations.

But I didn't ask. I withdrew into the Twilight again. I certainly didn't want to drag myself over the frozen snow again. And what had been good for the previous day, when I thought I was running away from Gesar, was no good today, when I was rested and full of fresh power.

There was something else I'd forgotten . . . Ah, yes, the hat. That wasn't mine either, and I was still wearing it. I tossed it onto the jacket, and set off.

I moved in leaps of a hundred or two hundred metres, opening weak little portals at the limit of my visibility and stepping through them, eating up the distance like a giant.

By day the cutting looked perfectly ordinary, all of its magical charm had completely disappeared. It was obviously no accident that the genuine romantics and lovers of freedom – the Dark Ones – had chosen the night as their time, and not the day, when all the dirt and rubbish of the world assaults your eyes, when you can see how unattractive and cluttered our cities are, when the streets are full of stupid people and the roads are full of stinking cars. Day is the time of bonds and chains, of duty and rules, but night is the time of freedom.

And for a genuine Other, nothing can take the place of that freedom. Neither ephemeral duty, nor service to cheap, fuzzy ideals invented by someone else long before you were even born. That's all a myth, a fiction, 'ucho od sledzia' as our Slav brothers the Poles say. There is only freedom, for everyone alike, and there is only one limitation: no one has the right to limit the freedom of others. And let the cunning and hypocritical Light Ones seek apparent paradoxes and contradictions in this – everyone who is free gets along just fine with others who are just as free, and they don't get in each other's way at all.

I had to use my Other powers to stop a car – for some reason no one wanted to pick up a man without jacket or coat. I had to touch the mind of a driver in his dolled-up Zhiguli 9 the colour of 'wet tarmac'.

Naturally, he stopped.

The driver was a young guy of about twenty-five with cropped hair and absolutely no neck. His head was simply attached, in a very natural way, directly to his body, and his eyes were blank. But his reflexes turned out to be quite fantastic. I seriously suspected that he could have driven the car even if he was unconscious.

'Eh?' he said to me when I'd made myself comfortable in the back, beside his huge leather jacket.

'Straight on, straight on. To Moscow. You'll let me out on Tverskaya Street.'

And I touched him gently, again through the Twilight.

'Ah,' the young guy said, and got his Zhiguli moving. Despite the slippery road and the trance he'd been put in, he drove at over a hundred kilometres an hour. The car held the road so superbly, I wondered if he had special tyres on it.

We drove into Moscow from the north-west after turning onto the Volokolamsk Highway, which meant we sliced through half of the megalopolis very quickly, driving in a straight line almost the entire time. Straight to the Day Watch office on Tverskaya Street.

I was lucky to have found such a remarkable driver, and the

Highway encouraged him to put his foot down. And on top of that, we rode a wave of green lights.

As we were driving past the Sokol metro station, I realised they'd spotted me.

Me and the Talon.

But in the middle of Moscow it's almost impossible to catch a Zhiguli 9 hurtling along in a straight line without changing lanes.

I got out on Tverskaya Street and handed the neckless driver a hundred. Roubles, not dollars.

'Eh?' he gasped and started gazing around. Of course, he didn't remember a thing and now he was straining his meagre intellect to solve the almost insoluble puzzle of how he'd got from a suburban Moscow motorway to the very centre of the city.

I didn't interfere and left him alone with his unsolved mystery.

He had really first-rate reflexes: the Zhiguli set off almost immediately. But the young guy's face was turned towards the side window, his jaw hanging open. It was still like that as he drove out of sight. I crossed the street and headed for the entrance.

The lobby was full of cigarette smoke and a tape-deck – a Phillips 'boom-box' – was quietly playing some song with a laid-back, powerful melody. The voice was so hoarse and low I didn't realise at first that it was Butusov:

> The wind is cold through the open window,
> And long shadows lie on the table,
> I am a mysterious guest in a silver cloak,
> And you know why I have come to you.
> To give you strength,
> To give you power,
> To kiss your neck,
> Kiss to my heart's content!

The young vampire was blissfully mouthing the words of the song with his eyes half-closed. At the sight of me he was struck dumb. But the other guard on duty, an equally young alchemist-magician, was already gabbling into the phone.

'They're waiting for you,' he told me. 'Ninth floor.'

Even though he was dumbstruck, the vampire had managed to call the lift.

But I suddenly got the feeling I shouldn't get in, and I certainly shouldn't go up in it. I just shouldn't, and that was all.

'Tell them I'm alive and everything's okay,' said that something inside me.

I went back out onto the street.

I was being guided again. Without the slightest hesitation I turned left – towards Red Square.

I still didn't know what was leading me there and what for. But I could only obey the power inside me. And I could also feel that Fáfnir's Talon had come to life, it was breathing.

Every metre of ground here, every square centimetre of tarmac, was saturated with magic. Old magic that had eaten its way into the stone of the buildings and the dust on the street.

The massive shape of the Historical Museum towered up on my right. I didn't even know if it was still open or whether it had been transformed into a casino by the latest sea change in the history of long-suffering Russia. But in any case, I had no time to find out. I walked on.

The cobblestones of Red Square, which remembered the leisurely paces of the tsars, the tramping boots of revolutionary soldiers, the caterpillar tracks of Soviet armoured monsters and the columns of May Day demonstrations, seemed to embody Moscow's unshakeable permanence. The city had stood here through the ages, it would always stand here, and nothing – not the squabbles of ordinary human beings, or even the eternal altercations between the Watches – could shake its calm grandeur.

I walked out into the square and looked around. On my left GUM – the old State Department Store – was teeming with life. On my right were the battlements of the Kremlin wall, with the pyramid of Lenin's Mausoleum rising up in front of it. Could that be where I was being led?

No, not there. And that was good. No matter what people in Russia felt about their former leader, it was a sin to disturb the peace of the dead. Especially of those who had died irrevocably, for ever – he wasn't an Other . . . and it was a good thing he wasn't.

I walked across the square without hurrying. A line of official government cars snaked out of the Kremlin and tore off into the side streets. The Execution Site greeted me in silence. Citizen Minin and Prince Pozharsky watched as I walked by. The bright-painted domes of St Basil's Cathedral breathed a sigh.

Power. Power. Power . . .

There was so much of it here that an Other who had exhausted himself could restore his strength in moments.

But nobody would ever do anything of the kind. Because it was strange, alien power. It belonged to no one. It was unruly and uncontrollable, the power of the past centuries. The power of dethroned tsars and general secretaries of the Communist Party. Touch it and it would blow you to pieces.

I looked around again.

And I spotted him.

The Inquisitor.

It's impossible to confuse an Inquisitor with anyone else, either a Light One or a Dark One, let alone an ordinary human being.

The Inquisitor was looking straight at me and I couldn't understand why I'd only just noticed him now.

He was alone, completely alone, outside and above any worldly balance of power, alliances and treaties. He embodied Justice and the Inquisition. He maintained equilibrium. I didn't need to ask what he was there for.

I walked up to him.

'You did right not to disobey,' said the Inquisitor.

Somehow I knew his name was Maxim.

He reached out his hand and said:

'The Talon.'

There was nothing imperious about his tone, not even a hint of pressure. But I had no doubt that anyone would obey that voice, up to and including the chief of either of the Watches.

I reached gloomily inside my sweater, with obvious regret.

The Talon was seething, processing the surrounding power. The moment I held it in my hand I was swamped by a dense wave of it. The power given to me by the Talon rushed into every cell of my body, it felt as if the whole world was ready to go down on its knees and submit to me. To me. The possessor of Fáfnir's Talon.

'The Talon,' the Inquisitor repeated.

He didn't add anything more or tell me not to do anything stupid. The Inquisition is above giving meaningless advice.

But I still hesitated. How was it possible to give up a source of such inexhaustible power voluntarily? An artefact like that was every Other's dream.

I automatically noted the redistribution of energy as a Light portal opened up nearby. Of course, it was Gesar, the chief of the Moscow Night Watch.

The Inquisitor didn't react to the appearance of the unexpected witness. Not at all. As if no portal had opened up and no one had surfaced out of the Twilight.

'The Talon,' the Inquisitor said for the third time. The third and last. He wouldn't say another word. I knew that.

And I also knew that even if all the Dark Ones of Moscow appeared beside me, it wasn't worth trying anything. They wouldn't help me. On the contrary, they'd take the Inquisitor's side. The intrigues played out around the Talon could only continue until the guardians of the Treaty put in a personal appearance.

I squeezed my eyes shut and drew in as much power as I could hold within myself, almost choking on the pressure; with a trembling hand, I held out the case holding the artefact to the Inquisitor. As I did so, I could just sense the amorphous desire that Gesar was struggling to control – to dart forward and take possession of the Talon. But naturally, the chief of the Night Watch didn't move a muscle. Experience is primarily the ability to restrain our fleeting impulses.

The Inquisitor glanced at me. I probably ought to have been able to read satisfaction and approval in his glance: well done, Dark One, you didn't flinch, you did as you were told, clever boy.

But I couldn't see anything of the kind in the Inquisitor's eyes. Not a thing.

Gesar was gazing at us with open curiosity.

Without any hurry, the Inquisitor put the case into the inside pocket of his jacket and then disappeared into the Twilight without even saying goodbye. I stopped sensing him instantly. Instantly. The Inquisition has its own paths.

'Ha,' said Gesar, looking away to one side. 'You're a fool, Dark One.'

Then he looked straight at me, sighed and added:

'A fool, but clever. And that's remarkable.'

Then he left too, quietly this time, without using a portal. I could still sense him for some time in the deeper layers of the Twilight.

And I was left on Red Square, out in the piercing wind, alone, without the Talon after I'd already got used to its power, with no warm clothes, still wearing the same sweater, trousers and shoes, and my hair was as tousled as a film actor's in some dramatic solo scene. Only there weren't any viewers to appreciate this fine shot, now that Gesar also had gone on his way.

'You really are a fool, Vitaly Rogoza,' I whispered. 'A clever and obedient fool. But then, maybe that's the only reason you're still alive?'

But the person inside me suddenly came to life and reassured me: 'Everything's happening as it should. You did the right thing by getting rid of Fáfnir's Talon.' I was so overwhelmed by such a blissful, unshakeable certainty that I was right, that I even stopped feeling the cold, piercing wind.

Everything was just fine. Everything was right. Children shouldn't play with atom bombs.

I twitched my shoulders, turned round and strode off in the direction of Tverskaya Street.

I'd only gone a few steps when I came across the entire senior grade of the Day Watch (apart from the magician Kolya and – naturally – the chief), plus about fifteen mid-grade agents, including Anna Tikhonovna's young witches, three vampire brothers and a rather tubby werewolf. The entire company was staring at me like bystanders idly gaping at a penguin that has escaped from the zoo.

'Hi,' I said in a surprisingly cheerful voice. 'What are you all doing here, eh?' I'm getting carried away again, I thought miserably. Oh-oh . . .

'Tell me, Vitaly,' Edgar asked in an odd, unnatural voice, 'why did you do that?'

His attention was distracted for a second as he diverted an over-vigilant militiaman all set to approach a gathering that he thought looked suspicious. Then he gazed back at me:

'Why?'

'Do the Dark Ones really want a needless fight? Do they want needless casualties?' I said, answering a question with a question, like some joker from Odessa.

'I think he's lying,' Anna Tikhonovna said aggressively. 'Maybe we should probe him.'

Edgar frowned darkly. As if to say: How can we probe him?

So they were already afraid of me in the Day Watch. Would you believe it?

'Anna Tikhonovna,' I said, addressing the old witch sincerely, 'Fáfnir's Talon is an incredibly powerful destabilising force, capable of disrupting the balance of power like nothing else. If it had remained in Moscow, a bloody battle would have been inevitable. As a law-abiding Other, I accepted the Inquisition's verdict and returned the Talon. That's all I have to say.'

I was keeping quiet for the time being about the power that had settled in me after my contact with the Talon. Until the right time.

'Surely you wouldn't have done anything else?' I added, realising that no one would dare object to that. All of them had wanted to touch the artefact . . . to draw power from it.

And all of them had been afraid of the consequences of doing so.

'Why don't we go back to the office?' the magician Yura growled. 'Instead of standing around in the wind like the three poplars on Plushchikha Street in that old film.'

That made sense – I was beginning to shiver again, and it would have been unforgivably stupid to waste the power that I'd stored up.

With Edgar's support, Yura called up an economical portal, and two minutes later the entire Watch had divided into groups and taken the lift up to the office. I couldn't help remarking that my portal would have been more stable and would have worked for longer. Apparently I'd taken another step up the stairway to nowhere when I parted with Fáfnir's Talon. And apparently I was now more powerful than everyone else there, all of them together. But I was still as inexperienced and naïve as ever, and I still had to learn the most important thing of all – how to use my power appropriately.

The technicians, led by the unsleeping Hellemar, were hard at work on their HQ laptops. When on earth did these young guys ever rest? Or was it just that they all looked alike?

'What's going on, Hellemar?' Edgar asked.

'The Light Ones are withdrawing their outposts,' the werewolf reported cheerfully. 'One after another. Not just changing them, but removing them completely. And they've lifted the cordons at the entrances to the city and the railway stations.'

'They've calmed down,' sighed Anna Tikhonovna.

'Of course they've calmed down,' Yura snapped. 'The Talon's gone now. They've probably already transferred it to Berne. In fact I'd bet on it.'

He was right. A few seconds earlier I'd sensed the source of my power suddenly disappear into the Twilight and move somewhere far, far away. I wondered if I was fated ever to hold it in my hands again, just one more time . . . I had no idea.

'For the life of me, I don't understand why all this fuss over the Talon started in the first place. What were the Regin Brothers trying to achieve? Why didn't they let us know what they were doing? It's all some crazy nonsense, absolute nonsense.'

'And what makes you so sure the Regin Brothers didn't achieve their goal?' I asked innocently.

They looked at me as if I was a child who'd asked an awkward question in adult company.

'You have a different opinion?' Yura enquired cautiously, exchanging a quick glance with Edgar.

'Yes,' I said honestly. 'Only don't ask me about the details – I don't know them anyway. There was a serious imbalance of power developing in Moscow in the Light Ones' favour. So serious that all Europe was beginning to feel concerned. Measures were taken. The Regin Brothers' escapade is one piece of a jigsaw that will eventually add up to a new equilibrium.'

'And your appearance is another piece of the jigsaw?' Edgar surmised.

'Obviously.'

'And Zabulon's absence from Moscow?'

'Probably.'

The Dark Ones looked at each other, wondering.

'I don't know about that,' Anna Tikhonovna drawled, displeased. 'It all looks pretty strange. If we had the Talon, we'd soon have the Light Ones in a tight corner.'

'But would we be able to keep it under control?' Yura remarked.

'I don't know.'

'In any case,' said Edgar, after thinking for a while, 'we still have the right to demand satisfaction from the Light Ones. There were several serious interventions committed. What they've done over the last two days goes way beyond the recent killings. Tiunnikov's death should really be classed as an accident, and if Gesar tries to dispute that, the Tribunal will soon demolish his case. And the vampire poacher and the shape-shifting whore aren't such very serious violations, only sixth-level, or fifth at most. They were acting independently, the Day Watch had nothing to do with it. Now we have the right to demand several second-degree interventions at least. That's what I think. So all in all the Day Watch has still come out on top from everything that's happened. Even without the chief and his powers.'

'Better hold the fanfares for a while,' Yura remarked sceptically. 'Wait and see.'

Edgar shrugged and spread his arms in the gesture of a man

sticking to his guns. He really believed what he'd just said. And he had a point.

There's no way of knowing how the argument would have ended. The mobile on Edgar's belt trilled and everyone automatically turned towards him.

It could have been a private call, or a call from the technical section. But the Others gathered in the office were pretty powerful. Almost all of them were capable of calculating probabilities and the consequences of simple events.

This call had a dense central thread that was clearly visible. A thread connecting it to events of the greatest importance.

Edgar put the phone to his ear and listened for a while.

'Show him through,' he said, then ended the call and put the mobile back on his belt. 'An Inquisitor,' he said with a stony expression. 'With an official announcement.'

Less than thirty seconds later the warlock from the duty watch opened the door to the Day Watch main office. And a second after that the impassive Inquisitor called Maxim strode in through the doorway.

'In the name of the Treaty,' he declared – there was absolutely no emotion or colour in his voice, his tone was strictly neutral. And it would have been foolish to suspect an Inquisitor of sympathising with one side or the other – 'tomorrow at dawn there will be an extended session of the local board of the Tribunal, under the patronage of the Inquisition. The subject is a number of actions taken by Light Others and a number of actions taken by Dark Others that are incompatible with the stipulations of the Treaty. Attendance is compulsory for all who have been informed. If anyone who has been informed fails to attend or arrives late, it will be regarded as an act incompatible with the stipulations of the Treaty. Until the session begins all magical interventions at the fifth level of power and above are prohibited. May equilibrium triumph.'

When finishing this pronouncement, the Inquisitor turned unhurriedly and walked out to the lifts in the lobby.

The warlock cast a fleeting glance at his superiors and closed the door behind him. He obviously regarded it as his duty to show the Inquisitor out.

The office was quiet for a while, even the technicians and their laptops had fallen silent.

'Just like in forty-nine,' Anna Tikhonovna remarked quietly. 'Exactly the same.'

'Let's hope so,' the magician Yura said in a low voice. 'Let's hope so, Anna Tikhonovna. Let's hope very hard.'

# CHAPTER 5

EVERYBODY GETS the feeling sometimes that what is happening just at the moment has already happened before. There's even a special term for it, *déjà vu*, a kind of false memory.

Others have it too.

Night Watch agent Anton Gorodetsky was standing in front of the door of his apartment and struggling with his memories. He had hovered in front of this open door in exactly the same way before, wondering who could have got inside. And when he went inside that time, he'd discovered that his uninvited guest was his sworn enemy, the chief of the Day Watch, known to the Light Ones as Zabulon.

'Déjà vu,' Anton whispered and stepped inside the door. The defence system again remained silent, but there was definitely a visitor in the room. Who was it this time?

Anton squeezed his talismanic medallion tight in his hand as he entered the room.

Zabulon was sitting in an armchair and reading the newspaper *Arguments and Facts*. Wearing a severe black suit, a light-grey shirt and black shoes with blunt, square toes, polished so that they shone like mirrors. He took off his glasses and greeted Anton.

'Hello, Anton.'

'Déjà vu,' Anton muttered. 'Well, hello.'

Strangely enough, this time he wasn't scared of Zabulon at all. Maybe that was because the last time Zabulon had conducted his surprise visit in an entirely correct manner.

'You can take my amulet. It's in the desk – I can sense it.'

Anton let go of the talisman hanging round his neck, took off his jacket and went across to the desk. Zabulon's amulet was hidden in among some papers and all the other office clutter that always seems to appear out of nowhere with fatal inevitability.

'Zabulon, you have no power over me,' Anton declared in a voice that didn't sound like his own.

The Dark Magician nodded in satisfaction.

'Excellent. Allow me to compliment you. That other time you were trembling like a dry leaf. But today you're calm. You're growing, Anton.'

'I suppose I ought to thank you for the compliment?' Anton asked coolly.

Zabulon threw back his head and laughed soundlessly.

'All right,' he said a few seconds later. 'I see you're in no mood to waste time. Well, neither am I. I came to offer you the chance to commit an act of betrayal. A small, calculated act of betrayal from which everyone will benefit, including you. Sounds paradoxical, doesn't it?'

'It does.'

Anton looked into Zabulon's grey eyes, trying to understand what trap he'd fallen into this time. Trust a human being halfway and a Light One a quarter of the way, but don't trust a Dark One at all.

Zabulon was the most powerful, and therefore the most dangerous, Dark One in Moscow. And probably in the whole of Russia.

'Let me explain,' said Zabulon, unhurriedly, but without hesitation as well. 'You already know about tomorrow's session of the Tribunal, do you not?'

'I do.'

'Don't go to it.'

Anton finally decided to sit down – on the sofa by the wall. Now Zabulon was on his right.

'And for what particular reason?' Anton inquired.

'If you don't go, you and Svetlana will stay together. If you go, you'll lose her.'

Anton felt a sudden burning sensation in his chest. It wasn't a question of whether he believed Zabulon or not. He wanted to believe him. He wanted to very much.

But he couldn't forget that Dark Ones can't be trusted.

'The leadership of the Night Watch is planning yet another global social experiment. You must know that. And Svetlana has been assigned a rather important role in this project. I shan't try to change your convictions or win you over to the Dark – that's an entirely hopeless proposition. I shall simply tell you what the danger of realising such an experiment is: the disruption of the balance of forces. Obviously a rather desirable thing for the side that grows stronger. In recent times the Light has been growing stronger and, naturally, I don't like it. It is in the Day Watch's interest to restore the equilibrium. And you are the one who can help us.'

'Strange,' Anton said thoughtfully. 'The head of the Day Watch asking for help from a Night Watch agent. Very strange.'

'Well, your help isn't absolutely necessary to us. We could manage on our own. But if you help yourself in the first instance, then you will also help us. And Svetlana, and everyone else who will inevitably suffer from the next global experiment.'

'I don't understand, how can I help myself and Svetlana?'

'What don't you understand? Svetlana is potentially a very powerful enchantress. As she grows stronger, so the gulf that separates you grows wider. Her power is the factor that is shifting the balance in the favour of the Light. If Svetlana is deprived of her power for some time, equilibrium will be restored. And there will be nothing to keep you apart, Anton. She loves you – anyone can see that. And you love her. Surely you wouldn't sacrifice your happiness and that of the woman you love to the Light? Especially since the sacrifice is meaningless in any case. That's why I'm proposing you commit this little, perfectly painless act of betrayal.'

'Betrayal is never little.'

'Sometimes it is, Anton. It most certainly is. Loyalty itself is built up from a series of little, calculated acts of betrayal. You can trust me on that – I've lived in this world long enough to be quite sure of it.'

Anton paused for a while before he spoke.

'I'm a Light One. I can't betray the Light. By my very nature I can't do it – and you should understand that.'

'No one's trying to make you go against the Light. And what's more, if you do this, you'll be helping many people. Very many people, Anton. Isn't that the goal of a Light Magician – to help people?'

'And how will I be able to look my colleagues in the eye?' Anton asked with a bitter laugh. 'After that?'

'They'll understand,' Zabulon said with an assurance that seemed strange to Anton. 'They'll understand and they'll forgive. And if they don't – what kind of Light Ones are they after that?'

'You're good with the sophistry, Zabulon. Far better than I am, no doubt. But just calling things by different names doesn't change their essential nature. Betrayal is always betrayal.' .

'All right,' Zabulon agreed with surprising readiness. 'Then betray love. Basically you have a choice between two betrayals, surely you can understand that? To betray yourself or to prevent yet another cycle of bloodshed from happening: to forestall the inevitable battles between the Watches or to allow them to happen. Or haven't there been enough deaths for you yet? You went out on patrol with Andrei Tiunnikov more than once. You were friends with the girl shape-shifter, Tiger Cub. Where are they now? Who else are you willing to sacrifice in the name of the Light? Don't go to the Tribunal session tomorrow, and your friends will stay alive. We don't need any more deaths, Anton. We're willing to avoid conflict. To settle things peacefully. That's why I'm suggesting you should help everybody. Everybody. Dark Ones and Light Ones. And even simple, ordinary people. Do you understand?'

'I don't understand how my absence from the Tribunal session will help restore equilibrium.'

'You've already run into the Dark One from Ukraine, haven't you? Vitaly Rogoza?'

'Yes, I have,' Anton replied reluctantly.

'He's not an Other.'

Anton was startled.

'How do you mean, not an Other?'

'He's not entirely an Other. He's only a Mirror. And he doesn't have long left to live.'

'What – or who – is a Mirror?'

'Definitely "what",' Zabulon said with a sigh. 'Alas, only a "what" . . . That's not important, Anton. It's more useful for you to know something else. If you stay away from the session of the Inquisition, no more blood will be spilled. If you go, a bloodbath is inevitable.'

'Failure to appear at a Tribunal is punished by the Inquisition.'

'The Inquisition will regard your reluctance to engage in combat with Rogoza as legitimate. There have been precedents; if you wish, I can even show you the relevant documents. But you can take my word for it. I've never deceived you yet.'

'I don't like the sound of that "yet".'

Zabulon smiled with just the corner of his mouth.

'That can't be helped. I am a Dark One after all. But I don't happen to think it's useful to lie without any reason.'

Zabulon stood up, and Anton also got to his feet.

'Think, Anton. Think, Light One. And remember: your love and the lives of your friends depend on your decision. That's the way it goes sometimes: in order to help your friends, first you have to help your enemy. Better get used to it.'

Zabulon walked rapidly out of the room, and then out of the apartment. That very instant the sentry sign started howling in the Twilight, and the mask of Chkhoen on the wall pulled a terrifying face. As Anton listlessly tidied up, he tried to gather his thoughts.

Should he believe Zabulon or not?

Should he be with Svetlana or not?

Should he call Gesar and tell him everything or should he keep quiet?

Every conflict, from a simple, crude brawl to high-level intrigues between states and the Watches, is a battle of information. Whoever has the more precise idea of his enemy's strength and aims will win.

Zabulon's aims and Anton's could not be the same. That was absolutely impossible. But what if the head of the Day Watch had told Anton what he had precisely in order to make him reject the very idea of missing the Tribunal?

Where was the truth, and where was the lie? Zabulon's words were a cage, but inside the cage there was a man-trap, and inside the man-trap there was a mousetrap, and inside the mousetrap there was poisoned bait . . . How many layers of falsehood had to be peeled away in order to expose the truth?

Anton took a coin out of his pocket. He tossed it in the air and caught it, then laughed and put it back in his pocket, without even looking to see if it had come up heads or tails.

That wasn't the right way.

If one of the two choices was a trap, then he had to look for a third choice.

In order to get to the Tribunal at dawn, I either had to get up very early, or not go to bed at all. I chose the second option. I could catch up on my sleep later.

My Dark colleagues had grilled me stubbornly for a while, trying to establish my motives, but since I myself didn't understand very much about why I behaved the way I did rather than some other way, they didn't get much out of me.

Nothing really interesting happened until the evening; I went to the shop where they burned minidiscs for my stylish little player and asked if they kept the lists of tracks ordered by their customers. It turned out they did. And for some reason I chose to order a copy of the last disc they'd done for Anton Gorodetsky, the Light Magician. Maybe I was trying to get an idea of his view of the world from his choice of music. I don't know . . . Just recently I'd got out of the habit of asking questions, because most of the time I didn't get any answers. And correct answers were even rarer.

And there was one other thing that stuck in my memory that evening: someone I met in the metro. I was on my way back from the music shop. On the metro. Sitting there with my hands in the pockets of my jacket (my Dark colleagues had kindly brought my things back from the field HQ at the airport) and listening to the disc I'd just bought. I was in a good mood, feeling calm.

The essence of things and the sequence of years,
The faces of friends and the masks of enemies
Are clearly visible, they cannot be concealed
From the sight of the poet – he owns the centuries.
The light of distant stars and the beginning of dawn,
The secrets of life and the mysteries of love
At the moment of inspiration, warmed by the sun,
All is reflected in the poet's soul,
In the mirror of the world . . .

Suddenly there was a subtle change of some kind in my surroundings. The announcer was just warning the unfortunate passengers to be careful, because the doors were closing. I pressed 'pause' and raised my head, glancing around.

And I saw him. A teenage kid, fourteen or fifteen years old. There was no doubt that he was an Other. He must have been initiated, because he was staring at me in fascination through the Twilight and also shielding himself against it pretty skilfully. But his aura was absolutely pristine and clear. As pure as newly fallen snow, halfway between the Light and the Dark. He was an Other, but at the same time he wasn't either Light or Dark.

We looked at each other for a long time, all the way to the next stop. Probably we would have carried on looking at each other for even longer, but a rather attractively built woman, obviously his mother, roused the kid from his trance.

'Egor! Are you asleep? We're getting off.'

The teenager started, looked at me one last time with obvious anguish in his eyes and stepped out onto the platform. I was left behind in the carriage.

It took me about a minute to gather my thoughts. I was still wondering what had struck me so much about this Other. He had reminded me of something. Something very important, but elusive – I just couldn't think what it was.

Then I went back to Nikolsky and his 'Mirror of the World', and that calmed me a little:

> The mirror shows me how a man has lived,
> Who has composed his song out of lies,
> Who wants it to be night everywhere,
> Shows me that I must help people.
> I have the mirror of the world,
> If you want to look – don't fear the fire,
> The fire that I will glorify in song,
> Let people know there is a good power
> In the mirror of the world . . .

Strange. This song would suit the Light Ones better. So why did I, a Dark One, feel that strange ache in my heart?

I carried this vague, uncertain feeling back to the Day Watch office with me. The elderly, worldly wise vampire at the entrance started away from me like a sanctimonious hypocrite from sudden temptation. Shocked, I suddenly realised that there were a few bluish-white streaks glowing in my own aura.

'I'm sorry,' I said, putting my aura in order. 'It's a disguise.'

The vampire gave me a suspicious look: a female vampire stuck her head out of the duty office – she was almost certainly his wife.

They checked my seals very thoroughly and it looked as if they were going to stall me as long as they could, but at this point Edgar came into the office with a pretty young witch. He understood what was happening at a glance, and a single twitch of his eyebrow was enough for the over-vigilant couple on watch. Edgar nodded to me and walked towards the lifts. The witch was devouring me with her eyes.

In the lift she plucked up her courage and asked:

'Are you new here?'

Her voice expressed an entire spectrum of emotions and aspirations that I felt no desire to analyse. Somehow I didn't feel like demonstrating my own power in front of Edgar and the other powerful Dark Ones.

But Edgar's attention had been caught, and I could see he was genuinely interested in how I would answer.

'Well, in a certain sense I'm new.'

The young witch smiled.

'Is it true that you defeated four Light warriors single-handed and killed the tiger-woman?'

Edgar curved his lips very slightly in a sarcastic smile, but he still said nothing, listening with interest.

'Yes.'

The witch had no time to ask any more questions. We'd arrived.

'Alita,' Edgar said in a deep, hollow voice, 'you can pester our guest later. First go and report to Anna Tikhonovna.'

Alita nodded enthusiastically and then turned to me:

'Can I come round and see you for coffee? In about an hour?'

'Yes, okay,' I agreed. 'Only I haven't got any coffee.'

'I'll bring some,' the pretty witch promised. And she set off for the office.

She didn't ask where I was staying. Which meant she already knew.

For a few seconds I watched the witch from behind. Her stylish silver jacket, the kind that mountain skiers and tourists wear (I was immediately reminded of my acquaintances from the forest) was decorated in bright colours, a cartoon of a girl with big eyes and her foot thrust out in a kick, with the caption 'Battle Angel Alita'. The drawing and the caption were partly covered by the witch's long hair, which was hanging down over the jacket.

Edgar also looked as Alita walked away. There was plenty to look at, despite the winter outfit.

'She'll come,' Edgar said thoughtfully. 'She's already asked about you.'

I shrugged.

'The Tribunal's tomorrow,' I said, changing the subject. 'What should I do? Skip it? Go with everyone else?'

'Go with everyone else, of course. You're a witness.' Edgar looked around. 'Would you come into the office for a moment?'

'All right.'

Somehow I was quite sure this office had never been used to run things by the actual head of the Day Watch. It was more likely Edgar's office or the office of one of the other senior Dark Ones. I slumped gratefully into an armchair, noting to myself that it was far more comfortable than the sagging seats on the metro. Edgar took an already opened bottle of cognac out from somewhere under the desk.

'Shall we have a shot?' he suggested.

'Sure.'

Who would want to refuse old Koktebel?

'I'm glad you've come back,' said Edgar, pouring the cognac. 'Otherwise we would have had to go looking for you.'

'In order to agree our tactics and strategy at tomorrow's session of the Tribunal?' I asked, guessing.

'Exactly.'

It was good cognac. Smooth and aromatic. Maybe it wasn't the most famous and prestigious brand (which one is, anyway?), but I really liked it.

'I won't even ask any more why you behave so strangely. To be quite honest, I've been instructed not to. From up there.' Edgar raised his eyes expressively to the ceiling. 'And I'm not going to try to figure out who you really are, either. For the same reason.

All I want to ask is: Are you on our side? Are you with the Day Watch? With the Dark Ones? Can we count on you as one of ours tomorrow?'

'Definitely,' I said, without even pausing for thought. Then I made it even clearer: 'And that's the answer to all your questions.'

'That's good,' Edgar said with a rather weary sigh and drained his balloon glass in one gulp.

I didn't think he believed me.

We finished the cognac in silence. Edgar didn't find it necessary to advise me on how to behave at the following day's session of the Tribunal. He had clearly decided that I'd behave however I wanted to anyway. And he was absolutely right.

I spent the night with Alita. Over coffee – the young witch had even managed to get hold of that long-forgotten brand Casa Grande – we settled down in the armchairs and talked, about everything and nothing. It was a long time since I'd had such a good time, just sitting and chatting. About music, which I turned out to know quite a lot about. And literature, which I knew rather less about. And films, which I knew absolutely nothing about. Every now and then, Alita tried to get me to talk about myself and my powers, but she did this so artlessly that I never even suspected she could have been sent by the vigilant Anna Tikhonovna.

An hour before dawn there was a knock at the door.

'It's open,' I shouted.

Edgar and Anna Tikhonovna came in.

'Are you ready?' Edgar asked.

'Always prepared, like a young pioneer,' I assured him. 'Are we moving out in close formation? In armoured vehicles or in marching order?'

'Don't play the clown,' said Anna Tikhonovna, pursing her lips and giving Alita a severe look. Alita gazed back innocently.

'All right, I won't,' I promised. 'Where are we going? I don't even know.'

In fact, I had no doubt that the reliable internal guide buried somewhere in the depths of my mind would tell me where we were going and which direction to follow. But I asked anyway.

'The main building of Moscow University,' Edgar told me. 'Up in the tower. Shagron's waiting downstairs with his car, you can go with him.'

'Okay. I'll go with him.'

'Good luck,' said Alita, heading for the door. 'I'll call round tomorrow, okay, Vitaly?'

'No,' I said gloomily. 'You won't.'

I knew for certain that I was right. But as yet I didn't understand why.

Alita shrugged and walked away. Anna Tikhonovna slipped out after her. Hmm . . . Maybe the old hag had sent the girl after all? But then she'd decided to do her own thing and not tried to get anything out of me. If I was right, I had to feel sorry for Alita. Anna Tikhonovna would extract her very soul, squeeze it out and hang it up to dry. She'd regret she'd ever been born.

I reached for my mobile and dialled Shagron's number, too fast even to be surprised that I knew it.

'Shagron? This is your guest from the south. Can you give me a lift? Uhuh, I'm on my way.'

'Okay, I'll get going too,' said Edgar. 'Don't hang about. The Inquisition gets very touchy when someone's late.'

I put my coat on, locked my door and went down in the lift. The vampires on watch looked at me a lot more calmly this time – either their immediate superiors had had a quiet word with them, or they'd realised the truth for themselves. But then, what was the truth? It refused to reveal itself even to me. There were only sudden, brief glimpses of one piece of the mosaic when the curtain was raised for an instant only for it to descend again, and that impenetrable, misty shroud to obscure my sight.

Shagron's BMW was snorting out exhaust fumes about twenty metres away, right under the 'No stopping' sign. I got in on Shagron's right:

'Good morning.'

'I hope it's a good one,' Shagron barked. 'Shall we go?'

'Yes, if we're not waiting for anyone else, let's go.'

Shagron slid into the dense stream of traffic without saying another word.

Driving round snow-covered Moscow in the rush-hour is a unique experience. Occasionally Shagron used the Twilight to calm the over-aggressive drivers around us. Otherwise they would have been cutting in front of us, forcing us over into the next lane and squeezing us out of the gaps that suddenly opened up. I put my safety belt on just in case. Shagron muttered something with his teeth clenched. He was probably swearing.

After my sleepless night it was almost impossible for me not to yearn to doze blissfully off, which was just what these top-end German car seats wanted me to do. And if I'd tried listening to music, I'd definitely have been lulled asleep. But I didn't feel like listening to music just then, so I remained in this world, filled with the roar of dozens of engines, the quiet hum of the air-conditioning, the shrill honking of car horns and the swish of dirty-grey slush under our mudguards.

If we'd gone by metro, we would have got there a lot sooner. But as it was, half an hour later we were still crawling along a jam-packed Ostozhenka Street towards Vernadsky Prospect. The traffic jam was getting bigger, sprouting a tail that reached back towards the centre of Moscow.

'Hell's bells,' Shagron hissed angrily. 'We could get stuck in this.'

'Let's open a portal,' I said with a shrug.

Shagron gave me a strange look.

'Vitaly! We're on our way to a session of the Tribunal under the patronage of the Inquisition! Your portal would collapse two kilometres away from where we're going!'

'Ah, yes,' I said lightly. 'That's right. I forgot.'

Actually, I could easily have guessed that for myself. Magical interventions and any use of magic were forbidden while the Tribunal was at work. The alter ego inside me helpfully informed me that there been violations in the past, but only during times of violent upheaval that was the direct cause of the violations themselves.

But then, this was a time of change too. The end of the millennium. A turning point. I remembered how terrified people had been in the summer, as they waited for the eclipse, how badly the earthquake in Turkey had frightened them. But everything had turned out okay, we'd survived.

Only, of course, in surviving we'd become slightly different. All of us, Others and people, especially people.

'Shi-it!' Shagron yelled, jolting me out of my reverie.

I didn't even have time to glance through the windscreen. There was a deafening crash and in the same instant I was thrown forward and my ribs were squeezed together painfully as the safety belt bit into my chest; with a repulsive, shrill squeak, a fat, round cushion sprouted from the driving wheel, and Shagron's face and chest slid up round it until he crashed into where the windscreen met the roof. There was an unpleasant jangling sound outside the car and a fine shower of crumbs of glass shot up in the air, falling silently on the snow, but drumming an irregular tattoo against the bodywork of the cars around us.

Then, to add insult to injury, we were rammed from behind. Someone had run straight into our boot.

For two or three seconds it felt like the launch of a space shuttle, and then I was no longer twisted and tossed about. The blissful moment of dynamic equilibrium.

Shagron slid back down off the steering wheel into his seat, leaving a trail of blood on the balloon. I thought his arm was broken too. The idiot hadn't fastened his belt. How long would he be regenerating now?

All around us there were car horns blaring.

With mixed feelings, I unclasped my belt, pushed the door open and got out onto the road covered in compressed snow and sprinkled with broken glass.

The front of our car had been rammed at a slight angle by a red Niva. The boot had been crumpled so badly it looked as if someone had taken a bite out of it: the front end of a well-cared-for Japanese 'jeep' was stuck into it. Well it had been well-cared-for. In fact, the jeep hadn't suffered all that badly: one headlight on the impact bar was broken, and the bar itself was slightly bent. He'd obviously had enough time to brake.

'You stupid or something, you prick?' someone from the jeep yelled as he charged at me: he seemed to consist of dark glasses, a shaved head, a barrel-like torso squeezed into something crimson and black, and stylish shoes that were size forty-something plus.

His eyes were as pale as the aura of a young infant . . . or of that kid Egor in the metro.

Couldn't he see the Niva that had rammed us?

And then this human barrel's crimson outfit suddenly flared up in a dull-bluish flame, and he squealed like a hog under the knife.

I recognised a transatlantic spell popularly known as 'spider flame'. And then, before I could recover my wits from the attack by the man-in-crimson, someone took me by the collar and swung me round.

If there was one person I hadn't expected to see, it was him. The Light Magician and music-lover, Anton Gorodetsky.

'Who are you?' he whispered furiously. 'Who are you, may the Dark take you? Only don't lie!'

His eyes were even paler than the eyes of the individual from the jeep, who was now furiously dancing a strange kind of jig.

Something seemed to click inside my head. And my lips whispered the words of their own accord:

'The mirror of the world . . .'

'The mirror . . .' the Light One echoed. 'Damn you! Damn everything!'

I felt like replying that curses were the province of the Dark Ones, but I restrained myself. And I was right. Anton's aura was a blaze of crimson and purple. I was certainly more powerful than Gorodetsky . . . but just then he seemed to be supported by some incomprehensible force that was neither Light nor Dark, but no less powerful. And if there had been a duel, I couldn't have told which way it would go.

Anton let go of my jacket collar, swung round and wandered off blindly, squeezing his way between the cars, ignoring the horns and the curses hurled at him through the wound-down windows. Traffic police sirens began howling somewhere quite close. The traffic jam had completely blocked Ostozhenka Street, except for a narrow channel in the oncoming stream of traffic, through which a few lucky drivers were squeezing their cars one by one, swearing and beeping their horns.

I looked at my watch. I had fifteen – no, now it was fourteen minutes left to get to the university. And I knew for sure that I couldn't use any transport magic.

But first things first – how was Shagron?

I walked round the Niva, its door hanging open, and approached the BMW from the driver's side. Shagron was unconscious, but in the first instant of danger his immediate reflex response had been to set up a protective membrane and slip into the Twilight.

And now he was regenerating, like a pupa, and the greedy Twilight could do nothing to him.

He would survive. He'd recover, and fairly quickly too. Most likely in the ambulance, if it could get here through the traffic jam. Shagron was too powerful a magician to be seriously hurt by something as minor as a traffic accident.

All right then, till we meet again, Shagron. I don't think the Inquisition will charge you with anything. It was *force majeure*, after all.

And just then I saw my salvation. A young guy deftly manoeuvring his way along the very edge of the road on a weedy little orange moped. There was someone who didn't have to worry about traffic jams . . .

Of course, it was hardly the season for that kind of transport. But even so.

I slipped into the Twilight.

In the Twilight the moped looked rather like the little humpbacked horse in the fairytale. A small animal with handlebars for horns and one big headlight-eye.

'Get off,' I told the young guy.

He obediently dismounted and stood there.

Leaping over the bonnet of a beige Opel, I took hold of the handlebars. The moped's engine was idling and snorting devotedly.

Okay then, on we go. The young guy was standing there frozen like a dummy on the pavement, clutching the dollars I'd stuffed in his hand. I twisted the accelerator grip towards me and just avoided scraping the polished side of the nearest car as I set off, squeezing my way through the traffic towards the edge of the jam. Towards the Garden Ring Road. It was fairly simple to get the hang of the tiny Honda, even though it was meant for the warm tarmac of Japan and not the icy roads of Moscow. And I managed to manoeuvre between the cars pretty smartly too. But the moped couldn't give me any real speed – thirty kilometres an hour at most. I realised I still wouldn't get there in time. Even if I abandoned the labouring Honda and dived into the nearest metro station – it was still a long way from the University metro to the spire of the central building of the university itself. Of course, I could take over any driver's mind on the way, but what guarantee was there that we'd escape the morning traffic jams? I remembered vaguely that around the university the main roads were immensely wide, but I still wasn't certain. If I rode the Honda further, I would be mobile almost all the way to my destination. But on the other hand, I only had a very general idea of the route. I was no Muscovite, unfortunately. Maybe I should just rely on my inner helper, who had never let me down so far. I could, of course. But what if this was the very moment he chose to let me down? The most critical moment of all? That was the way things usually happened.

I listened for an inner voice. The cold wind lashing my face was full of exhaust fumes. Moscow was breathing carbon monoxide.

My faithful assistant was obviously asleep.

I passed the Garden Ring Road and the Park of Culture metro station. But when I saw the Frunzenskaya station up ahead, I decided to go underground. Time was pressing.

Before I even reached the metro steps, the moped had already been stolen. The motor gave a brief grunt as it started and some quick-thinking thief drove the reliable little Japanese machine away, disappearing into the side streets as quickly as possible. Ah, humanity, humanity . . . The Light Ones take care of you, protect you, cherish you, but you're still the same old trash you always were. Animals with no conscience or compassion. Elbow everyone aside, steal, sell, stuff your belly, and the world can go to hell. It's so disgusting . . .

I simply jumped the turnstiles – in the Twilight, an invisible shadow. I had no time to buy a ticket and stick it in the slot of the magnetic reader. That was okay, the country wouldn't go bankrupt because of me.

I slid down the escalator too, without leaving the Twilight. Jumped up onto the slow-moving handrail and went hurtling downward, barely managing to set one foot in front of the other in the grey stickiness. A train was just about to leave the platform; while I was still working out whether it was going in the right direction, the doors closed. Never mind, that wasn't a problem. But travelling back into the city centre certainly wasn't what I wanted.

I jumped into the carriage straight through the closed door – in the Twilight. Then gently moved aside the astonished passengers as I seemed to appear out of nowhere.

'Oh!' someone exclaimed.

'Tell me, is this Moscow?' I blurted out for some reason. Probably out of a boisterous sense of sheer silly mischief.

No one answered. Well, all right. At least now there was noticeably more space around me. I took hold of the handrail and closed my eyes.

Sportivnaya station, Sparrow Hills station, still closed – the train was barely crawling along; every now and then, in the cracks between the metal doors, I caught glimpses of electric light and the grey half-light of early morning. Dawn already . . .

Finally, here was the University station. The escalator, very long and very crowded. I had to wait again. That was it. I was definitely late.

Up at the top it was almost light. Finally realising that I wouldn't get there before the beginning of the session, I suddenly felt completely calm and stopped hurrying. Completely. I took the headphones out of my pocket, switched on the player with Anton Gorodetsky's disc in it and walked off to stop a car.

*         *         *

'It's time,' the Inquisitor announced quietly. 'All those who have not arrived on time will answer for it later, in strict accordance with the terms of the Treaty.'

Everyone present got to their feet. Dark Ones and Light Ones alike. The members of the Watches and the judges. Gesar and Zabulon, who everyone had thought was away from Moscow. The Inquisitor Maxim and the Inquisitors who were there as observers, shrouded in their long loose grey robes. Everyone who had gathered in the turret of the main building of Moscow University. The small, five-sided chamber of the invisible Twilight storey stood on top of the agricultural museum and was used exclusively for holding the infrequent sessions of the Inquisition's Tribunal. In the post-war years it had been quite common to include Twilight structures in buildings – it was cheaper than putting up with the constant opposition from the state security forces and militia, who were always sticking their noses into other people's business. There was an excellent view of the scarlet glow of dawn creeping out from behind the horizon and the incredible shimmering streaks of light that had been dancing above the university building, slowly fading, ever since Jean-Michel Jarre's concert for Moscow's anniversary celebrations. The Others would be able to see the traces of that laser show for a long time yet, even without entering the Twilight, where colours fade and disappear. Huge numbers of people had gazed in rapture at the colourful show, pouring their emotions into the Twilight.

Maxim, wearing an ordinary business suit, not the loose robes of the other Inquisitors, waved his hand, unfurling in the Twilight a grey canvas covered with letters of red flame. Thirty voices began chanting together:

'We are the Others. We serve different powers. But in the Twilight there is no difference between the absence of Dark and the absence of Light . . .'

The immense city and the entire vast country were unaware that almost everyone who decided the fate of Russia was gathered here now, and not in the Kremlin. In a neglected, crowded chamber under the very spire of the Moscow University building, with wooden chairs, light armchairs and even sun-loungers set in the old, thick dust – everyone had brought what they could manage. No one had bothered to bring a table, so there wasn't one.

The Others are not very prone to cheap ritual: a court is action, not spectacle. And so there were no gowns, wigs or tablecloths. Only the grey robes of the observers, but no one really remembered why the Inquisitors sometimes wore those.

'We limit our rights and our laws. We are the Others . . .'

The scarlet letters of the Treaty blazed in the semi-darkness, the embodiment of Truth and Justice. And the voices rang out:

'We are the Others.'

Thirty voices:

'Time will decide for us.'

After the Treaty had been read, the Tribunal proper began, by tradition, with the least important cases.

Without getting up off his rotating piano stool, a judge, one of the robed Inquisitors, announced in a perfectly ordinary voice, with no special solemnity:

'Case number one. Poaching by the Dark side. Bring in the guilty party.'

Not even the accused, but the guilty party. Guilt had already been proven. The Witnesses would only help to determine the circumstances and the degree of guilt. And the court would give its verdict. Pitiless and just.

'Unfortunately, not all the witnesses are present. We are missing Vitaly Rogoza, an Other registered in Nikolaev in Ukraine and temporarily registered here in Moscow, who is absent for reasons unknown; and also Andrei Tiunnikov and Ekaterina Sorokina, who were killed in cases that will be considered a little later . . .'

The trial was brief and strict:

'Victoria Manguzova, Dark Other, registered in Moscow, is guilty of the offence of unlicensed hunting. The verdict is dematerialisation. Are there any objections or proposed amendments to the verdict from the Watches?'

There were no objections from the Dark Ones and, of course, not from the Light Ones either.

'The sentence will be carried out immediately,' said the Inquisitor. He looked at the Light Ones – verdicts were traditionally carried out by members of the Watches.

Ilya stood up and adjusted his glasses. He looked intently at the female vampire, who howled, because she knew there was no escape. There was neither hate nor joy in the magician's glance. Only concentration. He reached out his hand and touched the registration seal on the vampire's chest through the Twilight.

A moment later Victoria slumped onto the floor. She didn't crumble to dust as an older vampire would have done, her body still hadn't lived out its time yet. But the force that replaces life in vampires, drawn over the years from human beings, had dissolved irretrievably into the Twilight. The room had became a little bit colder. Ilya frowned and dispatched the body into the Twilight with another restrained gesture.

For ever.

Thus is the verdict of the Others applied.

'Case number two. The killing of an uninitiated Other by a Dark Other, a shape-shifter. Bring in the guilty party.'

Questions. Answers. A brief consultation by the Inquisitors.

'Oksana Dashchiuk, Dark Other, registered in Moscow, is adjudged not guilty of premeditated murder; her actions are categorised as self-defence. But she is found guilty of using excessive force to defend herself and therefore deprived of her licence to hunt for a period of ten years. In the event of a repeat offence or any violation of the fifth level or above, she shall be subject to immediate dematerialisation. Are there any objections or proposed amendments to the verdict from the Watches?'

Ilya looked at Gesar and rose to his feet again.

'We have objections. There was no actual threat to the life of this Other. There was no need to kill the man. We demand that she be deprived of her licence for a period of fifty years.'

'Thirty,' replied Maxim, as if he'd been expecting this demand. As in fact he had been.

'Forty,' Gesar said in a cold voice, without getting up. 'Shall I present all the necessary grounds?'

'Forty,' Maxim agreed. He looked at the Dark Ones, but they said nothing, believing that the shape-shifter's fate wasn't worth arguing about.

'Release the prisoner from custody.'

The door opened in front of the pale, frightened girl and she ran out happily, still unaware that she might as well have been sentenced to execution. Forty years is a very long time for a shape-shifter who can only draw power from human lives. Long enough for her to grow decrepit and maybe even die, without any way of opposing the implacable advance of age.

'Case number three. An attack on a Dark Other by members of the Night Watch. Since the victim is not present, the court judges it appropriate to cross-examine the surviving guilty parties and the head of the Night Watch, who permitted the unsanctioned use of force against a Dark Other. All protests from the side of the Light Ones are rejected in advance.'

Gesar frowned. Zabulon permitted himself a restrained smile.

Svetlana Nazarova, Light Enchantress, glanced at her watch in concern. She was feeling nervous because the Light Magician Anton Gorodetsky was late.

'Might it not be more expedient to establish the reasons for the absence of three individuals who were invited to attend?' Gesar asked cautiously, involuntarily adopting the judges' official style of speech. 'I assure you that I am not trying to play for time. I am alarmed by the absence both of a member of the Night Watch and of one of the greatest troublemakers of these recent weeks.'

The Inquisitors exchanged glances, as if they were silently taking an official decision.

'The Inquisition has no objection,' Maxim said dispassionately. 'Permission is granted for the necessary magical intervention.'

The Inquisition observers' robes swayed as they moved their protective amulets. Maybe that was why they wore the robes, so that no one could see how they used the amulets and exactly what kind of amulets they had? The Inquisition has its own methods, its own laws and its own weapons.

An observation sphere suddenly appeared in mid-air. Grey haze, streaked with wavy lines. Most of them disappeared, leaving only three.

Three threads of fate that had recently crossed at a single point. One thread was faded and barely glowing at all. An Other was hurt . . .

'That's Shagron,' said Edgar, who had now relinquished the responsibilities of deputy-chief of the Dark Ones. 'That's Shagron!'

The two other threads separated, but they were about to cross again at any moment – right outside the university building.

A clash. Another clash between Dark Ones and Light Ones. But so far with no fatalities.

'The Night Watch requests the Inquisition to intervene!' Gesar barked. 'Maxim, Oscar, Raoul – they'll kill each other!'

A woman stood up beside the head of the Night Watch – it

was the Light Other Olga, who had only recently reacquired her abilities as an enchantress, and a very powerful one, which meant that she had lost her right to a surname, but not yet acquired the right to a Twilight name. She touched Gesar's elbow and looked at the judges inquiringly.

Svetlana had turned pale and her face looked as if it was made of wax.

The Dark Ones said nothing. Zabulon scratched the tip of his nose thoughtfully.

'The Tribunal forbids any intervention,' one of the judges announced dryly.

'Why?' Svetlana asked helplessly. She tried to get up out of her wicker armchair, but she didn't have the strength. The physical strength. But Svetlana's real strength, the magical power of an Other, began circling around her in a dense spiral.

Just like people, when Others are angry, or in extreme situations, they are often stronger than when they're calm.

'Why?' Svetlana's voice rang out insistently. 'Everywhere this Dark One has appeared, Others or people have died. He's a killer! Are you going to allow him to carry on killing?'

The judge remained imperturbable.

'While he has been in Moscow the Dark One Vitaly Rogoza has not once violated a single stipulation of the Treaty and he has not once exceeded the limits of permissible force to defend himself. He has nothing to answer to the Inquisition for. We have no grounds to intervene.'

'When the grounds appear, it will be too late!' Gesar said harshly.

The Inquisitor merely shrugged.

'He's going to take revenge for Shagron,' one of the Light Ones said quietly and coughed.

Two magicians – a Light One and a Dark One – were approaching the entrance to the Moscow University building, and as the distance between them melted away, everyone at the Tribunal felt more and more certain that only one of them would make it up into the turret.

But who would it be?

I don't know why, but I got out of the car about three hundred metres from the entrance to the university building. I could see spots of colour, rays of light and three-dimensional figures flickering above the building; I could sense that a power I didn't understand was restraining ordinary higher magic, not allowing it to be used. And I sensed that up there at the very top, just where the sharp steeple of the Moscow skyscraper began, there was a light grey cloud gradually swelling, and it reminded of a time-bomb.

I looked round as I set off along the pavement. In theory I ought to have been hurrying, but I walked at a medium pace. That must have been the way I was supposed to do it.

Just don't ask who had decided that.

My minidisc player was oozing out another tune: I didn't like it, so I found the skip button by touch and pressed it. What would it be this time?

> My name is an effaced hieroglyph,
> My clothes are patched by the wind . . .
> What I carry in my tight-clenched hands,
> No one asks, and I will not answer . . .

Picnic and their song 'Hieroglyph'. That would do – a leisurely melody for someone who is already late anyway and whose only option now is to focus his mind and acquire the all-embracing, imperturbable calm of the Eastern sages.

I wondered if there were any Others among the sages? Or

maybe the question should be the other way round – were there any human beings among them?

It would be interesting to find out.

I managed to adjust the security guards' minds – clearly the simplest, 'everyday' spells were permitted even during a session of the Tribunal.

I walked across to the lifts – the lobby was strangely deserted. Maybe subconsciously people had sensed the presence nearby of all the most powerful Others in Moscow and were avoiding this place? I pressed the call button and the doors of one of the lifts opened immediately. I got in automatically looking round to see if anyone else was hurrying for the lift.

And I saw Anton. He'd just walked past the security guards, who were still out of action.

I wondered how he'd managed to catch up with me. Had he requisitioned a moped or a motorbike as well?

I stood there, waiting. Anton looked at me, as if he were pondering some thought, and waited too.

After a brief pause, I pressed the button, the lift doors closed, and I went up. But not all the way to the top of the building straight away, only about two thirds of the way up. It turned out that the only way I could go higher was on another lift that just served the upper floors. And then the only way to get where I needed to go was to follow a wide marble stairway covered in old blotches of whitewash. The stairs led to a door that was open in the Twilight but, naturally, firmly closed and locked in the ordinary world.

Just before the stairs the Picnic song came to an end and the player selected another at random:

I dream of dogs and of wild beasts,
I dream that animals with eyes like lamps

> Bit into my wings high in the heavens,
> And I fell clumsily, like a fallen angel . . .

I'd only heard snatches of this Nautilus Pompilius song before, but now it suddenly struck an echo in my very soul. As I walked up towards the locked door and slipped into the Twilight, I sang along with Butusov.

> I don't remember the fall, I only remember
> The impact as I struck the cold stones.
> How could I have flown so high and then
> Tumbled down so cruelly, like a fallen angel?
> Right back down into the place that we
> Had left behind, hoping for a new life.
> Right back down into the place from where
> We stared avidly up into the blue heavens.
> Right down . . .

Any Other could have heard me and Butusov, even though the only real sound was coming from the earphones and faded away completely only one step away from me.

We entered the chamber where the Tribunal was taking place together. Me and the fallen angel.

> I tried to be just and kind,
> And I wasn't frightened or surprised
> By the people gathering down on the Earth
> To watch an angel fall . . .

Gesar. Zabulon. The Inquisitor Maxim. The Dark Ones I'd been drinking coffee with and talking to over the last few days: Edgar, Yury, Kolya, Anna Tikhonovna . . . The Light Ones I had been sparring and fighting with recently, bending the rules almost to breaking: Ilya, Garik, Tolik, the shape-shifter bear. Others I didn't know, both Dark and Light, including some who were obviously not connected with the Watches. Two in loose robes – Inquisitors, I supposed.

And a Light Enchantress with a face contorted in grief. Both people and Others have expressions like that when they've just lost someone they love.

> And the wind swirls into their open mouths,
> Filling them with white snow, or sweet manna,
> Or simply feathers flying down after
> The one who has fallen, like a fallen angel . . .

And then I was dragged, unable to resist, up the invisible steps, to the top of the mysterious pyramid I had been climbing all this time; and at almost the same moment, the two Inquisitors in robes rescinded the prohibition on higher magic. And Svetlana hit me with that cloud I had seen, which had been ready to burst and explode at any moment. A field of power that made a multi-megaton explosion seem tiny and insignificant.

Time stopped.

And I understood everything. Everything that had happened. Everything that was happening now and everything that was destined to happen in the immediate future. I understood, and swallowed hard to keep down the lump that had suddenly risen in my cramped throat.

I had become the most powerful magician on Earth. A magician beyond classification. A Caliph for an hour – no, only for an instant – the only one in this dilapidated round hall who had no future.

There are some Others who have no future . . .

A mirror! I was nothing but a mirror. The Mirror of the World. A weight cast into the dangling pan of the scales when the balance between the Powers of Light and the Powers of Dark is disrupted.

The Light had acquired a new Great Enchantress, but the Dark had not been granted an equally powerful adept. The Light had been given a chance to settle accounts with the Darkness once and for all.

But there is no Light without Dark. And so the Twilight had produced me. It had found a strange Other who had not yet inclined to one side or the other, an Other with a pristine, pure aura, and then coloured that aura Dark. It had taken away my former memories and given me the ability to reflect and absorb others' power. The more powerfully I was struck, the more powerful I had become, each time jumping up onto the next step. And when there was nowhere left to go, that was the summit, and beyond that there was only eternity and the Twilight – the Mirror was no longer needed. Because the Mirror had itself become capable of disrupting the equilibrium.

The Twilight was waiting for me. Eternal Twilight. I didn't know what would happen to the body of Vitaly Rogoza, who until only recently had been an Other with no destiny. I didn't know what would happen to his memory and his personality, it all happens differently every time a Mirror comes. I only knew that the one who had become aware of himself in that frozen park in Nikolaev on his way to catch a train to Moscow would disappear for ever, be transformed into an incorporeal, powerless shadow, a ghostly inhabitant of the Twilight.

Or simply into a part of the Twilight . . . the Twilight that is not as inert as we are all used to thinking.

I understood all this in the brief instant before I drew in all of Sveltana's power. She imagined that she had lost Anton Gorodetsky. And she imagined it because of a freak coincidence, because I walked into the Tribunal hall with a minidisc player exactly like Anton's, with a copy of his disc in the player and with Anton's favourite song in my ears and my soul. And I also understood that the Inquisition knew the truth. But none of the Inquisitors would say a word to reassure the Others of Moscow, who believed I'd had a skirmish with Anton and Anton had been killed.

The Light Ones knew his favourite songs.

'Die!'

No, I won't die, Svetlana. Or rather, I will, but not right now. I am a Mirror. In trying to destroy me, you grow weaker, and I only grow stronger. I can already see what lies ahead of you – thirty or fifty years spent slowly restoring the power you've squandered so insanely. You'll have to collect together what you've lost, piecemeal. For three, or maybe more, decades – long enough for the Dark, enough time to prepare for another attempt to disrupt the equilibrium by whichever side it happens to be. You have long years ahead of you to find happiness with Anton, or not to find it.

But in any case, throughout those years you will be equals.

Maybe you have lost your powers, but I'm giving you a chance . . . a chance that I don't have.

The music stopped. The magical blow had been too much for the player – in general, technology reacts badly to powerful magic – and it shattered into shards of plastic. My cap went flying towards the door, and my jacket split in several places at once.

I was barely able to keep my feet, but I managed it.

'A Mirror!' Gesar exclaimed, his voice filled with an entire gamut of indescribable feelings and intonations. 'The third time, and the third time for the Dark Ones!'

'Well, we don't set up global social experiments, my dear colleague!' said Zabulon, making no effort to conceal his triumph.

Today he was one of the victors. And the Light Ones had suffered a defeat.

But just how many times had this already happened – or the exact opposite?

Svetlana, drained and shattered, had been crushed by grief only a moment earlier, but now she cried out, unable to conceal her joy:

'Anton!'

He was standing by the door. Anton Gorodetsky. Light Magician. Alive and unharmed. He had followed me up the stairs.

'Thank you, Anton!' Zabulon said to him in a tone of immense satisfaction. 'You carried out my assignment perfectly. I hope you're pleased with your reward?'

'Assignment?' Gesar exclaimed. 'Anton?'

Zabulon laughed quietly as he stood up. The head of the Night Watch gave his triumphant enemy a swift glance and then looked back at Anton.

But Anton walked up to Svetlana, who was so happy she couldn't see anything else, put his arms round her, whispered, 'Just a moment' and moved towards me.

For a few seconds we looked each other in the eye. Enemy to enemy. Other and non-Other. I don't even know how to put it so that it sounds right. There are always at least two truths, after all.

'Take this,' said Anton.

And he handed me his minidisc player to replace the broken one.

'Thank you,' I whispered. I took the remains of mine off my belt, took out my disc without speaking and stuck it into the player he had given me, as if that was the most important thing of all now. And I thought: 'Now the Inquisitor will get up and say that I can go'.

I was right, of course. Magicians of that level don't make mistakes, even if they are non-Others.

'In the name of the Treaty,' Maxim declared as dryly and dispassionately as ever, 'since it has been demonstrated beyond any doubt that Vitaly Rogoza is not an Other in the ordinary meaning of that word, the actions of the Night Watch relative to Vitaly Rogoza are not a matter for investigation by the Inquisition. Likewise, Vitaly Rogoza does not come under the terms of the Treaty. He is free to pursue his own destiny.'

As if I'd ever really had one! Me and the other Mirrors who had come before me, and the young boy Egor, whose time had not yet come.

'The Inquisition has concluded its consideration of the cases before it,' said Maxim, glancing round the magicians present. 'Do the Watches have any comments or suggestions?'

I pressed 'Play' and walked away. In my tattered jacket I looked like a cross between a street bum and a bizarre scarecrow. But who cared?

The minidisc player I'd been given was working in random mode. And yet again it picked just what was wanted. Kipelov and Mavrin 'Troubled Times'. All I had to do now was sing along.

So I did.

> Troubled times!
> The spectre of freedom on a horse.
> Blood up to your knees,
> Like in some crazy dream.
> The people amuse themselves
> Killing the Old Gods,
> The people pray,
> Waiting for Righteous Words!
> A comet in the sky,
> A sure sign of imminent disaster.
> Fallen Warriors of the Light

Are burned on bonfires.
Warriors of the Darkness
Have encircled the world.
Thousands of birds
Fall down like rain.

Troubled times for the one who no longer has the right to call himself Vitaly Rogoza. For the one who rose, only to fall. For the fallen angel . . . the Dark angel. Troubled times for you and for the Others. The end of the millennium. The time when it's impossible to tell the Light from the Dark, or the Dark from the Light. A time of deaths and battles. Troubled times.

We don't know who we are –
Children of the red star,
Children of the black star,
Or of the fresh graves . . .
The dance of Death is simple and terrible,
But until the hour strikes,
The sins of all our lives
Are punished by these troubled times!

I don't know whose child I am either. I only know one thing: the troubled times usually punish those who have not committed any sins for the sins of others. Or if they have committed any sins, they're not the ones they're punished for. But I wasn't allowed any choice. I wasn't given destiny.

We're still alive.
Some will be saved, some will not
On a wild impulse
They put the lights out in our fortress,

The flag torn down
Is the sign
Of surrender to our enemies,
But you will not take it,
It's a lie —
For now we're still alive!

I am alive for now. And I'm singing. I'm singing, even though I know that Kipelov and Mavrin's next song contains the following lines:

Don't ask — I won't take you with me.
Don't look — I don't know the meaning of life.
Don't wish to learn another's secret.
That's all — I am only a spirit, I am vanishing!

I'm only a spirit. I'm only a Mirror. A Mirror that has reflected everything it was made to reflect. But I can't help asking and believing. I am leaving now, only to vanish, but I ask, I hope, I want to believe — take me with you! Take me!
I believe.
I hope.
I believe,
I . . .

# ANOTHER POWER

# PROLOGUE

YUKHA MUSTAIOKI flagged down the car – he was the senior member of their little group now – Yari Kuusinen and Raivo Nikkilya squeezed into the back seat of the old Zhiguli without a word, Yukha took the seat in front.

'Take us to She re me tie vo,' he said, speaking with emphatic clarity. Oddly enough, Russian had been the language of Mustaioki's childhood, although he'd managed to forget most of it afterwards. But then he'd always had a talent for languages, and now he lived near the Russian border and made regular drinking trips to St Petersburg. The others preferred the ferry to Sweden – on the overnight trip you could get really drunk on spirits from the duty-free shop, sleep it off during the day (who needs Stockholm, anyway?) and then indulge yourself expensively again on the way back. But Mustaioki had stubbornly kept on travelling to St Petersburg. 'Drive quick-ly and care-ful-ly,' he said.

The driver drove. Quickly and carefully. Taking foreigners to the airport was a serious bonus for him. An out-of-work engineer making a living as a freelance taxi driver didn't often land such a plum job. Especially at a time like this, just before the New Year, with the millenium coming up and everybody out working, trying to make sure there'd be food for the festive table and nice presents for the family.

The three Others sitting silently in the car weren't listening to the driver's thoughts. Although they could have done, of course.

After they'd already passed the ring road, Yukha turned to his comrades and said:

'Are we really leaving then, Brothers?'

Yari and Raivo nodded understandingly. It really was hard to believe that it was all over – the interrogations by the Night Watch, the visits from sombre members of the Inquisition staff, the exertions of the Day Watch's adroit female vampire advocate, who was as well known among human beings as she was among Others.

They were free. Free, released from this terrible, cold, inhospitable city of Moscow. Although they couldn't go home just yet, they were on their way to Prague, where the Inquisition's European Office had just relocated. But they had been released. With their rights restricted and the obligation to register when they arrived anywhere, but even so . . .

'Poor Ollikainen,' Raivo sighed. 'He was so fond of Czech beer. He used to say Lapin Kulta was the best beer in the world. He'll never drink beer again . . .'

'We'll drink a jug of beer for him,' Yari suggested.

'Three,' Yukha added. 'He was the most worthy of the Regin Brothers.'

'And what about us?' Yari asked after a moment's thought.

'We are worthy too,' Yukha agreed. 'We did our duty.'

For some reason, as he said this all three lowered their eyes.

The small sect of Dark Others that called itself the Regin Brothers had existed in Helsinki for almost five hundred years. They were among the few Others who had not officially accepted the Treaty, but since they never committed any serious violations of its provisions, the Watches turned a blind eye. The Light Ones even seemed to be quite glad that twenty or thirty Dark Ones occupied themselves with harmless rituals, chanting and archaeological exploration. The Dark Ones had made a couple of attempts to involve the Regin Brothers in the work of the Day Watch, but then just given up on them.

Until only recently Yukha and Yari and Raivo and their friend who had been killed, Pasi Ollikainen, had regarded their involvement in the sect as a kind of curious, even amusing, game. Their grandfathers and great-grandfathers had spent their entire lives as members of the sect, and their children would be Regin Brothers too . . . Their adopted children, that is. An Other is rarely fortunate enough to have a child who is also born with the abilities of an Other. That's only the norm for the lower orders of Dark Ones, the vampires and shape-shifters.

It wasn't at all easy for the magicians of the small Finnish sect. They had to scout round the world, searching for Other children they could adopt, educate and introduce to the great cause of service to Fáfnir. As a rule, these children were found in the more underdeveloped and exotic countries.

Raivo, for instance, came from Burkina Faso. The little boy with the bulging eyes, legs bandy from rickets and swollen, flabby stomach had been bought from his impoverished parents for fourteen dollars. He had been cured of his illness, educated and taught Finnish. And now, no one looking at this handsome, well-built young black guy could ever have guessed how strange his destiny was.

Yari had been found in the slums of Macao. At the age of four, with the help of his magical abilities, he was already a remarkably successful thief, which was how he was discovered by his future adoptive parents. They hadn't even had to pay for him. Yari hadn't grown very tall, but the Regin Brothers had been delighted with his sharp, tenacious mind and natural talent for magic.

Then were was Yukha, from Russia. Or rather, from somewhere

in the south of Ukraine. He had suffered from wanderlust since he was a child and at the age of seven he had travelled right across the country by jumping goods trains and hitchhiking, then crossed the border on foot, and one day he'd knocked on the door of the small town house owned by the Mustaiokis, devoted members of the sect. There was no way that could be explained except by magical predestination.

Ironically, only the deceased Ollikainen had been a genuine Finnish boy.

The driver had never had such an odd group of passengers before – a young white guy with Ukrainian facial features, a tall guy with skin as black as pitch and a short Asiatic with slanting eyes. And all three of them were speaking Finnish, or maybe Swedish, absolutely fluently. But then, you saw all sorts of things nowadays.

The first thing the Brothers did at the airport was study the timetable, but even here Russia's muddle-headed cunning had a snag in store for them: the flight to Prague had been delayed for the fourth time. True, there was another flight, to Duisburg with a stopover in Prague. But the transit flight wasn't in the timetable, of course, while the plane to Madrid, also with a stopover in Prague, left at a very inconvenient time, and they had to redraw their plans right there at the ticket office. This reduced a burly young guy in a track suit, wearing a gold chain as thick as a finger and clutching a mobile phone in his massive hairy hand, to a state of inexpressible fury. He was on the point of pushing little Yari out of the way, but Raivo concocted a hasty spell of respect, and after that the line that had grown behind them stopped complaining about the leisurely manner in which the Finns were making their decision.

'We'll take the Duisburg plane,' Yukha decided at last. 'It's more convenient. And we won't have to wait so long. They'll postpone the Prague flight another three times at least, won't they?'

Of course they would. The reality lines were woven into a tight knot, and the ill-fated flight wouldn't leave until late that evening.

The almost forgotten sensation of freedom was as intoxicating as their favourite Lapin Kulta beer. While Yukha talked to the pretty girl at the ticket desk, who was already hassled out of her mind, Yari and Raivo enjoyed themselves staring round the hall, looking at the passengers walking by, the sales assistants in the brightly lit aquariums of their little shops, the international airline offices that are always there in any major airport.

It was Yari who spotted the Other.

'Look!'

There was a Light Magician standing at a counter near the way out to the departure gates, drinking coffee from a small, dark-green cup. And there was a half-empty travel bag lying beside his bar stool.

Yari and Raivo studied the Light One's aura for a while – he was perfectly composed and completely in control of his emotions. He must have noticed them, but he didn't give any sign.

'When are they ever going to leave us in peace?' Raivo sighed. 'Do you think he's following us?'

'Of course,' Raivo said with conviction. 'We have to present ourselves at a session of the Tribunal. And the Moscow Night Watch has to be certain that the witnesses they released have left for Prague. You'll see, he'll follow us all the way to the boarding ramp.'

'But there's almost five hours left until our flight!'

'The Other's in no hurry. He's working.'

Yukha joined them with the tickets. There was a faint breath of magic from him – of course there hadn't been any tickets left for today's flight, so he'd had some taken out of the special reserve by influencing both the girl at the desk and the airport manager.

'Here, take them,' he began, but suddenly broke off. He looked closely at the other Brothers and asked: 'What's wrong?'

'A spy. Over there at the counter, drinking coffee.'

Yukha looked and saw the Light Other.

And just at that moment a murky red stripe cut across the even azure tone of the spy's aura.

'Something's upset him,' Yari said.

'Another Other!' said Raivo. 'Over there, by the way out!'

And there was a dark-haired, stocky thirty-something man standing right beside the glass doors, wiping his forehead with the handkerchief in one hand and holding a mobilephone to his ear with the other. He wasn't saying anything, either, but obviously listening to lengthy instructions from someone. There was a small black briefcase standing beside him.

This Other was a Dark Magician.

'And they're following us too,' muttered Raivo.

'Why would anyone be interested in us?' Yukha asked doubtfully. 'Any number of Others could have business at Moscow's international airport.'

'Remain vigilant, Brother!' Yari reminded him. 'Fáfnir is saddened and alarmed by carelessness.'

Yukha thought glumly that after the hopeless failure of the operation to deliver the Talon to Moscow, the resurrected Fáfnir ought to incinerate all four of them. Or at least the three survivors. But, as usual, he didn't say anything out loud.

Meanwhile the Light One finished his coffee, cast a displeased glance at the Dark One and set off in the general direction of the restaurant. His aura had returned to its even azure colour, with a barely visible hint of cherry red where the stripe had been.

The Dark One was still talking on his mobile. Or rather, listening.

'They want to make sure we leave!' said the shrewd Raivo. 'As if we weren't delighted to go – what have we got to do here!'

But Raivo was wrong.

The Light Magician wandered around the airport for a while and then settled at the counter again, reading a book and sipping coffee. The Dark Magician finished his conversation and walked across to the ticket desk, and the Brothers sensed a trace of magic. Quite strong magic, too — fourth grade or so.

'What's he doing there?' Raivo asked, getting worried. 'Is he getting a ticket too? Eh? Yukha, he's not going to bother us, is he?'

'Why would he?' Yukha asked. 'Look!'

The Dark Magician walked away from the counter window with a ticket in his hand.

'They've cancelled a ticket someone had already paid for!' Raivo guessed. 'Would you believe it! There'll be a fuss.'

And there was a fuss, when the passengers were checking in for the flight four hours later, when they all found themselves in the same queue. Including the Light Magician. One of the passengers was politely informed that his ticket had been sold to him by mistake, that the airline apologised to him and offered him a seat in business class on the next flight.

The Dark Magician watched the outraged passenger's complaints as if nothing untoward was happening. He actually seemed to be smiling. But the Regin Brothers had no reason to smile — the Dark Magician and the Light Magician were flying on the same plane as them.

'They've decided to see us all the way to Prague,' Raivo eventually announced. 'They're taking this business seriously.'

Yukha shook his head.

'No, Brother. No. Something's not right here. You'll see — they'll come up and want to talk to us . . .'

# CHAPTER 1

GESAR HAD summoned Anton in the evening, when the analysts and the technical staff had already gone home, and the field operatives who happened to be on duty that night had only just begun arriving at headquarters. The corridors on the second floor smelled of freshly brewed coffee, hot cinnamon buns and mild, fragrant tobacco – that year a fashion for smoking pipes had swept through almost the entire Night Watch staff. Even the women hadn't escaped it.

It was already about a year since Anton had worked in the IT department. He had been replaced as boss of the computer section by Tolik. A second-grade magician – Anton had been classed as second grade at the beginning of the year – was too important a figure to be spending his time stuck in a chair, tapping away at a keyboard and debugging programs.

'Like some coffee?' Semyon asked. Anton nodded, and just at that moment the phone rang. Silence fell instantly in the small room where the four field operatives – Anton, Semyon, Garik and Bear – were sitting. They could all sense a call from the boss.

And who it was for.

Anton's colleagues watched closely as he picked up the receiver.

'Call in to see me as soon as you're free,' Gesar ordered without saying hello. 'Finish your coffee and then come up.'

'Very well,' Anton replied steadily. 'As you wish, Boris Ignatievich.'

He thought for a moment and then lit his pipe. If Gesar hadn't warned him time was short, it meant there was no great hurry.

'You in line for a dressing down?' Garik inquired. Anton just shrugged. He could be in line for anything, from a charge of betraying the cause of the Night Watch to a promotion. From being told to stay in the office and not stick his nose outside to being ordered to storm the Dark Ones' headquarters. When a magician of the highest grade got some idea into his head, it was pointless trying to guess his plans. Especially if that magician was in the kind of bad mood that Gesar had been in for the last few months.

Basically they were all feeling pretty lousy. This year had been one failure after another. It had all started in the summer, when the workaday, humdrum arrest of a witch practising magic illegally had spilled over into conflict with the Dark Ones. Then the fine young magician Igor Teplov, who had drained his powers in that conflict, had been sent to the Artek children's camp to recover and run foul of a deliberate provocation by the Dark Ones. A witch called Alisa Donnikova had managed to enchant him and make him fall in love with her. She was Zabulon's girlfriend, the same Dark bitch who had interfered time and again in the Night Watch's most complex intrigues. This time Alisa hadn't gone unpunished – Igor had killed her. But in the process he had exceeded the limits of force permissible in self-defence, and now his fate hung by a thread.

A few months later Vitaly Rogoza had turned up, and that had proved to be a real disaster. At first they'd taken him for an ordinary Dark One, then they'd begun to suspect the visiting Ukrainian was an emissary, sent to assist the Day Watch. But Rogoza had turned out to be a Mirror – that very rarest of phenomena, which had been recorded less than ten times in the entire history of the Watches. He was a direct creation of the Twilight, moulded out of a quite unexceptional individual, who might not even have been an Other, into a monstrous fighting machine. If only they'd realised that straight away . . . but they hadn't. And in the struggle with the Mirror, Tiger Cub had been killed, Svetlana had lost her powers, and several other magicians had suffered to a greater or lesser degree.

Things were very, very bad.

Anton had cursed himself over and over again for not realising the need to conduct a detailed analysis of the circumstances in which the Mirror had appeared. After all, there were similar cases in the secret archives – the appearance of a magician who evaded classification, a rapid increase in his powers, a decisive skirmish – and then he disappeared. Everything fitted. Right down to the final moment, when Vitaly Rogoza had melted into thin air, dematerialised and vanished into the depths of the Twilight that had given birth to him.

But never mind Anton, never mind even Garik or Semyon. For them a Mirror was just one of those numerous exotic occurrences they'd only heard about in lectures or read about in the archives. Why hadn't Gesar or Olga, with all their experience, realised what was going on immediately? They'd run into Mirrors before, after all.

Things were bad. Nothing was going right. As if the Dark had been infuriated by the Night Watch's recent successes and was striking blow after blow. And very successfully too, it had to be admitted.

Anton shook his head to refuse the second cup of coffee that Semyon offered him. He carefully cleaned out his pipe, casting an involuntary sideways glance at Bear.

He was cleaning out his pipe too. The little pipe with a long, thin stem that had belonged to Tiger Cub. She had only smoked it occasionally, mostly to keep her friends company. But now that Tiger Cub was gone, Bear smoked his own pipe and hers in turn. It was probably the only way he had expressed his feelings since Tiger Cub's death – the gentle way he handled that pipe . . . and perhaps that fixed stare when Vitaly Rogoza had begun to dematerialise. A gaze full of regret: Bear hadn't had a chance to get his hands on Rogoza, he hadn't been able to satisfy his thirst for revenge.

Like Alisher, the Light One from Uzbekistan, whose father had been killed a year earlier by Alisa.

Anton had his own accounts to settle with the Day Watch and its chief, too. But of course the accounts would never be paid. The Treaty shackled both Watches, the Inquisition made sure it was observed, and the only way round it was to get straight to the point and challenge an enemy to a duel, which was what Igor had done, for instance. And what was the result? The witch was dead, but now the magician was facing dematerialisation, waiting for the judgement of the European Office of the Tribunal. And it wasn't hard to guess what it would be.

Anton got up, nodded to his friends and made for the boss's office on the third floor.

He was feeling really sick at heart, not looking forward at all to the New Year festivities that people everywhere round the planet were awaiting so eagerly, as if the number 2000 could change anything. What did it all really matter? But when Anton reached the door of the office, he felt a faint stirring of interest.

The magical defences there were very strong. The Night Watch building itself was protected against observation, and the employees' offices and conference rooms had additional screening. But today it seemed as though Gesar had put in a lot of extra effort to ensure confidentiality: the air in the corridor was still and stifling, saturated with energy. And this invisible wall extended into the Twilight, much deeper than the first two levels that were accessible to Anton.

He walked into the office and closed the door firmly behind him. He sensed a slight movement behind his back as the defensive field closed up after having been torn for a moment.

'Sit down, Anton,' said Gesar, and asked in a perfectly friendly voice: 'Tea, coffee?'

'Thanks, Boris Ignatievich,' Anton replied, calling Gesar by his human name, 'but I've just had one.'

'A mug of beer then?' Gesar asked unexpectedly.

Anton had to stop himself rubbing his eyes or even pinching his arm. Gesar had never shunned life's pleasures. He could leap about with the young people at a club, flirt a bit with the silly young girls and even take off with one of them for the night. And he enjoyed sitting in a restaurant over dishes of exotic food, driving the waiters backwards and forwards and unnerving the cooks with his international culinary knowledge. He could even go out with his staff, acting like one of the lads and drinking beer with smoked bream, vodka with freshly salted pickles and wine with fruit.

But there was one thing Gesar never did, and that was to have parties in the office. The ten members of the analytical section who drank a bottle of cognac to celebrate the birthday of Yulia, the Watch's youngest enchantress and a universal favourite, had been punished with genuinely brilliant originality. Not even an intercession by Olga, who had been involved in the misdemeanour along with the Others, had helped. The punishments had been individually devised for them, and each had been the most hurtful possible. Yulia, for instance, had been made to stay away from the Watch offices for a week and attend an ordinary school with teenagers of her own age, go for ice-cream with the girls in her class and to films and clubs with the boys. Yulia had returned to the Watch, fuming with indignation, and for ages she'd kept repeating: 'God, if you only knew how stupid they all are. I hate them.'

For those three words, 'I hate them,' she received another day's penalty and a long lecture from Gesar on the subject of 'Can a Light Enchantress entertain negative feelings for people?'

So now Anton was standing there in front of Gesar, frozen over the chair he'd been about to sit down in. He'd forgotten what he was doing.

'Sit down, will you,' Gesar prompted him. 'No point in standing. So will you have a beer?'

'It's not quite the weather for it,' Anton replied, indicating the window with his eyes. Outside large, heavy flakes of snow were swirling through the air. A genuine Christmas blizzard. 'Not the right weather . . . and not the right place?'

He surprised himself by making the last phrase sound like a question.

Gesar thought for a moment.

'Yes, we could go out to some amusing little place,' he said, with a note of real interest in his voice. 'For instance, that little café in the South-West district, where all the dentists go. Can you imagine it? The favourite café of Moscow's tooth-pullers? And there's a little pizzeria at the Belorussian station that's a real blast.'

'Boris Ignatievich,' Anton asked, unable to resist, 'where do you dig all these places up from? The mountain-skiers' restaurant, the lesbian bar, the plumbers' snack bar, the philatelists' *pelmeni* joint . . .'

Gesar shrugged and spread his arms:

'Anton, my dear fellow, let me remind you once again what we work with. We work with—'

'The Dark Ones,' Gorodetsky blurted out and sat down in the chair.

'No, my boy, you're wrong. We work with people. And people are not a flock of cloned sheep chewing their grass in unison and all farting at the same time. Every human being is an individual. That is our gift, because it makes the work of the Dark Ones harder. And it's also our misfortune, because it makes our work harder too. And in order to understand these people, whose souls, after all, are what the endless battle between the Watches is fought over, we have to know them all. It's not just that I have to, you understand. We have to! And we have to understand every one of them — from the kid with acne who swallows ecstasy in a club to the ancient professor who's the last in a dying line of blue-bloods and spends all his time growing cacti . . . Oh, by the way, the bar where cactus-lovers get together has rather interesting cuisine and highly original décor. But you and I can't go anywhere just now. Did you sense the defences?'

Anton nodded.

'Believe me, I had good reason to install them. And sound security arrangements in a crowded place would be far more complicated. I don't think I can really afford to waste that much power at the moment.' Gesar rubbed his hand across his face and sighed. He looked really tired, all right. 'By the way, take this. A little present.'

Anton accepted the small object from his boss's hands with a surprised expression. It was something like a globe: a ball that was made out of thin needles of bone . . . yes it was bone . . . bent into arcs and stuck into two little discs of wood at the poles. The ball was empty . . . But no, it wasn't. It was full of power. Power that was dormant, constrained.

'What is it?' Anton asked, almost in a panic.

'Don't worry. It's not liquefied bliss.'

'Er, what's liquefied bliss?'

Gesar sighed:

'How should I know? It was a joke. A figure of speech. A turn of phrase. A metaphor. I'm not even sure that bliss exists, let alone whether it can be liquefied. What you're holding in your hands is something like a magical white noise generator. If you need to have an absolutely – let me emphasise that – *absolutely* secret conversation, one that nobody can listen into, no matter what means they use, simply break the ball in your hand. You'll probably cut your hand, but that's just the unavoidable price. But then for the next twelve hours there'll be no way anyone can monitor or check what's happening in a sphere ten metres across, with you at the centre, no matter what technical or magical means they use.'

'Thanks,' Anton said gloomily. 'Somehow a present like this fails to inspire me.'

'You'll thank me for it yet. So, will you have a beer or not?'

'Yes. But why does it have to be beer?'

'To avoid too serious a violation of my own rules,' Gesar said with a contented smile. 'We're at work, after all.'

He pressed a button on the intercom and said quietly:

'Olya, bring us some beer.'

Nothing in the world was going to surprise Anton now. But Gesar released the button and explained anyway.

'Galochka's a magnificent secretary. But she's a fourth-grade enchantress. And she could give information away to the enemy without even realising it. So just for today I changed my secretary.'

A minute later Olga came in. With a tray on which there were two immense glass jugs full of pale beer, an impressive crystal jug holding about two litres of the same, and a plate with an assortment of cheeses.

'Hi there, Antoshka,' Olga said in a very friendly tone of voice. 'You like Budvar, don't you?'

'What Light One doesn't like light Czech beer?' Anton asked, trying to make a joke. It fell flat, but even attempting a pun was quite something. He hadn't felt up to that for ages.

'How's Sveta doing?' Olga asked, still in the same tone.

Anton gritted his teeth. The weight that had fallen from his heart returned for a moment.

'Still the same.'

'Nothing?'

Anton nodded.

'I'll call round to see her this evening,' Olga told him. 'I think she's ready for visitors now. And I'll find some way to make her feel better . . . trust me.'

It was true. Who better to console a Great Enchantress who had lost her magic powers for a long time than another Great Enchantress who had once been deprived of her powers for many decades as punishment for a misdemeanour?

'Yes, come round, Olya,' said Anton. 'Sveta will be very glad to see you.'

Gesar cleared his throat gently.

'You've got plenty of time,' Olga snapped. 'Anton, you know . . . I wish you luck. I sincerely wish you luck.'

'Luck with what?' Anton asked, puzzled.

Instead of answering, Olga leaned down over him and kissed him tenderly on the lips.

'Well now!' was all Gesar could find to say.

'Ever since Anton and I swapped bodies,' Olga remarked casually, 'you don't really have any right to be jealous of me with him. And especially over such a tiny thing. Right boys! Behave yourselves, don't drink too much, and if there are any problems – call me.'

'Any problems?' Gesar echoed with a frown. But Olga was already on her way out. The Great Magician watched her go and when the door closed, he sighed and said:

'Living with a Great Enchantress is a real ordeal. Even for me. How do you manage it, Anton?'

'Svetlana didn't have time to become a genuinely Great Enchantress,' Anton remarked. He picked up one of the jugs and took a mouthful of beer. It was excellent. Just the way real beer ought to be.

'But you're glad of that, surely?' Gesar inquired.

'No.' Anton took a piece of strong goat's cheese. 'I'm not.'

'Why not?' Gesar asked with gentle curiosity. 'Now you have several decades of happy life as equals ahead of you. Ideally fifty years.'

'Gesar, what happiness can there be if the woman I love feels like a worthless cripple?' Anton asked sharply. 'And if it's my fault, at least partly.'

'Partly?'

Anton nodded:

'Yes, exactly. Partly.'

Gesar paused. Then he asked the question Anton had been expecting three weeks earlier and had already ceased to expect.

'Tell me, what happened between you and Zabulon?'

'He came to my apartment again. Like the first time.'

'And he entered with the help of your vampire friend again?' Gesar inquired.

'No, after the other time I closed my home to him. I simply don't understand how Zabulon could have got through.'

Gesar nodded and took a drink of beer.

'Then Zabulon suggested I should commit . . . an act of betrayal. He said that Vitaly Rogoza was a Mirror-Magician created by the Twilight in response to the increasing strength of the Night Watch. That his main goal was to kill Svetlana or deprive her of her powers. And if I was late for the session of the Inquisition, then Rogoza would strip Svetlana of her power and dematerialise.'

'And you agreed?'

Anton thought before he formulated his answer. He'd run through this conversation with Gesar plenty of times in his head. But he'd never found the right words.

'Gesar, the only other alternative would have been continuing confrontation. Obviously, either Svetlana would have been killed, or . . .'

'Or?' Gesar was clearly interested.

'Or many others would have been killed . . . weaker members of the Watch. To weaken us to the same extent overall.'

Gesar nodded.

'You worked it out for yourself?'

'No, not entirely. I dug around in the archives and found a few similar cases, one of which ended with the annihilation of the entire Kiev division of the Night Watch, apart from its leader, Alexander von Kissel. That time, the Mirror's target was apparently von Kissel, but he managed to protect himself. The result was that ordinary operatives and magicians died.'

'But why didn't you contact me?' Gesar asked. 'Why didn't you warn me about Zabulon's visit?'

'How could I know what he was expecting to happen? Maybe just that – for me to go rushing to you for advice. Zabulon was clearly trying to trick me, but I couldn't work out what the trap was. It could have been a mistake to contact you, or to keep quiet. So I chose a third way. I tried to prevent the Mirror getting to Svetlana. Using a very primitive method – I rammed his car.'

'Bravo,' said Gesar in a strange, squeaky voice. 'Well done, Anton. It didn't work, but it was a good try. But why didn't you tell anyone who Rogoza was?'

'Why didn't you tell anyone, Boris Ignatievich?' Anton asked, raising his head. 'Or are you trying to tell me it wasn't you who led the investigation into what happened in Kiev in October 1906?

Or is one lousy century too much for your memory? The entire situation was a perfect parallel! A Vladimir Sobolev came to Kiev from Poltava and registered with the Night Watch. He was later found at the scene of the murder of a young streetwalker, where there were clear signs of vampirism, then he was caught near where a witches' coven was dispersed.'

'What did I summon you for?' Gesar asked in a very loud, indignant voice. 'To question you about the dubious circumstances of your relations with Dark Ones or to hear you accusing me?'

'You summoned me, Boris Ignatievich, to have a drink of beer with me. And to ask me to do something for you.'

Gesar started breathing heavily. Then he shook his head:

'No, I'm not going to ask. I still have the right to order you.'

'Go ahead,' Anton said, pleased. 'I won't argue, I'll carry out my orders. Right down the line. Only that's not what you want, is it? An obedient agent without any initiative?'

Gesar shrugged.

'All right. You win. I want to ask you to do something for me, Anton.'

'First answer me . . . about the Mirror.'

'Then listen. Mirrors have appeared nine times before – if we take just the documented and proven instances. Only two of them have been on our side. The last three appearances of a Mirror have been on the side of the Dark Ones, every time in a place where the forces of Light have had a significant advantage and plans were being made for . . . for a large-scale operation of some kind. It's impossible to fight a Mirror, he beats off any magical attack by rising to the level of his enemy and defends himself against ordinary attacks by using magical means. All you can do is choose who to sacrifice – a dozen of the rank-and-file magicians or one of the Great Ones.'

'And you decided to let him have Tiger Cub and Svetlana.'

'I didn't decide any such thing. In the first place, until Tiger Cub was killed I wasn't even sure that what we were facing really was a Mirror.' Gesar smashed his fist down on the desk, spilling the beer. 'And nobody was supposed to die. It was all supposed to end with Rogoza being captured – which would have meant he wasn't a Mirror at all, just an ordinary visiting emissary – or with us retreating. I didn't expect Tiger Cub to blow her top like that!'

'She was a very impulsive girl.'

'No, Anton. You're wrong. She was an energetic, impulsive Other, but she had excellent self-control. And this outburst of hers . . .' Gesar paused. 'It seems like I underestimated her feelings for Andrei Tiunnikov.'

'They'd been seeing each other a lot just recently,' Anton admitted. 'He even went to her place out in the country, and Tiger Cub was very fond of her privacy. And when Andrei . . . well, just why did he go into Rogoza's room?'

'To show off to Tiger Cub.' Gesar sighed. 'Ah, you boys and girls, still green, boasting to each other, showing off your magic, your battle scars, talismans and amulets . . . why is there so much human stupidity in all of you?'

'Because we are people. People who are Others, but still people. And we don't become true Others straight away.'

Gesar nodded:

'You're right again, Anton. You have to live an entire human life, eighty years or a hundred, lose your family and all your human loved ones, see how ridiculous the politicians are, building their empires to last a thousand years, and the philosophers, creating their eternal truths for one or two generations . . . that's when you become an Other. But while you live your first, human life, you're still a human being. Even if you can enter the Twilight, cast spells and read the reality lines, you're still a human being, Anton.

And so is Svetlana. And Tiger Cub and Andrei were human beings. And your human side is where the Darkness catches you out. Your weaknesses, your emotions.'

'Is love really a weakness?'

'If you have love in you, it's a strength. But if you are in love, it's a weakness.'

'We can't do it any other way yet.'

'Yes you can, Anton. It's hard for you, but you can.' Gesar looked into his eyes. 'Well, are you still angry with me?'

'No. I believe you tried . . . your best.'

'Yes, I tried. And I pulled it off – that's the amazing thing.'

'Tiger Cub and Andrei dead, Svetlana powerless – and you say you pulled it off?' Anton exclaimed indignantly.

'Yes. Because all the other options were far worse. And surprising as it may seem, what's happened doesn't simply play into the hands of Zabulon and his mangy curs.'

Gesar smiled. A cold, ironic smile. A very disturbing, suggestive smile.

'That still won't do Svetlana any good . . .' Anton began. Then he stopped, because Gesar shook his head:

'It's not finished yet, Anton. In fact, it's only just begun.'

The chief of the Night Watch poured them each a second mug of beer, took a sip and leaned back in his armchair.

'Boris Ignatievich . . .'

'Anton, I understand everything. You're tired. I'm tired too, we're all tired, we're full of bitterness, pain, anguish. But we're at war, and this war's a very long way from over yet. If you want to withdraw from it – then go. Live as an ordinary Light One. But while you're in the Watch . . . you are in the Watch, Anton?'

'Yes!'

'Well, that's excellent. Do you like the beer?'

'Yes,' Anton muttered.

'Well, that's excellent too. Because you're flying to the home-land of this wonderful drink. To Prague.'

'When?' Anton asked stupidly.

'Tomorrow morning. Or rather, afternoon, the morning flight will be postponed until six in the evening and you'll take another flight with a stopover in Prague.'

'Why?'

'You know that the European Office of the Inquisition has moved from Berne to Prague?'

'Yes, of course. Because of Fáfnir's Talon, the artefact that those idiots stole.'

'Precisely. But even without that the Inquisition has a tradition of changing its location every fifty or a hundred years, and it was a very serious embarrassment for the Berne Watches. Anyway, they've settled in now and finally got round to considering our case.'

'So that's why I got this present . . . Igor?'

'Yes. He's already there. We've lodged an official complaint, claiming that the Dark Ones organised a deliberate provocation and Alisa Donnikova enchanted Igor, which was the reason for his nervous breakdown . . . and . . . that unfortunate incident in which a boy drowned. The Dark Ones, of course, are claiming that Igor enchanted Alisa in an attempt to recruit her to our side.'

Andrei snorted at the absurdity of the accusation – recruiting a witch! As if a Dark One could ever stop being Dark. Frighten her, force her to collaborate, bribe her or blackmail her – all that was possible. But to recruit a witch . . .

'Well then, the Tribunal will decide who was to blame and what degree of responsibility Igor bears. The lad challenged Alisa to an officially registered duel, so the Watch has nothing to answer for. But if the Inquisition accuses him of exceeding the limits of force required for self-defence or of deliberate provocation – there's only one outcome for him. Into the Twilight. He's only half-alive as it is . . . and he doesn't even seem to want to fight. But we need Igor, Anton. You have no idea just how badly we need him!'

'Boris Ignatievich, what really happened down there?'

'Really? I don't know. We didn't arrange any provocations, you can trust me on that. I sent Igor on holiday because the lad had drained himself completely. Do you know how good working in a young pioneer camp is for restoring your powers? Smiling children's faces, happy laughter, cheerful voices . . .' Gesar's voice had warmed so much that Anton was expecting the serious boss of the Night Watch to lick his lips and start purring at any moment. But Gesar broke off and then continued: 'Either our accusation is just, and then there's a chance of saving Igor. Or everything that happened was just a tragic coincidence. In that case, there's nothing the Inquisition can accuse us of, but Igor won't survive the business. He's punishing himself for the death of that boy . . . and Alisa.'

'What does Alisa matter?'

'He really did fall in love with her . . . yet another half-baked Other.' Gesar watched as the expression on Anton's face changed and nodded. 'Yes, he fell in love, no doubt about it. So, you're going to Prague. As our representative at the Tribunal. Defender and prosecutor in the same person. I'll give you all the necessary documentation in a moment.'

'Ah . . . but . . .' Anton was confused. 'I don't have any experience!'

'Nobody has. But you'll acquire it. My heart tells me that as things develop there are going to be more and more of these . . . legal conflicts. Instead of honest battle and open combat. And don't you look so worried, I'll probably come to Prague for when the session starts. Possibly even with Olga and Svetlana.'

'Why bring Svetlana?'

'Perhaps we'll be able to prove that Svetlana lost her powers because of a provocation by the Dark Ones and receive permission to restore her.'

'How?'

'The same way as we did with Igor. The problem isn't that Svetlana can't restore her powers rapidly, in just a few months. She can! The problem is that I can obtain permission to heal a second- or third-grade magician, but restoring the powers of a Great Enchantress is an extreme case. To do that, we need direct permission from the Inquisition. And not the Moscow branch, it has to be the European Office at least.'

Gesar raised his jug and smiled.

'Prosit, Anton. Let's drink to your success.'

'Boris Ignatievich, even now you're still not telling me everything,' Anton almost shouted.

'No, I'm not. Although I've already told you more than I ought to. But if you really want to lie awake all night with insomnia . . .' Gesar thought carefully. 'Then put together everything that's happened over the last year. The Chalk of Destiny,* the death of Alisa Donnikova, the appearance of the Mirror, those ludicrous buffoons the Regin Brothers and Fáfnir's Talon . . . and the hysteria everywhere over the end of the second millennium.'

'But there isn't a single thread connecting all these things,' Anton blurted out.

'Then sleep well,' Gesar said with a smile.

Late December is a time of frivolity and bustle. A time of frantic preparation for the holidays, a time for presents and drinking champagne with colleagues at work, even during the working day. A time of bright lights in the streets, a time for New Year tree

* See 'All for My Own Kind', Part 3 of *The Night Watch*.

bazaars. With the approach of Christmas and the New Year, even the eternal confrontation between the Others dies down, when Light Ones and Dark Ones suddenly slip into a short-lived dreamy state and sometimes even feel like forgiving their rivals their old offences. The less serious and deeply felt ones, at least.

Edgar, the Dark Magician, was late for a daily operational briefing for the first time since he had moved to the Russian capital from Estonia. The reason was trivial, but any self-respecting magician would have been ashamed to admit it.

Edgar had been feeding the ducks at the pond on Chistoprudny Boulevard. He'd surrendered completely to the memories that had suddenly come flooding back and completely forgotten the time. He'd got lost in his dreams, like a teenage kid after a glass of beer. And when he finally surfaced, he realised the briefing had already begun.

If age teaches you anything, then one of its lessons is certainly not to hurry if you're already late. So Edgar didn't rush off to flag down a car or make a headlong dash for the metro; he calmly finished crumbling the bun he'd bought for the mallards darting nimbly about at the edge of the unfrozen patch of water, or even scrambling across the ice, and only then set off towards the Chistye Prudy metro station, with the Christmas snow crunching cheerfully under his shoes.

Twenty minutes later Edgar arrived at the Day Watch office in no hurry and with his dignity intact. The elderly vampire couple on watch were decorating the New Year tree. They greeted Edgar as they were supposed to – deferentially and respectfully.

'The chief's been asking for you,' the vampire husband told him. 'He said to go and see him as soon as you turn up.'

'Thank you, Filippich,' said Edgar. 'Is he in his office?'

'He is now.'

'Uhuh. Enjoy the holiday.'

'And you, Edgar.'

Edgar took the lift to the top floors and sent Zabulon the sign of Hojd through the Twilight.

'Come in,' Zabulon replied.

The chief of the Day Watch required a strict observance of hierarchical discipline from his subordinates. But at the same time he somehow managed both to respect the freedom of even the shabbiest werewolf security guard and to trust the senior Watch magicians. He didn't question Edgar directly about why he'd missed the daily briefing. If he'd missed it, there must have been a good reason.

But there hadn't been any good reason. And so Edgar thought he'd better simply tell Zabulon the way it was and leave it at that. Especially since there hadn't been any serious operations planned for today; if a difficult situation had come up they would have reached out to him through the Twilight or simply called him on his mobile, so he wasn't feeling particularly guilty.

'Good evening, chief.'

'Good evening, Edgar. How do you like this weather?'

'Snow and no wind. I like it. I'm sorry I missed the planning meeting, chief. There wasn't anything urgent, was there?'

'No. But there will be now.'

Zabulon was dressed as usual in his favourite grey suit and grey shirt. Edgar thought he'd never seen the boss dressed any other way. Always a suit and a grey shirt when he was in the ordinary world. And without any clothes at all in his Twilight form.

'Would you believe it, chief, I was daydreaming? Walking along the boulevard at Chistye Prudy, remembering Samara and nineteen-twelve.'

Zabulon gave a faint smile and sang quietly:

'The photo studio ... Samara wrapped in mist again, it's nineteen-twelve ...'

The chief of the Day Watch had a clear, resonant baritone voice. Even though the Dark Magicians had known each other for many years, it was the first time Edgar had ever heard Zabulon sing.

'Were you feeding the ducks?' Zabulon asked.

'Yes.'

Zabulon sighed as he too briefly indulged his memories. Very briefly. Literally for half a minute.

'Okay, Edgar. Tomorrow you fly to Prague.'

'For the Tribunal?'

'Yes. It's going to hear several cases, including Alisa's murder and the Regin Brothers' case.'

'But weren't they going to release them tomorrow?' Edgar asked in surprise. 'Or have the Light Ones changed their minds?'

'No. They've handed the case over to the European Office of the Tribunal. And I think Gesar will try to lay the responsibility for what they did at our door. As if we'd planned it. Or incited them.'

'But they don't have any evidence. Not a shred.'

'Well, that's why I'm sending you to Prague. You can take a look, see what's what. And don't take it easy on anyone. We've taken enough, we've given way to them over the last two years, it's time we held our heads up higher.'

'It was the circumstances. That's what we gave way to,' said Edgar. The prospect of spending Christmas and seeing in the millennium in the ancient Gothic city of Prague had really fired his enthusiasm. Edgar loved the solemn city, it was the embodiment of the European spirit, a city where Dark Ones felt free and at ease.

'By the way. You'll probably be flying on the same plane as those Regin Brothers. Take a moment to let them know that the Moscow Day Watch has no intention of abandoning Dark Ones who have suffered on its territory. Tell them not to panic or lose heart.'

'And are we really going to defend them?'

'Yes, we really are. You see, Edgar, I have some plans that involve that absurd trio. For the time being I need this international alliance. So pay a bit of attention to them as well. The Light Ones will probably have a spy on their trail. Keep an eye on him too. Don't let him interfere. Don't get involved in any unnecessary violence, just keep him at a distance, that's all.'

'I understand, chief.'

'Take these,' said Zabulon, opening the safe beside the desk and handing Edgar two amulets and a charged wand. 'I don't expect you'll need to use the Mist. But just in case . . . And you know where to recharge the wand.'

'At Kostnitsa? At that chapel built out of bones?' Edgar asked immediately.

Zabulon nodded.

'Dark!' said Edgar, almost feeling envious of himself. 'I haven't been there for seventy years.'

'And you can purge yourself at the same time,' Zabulon advised. 'Do you know how?'

Edgar frowned. They might be friends, but after all, Zabulon was a magician beyond classification, and Edgar hadn't even reached the first grade yet, although he obviously had the potential to. Edgar still had to use his ordinary human name, but on the other hand, his surname had been completely forgotten by now.

'I've mastered the general technique.' It was obvious that Edgar would rather not have had to say that.

'Then you can practise it,' said Zabulon, closing the subject. 'That's all, now go and get ready. If you have any business outstanding, hand it over to someone else. Shagron or Belashevich.'

'I understand, chief, I will.'

'Good luck.'

Edgar left the chief's office, then called into his own for a moment, composed a message for Shagron and suspended it in the Twilight, before he set off home.

On his way out he ran into Alita.

'Hi there, beautiful!'

'Hello, Edgar. Do you fancy going skating?'

'I don't have time.'

'Oh, come on,' said the young witch. 'It's almost New Year, what work can you have to deal with? The Light Ones are more bothered about the quality of the Russian champagne is than with their usual tricks. Holidays are for fun, not for work.'

'Maybe, maybe,' Edgar said with a sigh. 'But anyway, I don't have time. I'm going away.'

'Where to?'

'To Prague.'

'Ooh!' Alita said enviously. 'For long?'

'I don't know. A week or so.'

'New Year in Prague!' Alita sighed. 'And not just any New Year – the year two thousand . . . Perhaps I should go with you?'

'Go if you like.' Edgar didn't try to dissuade her. 'But not with me. I'm not going to have fun.'

He felt a little envious too: if the witch went to Prague, she'd be able to relax with a clear conscience. But Edgar had been on too many of these work trips to entertain any illusions that they wouldn't involve much work.

There was always plenty of work. And especially at holiday times, as bad luck would have it. And during the most important holidays (who would suggest that the turn of a millennium wasn't an important event?) there was always more work than even the most pessimistic forecast might predict.

On his way home Edgar quickly reviewed the probabilities and established that the morning flight to Prague would be delayed until the evening and he would have to take an afternoon flight with a stopover in Prague. Of course, there weren't any tickets left, and he couldn't really count on the special reserve either. But that didn't bother Edgar too much – what could be simpler than the old double-booking trick? And, of course, the 'right' ticket would turn out to be the one held by the Other. Even if he only bought it a minute before check-in.

Packing for a trip doesn't take an Other long. Why bother taking things with you when it's simpler to buy them on the way? His entire luggage consisted of the amulets, the wand and a briefcase containing a solitary magazine and several wads of American dollars.

Of course, an Other can get anything that money can buy without spending a kopeck. But it's not worth wasting the power. And not all interventions are the same. Manipulate a sales assistant's mind for a piece of cake, and the Night Watch would nail you for an unsanctioned intervention. That would be just like them.

And apart from that, Edgar would simply have felt sorry for the sales assistant. The cake wouldn't have bothered him, of course. But what if he suddenly needed a jeep from a car sales room? People were the Others' foundation. Their feed base and substratum. They should be treated with consideration. And there was no need to worry about that kind of attitude sounding too much like that of the Light Ones.

The Dark Ones could tell the difference between treating human beings with consideration and doting on them.

They could tell it very clearly.

Edgar used the night to catch up on sleep, although it was harder than he expected to get to sleep at such an unaccustomed time. Even as he was nodding off, Edgar regretted that he hadn't gone skating with Alita.

In the morning Edgar discovered that someone had put a lot of work into improving his natural magical shell, strengthening it and weaving in stiff, tightly connected reinforcing threads. Zabulon, of course, who else? It couldn't be anyone else. 'Hmm,' thought Edgar. 'Could this mission really turn out to be complex and dangerous? Or is Zabulon simply playing safe?'

Since clashes with the Light Ones had become more frequent, Zabulon had installed personal protection for many members of the Day Watch. Just where did he get all the energy to maintain so many shields?

There were probably only two Others in Moscow who knew the answer to that – Zabulon himself and his constant opponent Gesar. And maybe the Inquisition. At least its top echelons.

Shagron offered Edgar a lift to the airport. It seemed like the newly repaired magician simply enjoyed driving his newly repaired BMW round Moscow when the city was in holiday mood. His excuse couldn't have been any simpler or more convincing: a briefing on current business. Not that there was much business for Edgar to brief him on. The hysteria of a thirteen-year-old girl who had discovered that she could enter the Twilight and accidentally looked at herself in a mirror while she was there. Win her confidence, talk some sense into her, support her . . . a beginner's assignment. And some gerontophilic succubus who was the laughing stock of half of Biruliovo.

This wasn't even work, just a couple of trifling problems. Minor domestic turbulence.

As he was walking into the airport terminal, Edgar got a call from another senior Day Watch magician – the magician that his colleagues knew as Yury, although he could obviously have used a Twilight name quite openly. Shagron had one for his special services to the Watch. And Yury was significantly more powerful and much older than Shagron.

'Hi, Edgar. On your way to Prague?'

'What of it?' Edgar asked, Odessa-style.

'Listen, and don't interrupt. I know a thing or two about the boss's plans. And why you're being sent there. It's not all as simple and clear-cut as it seems. A number of Light Ones are leaving for Prague today and tomorrow, and I wouldn't be surprised if Gesar himself follows in a few days. There are signs that the Light Ones are setting up a large-scale operation. And of course, Zabulon is planning an appropriate response. So you just be careful. Especially while you're travelling.'

Yury stopped, as if expecting a reply from Edgar, but Edgar said nothing – he remembered he'd been told not to interrupt. He just reached into the Twilight, attempting to locate Zabulon – but he couldn't find any trace of the chief. He couldn't tell where he was, what secret cranny he might be lurking in, what deep level of the Twilight he might be roaming. The most powerful magicians had their own paths and their own motives, incomprehensible to those around them.

'You remember the boss sent Alisa Donnikova on holiday?' Yury went on. 'Remember what happened to her. Of course, you want to know why I'm telling you all this, so I'll tell you. Because I'm a Dark One. And also because I've worked with you for a while already. Think what you like, but I'd prefer to see you as a live, healthy Other, and not just another shadow in the Twilight. See you, Edgar.'

Edgar stood there for a while, thoughtfully squeezing the mobile in his hand. Then he put it back on his belt, picked up his briefcase and set off for the ticket desks.

'Dark!' the magician thought to himself. 'What was that? A warning of some kind? And obviously behind Zabulon's back. And he brought up that business with Alisa?'

Zabulon had simply sacrificed the witch Alisa. Coldly and without any unnecessary pity. Like a pawn in a game of chess. In the games played between the Watches it was absurd to develop any feelings for the faceless figures on the board, but Others know how to feel and love as well. Edgar felt genuinely sorry for Alisa, but he wouldn't have lifted a finger to save her, not even if he had known everything in advance. Every game has its own inflexible rules, set once and for all. And nobody who has joined in a game can ever withdraw from it, or defy the rules. The witch Alisa had made her exit, and the witch Alita had made her entry. The law of conservation of energy in action. In fact, Alita even promised to be more likeable.

Edgar brainwashed the girl at the desk on autopilot, still absorbed in his own thoughts. They gave him a little blue booklet with his ticket and cancelled the ticket of some other unfortunate passenger. Unfortunately, he would just have to take a later flight. Because in the world of people and Others, it was the latter who made the rules. 'Why did Yury feel the need to warn me?' Edgar wondered as he stood at a bar counter with a glass of beer that was very expensive, but not very good. 'Surely not out of altruism? Nobody breaks the rules of the game *that* way.'

He recalled that when Zabulon left Moscow, he hadn't left Yury or Nikolai as his deputy in charge, although they were the Day Watch's next most powerful Dark Magicians. He had appointed Edgar, who was substantially less powerful than either of them. Yury had been acknowledged as a magician beyond classification back in the nineteenth century, and Nikolai just recently, after the war. Edgar still hadn't even reached first grade, and if he was honest, he hadn't even fully mastered the second grade. Sure, Edgar was a powerful magician. He was certainly more powerful than most of the Others in Moscow, Dark or Light. But he still couldn't equal Yury or Nikolai.

So why had Zabulon done that? Was Yury trying to take petty revenge? Out of mere envy? Trying to scare him or even (you could never tell!) simply having a joke at his upstart colleague's expense?

And the way Edgar had been brought in from Estonia had been hasty and illogical too. There he was, living a quiet life up in the small Baltic country, running its small, sleepy Day Watch and then – suddenly – the urgent summons to Moscow, the mad scramble to get his successor in Tallinn up to scratch – he was a classic 'hot-headed Estonian boy', barely even fourth grade. Edgar ought to give him a call, by the way. And then what had happened in Moscow? Edgar had been thrown straight into the crucible of a hectic two-week operation, and then, not long after that, he'd taken part in a wild cavalry raid to rescue a witch, who'd been practising without a licence, from the Light Ones. And that was all. After that, there'd been more than three months of routine work until the middle of November, when he'd suddenly been appointed acting chief of the Day Watch while Zabulon was away, and then there'd been the appearance of the Mirror and the Tribunal at Moscow University.

If he thought about it, it was quite possible that the old Day Watch magicians would try to teach this newcomer from the Baltic a lesson, because he was making a career for himself too fast, but they could hardly believe he was actually intriguing to take over from the boss. Zabulon didn't leave Moscow very often. And when Zabulon was there, Edgar was no more than just another operational agent. A powerful one, of course, an elite operative. But he only had the same rights as the others.

By the time his glass was empty, Edgar had decided to stop guessing at the reasons behind it all. His best bet was to try to plan a line of action that took account of . . . of everything. Even the very wildest possibilities.

All right. What was it that had done for Alisa? She hadn't gathered enough power in time. She hadn't recognised the Light Other, even though he was so close to her. She hadn't refused a duel that she was certain to lose. And most important of all – she'd given way to her emotions. She'd tried to appeal to a Light One's feelings.

Well, then, Edgar wasn't short of power, and Zabulon had even given him some of his own. The two amulets were a real treasure house of power. Especially the one charged with the Transylvanian Mist. If Edgar used that one, every Other in Europe would sense the monstrous discharge of energy. Plus the battle wand – a highly specialised weapon, but it was fast and reliable. Shahab's Lash was nobody's idea of a joke.

That meant Edgar had to keep as close an eye as possible on the Light Ones. Oh yes, the Light Ones . . . Just at that moment there were three of them in Sheremetievo. First there was his old friend from previous operations, Anton Gorodetsky, who lower-level Dark Ones had nicknamed 'Zabulon's favourite'. In that business with the Mirror for some reason he'd done just what Zabulon wanted, and helped the Dark Ones. Or had he just made everyone think he helped the Dark Ones? Probably that was it – otherwise how could he have stayed on in the Night Watch?

Second, there was a middle-aged female healer who had no connection with the Night Watch, thoughtfully sniffing perfumes in the duty-free shop. It was probably just coincidence that she happened to be travelling that day.

Third, there was a militiaman who was an Other on duty at the check-in. As there was supposed to be in any airport.

Apart from Edgar himself, there were four Dark Ones in the international terminal of Sheremetievo-2: his charges, the trio of Regin Brothers, who kept staring guardedly by turns at Edgar and Anton, who had installed himself in the bar at the far end of the hall; plus a low-grade magician over by the gambling machines who was paying no attention to anything. He seemed to be trying to earn a bit of extra cash by getting the mechanism to pay out the maximum winnings. His kind was perfectly described by the phrase 'cheap trash'.

The basic situation couldn't have been clearer.

Check-in and passport control were quickly over, no visas were required for the Czech Republic. But just in case, Edgar was carrying Estonian and Argentinian passports, both perfectly legal – Argentina was a wonderful country that traded in its own citizenship quite freely.

Edgar spent the rest of the time until boarding in one of the bars, though naturally not the one where Zabulon's favourite, the Light Magician Gorodetsky, had installed himself. Edgar's glance and his had met just once – I know you're here and you know I'm here, and both of us know that the other knows his opponent . . . and we're on similar missions. To defend our own at the trial and rout our enemies.

To Gorodetsky's credit, he'd made his position perfectly clear: when the trial starts, that's when we'll get to grips. Meanwhile let's just enjoy the flight and not get in each other's way.

Strange, how easily they understood each other. Maybe it was just a hangover from those ancient times before the Others were divided into Dark Ones and Light Ones, when they simply stood together against fate and the vicissitudes of life. Back then, of course, any healer was closer to a vampire than to a simple, luckless human being among the faceless mass of others like him. The Twilight can bring you together.

But the Twilight could separate you too. In fact, the Twilight was pretty good at it – nowadays you couldn't find more irreconcilable enemies anywhere on earth than Dark Ones and Light Ones. The trivial conflict between the USA and the Islamic world was nothing in comparison. Even the old 'cold war' between the USA and the USSR, now history, hadn't come close to the war of the Watches. They were just childish games for foolish human beings.

Edgar drank coffee that was extremely black, but not very good, thinking about everything at once and nothing in particular. For instance, why all these airport bars, which charged the earth and didn't seem to be skimping on their raw ingredients, managed to brew lousy coffee, serve bad beer and make absolutely inedible sandwiches. Plenty of the problems of human life could be attributed to the struggle between the Watches, but this wasn't one of them.

His charges – the entire ill-assorted trio – were peering at him disapprovingly from the waiting hall. Of course, the Regin Brothers regarded him as just another cop. Let them. They were boneheads. Brainless, heedless boneheads. And since that was what they were, they could be used to serve the cause of Darkness. And Zabulon had been quite right to decide to make use of them. That business with Fáfnir's Talon had certainly put the Light Ones off their stride during Rogoza the Mirror's appearance. Without even knowing it, the Regin Brothers had taken one of the blows intended for the Day Watch and allowed the Mirror, who had already grown strong, to charge himself up with power to the maximum. That was really what had made certain that Zabulon and his cohorts would win out in the latest clash with the Light Ones.

And serve them right.

Edgar watched without the slightest sympathy as courteous customs officers led away a furious gent in a prim, formal suit and expensive raincoat. It was his seat that Edgar would be occupying on the flight to Prague.

When they had taken off, Edgar waited until one of the Regin Brothers left his seat and then sat down next to the one who seemed to be the most sensible – the white one.

'Greetings, brother,' Edgar said warmly.

The Finn looked at him with big round eyes. A cautious look.

'We are Dark Ones,' Edgar went on quietly. 'We don't abandon our own. I've been sent to protect you if necessary. And we'll be able to defend you at the Tribunal – trust me. So hold your heads high, servants of the Dark. Our hour will come very soon now.'

With that, Edgar got up and went back to his seat without looking back.

There. Now let them rack their brains over that.

Rather dramatic. He'd had to work really hard to keep a solemn, stony face and avoid cracking a smile. But the expression in the Finn's big round eyes had been the opposite of a smile – he'd been genuinely frightened and concerned.

'I really shouldn't have,' Edgar muttered to himself. 'They're like children . . . And I tease them.'

Edgar sighed regretfully and opened his magazine. It was a nice short flight to Prague, not like flying to Yuzhno-Sakhalinsk, for instance. You were there before you knew it. Without any stops on the way or the hellish nightmare of having to sleep in your seat. But then, if you really thought about it, the most convenient form of transport was a Dark portal. Only setting up a portal from Moscow to Prague would be an unjustifiable extravagance. So he had to fly, like an ordinary human being.

But not quite like an ordinary human being. At least Others didn't have problems with tickets.

# CHAPTER 2

ANTON LOVED Prague. In fact, he simply couldn't understand how it was possible not to. There were some cities that confused you and suffocated you from the first, and there were some whose charm slowly and imperceptibly fascinated you. Moscow, unfortunately, did not belong in either category. But Prague was like an old, wise enchantress who knew how to pretend to be young, but did not see any need to, since she remained beautiful at any age.

Prague really ought to have become the abode of Dark Ones. A city overflowing with Gothic buildings, a city full of plague pillars – monuments to the medieval pestilence of the Black Death – a city that had a ghetto during the Second World War, a city that witnessed the opposition of the two superpowers during the 'cold war' . . . where could all those emanations of Dark, the nutritional substratum of the Dark Ones, have gone to? How had they been scattered, where to, and why had they been converted into memory, but not into malice?

It was a mystery.

Anton didn't know any members of the Prague Night Watch in person. They had occasionally exchanged information by courier or e-mail, when something in the archives needed clarification. And at Christmas and the New Year it was traditional to send greetings to all the Night Watches, but nobody made any distinction between the Prague Night Watch (active staff, one hundred and thirty Others; operational reserve, seventy-six) and the Night Watch of some small American 'town' (active staff, one Other; operational reserve, zero).

Anton had been to Prague twice on holiday. Simply wandering aimlessly round the city from one bar to the next, buying cheap little souvenirs on the Charles Bridge, travelling out to Karlovy Vary to swim in the pool filled with hot mineral water and take the hot wafers in the café.

But now he was flying to Prague on business. Really serious business.

Anton stretched out in his seat, as far as economy class in a Boeing-737 would allow – the standard of comfort wasn't so different from that in an old Soviet Tupolev – and examined the backs of the Regin Brothers' heads. They looked tense, their auras full of fear and impatience. They knew Anton was there and they were dreaming of getting as far away from him as possible, as soon as possible.

If it hadn't been for that incident at Sheremetievo, Anton might even have felt sorry for the luckless magicians. But once Anton had gone into combat with an enemy, he was an enemy for ever.

As if he could read Anton's thoughts – although, of course, that was beyond his power – one of the Regin Brothers, the tall, strong black guy, turned round, glanced warily at Anton and hastily averted his eyes. Raivo – Anton remembered his name. From somewhere in Senegal . . . no, from Burkina Faso, that was it. Picked up by one of the Regin Brothers' families and raised in the spirit of devotion to the great Fáfnir.

Just how had the Regin Brothers come up with all this nonsense?

Once, long, long ago, something had happened, something that often happened among the Others. A Dark Magician and a Light Magician fought to the death. The Light Magician was called Sigurd, Siegfried in German. The Dark Magician was killed . . . and he died in his Twilight form of a dragon. He was called Fáfnir. Later Sigurd was killed as well. Anton wondered if Gesar had known him.

After that, things took an unusual turn. The Dark Magician's disciples didn't scatter, as often happened, and they didn't fight among themselves, as happened even more often. Instead they decided to resurrect their master. They banded together to form a sect known as the Regin Brothers and withdrew almost completely from the usual struggle between Light and Dark, which suited the Light Ones very well, of course. They lovingly preserved the Talon, torn from the Twilight body of the Dark Magician. Later the Talon was confiscated by the Inquisition – just before the Second World War the Light Ones had lodged a successful protest against such an extremely powerful artefact remaining in the hands of Dark Ones. The Regin Brothers hadn't really argued about it, but they handed over the Talon with the words 'Fáfnir's time has not yet come . . .' And then the European Office of the Inquisition had suddenly been attacked. There had been a battle, in which almost all the magicians of the small sect had been killed, along with a substantial number of the Inquisition's bodyguards, who had grown idle and lazy. And then the remnants of the sect had made their bizarre arrival in Moscow.

It was well known that human beings didn't have a monopoly on idiots.

But then, were they really idiots?

Anton remembered what an intense charge of power the Talon had emitted. In part it was the power accumulated in the Talon as a result of the Regin Brothers' efforts over many years. In part it was the Power of the Dark Magician himself.

Others didn't die in the same way as ordinary people. They receded into the Twilight, losing their physical form and with it their ability to return to the world of human beings. But something was left behind – Anton had seen vague shadows and a quivering mist that sometimes appeared in the Twilight, marking the paths taken by dead Others. And once he had even met a dead Other. It wasn't one of his most pleasant memories. But there was something left, even there.

Was it possible to bring a dead Other back to life?

The answer was probably somewhere. In the labyrinth of the archives, classified as top secret, sealed by the Night and Day Watches, with access banned by the Inquisition. The higher magicians were bound to have wondered about where Others went when they died, the path that they themselves would eventually follow.

But Anton wasn't supposed to know the answer.

He looked through the window at the clouds stretching out below, at the faint glimmering of thousands of merged auras that indicated cities. The plane was already flying over some part of Poland.

Just supposing it was possible to bring Fáfnir back to life . . .

So what? Maybe he had been a powerful magician, maybe even a Higher Magician, a magician beyond classification . . . His resurrection wouldn't change the global balance of power. Especially since he would be estranged from human life; he wouldn't understand modern reality. And if he was stupid enough to set off round Europe in his Twilight form, he'd be torn to pieces by rockets, shot with lasers from satellites, they'd use tactical nuclear weapons . . . while the Japanese howled woefully that Godzilla had come back to life and been killed again.

What was it the Dark Ones wanted? Disorder, panic, people screaming about the Apocalypse?

Anton squirmed in his seat. He took the plastic cup and the two-hundred-gram bottle of dry Hungarian wine from the smiling stewardess. It was all very well for Edgar. Like any Dark One he was flying business class, so he had a crystal glass, and superior wine.

There was something to that last thought. Fáfnir . . . the Apocalypse. At least it made some sense of Gesar's remark about mass hysteria over the millennium. But why would the Dark Ones want to stage the end of the world? And what about everything else? The witch Alisa . . . The Chalk of Destiny . . .

Anton was sorry that he didn't have his laptop. It would have been interesting to lay it all out on the screen, shuffle the variants around and see what fitted with what. There was a standard program called Mazarini for analysing intrigues and it could have helped him understand a few things.

The Chalk of Destiny.

He took a gulp of wine, and it turned out to be surprisingly pleasant. Then he frowned. Gesar and Zabulon. They were really the two who would determine the whole business. They were far more mysterious and complex than ancient artefacts like the Chalk of Destiny and Fáfnir's Talon, or Others like the Mirror and Alisa. They probably understood everything that was going on . . . and were trying to outwit each other. As usual.

Gesar.

Zabulon.

The starting point for an analysis probably ought to be the Chalk of Destiny. When Svetlana, the new Great Enchantress, had appeared and joined the Night Watch, Gesar had attempted yet another intervention on a global scale. Svetlana had been provided with the Chalk of Destiny – an ancient and extremely powerful artefact that could be used to rewrite the Book of Destiny and alter human life. At first glance it had appeared that Svetlana was supposed to rewrite the destiny of the boy Egor – an Other with an indeterminate aura, inclined equally to the Dark and the Light – and make of him either a future prophet or a future leader. But, with some assistance from Anton, Svetlana had failed. All she had done was to bring Egor's destiny into equilibrium by removing all the influences exerted on him by the Watches in their struggle against each other.

But, of course, there had been more than one level to Gesar's plan. At a second level another Great Enchantress, his long-time lover Olga, recently rehabilitated after being punished by the leadership of the Light Ones, had recovered her magical abilities and used the other half of the Chalk of Destiny to rewrite someone else's destiny – while all the Dark Ones of Moscow were watching Svetlana.

That was the truth that Anton knew. The second level of truth.

But maybe there was a third.

He'd have to put that on hold for the time being. What had happened next? Alisa Donnikova, a capable witch and member of the Day Watch, if not one of the elite. Following a skirmish between Dark Ones and Light Ones that had obviously been engineered by Zabulon, she completely lost her magical powers. Then she'd been sent on holiday to the Artek young pioneers' camp to recuperate . . . and Gesar had sent Igor, who had suffered a comparable trauma, to the same place. A passionate love had sprung up between them – a terrible, deadly love between a Light Magician and a Dark Witch. And the outcome was that Alisa was dead, killed by Igor; and Igor himself was under threat of dematerialisation, brought down by his violation of the Treaty and the burden of his own guilt. And then there was the boy who had accidentally drowned because of him.

This wasn't one of Gesar's intrigues. Its ruthless and cynical style bore the signature of the Day Watch. Zabulon had sacrificed his lover, – but what had he sacrificed her for? To get Igor out of the way? That seemed odd. It had been almost a straight swap. Alisa Donnikova had been a powerful witch.

So it was one intrigue in response to another . . .

Then there was the appearance of the Mirror. Gesar was certain it had been impossible to predict, so it must have been a matter of chance. But no doubt Gesar and Zabulon had both immediately decided to exploit it, each for his own ends.

Anton suppressed the desire to swear out loud. There just wasn't enough data for an analysis. Nothing but conjectures, blanks, assumptions.

And not much was certain about the Regin Brothers either. They'd been lured to Moscow by Zabulon. Had he wanted to spread panic among the members of the Night Watch? Or feed the Mirror with power? The only thing that could have lured the Black Magicians into their insane attack on the Inquisition was a promise to resurrect Fáfnir. Naturally the old magicians, who had known Fáfnir when he was alive, had agreed – it was just about their last chance of victory. The young magicians had followed of course, . . . all those young Finns of African and Asian origin, collected one at a time – they were too isolated in their own little world, they thought of what was happening as a game, not an outrageous crime.

But what had Zabulon been after?

No. Anton didn't understand a thing. He shook his head and accepted his inability to fathom what was going on. Well then, he'd just have to do the job he'd been given. Try to save Igor.

Try to make the charges against the Day Watch stick.

The plane was already making its approach for landing.

*     *     *

The latest issue of *National Geographic* didn't help Edgar relax. He just couldn't get into an article about the Italian custom of throwing old things out of the window and other amusing European New Year rituals. The only thing Edgar took away from the opening paragraphs was a firm determination not to wander down narrow old Italian streets at New Year.

The smooth hum of the turbines set his thoughts vibrating in sympathy. And despite himself, Edgar's thoughts turned once again to his mission and the constant conflict between the Light and the Dark.

All right, he thought. Let's take it from the beginning.

In recent times the Day Watch had significantly strengthened its position and struck several substantial blows against the Light Ones, inflicting losses that could not immediately be made good. It would take time – not years but decades. Zabulon's obvious move should be to build on success right now, without giving the Light Ones time to re-gather their strength. To dash to victory while the enemy was still stunned.

What could weaken the Light Ones and strengthen the Dark Ones right now? When the Night Watch had lost a very powerful and highly promising enchantress? An attempt to take someone else out of the game?

Edgar pondered for a moment and again regretted he hadn't brought his laptop with him. He could have weighed up the possible variants, run through all the White Magicians of any real power and tried to identify their weak points. There was even a specialised program, called Richelieu – the Day Watch wasn't short of qualified programmers.

He would have to rely on his own natural computer – powerful but imperfect.

Who? Gesar was obviously not a candidate, he had already crossed that line beyond which an Other becomes almost invulnerable to his colleagues.

Objectively considered, the number two in the Night Watch hierarchy ought to be Svetlana Nazarova, but she would be out of the game for a long time, so Edgar had to award that honour either to the tricky Olga, an old specialist in combat operations, but who had only just returned from being out of the game herself; or to Ilya, a first-grade magician. But Edgar suspected that was not the limit of Ilya's abilities. Eventually, he could in all likelihood develop his powers and become a Great Magician, but such metamorphoses require time and colossal effort, primarily from the magician himself, and Ilya was still too young to abandon many of the simple, almost human, pleasures of life.

Who then? Olga or Ilya? Which of them should they tackle now?

Like Stirlitz, the Russian spy at Nazi HQ in the cult seventies film, Edgar pulled down his tray table and calmly sketched two symbolic portraits on napkins – a shapely female silhouette and a narrow face in spectacles. Olga or Ilya?

Olga. Intelligent, experienced, perceptive, worldly wise and cynical. Edgar didn't know her exact age, but it was reasonable to suspect that she was at least twice as old as he was. Edgar didn't know her true power – he'd never had a chance to test it to make sure. And to be quite honest, he didn't really want to try. To deprive her of her powers again would certainly be incredibly difficult – if you've just been released from imprisonment, you value your freedom very highly. Olga wouldn't think twice, she'd think a thousand times before taking another risk and ending up in front of a Tribunal. Apart from that, she was Gesar's long-time lover, and the boss of the Night Watch would certainly take great pains to protect her. In Zabulon's place Edgar would be wary of offending Olga, for an enraged Gesar was a far more dangerous enemy than the usual Gesar.

Edgar scratched his nose thoughtfully with the end of his felt-tip pen and drew a cross through the female portrait on the napkin.

Ilya. A very powerful magician with the face of a refined intellectual, who wore glasses for some reason, although he could easily have corrected his own sight. Just at the moment he wasn't in Moscow, or even in Europe. He was somewhere in Sri Lanka – for the last five years or so Light Ones from the Moscow Night Watch had been making trips to Sri Lanka with suspicious frequency. Edgar wondered what they got up. to there.

He made a mental note of that – he ought to pass the information on to the analytical section, let them rack their brains over it. Although most likely they were probably already monitoring this anomaly. But what if they weren't? Edgar would do better to play safe, even if he did make himself look stupid, than to feel sorry later, if no one had paid any attention to the Sri Lanka business.

Ye-es. But if Zabulon was plotting something against Ilya, he would hardly be likely to choose Prague to put his plans into practice at any time in the near future. Unless he could lure him there somehow.

Edgar pushed the napkin away and took a clean one. The last one. He divided it into four with two lines at right angles and began to draw a face in each quadrant. The first three were sketched in sparing strokes but were remarkably vivid, in the style of Bidstrup or Chizhikov.

In Edgar the world had probably lost a fine caricaturist.

Ilya, Semyon . . . Igor, the defendant at the Tribunal. Should he count him or not? Probably he should, especially since he was now the most vulnerable of all.

Edgar thought for a moment and then drew Anton Gorodetsky in the fourth quadrant. The only one who was still using his surname. But even so, he had already reached second grade, which made him Edgar's equal. If less experienced.

Which one? Of course it was simplest to exclude Igor. He already had one foot in the shadows of the Twilight.

And then there was Gorodetsky – he was flying to Prague too. But these were only the simplest variations. How many were there altogether?

The mere thought of the theoretically possible number set Edgar's teeth on edge. Ah, if only he had his laptop and the windows of Richelieu, with its heuristic module . . .

Stop, Edgar said to himself. Stop. How depressingly one-sided you are, Dark One!

The thought that had occurred to him was simple and surprising.

Eliminating one of their enemies from the game wasn't the only way to make the Dark Ones stronger. Why not the opposite approach – introducing a powerful Dark One into the battle?

But who was there to swell the all-too thin ranks of the Day Watch? Vitaly Rogoza, whose appearance had filled Edgar with childish delight, had turned out to be no more than a Mirror. And after he'd done everything the Twilight had created him to do, he'd disappeared for ever. Hunt down some promising young recruits? They were looking and they did find a few. But you couldn't mould any of them into a genuinely powerful Other overnight and the Dark Ones hadn't come across a prodigy like Svetlana Nazarova for a long time now.

Even so, thought Edgar, I'm on the right road. I'm flying to Prague. The capital of European necromancy. And in time for the Christmas just before the arrival of the millennium. At a time when countless prophets and soothsayers are frightening the world with all sorts of horrors, up to and including the end of the world itself.

Yes! That was it! Maybe Zabulon was planning to resurrect one of the disembodied magicians of the past? Prague, at a time like this! Dark upon Dark! As always, Zabulon had skilfully and unobtrusively hidden what was lying in open view.

Edgar breathed out heavily, crumpled the napkin and stuffed it in his pocket.

And so, in the city of necromancers, at a time of incredible energy instability, Zabulon could easily try to pluck someone out of non-existence. But who?

Think, Edgar. The answer should be lying on the surface too.

All right then, what have we got? Prague, the Tribunal, the case of the duel between Teplov and Donnikova, Gorodetsky and Edgar seconded to the trial. Possibly Alita too. Who else? The Regin Brothers.

Stop. That's it!

The Regin Brothers. The servants of Fáfnir. 'I'll find a use for them, Edgar,' Zabulon had said. 'I have some plans that involve them.'

Fáfnir.

Trying to maintain an appearance of calm, Edgar folded away his tray table and settled more comfortably into his seat.

Fáfnir. There was someone who would be very, very useful indeed to the Dark Ones. The mighty Fáfnir, the Great Magician, the Dragon of the Twilight.

The faint echo of his power, absorbed by the Mirror Rogoza, had allowed him to drain an enchantress like Svetlana with ease.

'And if Zabulon really is going to attempt to resurrect Fáfnir, he couldn't have chosen a better place and time during the last hundred years – or over the hundred years to come,' Edgar thought as his eyes wandered idly across the panelling of the Boeing. 'That's for certain, he couldn't have.'

The stewardess glanced at him, and Edgar fastened his seat belt. The plane was making its approach for landing.

Hello, Prague.

Edgar's ears felt like they were stuffed with cotton-wool, but that didn't stop him thinking.

So it was a resurrection. That was something the Dark Ones hadn't tried for at least fifty years – not since Stalin's time. There hadn't been any opportunity, because the level of energy turbulence hadn't been high enough at any time since 1933 and 1947.

Why hadn't Zabulon told Edgar? Was it too soon? But then what was he to make of Yury's cautious warning? And then, what had this to do with what had happened at the Artek camp that summer? Because it had to be connected somehow, it had to be. A pawn had been sacrificed, and now maybe a more weighty piece's turn had come. A knight or a bishop – which of those would Edgar be? The two rooks, of course, were Yury and Nikolai, the queen was Zabulon himself, and the king, defenceless but crucial – that was the cause of the Dark.

And so one of the rooks had hinted to Edgar that there was a chance the Crimean Gambit might be used again, this time with a rook. Somehow Edgar didn't feel like being a knight. Let that vicious old hag Anna Tikhonovna play the horse, that would be just about right for her.

The plane shuddered as the wheels touched down on the runway Once, twice – and their flight became a rapidly decelerating dash over the concrete.

But surely Zabulon hadn't set up another exchange of pieces while he furtively pushed forward a few pawns, the Regin Brothers, in the hope that another black queen would appear on the board or, at the very least, a bishop?

It was insulting to be a sacrificial piece.

'And what if it's a test at the same time?' Edgar wondered. 'A trial of endurance? Alisa let herself be squandered – Zabulon doesn't need pieces like that in his game. But if Edgar can manage to survive, and without disrupting the boss's plans . . . Yes, that's the result we need!'

But how could it be achieved?

The other half of the exchange was Anton Gorodetsky, Zabulon's favourite. There was no doubt about that. The boss of the Day Watch couldn't carry on using him for ever, and he understood that very well. It wasn't even really true that he could use him. Zabulon was always ready to put a good face on a poor result and make it look as if he'd tricked the Light Magician.

The passengers began moving towards the exit and the concertina bridge that was so unfamiliar to the inhabitants of the former USSR. Edgar took his raincoat out and put it on, left his magazine in the pocket on the seat in front, picked up his briefcase and followed the rest.

The feeling of being in Europe rather than Russia was instantaneous and strangely comprehensive. It was hard to grasp exactly what triggered it – the expressions on people's faces, their clothes, the cleanliness of the airport, the way it was laid out? Thousands of minor details. The announcements in Czech and English without a Ryazan accent. The far greater number of smiles. The fact that there weren't any of those private cabs that he detested on the square in front of the terminal building.

And there was a line of attractive yellow Opels at the taxi rank.

His taxi driver gabbled away equally freely in Russian and English and, of course, in his native Czech. Where to? A hotel. The Hilton, I suppose. Well, well. Russians don't often go straight to the Hilton. And the ones who do look different: lots of gold, bigwigs with bodyguards, in expensive limousines . . . I'm not Russian, I'm Estonian. Yes, that's not the same thing any longer . . . It wasn't the same thing before either. Well, even a Czech was almost the same as a Russian before . . . That's debatable. Yes, maybe it is.

The driver's chatter was diverting and Edgar decided to take a break from all his thinking. He wouldn't get any real work done the day he arrived in any case. He could actually relax – with a glass or two of beer, naturally. Who in his right mind wouldn't take a mug of real Czech beer, provided his stomach was in good shape (or even if it wasn't)?

Only a dead man.

Just as in any Hilton, a free room could be found without any great problem, even when Prague was crowded with tourists just before Christmas. But just as in any country that had not yet cast off the shackles of its recent socialism, it would cost crazy money for a non-Other. Edgar was an Other, and so he paid up straight away without even a frown, although they were obviously expecting one. He was Russian, after all, and he didn't look like a nouveau riche bandit. A hundred years earlier Edgar wouldn't have been able to resist sticking his Argentinian passport under the receptionist's nose. But he was a hundred years more mature now, and he made do with his Russian passport.

The person at the registration desk – the one that not everybody went to – was a Dark One. A very rare type, too – a *beskud*. He glanced at Edgar, licked his thin lips and opened his slit pupils wide. And then, at last, he smiled – his teeth were small and sharp, all the same triangular shape.

'Greetings! Here for the Tribunal.'

'Uhuh.'

'Here you go.'

He threw a small bundle of blue fire at Edgar – it was his temporary registration. The fire passed easily through Edgar's clothes and landed on his chest in the form of an oval seal that glowed in the Twilight.

'Thanks.'

'You give them a roasting at the Tribunal,' the *beskud* told him. 'A real roasting. It's our turn now.'

'I'll try,' Edgar promised with a sigh.

He went up to his room, just to have a wash and leave his brief-case there.

'And now,' Edgar thought enthusiastically as he rode down in the lift, 'I'm for the Black Eagle. And I'm going to order the *vepřová kýta pčeně.*' This dish, 'roast leg of pork', was so popular he'd even come across a description of it in a fantasy magazine he'd read once.

As he waited for his order, Edgar took small mouthfuls of his second mug of beer (he'd drunk the first one Russian-style, straight down, evoking a nod of approval from the waiter), and tried to focus on his thoughts. But something was preventing him. Or someone.

Edgar looked and saw Anton Gorodetsky, who was standing near the table and staring steadily at him.

Edgar shuddered, thinking he must have been followed. But there was a puzzled expression in Gorodetsky's eyes too and Edgar breathed a sigh of relief. A coincidence, nothing more than a coincidence.

And what's more, there weren't any places left. Except at Edgar's table.

Acting on a sudden impulse, Edgar nodded to the Light One and said:

'Sit down. I'm having a break. You should too – to hell with all this work!'

Anton hesitated and Edgar thought he was going to leave, but then he decided to stay. He walked over and sat down opposite Edgar, giving him a sullen look, as if he found it hard to believe that all his old enemy wanted to do was relax for a while. What was that saying the Light Ones had? Anyone you've fought with once is an enemy for ever.

Nonsense. Fanaticism. Edgar preferred a more flexible approach – if today it was advantageous to ally yourself with someone you hurled Shahab's Lash at yesterday, why not do so? But then, after Shahab's Lash there isn't usually anybody left to conclude an alliance with. Ashes don't make much of an ally.

'And not a word about the Watches?' Anton asked ironically.

'Not a word,' Edgar confirmed. 'Just two fellow-countrymen in Prague before Christmas. I've ordered the *vepřová kýta pčně*. I recommend it.'

'Thanks, I know it,' said Anton, still without a shadow of a smile, turning to the waiter.

These Europeans had no idea what a real frost was, a real winter. As Anton came out of the Malostranská metro station, he wondered if he ought to button up the collar of his jacket, but he didn't bother. Snowy weather, but there was no bite to it. Two degrees below zero at the most.

He set off along the street, strolling at a leisurely pace across the ancient cobblestones. Sometimes he gave in to curiosity and dropped into the souvenir shops – amusing wooden toys, curiously shaped ceramics, photographs with views of Prague, T-shirts with witty slogans. He ought to buy something, after all. Just to make his mark, so to speak. Maybe that T-shirt with the funny face on it and the words 'Born to be Wild'.

There was almost three hours to go before he was due to meet the Inquisition's representative. He didn't even need to take a taxi or the metro – he could have a long lunch and stroll over on foot. A rendezvous under the clock tower – what could be more romantic? What if the Inquisition's representative turned out to be a woman, maybe even attractive, and a Light One? Then romance would really be in the air.

Anton laughed at his own thoughts. He hadn't the slightest desire to play the field or start an affair. And anyway, the concepts of 'Light' and 'Dark' didn't apply to the Inquisition. It stood beyond the two great powers.

But maybe the concept of gender did apply? As far as Anton

knew, when Maxim, the Light Magician from Moscow, the one they'd nicknamed the Maverick, became an Inquisitor he had divorced his wife.* Apparently inquisitors simply lost interest in all that petty human stupidity – love, sex, jealousy.

The Black Eagle was one of Anton's favourite restaurants in Prague. Maybe that was simply because he'd been there a few times the first time he was in the city. It doesn't take much to make a Russian happy, after all. Good, unobtrusive service, fine food, excellent beer, low prices – last but not least. Only the Dark Ones can afford to throw their money around. Even Rogoza, that creation of the Twilight, had appeared in Moscow loaded down with dollars. It was possible to earn money honestly, but to earn a *lot* of money – you could never do that without compromising your conscience a little. And when it came to that, the Night Watch was definitely at a disadvantage compared to the Day Watch.

The street Anton was walking along divided into two, like a river, leaving a number of old, low buildings forming a long, narrow island along its centre – most of them restaurants and souvenir shops. The Black Eagle was the first in the row.

As he walked into the small courtyard, Anton saw a Light Other.

Not a member of any Watch. Just an Other who preferred an almost ordinary, almost human life to the front line of magical war. A tall, handsome, middle-aged man with a good figure, in the uniform of a US Air Force officer. He was leaving the restaurant, obviously feeling quite contented with his time there, with his girlfriend – a pretty Czech girl – and with himself.

He didn't spot Anton straight away – he was too absorbed in conversation. But when he did, he gave him a broad, beaming smile.

---

* The events in which Maxim was involved are described in 'All for My Own Kind', Story Three of *The Night Watch*.

There was nothing else for it — Anton raised his shadow from the snow-covered cobblestones and stepped into the Twilight. Silence fell, all sound was muffled in cotton-wool. The world slowed and lost its colours. People's auras shimmered into life, like rainbows — most of them calm and peaceful, not overloaded with unnecessary thoughts. The way it ought to be in a tourist spot.

'Greetings, Watchman!' the American hailed him happily. Here in the Twilight there were no problems with language.

'Hello, Light One,' Anton replied. 'Glad to see you.'

'The Prague Watch?' the American queried. He'd read the Watchman's aura, but not made out the details. But then, he was a pretty weak magician. Somewhere around sixth grade, and with a strong attachment to natural magic. There wouldn't have been anything for him to do in the Watch anyway. Except maybe sit somewhere out of the way and keep an eye on witches and shape-shifters whose powers were as weak as his own.

'Moscow.'

'Oh, the Moscow Watch!' There was a clear note of respect in the American's voice now. 'A powerful Watch. Allow me to shake your hand.'

They shook hands. The American airman seemed to regard the encounter as one more element of a pleasant evening.

'Captain Christian Vanover Jr. Sixth-grade magician. Do you need my assistance, Watchman?' The formal proposal was made with all due seriousness.

'Thank you, Light One, but I don't require any assistance,' Anton replied no less politely.

'On vacation?' Christian asked.

'No. A business trip. But no assistance required.'

The American nodded:

'This is my Christmas vacation. My unit's stationed in Kosovo, so I decided to visit Prague.'

'Good choice,' said Anton with a nod. 'A beautiful city.'

He didn't want to continue the conversation, but the American was full of bonhomie.

'A wonderful city. I'm glad we managed to save it in the Second World War.'

'Yes, we saved it,' said Anton, nodding again.

'Did you fight back then, Watchman?'

Anton realised Christian must be a really weak magician, not to see his real age, at least approximately.

'No.'

'I was too young too,' the American sighed. 'I dreamed of joining the army, but I was only fifteen. A pity, I could have got here fifty years earlier.'

Anton only just stopped himself from saying that Christian wouldn't have had the chance, as American forces never reached Prague. But he immediately felt ashamed of his own thoughts.

'Well, good luck,' said the American, finally deciding to move on. 'Some day I'll fly into Moscow to see you, Watchman!'

'Only not the way you flew into Kosovo.' This time Anton couldn't stop himself. But Captain Christian Vanover Jr didn't take offence. On the contrary, he smiled his broad smile and said:

'No, I don't think it will come to that, do you? May the Light be with you, Watchman!'

Anton followed the American out of the Twilight. Christian's girl hadn't noticed a thing. He took her by the arm and winked at Anton.

'And may the force be with you,' Anton muttered in Russian.

That was a stroke of bad luck. His good mood had completely melted away, like a lump of ice on a hot skillet.

He could tell himself a thousand times over that no arguments and disputes between states had anything to do with the concerns of the Light and the Dark. He could accept that in a war this airman–magician was far more likely not to aim his bombs at civilians. But even so.

Just how could he manage to go out on bombing raids and drop his explosives on people's heads, and still remain a Light One? Because he was a Light One, no doubt about that. But he almost certainly had human lives on his conscience. How did he manage not to fall back into the Twilight? What incredible faith he must have in his own righteousness, to be able to combine active military service and the cause of the Light.

Anton entered the Black Eagle in a melancholy mood.

He immediately spotted Christian Vanover's fellow airmen. About ten of them, all ordinary human beings. They were sitting at a long table, eating goulash and drinking Sprite.

They really were drinking Sprite!

In a Czech beer bar. On holiday.

And not because they were teetotallers. There were empty beer bottles on the table, American Budweiser, which Anton would only have considered drinking if he was dying of thirst in a desert.

Anton walked past the Americans. There were no more free tables – another stroke of bad luck. But there was someone over there sitting on his own, maybe he could join him.

The person at the table looked up – and started. Anton did the same.

It was Edgar.

# CHAPTER 3

ONE THING the Dark Ones certainly had was a lust for life. Anton had never had any doubt about that. He only had to look at the way Edgar was dealing with that tasty-looking leg of pork that no dietician would ever have approved, larding it generously with mustard – the kind the Russians liked, of course, sweetish, but still with a sharp bite – and horseradish too, and swilling it down with plentiful quantities of beer.

Anton had always found that astonishing. He had always been on perfectly friendly terms with his vampire neighbours, and even they sometimes looked more full of the joy of life than the Light Magicians. The higher magicians, that was – those whose powers were at Anton's level still hadn't finished 'playing at people'.

The unpleasant thing about it was that their love of life usually didn't extend beyond themselves.

Anton lifted his heavy mug of Budvar and muttered:

'Prosit.'

It was a good thing the Czechs didn't have the custom of clinking glasses. Anton wouldn't have liked to clink glasses with a Dark One.

'Prosit,' Edgar replied. He drained half of his mug in two swallows, savouring the beer, and wiped the foam off his upper lip. 'That's good.'

'It is,' Anton agreed, although he was still feeling tense. No, of course there was nothing reprehensible about them drinking beer together like this. The rules of the Night Watch didn't prohibit contact with Dark Ones; on the contrary, if a member of the Watch was confident that he was safe, it was welcomed. You never knew what you might find out, you might even be able to influence a Dark One. Not turn him to the Light, of course, but at least stop him pulling his next lousy trick. Anton surprised himself by saying: 'It's nice to find at least one thing we can agree on.'

'Yes,' said Edgar, trying to speak amicably and politely, so that the Light One wouldn't blow his top over some imaginary insult or get suspicious for no reason. 'Czech beer in Moscow and Czech beer in Prague are two different things.'

Gorodetsky nodded.

'Yes. Especially when you compare it with bottled beer. Czech beer in bottles is the corpse of real beer in a glass coffin.'

Edgar smiled in agreement and remarked:

'Somehow the rest of Eastern Europe seems to have lost the talent for brewing beer.'

'Even Estonia?' Anton asked.

Edgar shrugged. These Light Ones could never let slip a chance for a jibe.

'Our beer's good. But it's not exceptional. Pretty much like in Russia.'

Anton frowned, as if he'd just remembered the taste of the beer back home. But he said something quite different:

'I was in Hungary this summer. I drank Hungarian beer, Dreher. Almost the only kind they have.'

'And?'

'I'd have been better off drinking sour Baltika.'

Edgar laughed. Even when he strained his memory, he couldn't remember a single brand of Hungarian beer. But then, if Anton thought so poorly of it, it was better not to remember. Anton was a good judge of beer, an excellent judge, in fact. The Light Ones were fond of the pleasures of the flesh – you had to give them that.

'And these . . . valiant warriors . . . drinking their slops from back home,' said Anton, nodding towards the Americans. 'Peacemakers . . . Goering's aces.'

Both Edgar and Anton had finished their *vepřová kýta pčeně* long ago. They'd both drunk enough beer to set their eyes aglow and their voices were growing louder and more relaxed.

'Why Goering?' Edgar asked in surprise. 'They're not krauts, they're Americans.'

Anton explained patiently, as if he were talking to a child.

'Aces of the US Air Force doesn't sound right. Do you know any short, snappy term for the US Air Force?'

'No, I don't.'

'All right, then. They can be Clinton's aces. At least the Germans knew they were fighting airmen like themselves, but this crowd have dropped bombs on villages where the only defence is a Second World War anti-aircraft gun. And they get medals for it, too. But you just try asking them if there's anything in their lives they hold sacred. They still think they were the ones who liberated Prague.'

'Sacred?' Edgar echoed with a laugh. 'Why would they need to hold anything sacred? They're soldiers.'

'You know, Other, it seems to me that even soldiers should still be human beings first and foremost. And human beings need something sacred to cherish in their souls.'

'First you need to have a soul. The sacred bit comes later. Oh! Now we can ask one of them!'

One of the American airmen, a guy with rosy cheeks, his uniform glittering with braid and various kinds of trimmings, was trying to squeeze past their table. A fresh strawberries and cream complexion, the pride of Texas or Oklahoma. He was probably on his way back from the gents.

'Excuse me, officer! Do you mind if I ask you a question?' Edgar said to him in good English. 'Is there anything in your life that you regard as sacred? Anything at all?'

The American stopped as if he'd stumbled over something. His instinct told him that a soldier of the very finest country in the world had to rise to the challenge and give a worthy reply. He thought, his face reflecting the painful workings of his mind until suddenly it lit up. Inspiration. A proud smile spread across his face.

'Anything sacred? Of course there is! The Chicago Bulls.'

'It's like a game of chess, you get it?' Edgar explained. 'The bosses are just moving their helpless pieces – that's you and me   around the board.'

The waiter's face grew longer and longer, the more beer Anton and Edgar drank. The number of those big glass mugs he'd brought to this table would have been enough to get the entire American air squadron drunk, and the Chicago Bulls as well. But the two Russians just carried on sitting there, even though it was obvious they were finding it harder and harder to control their tongues.

'Take you and me, for instance,' Edgar went on. 'You're going to be the defender in this trial. I'm going to be the prosecutor. But we still don't carry any real weight. We're just figures on the board. If it suits them, they'll throw us into the thick of it. If it suits them, they'll set us aside for better times. If they want to, they'll exchange us. After all, what is this trial, really? It's a song and dance over a trivial exchange of pieces. Your Igor's been swapped for our Alisa. And that's all. They just set them on each other, like two spiders in a jar, and took them off the board. In the name of higher goals that are beyond us.'

'No, you're wrong,' Anton said sternly, wagging his finger at Edgar. 'Gesar had no idea that Igor would run into Alisa. It was one of Zabulon's intrigues!'

'And how can you be so sure of that?' Edgar asked derisively. 'Are you so powerful you can read Gesar's soul like an open book? As far as I know, the head of the Light Ones isn't too fond of letting his subordinates into his most important plans either. It's the high politics of the higher powers!' he said, loudly and insistently.

Anton really wanted to object. But unfortunately he didn't have any convincing arguments.

'Or take that latest clash, in Moscow University. Zabulon used you – I'm sorry, you probably don't like to hear me say that, but now that we've started . . . Anyway, Zabulon used you. Zabulon! Your sworn enemy.'

'He didn't use me.' Anton hesitated, but then went on anyway. 'He tried to use me. And I tried to use the situation to our advantage. You understand – after all, this is war.'

'Okay, so you tried to use the situation too,' Edgar agreed dismissively. 'Let's assume that. But Gesar did nothing – nothing! – to protect you. Why should he try to keep his pawns safe? It's wasteful and pointless.'

'You treat your pawns even worse,' Anton remarked morosely. 'You don't even regard the lower Others, the vampires and shapeshifters, as equals. They're just cannon fodder.'

'But they are cannon fodder, Anton. They're less valuable than us magicians. And anyway, it's pointless for you and me to talk about things and try to understand. We're puppets. Nothing but puppets. And we don't have a chance to become puppet-masters, because for that you need the powers of a Gesar or a Zabulon, and that kind of power doesn't come along very often. And anyway, the places at the chessboards are already taken. None of the players will give his place away to a mere piece – not even to a queen or a king.'

Anton drained his large mug sullenly and put it back down on the glass stand with the restaurant's logo.

He was no longer the same young magician who had gone out into the field for the first time to track down a poaching vampire. He had changed, even in such a short time. Since that first mission he'd had plenty of opportunities to observe just how much Dark there was in the Light. He was actually rather impressed by the gloomy position adopted by the Dark Magician Edgar – they were only grains caught between the millwheels as the big players settled accounts with each other, so the best thing to do was drink your beer and keep quiet. And once again Anton thought that sometimes the Dark Ones, with their apparent simplicity, were more human than the Light Ones, with their struggle for exalted ideals.

'But even so, you're wrong, Edgar,' he said eventually. 'There's one fundamental difference about us. We live for others. We serve, we don't rule.'

'That's what all the human leaders have said,' Edgar replied, obligingly falling into the trap. 'The Party is the servant of the people, remember?'

'But there's one thing that distinguishes us from human leaders,' said Anton, looking Edgar in the eye. 'Dematerialisation. You understand? A Light One cannot choose the path of Evil. If he realises that he has increased the amount of Evil in the world, he withdraws into the Twilight. Disappears. And it's happened plenty of times, whenever a Light One has made a mistake or given way even slightly to the influence of the Dark.'

Edgar giggled quietly.

'Anton, you've rebutted your own point. "If he realises . . ."

What if he doesn't realise? Do you remember the case of that maniac healer? Twelve years ago, I think it was.'

Anton remembered. He hadn't been initiated at the time, but he'd discussed and analysed the unprecedented case with every member of the Watch, with every Light One.

A Light healer with a powerful gift of foresight. He lived outside Moscow and wasn't an active member of the Night Watch, but he was listed in the reserve. He worked as a doctor, and used Light magic in his practice. His patients adored him – after all, he could literally work miracles.

But he also killed young women who were his patients. Not by using magic; he simply killed them. Sometimes he killed them using acupuncture – he had a perfect knowledge of the body's energy points.

The Night Watch discovered what he was doing almost by accident. One of the analysts started wondering about the sharp rise in deaths among young women in a small town just outside Moscow. One especially alarming factor was that most of the victims were pregnant. They also noticed a remarkably high number of miscarriages, abortions and stillbirths. They suspected the Dark Ones, they suspected vampires and werewolves, Satanists, witches. They looked into absolutely everyone.

Then Gesar himself got involved in the case, and the murderer was caught. The murderer who was a Light Magician.

The charming and imposing healer simply saw the future too clearly. Sometimes, when he received a patient, he could see the future of her unborn child, who was almost certain to grow into a murderer, a maniac or a criminal. Sometimes he saw that his patient would commit some monstrous crime or accidentally cause the deaths of large numbers of people. So he decided to fight back any way he could.

At his trial the healer had explained ardently that Light

magical intervention wouldn't have been any use – in that case the Dark Ones would have been granted the right to an equal intervention in response, and the quantity of Evil in the world wouldn't have been reduced. But all he had done was 'pull up the weeds'. And he had been prevented from sinking into the Twilight by the firm conviction that the amount of Good he had brought into the world was far greater than the Evil he had done.

Gesar had had to dematerialise him in person.

'He was a psychopath,' Anton explained. 'Just a psychopath. With their typical deranged way of thinking. You get cases like that, unfortunately.'

'Like that sword-bearer of Joan of Arc's, the Marquis Jules de Rey,' Edgar prompted eagerly. 'He was a Light One too, wasn't he? And then he started killing women and children in order to extract the elixir of youth from their bodies, conquer death and bring happiness to all humanity.'

'Edgar, nobody's insured against insanity. Not even Others. But if you take the most ordinary witch,' Anton began, fuming.

'I accept that,' said Edgar, spreading his hands in a reconciliatory shrug. 'But we're not talking about extreme cases here. Just about the fact that it's *possible*, and the defence mechanism you're so proud of, dematerialisation . . . let's call it simply conscience . . . can fail. And now think – what if Gesar decides that if you die it will do immense good for the cause of the Light in the future? If the scales are balanced between Anton Gorodetsky on one side and millions of human lives on the other?'

'He wouldn't have to trick me,' Anton said firmly. 'There'd be no need. If such a situation arises, I'm prepared to sacrifice myself. Every one of us is.'

'And what if he can't tell you anything about it?' Edgar laughed, delighted. 'So the enemy won't find out, so you'll behave more naturally, so you won't suffer unnecessarily. After all, it's Gesar's responsibility to preserve your peace of mind as well.'

He raised the next mug of beer with a satisfied expression and sucked in the foam noisily.

'You're a Dark One,' said Anton. 'All you see in everything is evil, treachery, trickery.'

'All I do is not to close my eyes to them,' Edgar retorted. 'And that's why I don't trust Zabulon. I distrust him almost as much as I do Gesar. I can even trust you more – you're just another unfortunate chess piece who happens by chance to be painted a different colour from me. Does a white pawn hate a black one? No. Especially if the two pawns have their heads down together over a quiet beer or two.'

'You know,' Anton said, slightly surprised, 'I just don't understand how you can carry on living if you see the world like that. I'd just go and hang myself.'

'So you don't have any counterarguments to offer?'

Anton took a gulp of beer too. The wonderful thing about this natural Czech beer was that even if you drank lots of it, it still didn't make your head or your body feel heavy. Or was that an illusion?

'Not one,' Anton admitted. 'Right now, at this very moment, not a single one. But I'm sure you're wrong. It's just difficult to argue about the colours of a rainbow with a blind man. There's something missing in you. I don't know what exactly. But it's something very important, and without it you're more helpless than a blind man.'

'Why am I?' Edgar protested, somewhat offended. 'It's you Light Ones who are helpless. Bound hand and foot by your own ethical dogmas. And those who have moved up onto the higher levels of development, like Gesar, control you.'

'I'll try to answer that,' said Anton. 'But not right now. We'll be seeing each other again.'

'Avoiding the question?' Edgar asked, laughing.

'No, It's just that we decided not to talk about work. Didn't we?'

Edgar didn't answer. The Light One really had got him there. Why had he bothered getting into such a useless argument? You can't paint a white dog black, as they said in the Day Watch.

'Yes,' he agreed. 'It's my fault, I admit it. Only . . .'

'Only it's very hard not to talk about the things that separate us,' Anton said with a nod. 'I understand. It's not your fault . . . it's destiny.'

He rummaged in his pockets and took out a packet of cigarettes. Edgar couldn't help noticing that they were cheap ones, 21st Century, made in Russia. Well, well. A Dark Magician of his grade could afford all the pleasures of life. But Anton smoked Russian cigarettes, and maybe it was no accident that he'd ended up in this small, cosy restaurant that was so inexpensive?

'Where is it you're staying?' he asked.

'The Kafka Hotel,' Anton answered. 'That's in Žižkov, Cimburkova Street.

That fitted, all right, it was a small, second-rate hotel. Edgar nodded as he watched the Light One light up. It looked awkward somehow, as if he hadn't been smoking long or didn't smoke very often.

'And you're in the Hilton, aren't you?' Anton suddenly said. 'Or the Radisson-SAS at the very worst?'

'Are you following me?' Edgar asked, suddenly on his guard again.

'No. It's just that all Dark Ones are so fond of famous brands and expensive hotels. You're predictable too.'

'So what?' Edgar said defiantly. 'Are you a believer in asceticism and the poor life?'

Anton looked round ironically at the restaurant, the pathetic remains of his leg of pork on the knife-scarred wooden board, his latest mug of beer — how many had there been? It didn't seem as if he even needed to answer, but he did:

'No, I'm not arguing that. But the number of rooms and staff that a hotel has isn't the most important thing. Nor are the prices on the menu. I could have stayed at the Hilton too, and drunk beer at the most expensive pub in Prague. But what for? And you — why did you come to this place? Not exactly five star, is it?'

'It's comfortable here,' Edgar admitted. 'And the food's good.'

'See what I mean?'

In a sudden fit of drunken magnanimity, Edgar exclaimed:

'That's it! I think I've got it! That's what the difference between us is. You try to limit your natural requirements. Maybe it's some kind of modesty. But we're more extravagant, yes . . . With power, money, financial and human resources . . .'

'People are not a resource!' Anton's eyes were suddenly piercing and angry. 'Do you understand? They're not a resource!'

That was always the way. As soon as the areas of common interest came up . . . Edgar sighed. The Light Ones really were deluded. How could they be so deluded?

'All right. Let's change the subject.' He took another mouthful of beer and couldn't help remarking: 'There was an American airman sitting in here . . . and he was a Light Magician . . . an absolute oaf, by the way, he didn't even notice me. I'll bet you he regards people as a resource. Or maybe as a stupid, dull-witted inferior race that can be nurtured and punished. The same way we regard them.'

'Our trouble is that we're a product of human society,' Anton replied gloomily. 'With all its shortcomings. And until they've lived many centuries, even Light Ones still carry around the stereotypes and myths of their own country: Russia, America or Burkina Faso — it makes no difference. What the hell, why can't I get Burkina Faso out of my head?'

'One of those idiots, the Regin Brothers, is from Burkina Faso,' Edgar suggested. 'And it's a funny name.'

'The Regin Brothers,' Anton said with a nod. 'What cunning business are your people up to with them? It was someone on the Moscow Day Watch who summoned them to Moscow. Promised to help them, to activate Fáfnir's Talon . . . What for?'

'I am not in possession of any such information, and that is an official statement of my position.' Edgar replied quickly. You couldn't afford to give these Light Ones the slightest hint of a formal violation to clutch at.

'Don't bother admitting it, there's no need,' Anton said with a dismissive wave of his hand. 'I'm not a little child. But the last thing we need is the appearance of an insane Dark Magician of immense power.'

'Us too,' Edgar declared. 'That would mean all-out war. No holds barred. In other words, the Apocalypse.'

'Then that means the Regin Brothers were lied to,' Anton said 'They were persuaded to attack the Berne office, steal the Talon and fly to Moscow, but what for? To feed power to the Mirror?'

'He's quick-witted,' Edgar noted to himself. But he shook his head as he came up with a superb denial:

"That's rubbish. We only found out who Vitaly Rogoza was after the Talon had already been stolen and the four survivors of the battle were on their way to Moscow.'

'That's right!' Anton suddenly exclaimed. 'You're right, Dark One! The appearance of a Mirror cannot be foretold, it's a spontaneous creation of the Twilight. But the Inquisition's official communiqué states that the sect began preparing to storm the artefacts repository two weeks before the actual event. Rogoza didn't even exist then, or, rather, he did, but he was an ordinary individual who was later transformed by the Twilight.'

Edgar chewed on his lip. Now it looked as if he'd given the

Light One an idea, passed on some information to him or simply pointed him in the right direction. That was bad. But then, why was it? He wouldn't mind being able to understand the situation better himself. It was a matter of vital importance to him too. Edgar mused out loud:

'Maybe someone wanted the Inquisition office moved out of Berne?'

'Or decided it ought to be moved to Prague.'

They gazed at each other thoughtfully – a Light Magician and a Dark Magician, both equally interested in understanding what was going on. The waiter was about to approach them, but he saw they hadn't finished their beer yet and went to serve the Americans.

'That's one possibility,' Edgar agreed. 'But we didn't need the actual operation with the Talon. Don't even think of blaming us for that kind of nonsense.'

'But maybe,' Anton exclaimed, 'you needed to ruin some other operation, one of *our* operations. And Fáfnir's Talon was a very good way to do that?'

Edgar cursed himself for being so talkative. Only in the figurative sense, of course. No Dark Magician would ever set an Inferno vortex spinning above his own head.

'Nonsense, what other operation . . . ?' he began. And then he suddenly realised that by starting to defend the Night Watch so unexpectedly, he had effectively confirmed Anton's guess.

'Thank you, Other,' the Light One said with sincere feeling.

Still mentally lashing himself, Edgar stood up. It was true what they said: before you sit down with a Light One, cut out your tongue and wire your mouth shut.

'It's time I was going,' he said. 'I really enjoyed . . . our little talk.'

'Me too,' Anton agreed. And he even held out his hand.

It would have been stupid to refuse, so Edgar shook it. Then he tossed a five-hundred-crown note onto the table and hurried out.

Anton smiled as he watched him go. It was amusing to give a Dark Magician a fright, especially one of the Day Watch's elite. The fat Watchman obviously thought he'd given away some terrible secret, but he hadn't given anything away; the explanation Anton had suggested was stupid, and even if it happened by chance to be the right one, Anton still hadn't learnt anything worth knowing.

He squinted at the waiter and gestured, as if writing on his palm with his finger. A minute later he was handed the bill.

Including the usual tip it came to one thousand and twenty crowns.

Oh, those Dark Ones . . .

It was only a trifle, but Edgar had still saved money. After all those jibes about the poor Night Watch and that invisible counting on fingers.

Anton paid, stood up (the beer had had an effect after all – his body felt relaxed in a way that was pleasant and alarming at the same time) and walked out of the Black Eagle. Towards Staroměstské Square, where he had an appointment with a representative of the Inquisition. He was only just in time.

There are always a lot of tourists here.

Especially on the hour, when the old astronomical clock begins to chime. The little double windows opened and little figures of the apostles appeared in them, moving out as if they were surveying the square, and then retreating into the depths of the mechanism again. The indefatigable Staroměstské Square clock.

Anton stood among the tourists with his hands in his pockets – they were feeling cold after all, and he'd never liked wearing gloves. All around him video cameras hummed quietly, camera shutters clicked and the multilingual crowd exchanged impressions of their visit to the latest obligatory attraction. He even thought he could hear their brains squeaking as they ticked off one more site on the tourist map of Prague: 'Watch the clock chime – done'.

Why was he walking along in this faceless crowd, as if he was also ticking off the points of a tourist itinerary in his mind?

Mental inertia? Laziness? Or an incurable herd instinct? Dark Ones probably never wandered around in the common crowd.

'No, I don't understand you,' someone in the crowd said in Russian, a couple of steps away from him. 'I'm on holiday, do you hear? Can't you decide for yourself?'

Anton squinted quickly at his fellow-countryman, but the sight wasn't a pleasant one. His compatriot was sturdily built, with broad shoulders and generously hung with gold. He'd already learned how to wear expensive suits, but not how to knot a Hermès tie. The tie was knotted, of course, but with a 'collective farm' knot that was awful to look at. A crumpled scarf dangled from beneath an unbuttoned coat of maroon cashmere wool.

The New Russian caught his glance and frowned as he put away his mobile. He turned to gaze at the clock again. Anton looked away.

The third generation, that was what the analysts said. You had to wait until the third generation. The grandson of this bandit who had got rich and somehow managed to stay alive would be a thoroughly decent man. You just had to wait. And unlike people, Others could afford to wait for generations. Their work went on for centuries . . . at least the work of the Light Ones did.

It was easy for the Dark Ones to make the changes they wanted to people's minds. The path of Darkness was always shorter than the path of Light. Shorter, easier, more fun.

'Anton Gorodetsky,' someone said from behind him. Someone

speaking a language that was obviously not his own, but which he knew perfectly.

And with that intonation that was quite impossible to confuse with anybody else's. The aloof, slightly bored intonation of the Inquisitors.

Anton turned round, nodded and held out his hand.

The Inquisitor looked like a Czech. A tall man of indeterminate age in a warm, grey raincoat, a woollen beret with a decorative pin in an amusing design of hunting horns, weapons and a deer's head. Somehow it was very easy to imagine him in a twilit park in autumn: strolling over a thick carpet of brown leaves thoughtfully, sadly, slowly – looking like a spy engrossed in his thoughts.

'Witiezslav,' said the Inquisitor. 'Witiezslav Grubin, let's go.'

They made their way out of the crowd easily – for some reason the people moved aside for the Inquisitor, even though he didn't make use of his powers as an Other. They set off along a narrow little street, gradually moving further and further away from the idle tourists.

'How was your flight, Anton?' Witiezslav inquired. 'Have you had a rest, some lunch?'

'Yes, thank you, everything's fine.'

A show of politeness from an Inquisitor, even if it was strictly formal, was a pleasant surprise.

'Do you require any assistance from the Office?'

Anton shook his head, quite certain that Witiezslav would sense the movement, even though he was walking in front.

'That's good,' the Inquisitor replied in the same indifferent voice, but quite sincerely. 'There's so much work to do. The Office coming to Prague is a great event for us. We feel very proud. But our department is very small and there's a lot of work.'

'I understand that the Inquisition hasn't had to intervene very often in Prague.'

'Indeed. The Watches here are law-abiding. They don't violate the Treaty very often.'

'Indeed,' thought Anton. The Inquisition's job had always been to resolve disagreements between the Watches, but crimes committed by individual Others were dealt with by the Watches themselves. The atmosphere of a normal European country was hardly likely to have a pacifying effect on the Dark Ones. But within the framework of an organisation they'd learned to respect the law.

Or at least to break it less obviously.

'The Tribunal session to consider the case of Igor Teplov, magician of the second grade, will commence tomorrow evening,' said Witiezslav. Anton appreciated the fact that he had used Igor's full name and given his status as a magician, and also the statement that the session would 'commence' and not 'take place'. That meant the Inquisition hadn't reached any conclusions yet. And it was prepared for a long hearing. 'Would you like to see him?'

'Yes, of course,' Anton said with a nod. 'I have some letters for him from the other guys, some presents.'

He stopped short – mentioning the letters and the presents had sounded somehow dismal. As if he really had brought a parcel for someone in prison. Or to the hospital bed of someone who was seriously ill.

'I've got a car,' said the Inquisitor. 'We can call round to your hotel for the parcel and then go to see the detainee.'

'Igor . . . is he somewhere in the Inquisition?'

'No, why would he be?' said Witiezslav, answering a question with a question. He stopped beside a Skoda Felicia parked at the kerb. 'We might have kept a Dark One who was detained under observation. But your colleague is in an ordinary hotel. He signed an undertaking not to leave the city.'

Anton nodded, acknowledging that it had been a stupid

question. It was true, what was the point of putting a Light Magician in a cell?

'Excuse me, Witiezslav,' he said. 'I know it has nothing to do with the work you do now, but I was wondering . . .just wondering, without any ulterior motive . . . I could probably try to probe you, but it's not appropriate somehow . . .'

'Who I used to be?' asked Witiezslav.

'Yes.'

The Inquisitor took out his keys and switched off the car alarm. He opened the door.

'I'm a vampire. Or rather, I was a vampire.'

'A higher vampire?' Anton asked, for some reason.

'Yes.'

Anton got into the front seat and fastened his seat belt. The vampire Witiezslav started the engine, but waited before driving off, giving it a chance to warm up.

'I'm sorry, it really was an idiotic question,' Anton admitted

'Of course it was. Absolutely idiotic.' The Inquisitor obviously didn't suffer from an excess of tact. 'As far as I'm aware, Anton, you are still extremely young.'

He drove the car out into the street, carefully and smoothly. Of course, he didn't ask what hotel Anton was staying in – he didn't need to. He said:

'You probably have certain illusions concerning the nature of the Inquisition and what kind of Others work in it. So allow me to explain a few things to you. The Inquisition is not a third force, as many ordinary members of the Watches believe. And we don't become some special kind of Other connected to neither the Dark nor the Light . . . We are simply Inquisitors. Selected from those Dark and Light Others who for various reasons have come to realise the absolute necessity of the Treaty and the truce between the Watches. Yes, we do possess certain information that you in the Watches don't have, apart, perhaps, from the very greatest magicians. And believe me, Anton Gorodetsky, when I tell you there is nothing comforting in what we know. We are *obliged* to stand on guard over the Treaty. Do you understand?'

'I'm trying to understand,' said Anton.

'I'm a vampire,' Witiezslav repeated. 'An absolutely genuine higher vampire who has often killed young girls . . . that's the most correct ener—'

'Please don't lecture me on the physiology of vampires,' said Anton. 'I find it unpleasant, believe me.'

Witiezslav nodded, keeping his eyes fixed firmly on the road. Anton suddenly realised that the car was still new, it had been well taken care of. The Inquisitor was clearly proud of it.

'Well, then, I don't possess a soul, and I'm not even alive in the sense that Light Ones use that word,' said Witiezslav. 'I regard the cause of the Light as a naïve, dangerous and frequently criminal doctrine. And on the other hand, I sympathise with the cause of the Dark. But . . .'

He paused for a moment, as if he were defining a complex pattern of thought.

'But I have a very clear picture of the alternative to the present situation. And that's why I'm a member of the Inquisition. That's why I punish those who have violated the Treaty. Note that, Anton. Not those who are wrong – after all, there are always at least two sides to the truth. The Light has sometimes acquired great power, and there have been times when the Dark has triumphed. All the Inquisition does is stand guard over the Treaty.'

'I understand,' said Anton. 'Naturally. But I've always wondered if a situation could arise in which the Inquisition would support one side or the other, not based on the letter of the Treaty, but on the truth.'

'There are always at least two sides to the truth,' the Inquisitor repeated. 'A situation . . .'

He thought about it.

'I've never come across a Light Inquisitor who would support his own Watch,' Anton added. 'But is the situation really the same with a Dark Inquisitor? Say what you will, but you have your own powers, your own esoteric knowledge. And I'm not talking about confiscated artefacts in the archives.'

'Anything is possible,' the vampire said unexpectedly. 'Yes, – I could imagine it. If open war broke out between the Dark and the Light, not just a clash between the Watches, but real war between the Dark and the Light. If every Other stood on his own side of the front, then what need would there be for the Inquisition? Then we would simply be Others.'

He nodded and added:

'Only by that time the Inquisition would probably have been destroyed. In the attempt to prevent such a situation arising. There aren't that many of us. And what a few surviving Others who once wore the Inquisitors' robes might decide to do wouldn't change anything.'

'I understand what makes the Night Watch observe the Treaty,' said Anton. 'We're afraid for people. And I know what motivates the Day Watch – fear for themselves. But what makes you Inquisitors go against your own essential natures?'

Witiezslav turned his head and said quietly:

'The only thing that restrains you is *fear*, Anton Gorodetsky. For yourself, or for people – that's not important. But we are restrained by *horror*. And that is why we observe the Treaty. You have no need to be concerned about the outcome of the trial – there won't be any fixes. If your colleague has not violated the Treaty, he will leave Prague alive and well.'

*     *     *

By the evening Edgar had somewhat recovered from his annoyance. Maybe a good dinner in an expensive restaurant had helped, with a bottle of vintage Czech wine (well, it wasn't French, or even Spanish, but it certainly wasn't bad). Or maybe the atmosphere of Prague at Christmas had a soothing effect. Naturally, Edgar didn't believe in God – not many of the Others, especially Dark Ones, suffered from such superstitions. But he found the festival of Christmas really very enjoyable, and he always tried to celebrate it accordingly.

Maybe it was the influence of memories from his childhood? When he was a simple country boy called Edgar who helped his father on the farm, went to church and looked forward to every holiday with his heart singing. Or maybe he remembered the nineteen-twenties and thirties, when he was already an Other, but not actively involved in the Watch, when he lived in Tallinn, had a good practice as a barrister, a wonderful wife and four little boys? His parents had died long ago, and he had buried his wife. One of his two surviving sons lived in Canada and the other in Pärnu, but he hadn't seen them for forty years. It would have been hard for the old men to believe that this youthful, sturdy man was their father, who had been born in the late nineteenth century.

'Yes, it must be the memories,' Edgar thought as he lit his cigar. There had been a lot of good things in ordinary human life, after all. Maybe he should play at being human again? Get married, have a family . . . take thirty years' leave from the Watch.

He laughed hollowly. That was all nonsense. You couldn't step into the same river twice. He'd lived as a man, lived as an ordinary Other, and now his place was in the Day Watch. It was all right for Anton, with his unspent passion and fresh, vital emotions, but all that fretting and fussing wouldn't suit Edgar any longer.

Edgar caught the eye of the young woman sitting bored and

alone at the next table. He smiled, and touched her mind with the gentlest of touches.

Not a prostitute, just a young girl out looking for adventure. That was good. He didn't like professionals. There was nothing they could surprise him with anyway.

He called the waiter over and ordered a bottle of champagne.

# CHAPTER 4

THE INQUISITION had not been mean with the detainees. The hotel was a perfectly decent one, and while Anton was not in de luxe accommodation, he had a suite with two good rooms.

Anton hesitated for a second before he approached Igor.

How he had changed.

Igor had always been an operational agent. He'd joined the Watch during the years after the war – there had been a lot of work to do then: on the one hand there was an upsurge of Light emotions, and on the other hand, during the difficult war years all sorts of petty riff-raff had multiplied. And with the general atheistic mood of the country, it wasn't easy for anybody to accept that he or she was an Other. But it had been easy for Igor to accept his true nature, he had been glad to. He didn't really see much difference between parachuting in behind the fascist lines to blow up bridges and hunting vampires and werewolves on the streets of Moscow. His power was an honest third grade, unlikely to advance any higher, but even the third grade is fairly substantial, if it's reinforced with experience, courage and good reactions.

Igor had all of those in abundance. Perhaps he was just a little bit short on experience, but then he had worked in the Watch at a time when you could easily count one year as three. Perhaps he wasn't as well-read or erudite as Ilya or Garik, and he hadn't taken part in as many impressive operations as Semyon, but there weren't many who could match him out in the field. And there was one other thing that Anton had always liked – Igor had stayed young. Not just physically – that was not difficult for a magician of his grade – but in his soul. Who would gladly accompany fifteen-year-old Yulia from the analytical department to some place in Tushino for the launch of the album *A Hundred and Fifty Billion Steps* by the hot band Tequila Jazz? Who was happy to spend time looking after a teenager riddled with complexes who'd just realised he was an Other? Who would enthusiastically devote five years to extreme parachuting simply in order to verify the theory about the high numbers of Others involved in extreme sports? Who was always first to volunteer to take a colleague's watch or take on the most tedious assignment (there was no lack of volunteers for the dangerous ones)? Maybe it was a mistake, but for some time already Anton had felt that it was safer to have your back covered by a partner who was reliable and cheerful, rather than powerful and worldly-wise. A powerful and wise partner could always be distracted by a more important job than covering someone else's back.

But the Other standing in front of Anton now looked neither powerful nor cheerful. Igor had lost a lot of weight, there was a strange dull, hopeless yearning in his eyes. And he didn't seem to know what to do with his hands . . . sometimes he put them behind his back, sometimes he clasped them together.

'Anton,' he said after a long silence. Without a smile, with only the faintest indication that he was glad. 'Hello, Anton.'

On a sudden impulse, Anton stepped forward and put his arms round Igor. He whispered:

'Hello . . . Now what are you doing in such a state?'

Witiezslav, who was standing by the door, said quietly:

'I shan't issue any official warnings about associating with detainees, since you're Light Ones. Shall I wait for you, Gorodetsky?'

'No, thank you,' said Anton, stepping back from Igor, but leaving one hand on his shoulder. 'I'll make my own way back.'

'Igor Teplov, the session of the Tribunal to consider your case will convene tomorrow evening, at seven o'clock local time. A car will come for you at six-thirty; be ready.'

'I've been ready for a long time,' Igor said quietly. 'Don't worry.'

'All the best,' the vampire said politely as he left.

The two Light Ones were left alone together.

'Do I look terrible?' Igor asked.

Anton didn't lie:

'Worse than that. I've seen corpses that looked better. Anybody would think you were being kept on bread and water.'

Igor shook his head seriously.

'Oh no, I've been well-treated.'

There was a hint of irony in his words. As if he was talking about some animal sitting in a cage in a zoo.

'I've got a parcel here for you,' Anton replied in the same tone, clutching at that hint of life. 'Is feeding the animals permitted?'

'Yes,' Igor said with a nod. 'I just . . . I just can't eat, you know? I can't read books, I don't want to get drunk . . . or see anybody either. I switch on the television and watch it until three in the morning. When I get up I turn it on again. You know, I've already pretty much mastered Czech. It's very easy.'

'That's terrible,' said Anton with a nod. 'Okay. As you can understand, when I left I was given confidential instructions – to give you the will to live again.'

Igor actually smiled.

'I understand. That's to be expected . . . Well, get the stuff out.'

Anton put a thick pile of letters on the table. There was one name on each envelope – the name of the person who had written the letter.

'These are from all our gang. Olga said you had to read her letter first. But Yulia and Lena said the same thing. So you choose for yourself.'

Igor looked at the letters thoughtfully and nodded.

'I'll throw dice. All right, get the rest of it out. I don't mean the letters.'

Anton smiled as he took a bottle wrapped in paper out of a plastic bag.

'Smirnov number twenty-one,' said Igor. 'Right?'

'Right.'

'I knew it. Go on.'

Anton carried on, smiling in embarrassment as he took out a small loaf of Borodinsky black bread, a whole salami, salted cucumbers in a polythene vacuum pack, several purple Yalta onions and a piece of pork fat.

'Why, you devils,' said Igor, shaking his head. 'Everything the way I like it. Semyon told you what to get, did he?'

'Yes.'

'The customs officers must have thought you were insane.'

'I made them look the other way. I'm on official business – so I have the right.'

'I see. Okay, I'll just get everything ready. And you can tell me what's been going on back there. I've been kept informed, but it's better coming from you. About Andrei, Tiger Cub . . . about that whole damn mess.'

While Igor was making the snacks, rinsing the glasses and drying them carefully and opening the bottle, Anton told him in brief about recent events in Moscow.

Igor poured vodka into four glasses without speaking. He covered two with slices of bread, set one in front of Anton and took the last one himself.

'For the guys,' he said. 'May the Light show them compassion. For Tiger Cub . . . for Andriuhka.'

They drank without clinking glasses, and Anton looked at Igor curiously. Igor began coughing and looked at his glass, perplexed.

'Anton . . . wait . . . this vodka's fake!'

'Of course,' Anton confirmed cheerfully. 'Absolutely genuine fake vodka, pure alcohol diluted with tap water. I chose it specially, you wouldn't believe how hard it is nowadays to buy fake vodka in the shops.'

'But why?' Igor exclaimed.

'What do you mean, why? Why did I bring you Borodinsky bread? I could have bought a loaf of fresh, tasty black bread in any shop in Prague. And the salami too, and the pork fat. The onions would have been the only problem.'

'So this is a greeting from the motherland, is it?' said Igor, still wincing.

'Precisely.'

'Oh no, I want to greet my last morning without a headache,' Igor said seriously. He frowned and passed his hand above the bottle and the two full glasses. The liquid glimmered a lemon-yellow colour for a moment. Igor explained in a slightly guilty voice: 'I'm allowed to use lower magic.'

'Then pour another glass.'

'Are you in some kind of a hurry?' Igor asked, frowning at Anton as he poured the transformed vodka.

'No, where would I be going in a hurry?' Anton replied. 'I'd rather sit here with you and have a chat. Do you know why I changed the bottle?'

'So it was you?'

'Yes, it was me. Semyon brought the right stuff. But I wanted to remind you that a beautiful bottle doesn't always contain something good.'

Igor sighed and his face went dark:

'Gorodetsky, don't moralise with me. I was in the Watch before you were even born. I understand everything. But it's my own fault, and I'll take my punishment.'

'No, you don't understand anything,' Anton shouted angrily. 'You adopt this grand pose of yours: "It's my fault, I'll take what's coming to me",' he said, mimicking Igor. 'But what are we supposed to do? Especially now, without Tiger Cub and Andrei? You know that Gesar's decided to give the programming girls intensive training?'

'Oh, come on, Anton. There aren't any irreplaceable Others. The Moscow Watch has hundreds of magicians and enchantresses in reserve!'

'Yes, of course. And if we whistle, they'll come running. Leave their families, drop their jobs and their everyday concerns. They'll take up arms, of course they will. If the active members of the Watch have disgraced themselves and given up.'

Igor sighed and began speaking abruptly and energetically, almost like the old operational agent:

'Anton, I understand all this. You're a bright guy, and you're doing the right thing now by making me angry. You're trying to inspire me with the will to live. You're trying to persuade me to fight. But understand one thing – I really don't want to fight. I really think I am guilty. I really have decided to . . . withdraw. Into nothingness, into the Twilight.'

'Why, Igor? I understand that any death is a tragedy, especially if it's your fault, but you couldn't have foreseen . . .'

Igor looked up at him with eyes full of pain and shook his head.

'No, Antoshka. It's you who doesn't understand a single thing.

Do you think I'm punishing myself because that kid drowned? No.'

Anton picked up his glass and drained it.

'I feel sorry for the boy,' Igor went on. 'Very sorry. But I've seen all sorts of things in my time . . . there have been times before when people died. And it was my fault. Children, women, old men. Have you ever, for instance, had to decide who to run to first, who to save – an uninitiated Other or an ordinary person? I have. Have you ever had to draw all the power from a crowd – drain it completely? Knowing there's a ninety per cent probability two people in the crowd won't be able to bear it and they'll kill themselves? I have.'

'I've had to do a few things too, Igor.'

'Yes, I understand. That hurricane . . . Then why are you talking such nonsense? Can't you believe it's not all about that unfortunate kid? That I fell in love with a Dark One?'

'I can't,' said Anton. 'I just can't! Gesar said that too, but . . .'

'You'd better believe Gesar,' Igor said with a bitter smile. 'I love her, Anton. I still love her, even now. And I'll go on loving her – that's the real tragedy.'

He picked up his glass.

'Thanks at least for not setting a glass out for her on the table.' Anton could feel the fury beginning to seethe inside him. 'Thanks . . .'

He broke off and followed Igor's glance to a glass-fronted cupboard. Inside, among the other glasses, was one half filled with vodka and covered with a stale piece of bread.

'You've lost your mind,' Anton muttered. 'Completely lost your mind. Remember, Igor – she's a witch.'

'She was a witch,' Igor agreed with a faint, sad smile.

'She provoked you . . . okay, she didn't enchant you, but she still made you fall in love with her.'

'No. She fell in love herself. And she didn't have the slightest idea who I was.'

'Okay. Let's accept that, you ought to know. But even so, it was provocation. By Zabulon, who knew everything that was happening.'

Igor nodded.

'Yes, very probably. I've thought about that a lot, Anton. That fight in Butovo was obviously well prepared in advance by the Dark Ones. At the very highest level, just Zabulon and another one or two of them. Lemesheva probably knew. Edgar and the witches didn't.'

He didn't even think it worth mentioning the vampires and shape-shifters.

'Well, if you agree . . .' Anton began.

'Wait. Yes, it was a deliberately planned operation. One of Zabulon's intrigues. And a successful one.' Igor lowered his head. 'Only what difference does that make to the way I feel about Alisa?'

Anton felt like swearing angrily. So he did, and then he said:

'Igor, you've looked at Alisa Donnikova's file. You must have looked at it.'

'Yes.'

'So you must understand how much blood she has on her hands. How much Evil she has done. I've clashed with her myself several times. She's been responsible for ruining our operations, she . . . she served Zabulon loyally.'

'You forgot to add that she was Zabulon's broad,' Igor said in a dull, lifeless voice. 'That the head of Moscow's Dark Ones had sex with her in his Twilight form, that she took part in covens with human sacrifices and sex orgies. Why don't you say it? Say it, I know it all anyway. Gesar gave me the full file . . . he tried really hard. I know all that.'

'And you still love her?' Anton asked incredulously.

Igor raised his head, and they looked into each other's eyes. Then Igor reached out and gently touched Anton's hand.

'Don't be angry with me, brother Light One. Don't despise me. And if you can't understand, you'd better go. Take a walk around Prague.'

'I'm trying to understand,' Anton whispered. 'Honestly, I'm trying. Alisa Donnikova was a perfectly ordinary witch. No better and no worse than all the rest. A clever, beautiful, cruel witch. Who left Evil and pain in her wake wherever she went. How can you love her?'

'She was different with me,' Igor replied. 'A nervous and unhappy girl who really wanted to love someone. Who had fallen in love for the first time. A girl who, unfortunately for us, the Dark Ones spotted before we did. And for her initiation they chose a moment when there was more Dark in her soul than Light. That's not too difficult with teenage girls – you know yourself. And after that it was all very simple. The Twilight drained all the goodness out of her. The Twilight turned her into what she became.'

'It's not Alisa herself that you love,' said Anton, failing to notice that he was speaking about Donnikova in the present tense. What you love is her idealised . . . no, her alternate image. An Alisa that never existed.'

'She certainly doesn't exist now. But you're still wrong, Anton. I love her the way she became when she lost her powers as an Other. When she was freed for just a moment from that sticky grey web. Tell me, have you never had to forgive somebody?'

'Yes, I have,' Anton replied after a pause. 'But not for something like that.'

'You've been lucky, Antoshka.'

Igor poured more vodka.

'Then tell me this.' Anton wasn't trying to spare Igor's feelings, but he still found it hard to get the words out. 'Why did you kill her?'

'Because she was a witch,' Igor said very calmly. 'Because she caused Evil and pain. Because "a member of the Night Watch always protects people against Dark Ones everywhere, in any country, regardless of his personal relation to the situation". Have you never wondered about why the Regulations include that specific phrase? About our personal relation to the situation? It ought to read "personal relation to the Dark Ones", but that sounds rather pitiful. So they used a eum . . . euph . . .'

'Euphemism,' Anton prompted him.

'A euphemism.' Igor laughed. 'Exactly. Remember when we caught the girl vampire on the roof, you were about to shoot at her point-blank, but then your vampire neighbour turned up. And you lowered your gun.'

'I was wrong,' Anton said, shrugging. 'She had to be tried. That was why I stopped.'

'No, Anton. You would have shot her. And any other vampire who came running to help the criminal. But you were facing a vampire who was your friend, or at least one that you knew. And you stopped. But imagine if the choice had been between shooting and letting the criminal escape.'

'I would have shot her,' Anton said abruptly. 'And Kostya too. There wouldn't have been any choice. I'd have felt very bad about it, I agree, but I . . .'

'And what if it hadn't just been someone you knew well, but the woman you loved? A human woman or an Other enchantress from either side?'

'I would have shot,' Anton whispered. 'I would have shot anyway.'

'And then what?'

'I wouldn't have allowed such a situation to arise. I simply wouldn't have allowed it.'

'Of course. The very idea of love never enters our heads if we see the aura of Dark. It's the same for the Dark Ones if they see the aura of Light. But we were caught by surprise, Anton. We'd lost all our powers. And we didn't have a choice.'

'Tell me, Igor . . .' Anton paused and took a breath. The vodka hadn't done the trick, and even though the conversation was certainly intimate, it wasn't bringing any relief. 'Tell me, why didn't you just throw Alisa out of the camp? Why didn't you ask Gesar for help and advice? That way you would have protected people and at the same time—'

'She wouldn't have gone,' Igor said sharply. 'After all, she had legitimate reason to be there at Artek. You know what's the most terrible thing about this whole business, Anton? Zabulon extracted Gesar's approval for her to restore herself in exchange for the same right for a third-grade magician. Me, that is. Do you see how everything was all tied up together?'

'But are you sure she wouldn't have gone away?' Anton asked.

Igor raised his glass without speaking. For the first time that evening they clinked glasses, but no toast was proposed.

'No, Anton, I'm not sure. That's the terrible thing, I'm not sure. I told her . . . I ordered her to clear out. But that was the very first moment, when we'd only just realised who was who. When my brain still hadn't kicked in, I was running on pure adrenalin.'

'If she loved you,' said Anton, 'she would have gone. You just needed to find the right words.'

'Probably. But who can say for certain now?'

'Igor, I'm really sorry,' Anton whispered. 'I don't feel sorry for the witch Alisa, of course . . . don't even ask me. I couldn't shed even a single tear for her. But I feel terribly sorry for you. And I really want you to stay with us. To get through this and not let it destroy you.'

'I've got nothing left to live for, Anton,' said Igor with a guilty shrug. 'You understand, nothing. You know, I probably fell in love for the first time in my life too. I had a wife once. I became an Other in nineteen forty-five . . . I came back from the front, a young captain with a chest full of medals, and not a single scratch on me . . . and I'd been lucky in general. It was only later I realised it was my latent abilities as an Other that had kept me safe. And then I learned the truth about the Watches. It was a new war, you understand? And an absolutely just one, it couldn't have been more just. I didn't really know how to do anything except fight, and now I realised I'd found myself a job for life. For a very long life. And that I wouldn't have to face any of those human afflictions and annoying illnesses, those queues for food. You can't even imagine what perfectly ordinary hunger is like, Anton, what genuinely *black* bread tastes like, or genuinely bad vodka . . . what it feels like the first time you laugh in the fat, well-fed face of a special agent from SMERSH and yawn lazily in response to his question: "Why did you spend two months in enemy territory if the bridge was blown up on the third day after you parachuted in?"'

Igor was beginning to get carried away now, he was speaking quickly and furiously, not at all the way the young magician from the Night Watch usually spoke.

'I came back and I looked at my Vilena, my little Lenochka-Vilenochka, so young and beautiful. She used to write me letters every day, honestly, and what letters they were. I saw how glad she was that I'd come back – I wasn't hurt, I wasn't crippled and I was a hero as well. Very few women were so fortunate then. But she was very afraid that her envious bitches of neighbours would tell me about all the men she'd had during those four years, that my officer's warrant wasn't the only reason she'd been getting by quite comfortably . . . even now you don't understand half of what I'm saying, do you? But I suddenly saw it. All of it at once. The longer I looked at her, the more I saw. Every detail. And not only all her men – from lousy speculators to others like me, soldiers who hopped over the hospital fence and went absent without leave. And the way she whispered to one colonel: "He's probably been rotting the ground for ages . . ." – I heard that too. And by the way, that colonel turned out to be a real man. He got up off the bed, slapped her across the face, got dressed and walked out.'

Igor poured himself some vodka and drank it quickly, without waiting for Anton, then filled the glasses again. He said:

'That's when I became what I am. When I left my home, with my medals jangling and Vilena roaring: "It's all lies what they told you, those bitches, I was faithful to you!" I walked along the street, with something burning away in my soul. It was May, Anton. May nineteen forty-five. Immediately after Germany capitulated, Gesar pulled me back from the front and told me: "From now on your front line is here, Captain Teplov." And back then people were . . . they were different, Anton. Their faces were all shining! There were plenty of foul Dark creatures around, no denying it, but there was a lot of Light as well. And as I walked along the street the little kids darted round me, looking at my chest full of medals, arguing about which one was for what. Men shook my hand and invited me to take a drink with them. Girls came running up to me . . . and kissed me. Kissed me like their own boyfriends, who hadn't come back yet, or had already been killed. Like their own fathers, like their own brothers. Sometimes they cried, kissed me and went on their way. Do you understand me? No, how could you? You worry about our country too, you think how bad everything is right now, what a bloody mess we're all in. You suffer because the Light Ones won't all get together to help Russia. Only you don't know what it's like to be in a real hole, Anton. But we do!'

Igor drained his glass again. Anton raised his glass without speaking and nodded in support of the toast that had not been spoken aloud.

'That was when I became what I am,' Igor repeated. 'A magician. A field agent. Eternally young. Who loves everybody . . . and nobody. I'd already made up my mind that I would never fall in love. Never. Girlfriends were one thing, love was something quite different. I couldn't love a human being, because human beings were weak. I couldn't love an Other, because any Other was either an enemy or a comrade-in-arms. That was the principle I adopted for my life, Antoshka. And I stuck to it as closely as I could. It seemed like I was still the same young man who came back from the front, who still had plenty of time to think about falling in love. It's one thing to take a whirl with a girl on the dance floor,' he said and laughed quietly, 'or leap about in cool clothes in the ultraviolet light at the disco. What difference does it make if it's jazz, rock or trash, what length the skirt is and what the stockings are made of? It's all good. It's the way things ought to be. Have you seen that American cartoon, about Peter Pan? Well, I became like him. Only not a stupid little boy, but a stupid young man. And I felt just fine for a long time. Supposedly I've outlived the time granted to a man, and it would be a sin to complain I haven't had a helpless old age or any other problems like that. So don't you torment yourself unnecessarily, Anton.'

Anton sat there with his head in his hands, not speaking.

It was as if he'd opened a door and seen something behind it . . . not something taboo, and not something shameful either. Just something that had absolutely nothing to do with him. And he realised that behind every door, if — may the Light forbid! — he was able to open it, he would see something equally alien and . . . personal.

'I've reached the end of my road, Anton,' Igor said almost tenderly. 'Don't be so sad. I understand that you came here hoping to shake me up, to get all this nonsense out of my head, to carry out your instructions. Only it won't work. Like a fool, I really did fall in love with a Dark One. I killed her. And it turns out I killed myself too.'

Anton didn't say anything. It was all pointless. He was overwhelmed by another's anguish, another's grief. Instead of simply bringing a parcel to a sick friend, here he was sitting with him at his own wake.

'Anton, don't go away today,' Igor said. 'I won't sleep anyway . . . soon I'll catch up on my sleep for ever. To be honest, I've got another three bottles of vodka in the fridge. And there's a restaurant five floors down.'

'Then we'll fall asleep at the table.'

'We'll be okay, we're Others. We can take it. I want to talk. To cry on someone's shoulder. I've started feeling afraid of the dark. Can you believe that?'

'Yes.'

Igor nodded.

'Thanks. I've got my guitar here, we can sing something. Or I'll sing. You know, singing for yourself is just the same as . . . well, you understand. And apart from that . . .'

Anton looked at Igor – his voice had suddenly become more focused. Stronger.

'I'm a Watchman, after all. I haven't forgotten that, you can be quite sure. And it seems to me that in all this mess, I'm no more than a pawn. No, probably not a pawn . . . a rook who has taken one of the other side's pieces and occupied a square in the line of fire. Only unlike the other pieces, I can think. I hope you haven't forgotten how to do that, either. I don't care about myself any more, Anton. But I do care who wins this game. Let's think together.'

'Where do we begin?' Anton asked, feeling amazed at himself. Surely he hadn't accepted what Igor had said and agreed to think of him as a piece who had already been removed from the board?

Or who at least was already doomed as the invisible player reached out his hand for him.

'With Svetlana. With the Chalk of Destiny.' said Igor, watching Anton's expression carefully. He laughed smugly. 'Well, have I guessed right? You've been having the same thoughts?'

'And so has Gesar,' Anton whispered.

'Gesar's a clever one,' Igor agreed. 'But we're no fools either, are we? Anyway, why don't we try thinking with our heads and not our hands for once?'

'Okay, let's try,' Anton said with a nod. 'Only . . .'

He fumbled in his pocket for the amulet that Gesar had given him. He crushed the little ball in his hand and felt the bone needles prick his skin. There was never any gain without pain . . . He said:

'Now for twelve hours no one will be able to see us or hear us.'

'Are you sure?' Igor asked. 'Won't the absence of information alert the Inquisition?'

'There won't be any absence,' said Anton. 'As far as I understand it, if they have any observational devices here, or if they've cast any tracking spells – they'll provide false information. It's a quality scam.'

'Gesar's a clever one,' Igor repeated with a smile.

Edgar sat by the window, smoking and slowly sipping a glass of flat champagne. It still tasted good.

The girl was sleeping peacefully in the next room, satisfied and happy. She had turned out fine. A German student with some Scandinavian blood, reasonably passionate and reasonably cheerful. But a bit too sexually inventive for Edgar's taste. Unlike most of his colleagues, Edgar was very conservative in such matters. He didn't do group sex, he didn't have underage girlfriends, and of all the possibilities he preferred the classic missionary position.

But there was no denying that in that position he had achieved perfection.

Edgar stretched sweetly and carefully opened the window. He stood up and breathed in the cold, frosty air. The new day had begun and perhaps the Tribunal would give its verdict that very evening. Then he'd be able to relax and enjoy the festive season, without worrying about all these intrigues.

But who was behind this intrigue, after all . . . the Day Watch or the Night Watch?

And most important of all – what role had been assigned to him?

Could Yury's hint really be right, was he supposed to be sacrificed, just like Alisa?

'Here, look.' Igor spread out a large sheet of paper on the table and took a pack of felt-tip pens out of his pocket. 'I've already drawn a few diagrams . . . and some things fit together. This is Svetlana.'

Anton looked thoughtfully at the circle drawn with a thick yellow line and said:

'It doesn't look much like her.'

Igor laughed:

'All right, very witty. But look at the way things fit together. We and the Dark Ones had a balance, a precarious one, but still a balance. Here are the magicians with first-to third-grade powers on our side, here are their equivalents on the Dark Side . . . both those in active service and others who can be easily mobilised.'

The paper was quickly covered with small circles. Then Igor divided the sheet in two with a broad stroke. At the top of one side he wrote 'Gesar', and at the top of the other 'Zabulon'. He explained:

'They're not really *in* the game. They're the players, but we're interested in the pieces. Look at how things changed with Svetlana's appearance.'

'It depends what piece we decide she is,' Anton said cautiously. 'Right now she's a first-grade enchantress . . . or rather, she was.'

'And what does that mean? Just look how many magicians there are at about the same level as her.'

'She's a pawn,' said Anton, surprised at his own words. 'Svetlana's no more than a pawn, for years to come yet. While she nurtures her power, learns to control her abilities, acquires experience. She's more powerful than me, or she was. But I'd have been able to handle her if I'd been on the other side.'

'Precisely, Anton,' said Igor, deftly pouring himself a glass from the second bottle of vodka – the first was already standing empty under the table. 'Precisely! Svetlana made the Night Watch significantly more powerful. And in the future she could certainly reach the same grade as Gesar. But that's a matter of decades, or even centuries.'

'Then why all this activity by the Dark Ones? They almost violated the Treaty, simply in order to get Svetlana out of the game.'

'Think,' said Igor, glancing into Anton's eyes. 'Let's take the chess analogy all the way.'

'A pawn that reaches the far side of the board . . .'

'. . . becomes any other piece.'

Anton shrugged.

'Igor, that's obvious anyway. We're all pawns, but some of us have a chance to become queens. Svetlana has. You don't, I don't, Semyon doesn't . . . but it's a long way to the far edge of the board, and the Dark Ones don't need to be in such a hurry to eliminate Svetlana!'

'The Chalk of Destiny,' said Igor.

'What about it? Gesar wanted to use Egor, the boy without any destiny, to make him into . . .'

'Into what?'

Anton shrugged:

'A prophet, a philosopher, a poet, a magician . . . I don't know. Someone who would lead humanity towards the Light. Or perhaps a Mirror? Another Mirror, like Vitaly Rogoza, only he would be on our side?'

'But Svetlana didn't want to interfere,' Igor said with a nod. 'The boy Egor was left with just his own destiny.'

'But then . . .' Anton began and stopped short. He didn't know if he had the right to tell Igor the truth he had uncovered, even under the protection of the amulet.

'But then Olga rewrote someone's destiny with the other half of the Chalk,' Igor said with a laugh. 'That's an open secret already. What's important thing is that the operation was successful. Svetlana didn't do it, but Olga did. And incidentally Gesar managed to have Olga rehabilitated.'

'Incidentally?' Anton queried, shaking his head. 'Okay, let's say incidentally. But that's the second level of the truth. I'm sure there's a third level too.'

'The third level is the person whose destiny Olga rewrote. As soon as Zabulon heard she'd been rehabilitated, he realised he'd been duped. Taken in by a simple diversionary manoeuvre. And the Dark Ones started to investigate. They checked poor Egor a dozen times — in case the Book of Destiny had been rewritten twice for him.'

'How do you know that?'

'I was keeping an eye on the boy. Gesar told me to — it was obvious the Dark Ones would start looking for a trick.'

'And?'

'There were no tricks with Egor. It wasn't his destiny that was rewritten.'

'Then whose was it?'

Igor looked into Anton's eyes without saying anything. As if he didn't have the right to say it himself.

'Svetlana's?' Anton exclaimed in sudden realisation. And he suddenly thought that in his place any Dark One would have squealed: 'Mine?'

'It looks like it. A brilliant and elegant move. There was such an ocean of Power raging around her that it was impossible for anyone to notice what was being done with her Book of Destiny. And the Dark Ones can't check her Book of Destiny – that would be as good as a declaration of war.'

'Gesar wants to accelerate Svetlana's transformation into a Great Enchantress?'

'Out of the question. That would be a violation of the Treaty. Dig a bit deeper.'

Anton looked at the circles on the paper. He took a felt-tip pen and drew a bright scarlet line upwards from Svetlana, ending in another circle. An empty circle.

'Yes,' said Igor. 'Precisely. You know what time this is now, don't you?'

'The end of the millennium.'

'Two thousand years since the birth of Jesus Christ,' Igor said with a laugh.

'Ieshua was a supreme Light Magician,' said Anton. 'I don't even know if we can call him a magician . . . he was the Light itself. But . . . Gesar wants a second coming of the Messiah?'

'You said it, not me,' Igor replied. 'Let's drink . . . to the Light.'

Anton drank a full glass in total bewilderment. He shook his head.

'No, but this . . . Igor, this is playing with the pure powers. With the foundations of the universe! How could he take the risk?'

'Anton, I'm certain that's the way it has all been planned. Judge for yourself – there's a boom in religious faith everywhere, one way or another everybody's expecting either the end of the world or the second coming . . . but then, they're the same thing.'

'Not everybody,' Anton protested. 'Don't exaggerate.'

'Not everybody, but enough for the level of human expectation to start reshaping reality. And if you could just help things along a bit, if you could rewrite someone's destiny . . . Gesar went for broke. Gesar wants to add someone new to our ranks, an Other so powerful that none of the Dark Ones will be able to match him. Not Zabulon, not a certain modest Californian farmer, not the owner of a small hotel in Spain, and not a popular Japanese singer . . . no one.'

'That might be true,' Anton admitted. 'But Svetlana's lost her power now, and for a long time.'

'And what of it? Does that prevent her from having a child?'

'Stop,' said Anton, waving his hands in warning. 'Now we're getting ahead of ourselves! We can believe any hypothesis, but let's look at everything else that's happened first. The Mirror, for instance.'

'The Mirror . . .' Igor frowned. 'A Mirror is created by the Twilight. Zabulon couldn't make use of him directly, but he certainly could bring those stupid sect-members to Moscow with that artefact of theirs and feed Rogoza with power. And the reason for that is obvious – to destroy Svetlana.'

'Rogoza didn't destroy her! He only drained her, but then that's . . .'

'One of us didn't play the game the way Zabulon had planned it,' Igor replied. 'Someone didn't make the move that would have led to the Mirror totally destroying Svetlana, as an individual. Maybe what saved her was the fact that Tiger Cub and Andrei had already died? A Mirror isn't exactly a Dark Other, and isn't directly involved in the confrontation between the Watches. You see, maybe he was expecting another blow of some kind? From you, for instance. From Gesar. But the blow never came, and he didn't strike back with all his strength.'

'Then explain to me, Igor – why did Zabulon set you and Alisa up?'

'That was an accident,' Igor muttered. 'I told you, Alisa—'

'Okay, so *she* didn't know! But Zabulon knew, believe me! And he sent her to her death, he exchanged one piece for another. Why?'

'I wish I knew,' said Igor with a shrug.

# CHAPTER 5

RAIVO BEGAN walking round the hotel room, gesticulating with atypical fervour.

'I still think there's going to be trouble. We have no reason to count on any help from the Day Watch of Moscow, or Prague or Helsinki – any of them.'

'But that Dark One promised to help us,' Yari objected.

Raivo frowned and waved his hands through the air picturesquely.

'He promised! Yes, of course he did. And who promised our Brothers that Fáfnir would be resurrected?'

'It seems to me,' Yukha said quietly, 'that it would have been more rational to serve the great cause of Fáfnir's resurrection than actually try to resurrect him.'

There was a moment of silence.

'Yukha —' Yari said reproachfully. 'You . . . you can't just say that.'

'Why can't I? The times when magicians used to play without any rules are long gone. Do you want a global cataclysm?'

'But our—'

'Our decrepit leaders were out of their minds! And that's why they were fooled by promises! That's why they were killed in

Berne . . . And we won't be getting any help, Raivo's right about that! Those who have departed can't be brought back. Pasi believed too – and where's Pasi now? Dematerialised in the Twilight by Gesar!'

The telephone on the table rang. Though clearly reluctant to stop talking, Yukha picked up the receiver.

'Yes?'

The next moment he leapt in the air, dropping his glass of Czech beer. He shouted:

'You? You . . . where are you calling from? What?'

He listened for a minute, the expression on his face growing ever more joyful and confused. The expression of a man given good news after he has already braced himself for bad and even managed to infect everyone else with his own pessimism. Finally Yukha put the phone down and whispered:

'Brothers . . .'

Anton couldn't decide if they'd been right or wrong to open the second bottle of vodka. On the one hand, it seemed as though they were getting close to the essential truth of what was going on . . . but on the other, it was getting harder and harder actually to discuss the problem. For instance, Igor had become extremely sceptical, and he just couldn't understand what Anton was trying to demonstrate to him:

'Igor, in such a complicated set-up, if even one episode doesn't fit in right, the whole thing collapses! There had to be a reason. Maybe you represented some kind of obstacle to Zabulon's plans?'

'Me?' Igor gave a bitter laugh. 'Don't be silly. I'm an ordinary field operative. Third-grade . . . second at a stretch . . . with no special abilities and no prospects. I couldn't have stood up to the Mirror. I don't know, Anton.'

'But you have an idea about something,' Anton muttered. He

poured some vodka, paused for a second and asked: 'Igor, was there something between you and Svetlana?'

'No,' Igor answered sharply. 'No, and don't even think about it. There wasn't anything, there isn't, and there won't be. And if you're thinking I was supposed to be the father of the future messiah . . .'

He burst out laughing.

'It was just an idea,' Anton muttered, feeling like a total idiot.

'Anton, think about it . . . that's your jealousy speaking, not your head, I'm sorry. The ordinary human process of reproduction has nothing to do with all this. If Svetlana's Book of Destiny has been rewritten, if she has to be the mother of the new messiah – that's a process that involves subtle matter, the energes of the Light and the Dark, the fundamental substance of the universe! What difference does it make who' – he faltered for a moment and went on – 'happens to be the biological father? It only even depends on Svetlana to some extent! No, that's nonsense. The only person Zabulon has to be afraid of is Svetlana.'

'Then I don't see the point in eliminating you.'

'Neither do I. But there probably is one.'

They drank in silence, without clinking glasses. And then they both began staring at the sheet of paper.

'Let's start with the essentials,' said Anton, noticing that he was slurring his words a little. 'So, a year and a half ago Gesar and Olga rewrote Svetlana's Destiny? And now she's supposed to give birth to a messiah?'

'Yes, that's the way it looks.'

'And Zabulon tried to use the appearance of the Mirror to destroy her, but he failed.'

'Yes, that's it.'

'Okay, let's leave your part in all this aside for the moment. What could Zabulon's next move be? Now, when Svetlana has no magic powers at all and is defenceless?'

'She's not defenceless,' said Igor, wagging his finger at Anton. 'Why do you say that? I'm sure she's been given the finest possible protection. And in any case, to attack her is a violation of the Treaty. The Dark Ones are fond of their own skins, no one wants to face dematerialisation.'

'What could his response be? Only one.'

'The appearance of an Antichrist, the only one capable of standing against the messiah.'

'And humanity is expecting the appearance of the Antichrist with no less eagerness,' Anton exclaimed. 'Thanks to mass culture.'

'Have you got a Bible?' Igor asked unexpectedly.

'With me? No, of course not.'

'Just a moment,' said Igor. He walked quickly, if not entirely steadily, into the other room and came back with a small, thick book. He gave Anton a rather embarrassed look and said: 'Of course, I'm an atheist. But the Bible . . . you understand. Now . . .'

'Igor,' said Anton, putting his hand on the book. 'It won't help us. Why don't we try thinking logically?'

'All right,' Igor agreed readily, setting the Holy Writ aside with some relief.

'Zabulon wants to live too. He doesn't want an Apocalypse . . . I hope. He needs a figure equal in power to a messiah of the Light.'

'Fáfnir,' Igor said thoughtfully. 'Fáfnir?'

'A powerful Dark Magician,' Anton agreed. 'But he's not the Antichrist.'

'Six six six,' said Igor, squirming in his chair. 'Come on, let's count what the letters in the name Fáfnir add up to!'

'I don't remember how the name Fáfnir is written in the original. But if we write it in Russian, then . . .' Anton thought for a moment '. . . then it's eighty-eight! Nothing like six hundred and sixty-six.'

'But eighty-eight is a strange kind of number too,' said Igor, looking at Anton with blazing eyes. 'Just think about it. Not eighty-seven. Not eighty-nine. Exactly eighty-eight. It's suspicious.'

'It is,' Anton agreed. The number really had begun to seem suspicious to him for some reason. 'And it probably is possible to resurrect Fáfnir, to bring him back from the Twilight. But . . .'

'Not just to resurrect him,' said Igor. 'This whole business depends on human beings, right? On their expectations, on their readiness to believe. And if Fáfnir's return to life can be staged in the appropriate way, the insane magician can be made into an insane anti-messiah.'

'But how?'

'The four horsemen of the Apocalypse . . . the emergence of the beast from the sea.'

Igor's eyes suddenly glazed over.

'Anton, Fáfnir was supposedly buried at sea. What if . . . Alisa and that boy, Makar, dying in the sea was some kind of sacrifice? What a release of Dark power . . .'

Anton shook his head and wiped his sweaty forehead:

'Igor, maybe we've had too much to drink? Yes, I agree that Gesar's intending to use . . . could use Svetlana as the mother of a new messiah, a reincarnation of Christ to some extent, or just a magician of unprecedented power. It looks very much that way. And to counter that, Zabulon might try to come up with a figure of equal power, but tying all this up with Armageddon, the Bible and religion — that's taking it all too far!'

'What about the millennium?' Anton almost shouted. 'You understand? Magicians might intend to do one thing, but human dreams and fears shape reality in their own way. So the figures who appear will possess all the required qualities. Let's go!'

'Where?'

'To get some vodka. In the restaurant.'

Anton sighed and glanced at the bottle. Yes, it really was empty.
'Why don't we just call and order some?'

'Oh no, I feel like a walk.'

Anton stood up and put the amulet in his pocket. He nodded.
'Okay, let's go.'

There was no one at the lifts, but they had to wait for a long
time. Igor leaned against the wall and declaimed:

'Look, this is how Zabulon can do it. Fáfnir's Talon is taken
from the vault.'

'How?'

'What does it matter how? If they've stolen it once, they'll
manage it somehow. Then they carry out the magical operation,
plus staging all the myths of the Apocalypse. The locusts, the star
Wormwood, the four horses . . .'

'I can just see Zabulon leading four horses by the reins . . .'

'He doesn't need any horses!' Igor said with a frown. 'You know
as well as I do what the magic of appearances can do. For instance,
let's take four people, or better still – four Dark Others. One from
Asia – he can be the red horse; one black – he can be the black
horse; the third a European – he can be the white horse; and one,
let's say, Scandinavian – the pale horse. We put them on wooden
toy horses . . .'

The door of the lift opened and Anton froze.

Staring out in fright at the Light Ones from within the mirror-
lined box were the Regin Brothers. The adopted children of the
sect: the African, the Chinese and the Ukrainian. Of course, where
else would they be but in this hotel? They'd come for the Inquisition
Tribunal too . . . Anton thought in a slow, leisurely way that the
fourth fighter commando had been a Scandinavian.

It was a good thing he wasn't around any longer.

Igor seemed to have had the same thought. He muttered:
'Three of them.'

In the deathly silence the doors of the lift began to close. But Yukha Mustaioki suddenly stepped forward and stuck his foot between them, just where the sensor was. The doors reluctantly parted again.

'I'd like to thank the Night Watch of Moscow,' he said unexpectedly. He was obviously agitated, but trying to maintain his dignity. 'It was very humane.'

'What was?' asked Anton.

'To spare Pasi Ollikainen. We . . . we appreciate the fact that he's still alive.'

'Where is he?' exclaimed Anton.

'Downstairs . . . in the bar,' said Yukha, gaping in surprise at the two Light Magicians.

'Four horses,' Igor said in a hollow voice. 'Four horses! Four horses!'

Mustaioki staggered back rapidly and exchanged puzzled glances with his comrades.

The Light Magicians were left alone.

'It all fits!' said Igor, turning to Anton. 'You see? Everything!'

'Hang on . . .'

Anton concentrated, remembering the movements. He raised his right hand, made a pass in front of Igor's face, then pulled his hand sharply downwards and back up again, curving his fingers and cupping his hand.

'Damn you,' Igor groaned in a choking voice and raced back to his room. Anton followed him slowly. He looked at Igor's hunched-over back through the open door of the toilet and reached out to him through the Twilight. Igor began groaning.

The sobering-up spell isn't very complicated, but it's not pleasant for the person it's cast on.

Two minutes later Igor came out of the bathroom. With his hair wet, his eyes sunk into his head, looking as pale as death.

'A pale horse,' Anton muttered. 'Okay . . . Now you do it to me.'

Igor eagerly made the passes, and then Anton leaned down over the toilet bowl. A few minutes later, after he'd washed his face and drunk some foul-tasting water from the tap (the thirst had hit him immediately), he walked back into the room. Igor was already clearing away the remains of their drinking session. He looked at Anton and said mockingly:

'A black horse.'

Anton went over to the fridge, took out several bottles of mineral water, pulled the top off one with his fingers and collapsed into a chair. Igor took a second bottle from him. They drank water for a while in blissful silence. Then Igor admitted guiltily:

'Yes . . . we got plastered.'

'Toy horses,' said Anton. He smashed his fist down on the table and swore. 'It's embarrassing, all that nonsense we came up with.'

'It all seemed very logical somehow,' Igor said in a humbled voice. 'Those bloody Brothers . . . so the fourth one's alive too.'

'He must be,' Anton said with a shrug. 'All I knew was that Gesar went after him in the Twilight and caught up with him.'

'Well, of course . . . why would he want to kill a suspect? He handed him over to the Inquisition. Probably right there in the Twilight. Anton, maybe we were right after all?'

'Are you still a bit tipsy?' Anton asked.

'No, I'm entirely sober now. Damn, I can't even get drunk properly! Yes, it's all nonsense. Zabulon wouldn't try to drag some ancient magician back out of the Twilight. What good would that do him? And as for staging the end of the world, creating an Antichrist . . .'

'And anyway, Fáfnir wouldn't do,' Anton said. 'He's not up to it. Wouldn't even come close.'

'So everything we came up with is nonsense?'

Anton looked at the sheet of paper, with its grease spots from the salami and wet rings from their glasses. At what point had they lost the plot? He thought they'd been very careful.

'I'm afraid the bit about Svetlana isn't nonsense. But as for all the rest . . . Why did we get so excited over the number eighty-eight? What's so mystical about that?'

'It's kind of smooth and rounded, it reads the same both ways.' Igor waved his hand through the air and burst into laughter. 'Yes, you're right. It was all drunken nonsense.'

Anton picked up a marker that had fallen on the floor and crossed out the circle with 'Regin Brothers' written inside it. He said:

'They're not in the game. It looks like they completed their mission by charging the Mirror with power. This is what we should be interested in, Igor.'

Igor looked at the circle with his own name in it. He sighed.

'I'd be glad to believe in my own special mission. To think I'd done something to really upset Zabulon and the Day Watch. But . . .'

He spread his hands helplessly.

'Igor, you're the key,' said Anton. 'Do you understand? If we can understand why Zabulon is trying to get rid of you in order to fight Svetlana, then we'll win. If we can't, then the game's his.'

'There's Gesar too. And from what I hear, he's coming this morning.'

'We'd better try to manage without him,' said Anton, sensing the note of irritation in his own voice. 'His decisions are too . . . too global.'

Edgar poured himself some flat champagne left over from the day before, took a swallow, grimaced and thought wryly: 'Only aristocrats and degenerates drink champagne in the morning. And you, my dear fellow, don't look much like an aristocrat.'

The old Watchman's habit of thinking all the time, in any situation, had not abandoned Edgar even during his nocturnal amusements. Last night Edgar had continued to wonder what the leaders of the Moscow Watches were planning for this Christmas . . . but that hadn't prevented him from enjoying what he himself was doing.

'Right, then,' Edgar thought. 'What have we got? We need to sort everything out neatly. Right down to the final detail.'

What could Zabulon squeeze out of the present situation? Edgar needed to construct a mental model of his boss.

A Tribunal that had drawn its forces from both Watches. Not the most powerful, but by no means the lowest either. Two magicians, both from the elite. Edgar and Anton. There would be observers too. There was no doubt of that. And there was no doubt that during the actual session of the Tribunal neither side would make a move — they would be manoeuvring to extract some advantage for themselves from the indifferent and disinterested Inquisition.

But was it indifferent? Edgar had no doubts about its being unbiased. He'd lived a long time as an Other, and never, not once, had he had even the shadow of a doubt over the actions of the Inquisition. The servants of the Treaty had always been both cool and decisive. Someone had once said that the Inquisition didn't judge who was in the right and who was in the wrong, but who had violated the Treaty. That was the essential worldview of any Inquisitor. Edgar had matured enough to understand that, but he still didn't understand what it was that made the Inquisition act that way and not any other.

He wondered if the higher magicians understood it. Gesar and Zabulon.

So, the Tribunal. The Light Magician Igor Teplov could either be acquitted (which was undesirable), or found guilty. In the first case, the Night Watch would keep a third-grade magician who was temporarily unfit for combat, but still powerful and, more important, highly experienced. Edgar had come up against Teplov before that battle in North Butovo, although only in passing. Immediately after the war, in the memorable 'Ashes of Belozersk' operation. Back then the Moscow and Tallinn Watches had operated in the most unlikely places, such as the Vologda region. They didn't have enough men . . . Or rather, Others. The Dark Ones and the Light Ones were both short of numbers.

The other option was that the Night Watch would lose the magician for ever. The question was: so what? Igor Teplov was clearly not who he seemed to be. Or rather, there was something about him that was only obvious to the senior magicians. All in all, it looked very much as if Zabulon was stubbornly and consistently aiming at two goals in the enemy's camp: Igor Teplov and Svetlana Nazarova. And in doing so he had been quite willing to sacrifice his own lover, Alisa. Edgar still hadn't made out any logical connection between the skirmish in Butovo, the duel at the Artek camp and the rather confused events that had accompanied the appearance of the Dark Mirror. But for him it was enough to sense very clearly that there was one. There was definitely a single thread running through all these skirmishes and intrigues, connecting them all together, and it led straight back into Zabulon's hand.

Of course, any attempt to eliminate a future Great Enchantress was quite justified and understandable. But why had Zabulon begun to intrigue against the magician Igor? Why him in particular? And why right now, and not earlier, when he was weaker and more careless?

There was only one answer that fitted: Igor had only become dangerous after Svetlana had joined the ranks of the Night Watch.

Okay. Let's move on.

The resurrection of Fáfnir. You couldn't imagine a better time and place: the eve of the millennium, the heart of European necromancy. But how was this connected to the Tribunal and the Teplov–Donnikova case?

That was the problem!

Edgar sipped glumly at his champagne, thinking that he was very short of time – he only had until the evening. So he took the only possible decision: to pay an immediate visit to the local Day Watch office and request all available information about the duel between Siegfried and Fáfnir, and also study the relevant section of the *Necronomicon*.

Edgar was a powerful enough magician to know of the mechanism for the resurrection of a Great Dark One and to understand which of the necessary conditions could currently be met and which couldn't.

The German girl was still sleeping serenely: Edgar took pity on her and didn't wake her up. He washed, shaved and dressed, gently touched her sleeping mind and went out into the morning snow of Prague.

The Day Watch office was located on Vysěhradská, right beside the Vltava, in a three-storey brick building that was a private house with a water pump that clearly still worked even though it was so old. The handle of the pump was like a twisted pointing finger. Following tradition, Edgar got out of his taxi some distance away, to give his colleagues a chance to identify him and decide what to do, if anything.

His colleagues were on the ball – they spotted Edgar about three hundred metres from the door. He felt a light touch on his aura and opened himself up – exactly enough for the magician who was scanning him to realise that a Dark One was approaching, a Dark Magician, a second-grade Dark Magician, coming on business. Just like that, a further level of information each time.

Of course, Prague was a European capital, but it wasn't Moscow. The *beskud* on duty – the only guard, as it happened – gave Edgar a toothy smile.

'Another *beskud*,' Edgar thought, surprised. 'Are they more common in Prague then? This is already the second one.'

There were only six *beskuds* registered on the territory of the former USSR: two in Turkmenistan and one each in the Crimea, Belarus, Yakutia and Kamchatka. Edgar knew that for certain, because fifteen years earlier he had had a case outside Estonia in which all six of them had testified as witnesses.

The *beskud*'s Twilight form was almost classical.

'Greetings, colleague!'

'Good morning.'

Of course, in the Twilight there were no language barriers.

'What brings you to our bastion? Business? Or simply a courtesy visit?'

'Business. Where's your archive here?'

'The second floor down, and then you'll see for yourself.'

'The second floor down,' thought Edgar. 'So they have a multi-level basement.'

'Thank you. So I can go on down?'

'Of course. A Dark One is free to go wherever he wants, isn't that so?'

Edgar sighed. That was so all right, but not entirely.

'The lift's over that way,' the *beskud* told him.

'Thank you,' Edgar repeated and set off as directed.

A very, very old lift took him down to two floors below street level. And that wasn't the deepest level: there were another five hidden further below. The Prague Watch was certainly firmly established.

The lift lobby was absolutely tiny: four metres by four. There was a door on the left and one on the right: the sign on one read 'Library', the other 'Computer Room'.

'Let's start with the library,' thought Edgar. 'In Fáfnir's and Al-Hazred's time there weren't any computers . . . at least not in the modern meaning of the word.'

Edgar stepped towards the door on his left. It was closed, but not locked.

It was a classical library: a large hall with about ten tables and long rows of shelves with books. One glance at their spines was enough to understand that these venerable tomes remembered more than many of the Others.

Edgar stopped, and just at that moment a strikingly thin Other emerged from behind the shelves. A vampire. And a higher vampire – Edgar realised that immediately.

The ordinary vampires that were quite common in Moscow were the junior members of the team, the cannon fodder that Anton Gorodetsky had mentioned. They had hardly any magic, and even a degenerate Dark Magician was still more powerful than they were. But higher vampires were a quite different matter, although for some reason there were none in Moscow, or anywhere in Eastern Europe – with the exceptions of the Czech Republic and Romania.

'Good morning. Can I be of any assistance?'

'Good morning. I'm interested in material on one of the magicians of the past.'

'Who exactly?' the vampire enquired.

'Fáfnir. The Dragon of the Twilight.'

'Aha,' the vampire said respectfully. 'He was a truly powerful magician. One of the most powerful Dark Ones in the history of mankind. What exactly are you interested in?'

'The circumstances of his death. The reasons for his duel with

Siegfried, the prehistory, all the details. In short, I want to make a comprehensive study of this outstanding figure. But unfortunately, I only have a few hours. I'd also like to model the operation of bringing him back from the Twilight.'

The vampire smiled sadly.

'Unfortunately, that is effectively impossible. It would require interventions of such power and intensity that the right to make them could not be earned even by placing all – let me emphasise that – all the Dark Ones of the world into hibernation for a hundred years.'

'Nonetheless,' said Edgar, with a sweeping gesture, 'I'd like to solve this problem, if only on paper.'

'Then you should take a look at Al-Hazred's *Necronomicon*,' the vampire advised him. 'It describes all the necessary interventions for the rematerialisation of essential beings with some precision.'

Then, without a pause, he asked:

'Are you a theoretical necromancer?'

Edgar smiled more broadly than before.

'Oh no! I've never really dealt with necromancy at all. But I've developed an interest.'

'Then you did right to come to Prague. People here know their necromancy, and there are any number of specialists. But unfortunately they are all theoreticians, and of course you understand why.'

Edgar really did understand why.

Because since the Treaty had been signed the Inquisition had only sanctioned rematerialisation twice, and both times only temporarily. The Tribunal needed to question witnesses, and sometimes there was an opportunity to bring a dematerialised Other back from the Twilight. On both occasions when such an opportunity had been exploited, but after questioning the witnesses had gone back to the Twilight.

Edgar couldn't believe that a magician of Fáfnir's power hadn't established in advance some loophole to allow for his own rematerialisation. He must have done so once he reached a certain grade – indeed, Edgar was hoping to reach that grade himself some day. Of course, he hoped with equal justification never to allow himself to be dematerialised, but life was such a strange business, it was always throwing up surprises. Especially in conditions of continuous war.

'Go on through,' said the vampire, indicating the tables. 'I'll bring you the books in a moment. I believe it's not the human experience of the time that interests you, but the chronicles of the Others, is that so?'

'Of course, dear colleague. Of course.'

'I'll just be a second.'

The vampire really did come back very quickly. He had obviously been working as the custodian of the library for more than a decade and knew his books very well.

'There,' he said, laying two large volumes on the table. The first was a huge, large-format book in an old binding of dull brown leather – the *Necronomicon* in Gerhardt Kuchelstein's translation; the second was rather more modest – not so big, with a florid title that covered half a page: *A Life and Exposition of the Glorious Doings and Also the Prophecies and Numerous Unparalleled Discoveries of the Great Dark Magician Well-known among Others by the Name of Fáfnir, or the Dragon of the Twilight* by Johann Jetzer. It looked like an original.

The title of Jetzer's book was probably even more archaic in style, but Edgar didn't know Old High German, so he had to read the book through the Twilight, where individual stylistic features are smoothed out and the text is levelled down, although it becomes much easier to understand.

Edgar ran his eye diagonally across *The Doings of Fáfnir*, as was only to be expected, the contents of the thick volume interpreted events rather differently from the two *Edda* and the *Song of the Niebelungen*. First, it was clear that Sigurd (a.k.a. Siegfried, a.k.a. Sivrit) and Regin and Hreidmar and Fáfnir himself were all Others. Naturally, Hreidmar wasn't Fáfnir's biological father and Regin wasn't his real brother. By means of long and careful intriguing, Sigurd managed to make the Dark Magicians quarrel and destroyed them all, some through the agency of Others and some with his own hands. Sigurd's goal, of course, was not treasure at all, not useless pieces of metal and glittering stones. Sigurd and the Others were searching for the legacy of the dwarf Andvari, but Jetzer's work did not explain what that was. It could have been ancient and powerful artefacts or simply knowledge (in the form of books, for instance). In any case, eventually Sigurd had killed all the Others and taken possession of the legacy of Andvari, but what happened after that, Edgar didn't have time to find out. Fáfnir had been Sigurd's penultimate victim, before Regin. It seemed that Fáfnir had taken certain secrets with him into the Twilight after all, but that didn't really bother the magicians of those times, who weren't bound by Treaties or codes of law and acted without regard for the Inquisition, since it did not yet exist.

The main thing that Edgar learned was that Fáfnir possessed certain forgotten knowledge in the field of higher battle magic (which didn't appear to have helped him much in his duel with the crafty Sigurd) and he had taken this with him into the Twilight. So, Zabulon could well be intending to get hold of that knowledge.

Having arrived at this essentially rather obvious conclusion, Edgar turned to the *Necronomicon*.

The first thing he learned there was that rematerialisation was not the resurrection of an Other who had been dematerialised. It all turned out to be much simpler and more banal.

It was more like castling in chess. Someone withdrew into the Twilight, and in his place someone else emerged from the Twilight. The higher the level of power of the individual rematerialised, the more powerful the person dematerialised had to be. But the levels didn't have to be identical – some leeway was allowed. If what Jetzer wrote about Fáfnir was true, it meant the Dragon of the Twilight could be exchanged for a second- or third-grade Dark Magician, but only if the overall available energy input was sufficient.

And the required input could for example be provided by acting out the Apocalypse – with the turbulent emotions of thousands of humans generating such a squall that Fáfnir would probably emerge reborn from the Twilight full of power, a mighty Dark Magician thirsting for vengeance and freedom. The freedom he had lost so long ago.

What would he do, this Great Magician from the past who had never even heard of the Treaty of the Inquisition? How was Zabulon planning to handle him? And was he planning at all? The Dragon of the Twilight in the skies over Europe at Christmas – what could possibly be more insane and terrifying?

Assume that Fáfnir runs wild, burning cities and causing all sorts of devastation; if he simply chooses stupid brute force, then even humans would be able to pacify him. With rockets. That Light flying ace who loved the Chicago Bulls could down him with some devastating explosive device from his Phantom or his Harrier. They wouldn't kill him, but they'd pacify him. But what good would that do Europe? What did Europe want with nuclear mushroom clouds and her cosy little towns burned to cinders by Fáfnir's flames?

But most likely Fáfnir wouldn't simply run berserk, he would use his experience and cunning, and then watch out, Europe. Then there would be far greater devastation and many more victims.

But why did Zabulon want all this?

Edgar didn't understand.

What else was required for the resurrection of the Dragon of the Twilight? A second- or third-grade magician in the right place . . . But what place was that?

Edgar spent about ten minutes calculating the answer from the stars and the shifting foci of energy. It was a problem of average difficulty: Fáfnir had been cast down into the Twilight in the north of Europe, so, the most convenient place to rematerialise him on the cusp of the millennium was . . . He had it.

Edgar wasn't very surprised by the result. The Czech Republic. Prague.

He was immediately struck by a dark sense of foreboding. A Dark Magician of the required grade in the right place . . . In Prague . . .

That was him! Edgar the Estonian!

Edgar wiped away the cold sweat that had sprung out on his forehead and went back to his reading.

Not every magician would suit Zabulon's purposes. For instance, the object of the castling move had to have been born in a specific place. It was rather unclear. What place exactly?

When he worked it out, the answer was Scandinavia, Northern Germany or the Baltic region.

The Baltic.

The chief of the Moscow Day Watch had suddenly summoned an Estonian to work in the Russian capital. And Edgar hadn't been able to identify any obvious need for his being there.

Who else had been born in Scandinavia, Northern Germany or the Baltic region and was in Prague just then?

No one. Only Edgar.

That was what Yury had warned him about before he flew to Prague. This had to be it. What else could it be?

All right. Easy now, easy. Just don't start getting nervous. Forewarned is forearmed. What else does the *Necronomicon* have to tell us?

Right, another four Dark Ones were required to form the Circle of Resurrection. Well, that was clear enough. The Circle was a kind of portal supported by the power of the four Dark Ones, who were referred to very elegantly as the horsemen of the Dark.

And the horsemen were red, black, white and pale. The precise scenario of the Apocalypse. Point for point.

And there were even magicians in Prague who would suit, although there were only three of them now – the Regin Brothers, who happened to be red-haired (the Asiatic), black (the African), white (the Slav) and pale (the Scandinavian that Gesar had killed).

Zabulon himself had said that the Brothers had a place in his plans. And now Edgar could reasonably guess exactly what those plans were. And Zabulon wasn't likely to be stopped by the absence of the fourth horseman.

Edgar read this section of the *Necronomicon* to the end and discovered another two details that were small but, in the general context, important.

Since Fáfnir was a dragon, the canonical form of his resurrection would be for him to emerge from the sea – though that wasn't absolutely essential. What was essential was the making of a sacrifice to the sea. In advance. Anywhere at all   it could be in China or the Falkland Islands.

Or even the Crimea.

The person sacrificed was supposed to be 'a youth or a maiden'. No longer a child, but not yet an adult.

'Artek,' Edgar thought immediately. 'The boy who drowned because of the duel.'

And then again, if Zabulon had set his sights on Edgar as the second piece in the castling move, then during the final twenty-four hours, no matter where Zabulon might be, he had to find an image of Edgar. A portrait or photograph. More likely a portrait. And keep this image with him. Until the moment when the move was made.

That was all – the library had no more help to offer Edgar. He hastily thanked the vampire librarian and hurried across to a computer.

Of course, he could have simply phoned Moscow. But a phone call was easy to trace, and Edgar didn't want to show his hand too soon. And he was absolutely certain that Alita was chatting on one of the IRC channels right at that moment.

The young IT manager – either a low-grade magician or a wizard – was glad to show him how to get onto the internet. Edgar thanked him, and the young guy instantly stuck his nose back into his own laptop, its screen covered in machine code. He was programming the old-fashioned way, without any of those new-fangled Delphi windows.

Edgar launched MIRC and connected in the usual way to the Getborg DALnet server, with the funny cow in its logo (of course, the cow was drawn in ASCII-art – in letters and numbers). He identified himself, but he didn't log on to any of the channels. He selected Query from the menu and put in the NIC he was interested in: Alita.

A new window opened.

What Edgar was most afraid of was a curt phrase appearing in the status window, saying: 'No such NIC or channel'.

But the Dark was merciful – the response came almost instantaneously. And from the right address – alita@ncport.ru.

'Edgar, hi! Are you in Prague?'

'Yes. Alita, I have an urgent question . . . it's rather strange. And not for everyone's ears. Will you help me?'

'Do you need to ask, Edgar? Of course.'

'Have you been in the chief's office during the last few days?'

In general, the likelihood of any witch being summoned by Zabulon himself was pretty low, but he had to start somewhere.

'Yes, I have, why?'

'Well, well,' Edgar thought to himself. 'I guessed right.'

He typed:

'You didn't happen to notice if he had a photograph or portrait of me in his office, did you? On the desk, for instance.'

'How did you guess?' And Alita sent him a generous scattering of smilies to symbolise her good mood.

'After you left the chief commissioned two drawings. One of you, the other of a dragon. They're both standing in frames on his desk. I went to the arts and crafts shop on Tverskaya Street to get the frames. The chief gave me a bottle of Veuve Cliquot as a thank-you.'

Edgar closed his eyes.

That was it. The final touch for the planned exchange of pieces. Your death sentence, Edgar the Estonian.

Now what are you going to do?

'Thanks, Alita,' he typed in stiffly. 'Got to run, I'm snowed under with work.'

'Cheers, Edgar. Kiss!'

Edgar couldn't even look at the smilies. He closed the window on the screen and got up from the table.

The young programmer glanced at him from behind his laptop.

'Is that it?' he asked without any real surprise.

'Yes,' Edgar replied. 'Thanks.'

He reached the exit without thinking about anything – his head felt strangely dull and empty.

He'd been specially selected, like a cow for Christmas kebabs. A reasonably powerful magician from the Baltic. He'd been lured in and treated well. Allowed to run things for a while – in the

Moscow Watch, not some dull backwater. But all the time he'd been nothing more than a sacrificial cow, to be slaughtered at the right moment. Used, just like a thing. Exchanged, like a mindless chesspiece.

After all, the game went on for ever, it was only the presence of the pieces on the chequered board that was temporary.

But so what? If the time had come for one more black queen to join the game, did that mean it was pointless for the rook hastily drafted in from the periphery to dig in and clutch hard at the slippery surface of the board?

'Oh no,' thought Edgar. 'I may not be a queen, but I'm certainly not a pawn. And I'm not leaving the board that easily. I'm going to kick up a fuss. And if I can manage it, I'll save half of Europe some serious problems.'

If all else failed, there was the Inquisition. Something told Edgar that the grey-robed officials were unlikely to be pleased by the idea of a visit from the Dragon of the Twilight.

Festive Prague seemed to have disappeared, faded and receded into the distance. Edgar caught a taxi and rode to the hotel without once looking out of the window. He paid the driver automatically and walked into reception, giving the doorman a look that probably made him wish he could disappear through the granite slabs of the floor.

Edgar strode towards the lifts so rapidly that his unbuttoned raincoat almost fluttered behind him. He walked towards the room that his intuition as an Other told him was the one he was looking for.

Then he suddenly stopped as if he'd run into something and swallowed convulsively.

The Finns had just come out of the bar. The Regin Brothers. All four of them. Four, not three – the Chinese, the African and the Slav had been joined by an ethnic Finn, the one everybody had thought was dead.

But there he was, alive and well.

But of course – why would Gesar have wanted to kill a witness?

No doubt an artist is overwhelmed by a whole range of inexpressible feelings when he puts the final piece of glass in place in a mosaic. But what are you supposed to do when the glass pieces of the mosaic form the stark words of your own death sentence?

'Brother!' one of the Finns said triumphantly to Edgar. 'We want to thank you and the Day Watch of Moscow for your support. Why don't you join us? We're celebrating the survival of our brother Pasi – everybody thought he was dead.'

The genuine Finn gave an embarrassed smile, his entire appearance showing how touched he was by his comrades' concern.

'Congratulations,' Edgar said in a hollow voice, although there wasn't really anything to congratulate them on – all four of them would be certain to die at Fáfnir's resurrection.

'Brother Dark One . . .' Seeing Edgar's hesitation, the magician stopped pressing him. 'Do you happen to know the Light One who is also a defendant? Why did he call us four horses?'

His colleagues all began nodding indignantly.

'Are we entitled to regard it as an unjustified insult?' the leader of the Regin Brothers asked hopefully.

'No,' Edgar replied. 'It's worse than an insult, it's the truth.'

And he sprinted for the lift.

# CHAPTER 6

By MIDDAY Anton had given up.

He and Igor hadn't drunk any more vodka, despite its remarkable ability to stimulate the imagination. Coffee already made him feel sick. And he didn't feel like drinking any of the wonderful Czech beer either.

Igor was standing at the window with a glass of Danone drinking yoghurt in his hand. He shook his head at Anton's latest suggestion.

'No, come on. What sort of dragon-slayer would I make? And I thought we'd abandoned the Fáfnir scenario?'

'But what if it's right after all?'

'It makes no difference. It's a battle of magic, not a duel with a fire-breathing dragon.'

Igor chuckled and added cynically: 'And anyway, in a fight between Fáfnir the Dragon and a pair of modern battle helicopters, I'd put my money on the choppers. There's no point in any more guessing, Anton. We won't come up with anything.'

'But even so, Igor, you're the key.'

'But what can we do about it? Nobody ever tells keys which doors they're to open. Anton, I'm a perfectly ordinary Other. Only

Zabulon knows what makes me significant. And Gesar probably knows too. He'll come upstairs and join us in a moment, then we can ask him.'

Anton looked through the Twilight and said enviously:

'Seriously? Is he already close? I can't sense him.'

'I can't sense him either, I just saw them through the window, walking into the hotel.'

There was a gentle tap at the door. Just a token gesture of politeness, no more than that, and a moment later the visitors entered through the Twilight. Gesar, his silent shadow Alisher, and Svetlana. Svetlana was led through the Twilight by the magicians, and she only saw Anton when all three of them emerged from the Twilight into the human world. She smiled and gave a slightly guilty shrug, as if to say: 'Just look what I'm like now.' And once again Anton was overcome by a miserable feeling of guilt and tenderness, mixed with shame and anger at himself. Even though he'd had no other option but to let the Mirror take away all of Svetlana's power. And the most important thing was that, as a result, Svetlana was still alive. But he couldn't rid himself of the cursed feeling that the game had been lost.

Could Igor really have similar feelings when he remembered Alisa? Similar, but far more bitter?

In that case Anton could only be surprised and delighted that he was still alive.

'Good afternoon, lads,' Gesar said softly.

He was wearing a modest, inexpensive suit and plain tie. Looking like a run-of-the-mill businessman who bought his clothes from Marks & Spencer and always sent his employees modest presents at Christmas. In this case, of course, Gesar regarded himself as the very best present.

'Hello, Boris Ignatievich,' said Anton. He couldn't bring himself to call this afternoon good. 'Hello, Alisher.'

He and Sveta simply exchanged glances again; he took her by the hand and led her across to a chair. As if she were an invalid. It was awful.

'Good afternoon, boss,' Igor said calmly. 'Good to see you. Hello, Sveta. Hi, Alisher.'

Gesar's bodyguard Alisher (that is, of course, if it was really possible to regard a third-grade magician as a bodyguard for a Great Magician) – or, perhaps more accurately, his orderly, the son of a devona and a human woman – nodded to the magicians without speaking and moved into the corner of the room, where he froze with his arms crossed on his chest and partially withdrew into the Twilight. Anton sensed that Alisher's ability to observe in the Twilight had been heightened artificially, clearly by the boss. And he also noticed that the young magician was trying not to look at Igor. That was another awkward complication – Alisher's father had been killed by Alisa Donnikova. And even though he hadn't been either a human being or an Other . . . it was hard to be precise about the status of a devona, a faithful helper of the Great Magicians. The devona himself did not perform any great feats of heroism, that was not his job. He merely served the heroes, removed minor obstacles from their path. And he strengthened family ties, facilitating the birth of great heroes.

Anton caught his breath.

As a rule, werewolves' children inherited the ability to transform, while magicians' children only became Others very rarely. But how did it work with devonas?

Who was Alisher, simply a magician or a devona like his father, who had been Gesar's assistant in Central Asia for many centuries?

And what did the boss need the young Uzbeki magician for? Was it only for sentimental reasons that Gesar had taken him into the Moscow Watch and made him his retainer?

'Anton!'

He looked at Svetlana and only then realised that he was squeezing her hand too hard.

'Sorry.'

Gesar was standing in front of Igor, looking into his eyes. He looked for a long time without saying anything. Then he sighed and walked away to a chair, hunched over and looking limp. He sat down and lowered his face into his hands.

'Boris Ignatievich,' said Igor, 'forgive me.'

'No!' Gesar barked, with his hands still over his face. 'I won't forgive you. So what if you fell in love with a witch? I won't condemn you for that — that's destiny. But you've given up on yourself — don't expect any forgiveness for that.'

Igor was clearly uncomfortable. As Anton looked at him, he suddenly realised he'd accomplished his mission after all. Not by simple, head-on tactics  it would have been stupid to expect to trick an experienced magician and restore his will to live by means of a simple drinking session and conversations about his friends. It would have been even more stupid to hope to convince him that the woman he loved was simply a repulsive, greedy bitch.

But their long nocturnal conversation, their attempts to understand what was happening and make sense of the latest stage in the war between the Watches had had their effect. Igor had been distracted from his misery and suffering. He had felt part of a team again.

Could that have been what Gesar was counting on?

In that case, all his behaviour, including the present scene, had been carefully calculated.

But after all, the boss was right, Igor's mind was simply clouded.

'Gesar, there are things that even you have no right to ask,' Igor suddenly said. He said it abruptly, with a reawakened fury. With life in his voice.

'Yes, of course, Captain Igor Teplov.' Gesar's voice was as cold as ice. 'I have no right! But who had the right to ask you to swim down the Dnepr under fire in November forty-two? And who had the right—'

'That's different!'

'Why is it?' Gesar stood up, walked over to Igor and stopped in front of him again. A head shorter than Igor, small and wiry, not looking at all heroic. 'Do I have to explain to you, Teplov, what a war requires? It's not bodies that a war devours, but souls. And you knew that in the glorious city of Berlin, when you used your knife on that poor snot-nosed kid from the Hitler Jugend to make him give his friends away – you knew that.'

Igor started as if he'd been slapped across the face.

'Conscience . . . love . . . honour . . .' Gesar said thoughtfully. 'No one has the right to make anyone go against their conscience. No one has the right to make anyone betray love. No one has the right to persuade anyone to betray their honour. No one. You're right. But we do it. Of our own accord. When one pan of the scales holds our love, conscience and honour, and the other holds a million loving, decent, honourable people. We're no angels, that's not for us. And I understand your pain, believe me. But you take a look at Alisher. And try to understand his pain. Ask Anton what he thinks about the one you love. Ask Svetlana.'

'I can't condemn Igor,' Svetlana said quietly. 'I'm sorry, boss. Forgive me, Alisher. Maybe I'm just a fool . . . unworthy of the Watch. But I can understand all of you.'

She said this in a very low voice, without emphasis, but Gesar stopped talking and moved away from Igor. He spread his hands and asked:

'Do you think I don't understand?'

The silence in the room was thick and heavy.

'Gesar, when it was my duty, I carried out my orders,' Igor said abruptly. 'Honestly, right down the line. Regardless of . . . what I thought or felt. But my duty's done now. I've reached the end of the line.'

'No. That's where you're wrong, Igor.' Gesar started walking round the room and took a cigar out of his pocket. He looked at it and frowned, put it back and took out a packet of democratic Pall Mall. He crumpled that and gestured in annoyance. 'The Watch needs you. We all need you. I need you.'

'Svetlana needs me,' Igor remarked casually.

'Svetlana, Alisher, Ilya, Semyon, Bear – all of us,' Gesar said very quickly. 'Of course.'

Igor smiled, as if reconciling himself to the fact that he couldn't finish what he wanted to say. And then suddenly he asked, in a businesslike, serious voice:

'For long?'

'Twenty years at most,' Gesar said quite calmly, as if he'd been expecting this question.

'Gesar, do you hope that will be long enough for me to stop loving Alisa?'

'That too,' Gesar admitted. 'But the Watch needs you right now. In the years immediately ahead.'

'What do you want me to do, Gesar?'

'Don't get in our way, Igor! We're going to try to get you out of this. And we will get you out of it, believe me, if you just don't get in our way . . . or even better, if you help us just a little.'

Igor considered this. Then he said:

'I won't accuse Alisa Donnikova of enchanting me. It's not true.'

'But you can express the suspicion that your meeting was set up by the Moscow Day Watch?'

'Yes, I can,' Igor said with a nod. 'That's probably the way it was.'

'That's enough,' said Gesar with a shrug. 'I don't ask anything else of you.'

And he really did look satisfied with that.

Anton cleared his throat and waited for Gesar to look at him.
Then he said:

'Boris Ignatievich, I'd like to ask you to do something for me.
Can you explain what role Igor plays in our current intrigue?'

'Just Igor?'

'Yes. What you need Svetlana for, and the devona Alisher, is
clear enough already.'

The young Uzbeki magician standing stock still in the corner
started.

'The new generation's coming along well,' Gesar said in a tired
voice. 'Shrewd. But stupid at the same time.'

He hesitated and looked round at them all. Then he shook his
head and Anton sensed the power spreading around them and
flooding the room. The elastic wall was pressing *something* back,
squeezing it out.

'I can't tell you,' Gesar admitted unexpectedly. 'I can't tell you
for one simple reason.'

'We'd refuse to co-operate?' Anton asked sharply.

Gesar shook his head:

'No. On the contrary. I swear on the Light that what is going
on will cause no harm to any of you. Neither to your magical or
to your human being. In fact, you would co-operate with genuine,
sincere zeal. But . . .' He was weighing every word now. '. . . what
is taking place now really is the final operation of the Moscow
Night Watch. It is also the final operation of the Day Watch. Too
much depends on the actions of everyone sitting here, as well as
on the actions of our enemies. We are making our moves and our
enemies are making theirs. They could be wrong, unsuccessful,
mistaken. But the victory will go to those who make the final
correct move.'

'The victors are never judged,' Anton agreed. 'And the pieces
on a chessboard have no right to move independently.'

'Zabulon will easily read any move that any of you make!' Gesar barked. 'And don't imagine, Anton, that when you rammed the Mirror's car it was a move that hadn't been foreseen. Yes, it was a successful move. The lesser of two evils. But even that was antici- pated. By Zabulon . . . and by me.'

He paused for breath and went on more calmly:

'To me you are not just pieces on a chessboard. Believe me. You're more than just tools.'

'But one of us,' said Svetlana with a smile that acknowledged that she was the only woman in the room, 'is the lathe for producing a tool?'

Anton didn't ask how she had realised. Maybe she'd been drawing diagrams too − without letting even him know? Or maybe she'd already sensed something when she still had her powers?

Gesar paused, lowering his head. He seemed to be thinking hard. And then Anton realised that the strength of the protective cocoon around them had increased to a quite extraordinary level. What was the limit to the power of the Great Magicians? Was there even a limit to it at all?

'All right,' Gesar said with a nod. 'Svetlana, you're right . . . but only partly . . . ah, Light and Dark!'

He lowered himself into an armchair, took out his cigarettes again and lit one. He took two drags and started speaking:

'Svetlana, you are a Great Enchantress. They're only born every few centuries. Potentially, you're more powerful than Olga . . . probably. But your value to the Light Ones − and I don't mean just our Watch, but Light Ones in general − is that you could become the mother of the messiah.'

'After Olga rewrote my Book of Destiny,' Svetlana said.

'No. Not after that. It's not possible to rewrite the destiny of an Other as easily as the destiny of a human being. It was prede- termined from the very beginning. We only corrected a few details.

Minor ones. That don't affect you or the future . . . the prospective child.'

'What details?' The anger could suddenly be heard in Svetlana's voice, the anger she'd restrained for so long. And now it was Anton who wanted to shout out as her fingers dug into the palm of his hand.

'Only the date.' Gesar had no intention of giving way to pressure from Svetlana. 'Nothing but the date. Two thousand years after the birth of Christ is the peak of human belief in the coming of the messiah.'

'Thank you very much,' said Svetlana in a voice trembling with fury. 'So you decided when I would have him and who his father would be?'

'In the first place, why "him?"' Gesar asked.

Anton had been on the point of putting in a few words, mostly to clarify what Svetlana had said about the father, but he choked on this swift rejoinder. Svetlana's hand went limp too.

'For some the father and mother decide, for some it's the drunken obstetrician, for others it's an extra glass of vodka,' Gesar said in a melancholy voice. There was no need for him to say 'in the second place'. 'Svetlana, my child! It's dangerous to play with such powers, with such predetermination! Even I'm not trying to do that. It is predetermined that you can give birth to a daughter who will become the greatest figure in the war between the Light and the Dark. Her word will change the entire world, her word will make sinners repent, at a glance from her the greatest magicians of the Dark will go down on their knees.'

'It's only a probability,' Svetlana whispered.

'Of course. There is no fate – which is both unfortunate and fortunate. But you must believe that an old, weary magician is doing everything he can to make it a reality.'

'I should have stayed a human being,' Svetlana whispered. 'I should have . . .'

'Have you looked at any icons recently?' Gesar asked. 'Look into Mary's eyes and think why they're always so sad.'

The room was very quiet.

'I've already told you more than I have any right to.' Gesar spread his arms in a guilty shrug and for the first time ever it seemed to Anton that he wasn't acting at all. 'But I have told you, I've put one foot over the line of what is permissible. It's up to you to decide. To think who is a piece on a chessboard, and who is a rational individual, capable of seeing past imaginary offences.'

'Imaginary?' Svetlana asked bitterly.

'When they told you that you had to wash your hands after playing in the sandpit or made you tie the ribbon on your plait in a bow – that was interference in your destiny too,' said Gesar. 'And I think it was justified.'

'You're not my father, Boris Ignatievich,' said Svetlana.

'No, of course not. But to me, you're all my children,' Gesar sighed. 'I'll wait for you in the hall . . . that is, Alisher and I will wait. Join us if you want to.'

He went out, and the devona followed him like a shadow.

Igor was the first to say anything:

'What hurts most is that he's right about some things.'

'If you'd been told that you have to give birth to a messiah, then I'd talk to you about what's right or wrong!' Svetlana replied abruptly.

'That would be rather, well . . . difficult for me,' Igor admitted in an embarrassed voice.

Anton was the first to smile. He looked at Svetlana and said:

'Listen, I remember how indignant you were about the injustice of destiny – that, generally speaking, Others only have children who are ordinary people.'

'That was just an abstract indignation,' said Svetlana, throwing her hands up. 'Boys, I think someone's already been smoking in here, so . . .'

Igor handed her a cigarette without speaking.

'Why do everything like that, behind our backs?' Svetlana complained as she lit her cigarette. 'And what sort of mother would I make . . . for a messiah? And a female one at that.'

'Well, messiah is just the appropriate term, that's all,' said Igor. 'Relax.'

'I'm no virgin,' Svetlana declared gloomily. 'And in general, I don't think of myself as a paragon of virtue.'

'Don't draw irrelevant parallels.'

Oddly enough, Igor seemed to have calmed down. For real. He was sharp and focused.

'Anton, why don't you say something!' Svetlana burst out. 'Doesn't this concern you at all?'

'I very much hope that it concerns me directly,' replied Anton. 'And I think we ought to go out now and join Gesar. It's tough on him sitting out there and waiting.'

'He already knows everything in advance,' Svetlana said and turned away.

'No. He doesn't. If we're really not pawns, he doesn't know.'

There was the soft sound of a guitar. Igor was leaning against the wall, playing. He began singing so softly that Svetlana and Anton both had to stop talking.

The devils ask me to serve,
But I serve no one.
Even myself, even you,
Even the one who has power.
If he is still alive,
I do not serve even him.

I have stolen just enough fire
Not to need to steal any more . . .

Igor held the guitar out and gently lowered it into an armchair, the way people put their instrument down when they're sure they'll be back soon.

'Shall we go then?'

Edgar was the first of the Dark Ones to enter the Tribunal's meeting hall. That was the procedure. He entered through one door just as Anton came in through the door opposite. They bowed their heads to each other in polite greeting. Edgar did not feel any particular resentment towards the Light One and he expected the feeling to be mutual to some extent.

Compared to the small, neglected room in Moscow University, this hall was certainly impressive. This was Europe, after all.

Stone vaulting – heavy and oppressive, but at the same giving a sense of security and calm. A simple metal chandelier, but with about two hundred candles, and Edgar could have sworn the candles had been burning for more than a century already. They said the Berne department of the Inquisition was located in an ultra-modern building, but the Prague department was in a truly ancient one.

Edgar liked the old style better.

The round hall was divided into two parts: one was faced with light marble, the other with dark. There was something at once naïve and exalted in this simple visual representation of the two powers. The little desks for the prosecutors stood at the centre, beside a circular metal grille covering a dark hole in the floor.

A wedge of grey marble reached almost to the very centre of the hall. That was the Inquisitors' area, and they, of course, were already in their seats. Seven of them. In principle the Inquisition was not regarded as a power equal to the two Watches, but Edgar knew that those seven included two Great Ones – one Dark and one Light. If it wished, the European Office could probably fight Gesar and Zabulon on equal terms.

That was good to know.

Anton was followed in by three Light Ones from Moscow. Gesar . . . well, of course, where would they be without Gesar? Svetlana . . . that was natural too. And that Uzbeki, Gesar's secretary or personal assistant.

The Dark Ones were already walking along the corridor behind Edgar. Zabulon . . . Sensing the approach of his chief, Edgar involuntarily looked round – and received a friendly nod from the head of Moscow's Dark Ones. Well, well . . . smile, you Judas . . . you're even worse than Judas, he betrayed his teacher, but you're betraying your disciple.

But then another two Dark Ones followed Zabulon into the hall. Edgar had been prepared to see Anna Lemesheva, but not Yury, who winked mockingly at him. The same Yury who had given Edgar the timely warning about Zabulon's underhand schemes – he hadn't been prepared for that.

Edgar forced himself to turn away from his colleagues and look straight ahead.

Igor was brought in last. Two rank-and-file Inquisitors walked in beside him and accompanied him to the circular grille, three metres across, in the centre of the hall.

There was no special magic in that circle, or at least Edgar couldn't sense any. And the mechanism that had once been used to invert the grille and plunge the accused into a deep well shaft looked as if it had rusted up long ago and was no longer used. Even so, standing in that circle could not be pleasant.

However, Igor paid such thoughts no heed and stood in the centre of the circle with his arms crossed on his chest.

'In the name of the Treaty . . .'

One Inquisitor came forward from the group. The only one who was not wearing grey robes. Witiezslav, the higher vampire.

'We are Others. We serve different powers . . .'

Edgar mechanically repeated the words of the Treaty, trying to work out what Witiezslav would start with. And how he could extricate himself from this mess now.

'Today the European Tribunal of the Inquisition has to consider a claim brought by the Night Watch of the city of Moscow, Russia, against the Day Watch of the city of Moscow, Russia,' the vampire announced after the reading of the Treaty. 'A counterclaim by the Day Watch of Moscow against the Night Watch of Moscow forms part of the proceedings. Its subject is the duel between the Light Magician, Igor Teplov, and the Dark Witch, Alisa Donnikova . . .'

There were no surprises so far. Edgar felt himself clutching the dark, cool wooden top of his desk and made an effort of will to calm himself. After all, he was an experienced lawyer. And how were legal proceedings between humans any different from legal proceedings between Others?

Except, of course, for the nature of the sentence.

'However, the sequence of proceedings will be somewhat altered,' said Witiezslav. 'The Tribunal is also obliged to resolve another two matters connected to the main claim. The first concerns a sect of Dark Ones who call themselves the Regin Brothers, who are guilty of attacking the Inquisition's vault and stealing the artefact known as Fáfnir's Talon, smuggling it into Russia and resisting the Night Watch of Moscow. Bring in the accused.'

Another two young Inquisitors led in the four Finns. Faint smiles appeared on the faces of all the Others present — it was impossible to imagine a more ludicrous-looking quartet.

'There is probably no need to recite the circumstances of the incident,' said the vampire. 'Everyone present is familiar with the materials collected by the Inquisition on this case. The Inquisition's job is to pronounce judgement. Just, impartial and strict.'

It was clear from the expressions on the faces of the four accused that they were not expecting leniency.

'The punishment for a crime as grave as attacking employees of the Inquisition and stealing a highly dangerous artefact from the vault is unconditional – dematerialisation,' the vampire declared. He paused and then added, making the Finns raise their heads: 'But . . . But the accused did not participate directly in the incident in Berne. As the materials of the case make clear, the leaders of the sect, who were unfortunately killed while being detained, compelled the four young magicians to act as couriers. Therefore, the Inquisition qualifies their actions only as smuggling and resisting the Night Watch of Moscow. There are also extenuating circumstances: profound and sincere remorse, assistance rendered to the investigation after detention, the youth of the accused and the absence of any previous offences. If the Night Watch of Moscow can adduce any further extenuating circumstances and will withdraw the personal accusations against the Dark Magicians, the Inquisition has the right to mitigate its sentence.'

Gesar stood to speak for the Light Ones. He spread his hands in a broad gesture:

'The Night Watch of Moscow has no . . . personal accusations to bring against the accused. In addition, we believe that the leadership of the sect of the Regin Brothers was provoked into committing its crime by a certain . . . a certain unknown Dark Magician.'

'That has not been proved,' said Witiezslav.

'Only the identity of the provocateur has not been established,' Gesar said with a smile. 'The fact of his existence is in no doubt.'

Witiezslav nodded and turned to face his colleagues. For a few moments the Inquisitors shared their thoughts with each other without speaking. Then Witiezslav turned back to the four motion-less Finns.

'In the name of the Treaty. Bearing in mind the clement attitude of the Night Watch, the absence of any grave consequences and the other extenuating circumstances, the Inquisition offers you the right to choose your punishment. The first option – you are condemned to death by hanging but your civil rights will not be affected . . .'

The large young black man sighed heavily and the Chinese and the Finn seized his elbows and held him up.

'The second possible punishment is that from this day until the end of your lives you will be forbidden to use magic. You will have the right to live ordinary human lives, without using magical means to prolong or improve the quality of those lives.'

The Finns looked at the Inquisitor, stunned. Zabulon giggled shrilly, but immediately assumed a serious expression.

'The second . . . the second!' Yukha Mustaioki said in a choking voice. The others nodded.

'Does anyone present have any objections?' Witiezslav asked.

Gesar got to his feet again.

'As a small gesture of goodwill, we consider it acceptable to permit the accused to use magic . . . minor magic . . . with inan-imate objects.'

It seemed as if Gesar had to struggle to pronounce every word, that he was forcing himself to show mercy.

'For, example, to find some . . . small item . . . that has been lost . . . a key or a coin . . . To drive flies out of a room . . . according to the regulations, flies are regarded as inanimate, are they not? To clean the carburettor in a car . . .'

The vampire's face expressed faint surprise. 'He doesn't under-stand,' Edgar thought.

'The Inquisition has no objections,' the vampire said eventually. 'Apply the seals to the accused!'

Two Inquisitors raised their right hands, and fine threads of glimmering energy streamed through the air towards the accused. The seals were applied permanently, leaving the condemned prisoners capable of only the very weakest forms of magic. In all probability the Inquisitors really hadn't understood that Gesar's unexpected kindness had only made the punishment worse. It was one thing to be completely deprived of all magic and gradually to come to terms with life as a human being. It was quite different to feel every day that you were a helpless cripple who had to manage life with a pale shadow of your former powers.

But then, the Finns hadn't thought about that yet. They were led out of the hall, beside themselves with joy. Yukha kept trying to break away and start shaking everybody by the hand, but the vigilant guards forced him to walk out by nudging and shoving him.

Edgar shook his head. He actually felt quite glad that the Dark Brothers had been spared. But what a price to pay. He would probably have preferred a quick death.

'The next matter this hearing needs to consider has not been announced in advance,' said Witiezslav. 'The Inquisition requests the leader of the Night Watch of Moscow, known under the name of Gesar, to step into the circle of the accused.'

Zabulon smiled in triumph.

'And also the leader of the Day Watch of Moscow, known under the name of Zabulon.'

Edgar was delighted by Zabulon's slightly perplexed expression. But just how genuine was it?

'The Inquisition's first question is for the Great Magician Gesar.' Witiezslav was speaking politely now, but very firmly. 'Gesar, have you carried out interventions in the Book of Destiny of the Great Enchantress Svetlana Nazarova, here present, with the intention of compelling the said Great Enchantress to become the mother of a Light Messiah?'

The hall fell silent.

'Rephrase your question, Witiezslav,' Gesar said in a soft voice. 'Or I shall take offence.'

The vampire bared his teeth in a smile.

'Answer the substance of the point, Great Magician Gesar.'

'Very well,' said Gesar with a nod. 'I was not expecting these accusations, but . . . I will explain for the benefit of the Tribunal.'

'You were expecting them,' thought Edgar. 'You were expecting everything, you cunning old intriguer.'

'An intervention of that kind is impossible in principle. Even for me,' Gesar declared modestly.

Witiezslav seemed confused by that.

'But, Great Magician Gesar, Svetlana Nazarova's Book of Destiny—'

'Shows that she will become the mother of the greatest of all Light Enchantresses; in poetical terms, a Light Messiah.' Gesar smiled contentedly. 'This is a matter of great joy for the Night Watch of Moscow . . . and, indeed, for all Light Ones. But the respected Inquisition must understand that such things cannot be *written into* a Book of Destiny. Absolutely not. There is no way. Not even by using a certain artefact familiar to you, which belongs by right to the Night Watch.'

'But interventions were made in Svetlana Nazarova's Book of Destiny?' the vampire continued to insist.

'Yes,' Gesar said and nodded. 'As everybody, or almost everybody, knows, it is possible to make a new entry in a Book of Destiny, but it has a direct effect on the balance between Light and Dark. It is fairly simple to introduce trifling changes to the destiny of an ordinary human being. It is rather more difficult to make even insignificant changes to the destiny of an Other. And the more powerful that Other is, and the more serious the change, the greater the disturbance suffered by the Light and the Dark.

Respected members of the Tribunal, can you calculate the consequences that would ensue from introducing into a Great Enchantress's Book of Destiny an entry that would make her the mother of a messiah?'

No one replied.

'Any one of us . . . all the Others taken together, would be dematerialised if that kind of meddling were to be attempted. We'd be reduced to dust. The world would collapse. And you accuse me of committing such an act!'

'Light Magician Gesar, what changes *were* entered into Svetlana Nazarova's Book of Destiny?'

Gesar shrugged.

'Nothing but trivial details! I am obliged to be concerned for my colleagues' well-being, am I not? A trip to some Italian resort or other, a course of lessons in a driving school . . . and something else. I can present a detailed list, if you wish. There was nothing serious. Just the little pleasures of human life.'

Witiezslav thought for a moment and asked:

'Where were the new entries made? *Before* or *after* the entry about the birth of the greatest of all Light Enchantresses?'

'I think, *before*,' Gesar said with a smile.

'And in that way, you adjusted the time of the event.' Witiezslav was not asking a question, he was thinking out loud. 'You maximised the probability that Svetlana's future daughter would be a Messiah of the Light.'

'Possibly,' Gesar agreed. 'But what of that? All I did was to improve the daily life of one of my colleagues.'

'And could you not have used other methods to improve Svetlana Nazarova's living conditions? Free holidays, bonuses, friendly advice?'

Gesar looked genuinely offended now.

'I made use of what came to hand. The Inquisition has a right to be surprised if I hammer in nails with a microscope. But you cannot possibly charge me with that.'

The Inquisitors exchanged glances. This time the silent consultation lasted for almost a minute. Edgar felt a trickle of cold sweat running down his back. It would really cause a commotion if the Inquisition accused Gesar. The dematerialisation of a Great Magician was not such a simple proposition as dealing with the four Finns.

'Not cognisable,' Witiezslav said eventually. 'Great Magician Gesar, having heard your explanations, the Inquisition accepts that you have not violated the letter of the Treaty—'

'The letter or the spirit!' Gesar corrected him sharply.

'The letter or the spirit,' the vampire agreed in a voice that betrayed his frustration. 'However, your actions are still considered to be dubious and dangerous.'

'No more so than the attempt by the Day Watch of Moscow to eliminate Svetlana Nazarova shortly before her initiation,' Gesar snapped. 'Do you have any more questions for me?'

'No,' said Witiezslav. 'You may return to your seat.'

Throughout the questioning, Zabulon had stood modestly on the very edge of the circular grille. He didn't seem upset that no charges had been brought against Gesar. And that made Edgar feel uneasy.

'Dark Magician Zabulon, the Inquisition also has some questions for you,' said Witiezslav. 'Was the attack by the sect of the Regin Brothers provoked by you?'

'No one is obliged to testify against himself,' Zabulon said dully.

'Is that a confession?' the vampire asked in a lively tone.

'No, it is a reminder of the law. You have no right to ask such a question. Therefore I shall not answer it.'

'Very well. Your objection is accepted. Great Magician Zabulon, have you been planning, in order to oppose the future Messiah of the Light, to resurrect the Great Magician Fáfnir, who was consigned to the Twilight and dematerialised more than a thousand years ago?'

Zabulon began blinking rapidly and exclaimed in an astonished voice:

'Where did get you a nonsensical idea like that?'

'Did you act to prevent the initiation of Svetlana Nazarova and carry out other actions directed against her?'

'Yes, within the limits permitted by the Treaty,' Zabulon replied briskly.

'And Fáfnir?'

'What about Fáfnir?' said Zabulon. He looked at Edgar and winked.

'Why did you send to Prague a certain member of the Day Watch, ideally suited for participation in the rematerialisation of Fáfnir?'

'I have no idea what you're talking about.'

'Did you plan to exploit the following parallels: Fáfnir as the Antichrist, the four Regin Brothers as the four horses of the Apocalypse?'

Zabulon burst into laughter. He laughed and wheezed happily for a long time, the way someone might laugh if they pulled off a risky but very amusing hoax. Then he wiped away the tears that had sprung to his eyes and said in a calmer voice:

'I am delighted by the sense of humour demonstrated by the members of the Inquisition. Fáfnir was an insane psychopath, I actually knew him personally and there is nothing I would like less than to meet him again. In any case, he would hardly be suitable as a Messiah of Darkness. That's beyond his grade . . . Eliminating Svetlana, now . . .' Zabulon smiled. '. . . that's a possibility. But at such a price . . . oh, no, never. And as for those half-witted Finnish magicians, what did you say they were – the horses of the Apocalypse?'

Edgar felt like a total idiot. He looked imploringly at Witiezslav. But the vampire hadn't given up yet.

'Why did you carry out the following actions: arranging the death of Alisa Donnikova, which could be interpreted as a ritual sacrifice for rematerialisation, and ordering two portraits from a well-known Moscow artist – one of the Dark Magician Edgar and one of the dragon Fáfnir?'

Zabulon became more serious:

'I would also like to understand the circumstances of Alisa's death better. As I understand, it is to be the subject of the next inquiry. Well, and as for the portraits . . .'

The head of Moscow's Day Watch reached inside his jacket and took out two small framed pictures, each about twenty by thirty centimetres. Edgar was horrified to recognise one as a picture of himself. The other showed a dragon contorted by convulsions.

'This is a small Christmas present for one of my finest employees, please pardon an old man's sentimentality.'

And with that Zabulon took a step towards Edgar and held the portrait out to him. It was a good portrait, no two ways about it. But Edgar was only frightened even more by Zabulon's whisper:

'Smart boy.'

Zabulon returned to the circle.

'And the second picture?' Witiezslav asked.

'Pure sentimentality,' Zabulon repeated. 'Those Regin Brothers stirred up old feelings. I remembered Fáfnir and . . . decided to have a portrait of him made as a keepsake.'

'You were not planning to bring him back to life?' Witiezslav asked again. This time Zabulon answered very seriously and apparently with absolute sincerity.

'Not for a moment. There are less disruptive ways to achieve my goal.'

The Inquisitors exchanged glances.

'Great Magician Zabulon,' said Witiezslav, 'the Inquisition has no charges to bring against you, you may return to your seat. However, we remind you that taken all together your actions appear extremely ambiguous and dangerous.'

'I understand, I understand,' Zabulon muttered as he walked out of the circle. 'Soon it will be impossible to pick your nose without permission.'

Edgar looked at Gesar, expecting the old intriguer to be angry.

But no. Gesar wasn't angry. He even seemed to have taken a genuine interest in what Zabulon had said. That is, he had clearly been quite convinced that the head of the Dark Ones would wriggle out of everything, but he was interested in the details.

They'd both known all of this beforehand.

Edgar struggled desperately to gather his scattered thoughts. That meant Svetlana really was going to be the mother of a Messiah of the Light . . . and a female one – that was a surprise. Zabulon was resisting it, but . . . but not by creating an Antichrist in the flesh. That had only been a diversionary manoeuvre, one in which Edgar had behaved like a naïve child.

But then what was the most important point?

'The Inquisition now moves on to the consideration of the most important matter of the day, which is of exceptional significance to both the Light and the Dark,' said Witiezslav, as if he were answering the question that Edgar hadn't asked. 'The case of Igor Teplov, a third-grade magician of the Moscow Night Watch. Is everyone familiar with the materials of the case?'

Nobody said anything. Everybody had been familiar with the materials for a long time.

'I offer the prosecuting counsel, Anton Gorodetsky, the floor.'

The Light One was standing opposite Edgar. He raised his head and nodded curtly to Witiezslav.

'I shall be brief. In essence, our charges are simple – we accuse the respected magician Zabulon, here present, of deliberately sending Alisa Donnikova to the Artek camp, knowing that Igor Teplov would be there, restoring his powers. Zabulon had in all probability read the reality lines and realised that for Igor and Alisa those conditions would inevitably lead to . . . to love between them. A tragic and hopeless love, since the young people served different powers. A love that would end in a duel that would lead to the death of either Igor or Alisa, while the surviving opponent would be condemned by the Inquisition. We accuse Zabulon of the deliberate and cynical elimination – attempted elimination – of the Moscow Night Watch agent Igor Teplov. We therefore request the Inquisition to withdraw the charge brought against Igor Teplov of violating the Treaty and murdering Alisa Donnikova.'

'Is that all?' Witiezslav asked after a pause.

'No. We also request the court to consider the matter of the death of a young boy – who was not an Other – as a result of the duel. Insofar as the duel was arranged by Zabulon—'

'Objection!' Zabulon exclaimed in a high-pitched voice.

'Objection sustained,' the vampire ruled.

'Since we believe the duel to have been arranged by Zabulon, he is also guilty of the boy's death, for which Igor Teplov cannot be held guilty. That is all.'

Witiezslav turned his head to look at Zabulon.

'Can you reply to the essence of the matter?'

'There will be no answer, I have already explained the reason,' Zabulon replied coolly.

'I offer the floor to the counsel for the defence.'

Edgar sighed. And began.

'My colleague's speculations are all highly diverting. We are witnessing an attempt to shield a criminal—'

'Objection!' Anton put in quickly.

'To shield the accused,' said Edgar, correcting himself. 'Igor Teplov is guilty of the murder of the young witch Alisa Donnikova. And the worst aspect of the case is that he truly loved her. And worse still, in the grip of his maniacal passion, Igor Teplov incidentally caused the death of the boy Makar Kanevsky. He killed a child. A human child, who also had a right to live. And there is more. As a result of his extensive gathering of power from children on holiday at Artek, seven of them suffered from nightmares for three months. Two cases of persistent incontinence were recorded. Nine-year-old Yurik Semetsky, a resident of Moscow, died of asphyxiation a month after his return from Artek, when he drowned in his bath. We do not know as yet if this was a result of the actions of Igor Teplov . . . the Light Magician Igor Teplov.'

He looked at the accused. Igor's face was stony. Impervious. Expressionless.

'The Light Ones can put forward their groundless accusations as long as they wish,' said Edgar. 'Without any proof, without even any cogent explanation as to why the Day Watch of Moscow would sacrifice a young and promising member of its staff, one who had already received several commendations from the head of the Watch, in order to eliminate a third-grade Light Magician who possesses no real talent . . . That is a matter for their consciences. We only request the Inquisition to consider the situation impartially and punish the guilty party for violation of the Treaty.'

Edgar took a breath and added his final, decisive words:

'Much is said about how Light Magicians who commit some ethically unjustifiable act dematerialise themselves voluntarily. They withdraw into the Twilight under the burden of their shame. We have all heard of this. But I, for instance, have never actually observed it. No doubt Igor Teplov regards the murder of a girl who was in love with him, and likewise the death and suffering of innocent human children, as ethically irreproachable actions.'

He stopped speaking.

The Inquisitors exchanged glances. Then Witiezslav asked:

'Do the parties to the case have any proof that their assertions are correct?'

Gesar said nothing, but Zabulon asked in surprise:

'Pardon me, but what proof can I offer that I am not a camel? Let those who have uttered such nonsensical claims attempt to prove them.'

'The Inquisition has heard the opinions of both sides,' said the vampire. 'Accused, do you have anything to add?'

Igor Teplov nodded.

'Yes. I admit that my actions were not entirely justified . . . and I profoundly regret their consequences. I . . . I had . . .' He broke off, then started talking more quickly. 'I had very strong feelings for Alisa Donnikova. But when I learned she was a Dark Witch, it affected the balance of my mind. I do not ask for clemency. I have already condemned myself. But . . .'

He turned sharply towards Zabulon.

'You are the murderer! You sent Alisa to her death! And that is why I have to remain alive. I have to, so that you will not profit from your villainy!'

Zabulon merely shrugged and gave a heavy sigh.

'Do you have any proof?' the vampire asked.

Igor shook his head.

'The Tribunal is aware of the significance of this case,' said Witiezslav. 'Although neither side has adduced any evidence, the Inquisition considers it important to determine who is genuinely the guilty party. Therefore . . .'

Edgar suddenly saw Zabulon's expression change: his face froze halfway through a sad smile.

'Therefore the Inquisition will continue to question witnesses. Alisa Donnikova will be temporarily rematerialised.'

'Objection!' said Zabulon, rising to his feet. 'This case is not important enough to disturb the peace of the departed!'

'Objection overruled. The Inquisition requests Anna Lemesheva, who has attended on the Inquisition's instructions, to advance to the centre of the hall. Her body will be used for the temporary rematerialisation of Alisa Donnikova.'

Lemesheva began to squeal. But a moment later two young Inquisitors were already leading her, twitching weakly, out into the centre of the hall.

'The expenditure of energy in this process will be borne by the Night Watch of Moscow and it will not be reimbursed regardless of the outcome of the trial,' Witiezslav continued. 'Great Magician Gesar, do you possess the required reserves of power?'

'Yes,' said Gesar, getting to his feet. 'I do.'

Edgar felt he was completely losing the thread of events. What was so important about this Igor Teplov that Zabulon would sacrifice his lover for him and Gesar would expend such a colossal amount of power?

'Proceed with the rematerialisation,' said Witiezslav. 'Any attempt to hinder it is punishable by immediate death.'

Several of the Inquisitors moved forward slightly and Gesar sighed and stepped towards Lemesheva. She squealed again, and then fell silent, staring at the Light Magician with glazed eyes.

And then Edgar had to squeeze his own eyes shut.

There was such a vast amount of energy raging in the centre of the hall that he simply couldn't look. He sensed the Inquisitors erecting magical barriers around Gesar and Lemesheva, one after another. He sensed the barriers crumbling under the pressure of unimaginable power. And he felt the Twilight shudder as it was torn open through all the levels that Edgar knew and those he had never even suspected existed. If this was temporary rematerialisation, then what must a permanent rematerialisation be like?

The storm died away. Gesar slowly stepped backwards.

Three figures remained in the centre of the hall – the Inquisitor Witiezslav, the Light Magician Igor Teplov and the Dark Witch Alisa Donnikova.

Alisa was trembling, coughing and clutching at her throat.

Edgar shuddered. He didn't know what happened to Others there . . . in the Twilight. And he didn't really want to know, if he were quite honest. But Alisa had just recovered consciousness at the moment when her human life had come to an end. She had come back to life with a searing pain in her lungs, still choking on sea water, struggling desperately against the pressure that Teplov had brought down on her.

'Alisa Donnikova,' the vampire began. Even his voice trembled – temporary rematerialisation was an infrequent procedure, highly infrequent. '. . . you have been temporarily rematerialised and are now on the premises of the European Tribunal of the Inquisition in Prague. Do you understand me?'

Alisa Donnikova straightened up, already controlling her wheezing. She was looking at Igor Teplov. And at nobody else.

'Do you understand me?' Witiezslav repeated.

'Why . . . in Prague?' Alisa asked. She was taking rapid, deep breaths, as if she simply couldn't get enough air – even the damp air of this dungeon.

'That is not important, Alisa Donnikova. You have been summoned to our world as a witness. A great deal depends on what you say.'

'Can . . . can I stay here? Again? For ever?' Alisa asked.

But she was looking only at Igor.

'No,' the Inquisitor replied honestly. 'Will you answer my questions voluntarily?'

Alisa shook her head to and fro. With a strange, desperate pride.

'Yes, I will, Inquisitor. Ask.'

But she was looking only at Igor.

'The questions concern your duel with the Light Magician Igor Teplov, here present. Was the challenge to the duel made in accordance with all the rules?'

'Yes.'

'Tell me, Alisa, do you accuse Igor Teplov of your death?'

Alisa smiled. She gestured with her hand – without turning round, but unerringly indicating Zabulon.

'No.'

Still she was looking only at Igor.

'Do you have any charges to bring against your . . . opponent?'

She only shook her head.

'Alisa Donnikova, can you accuse anybody who is present here of provoking the sad events that led to your death?'

'Zabulon,' Alisa said in an entirely indifferent voice. 'It was his operation.'

'You cowardly fool!' Zabulon shouted. 'They won't rematerialise you anyway! What are you doing, witch?'

It was only then that Alisa Donnikova turned towards Zabulon. And under her gaze the leader of the Dark Ones fell silent.

'Zabulon, have you forgotten what you said to me when I appealed to you as I was drowning?'

'Stupid, vengeful little fool,' Zabulon said in a calmer voice.

Alisa shook her head. She looked at Igor again and said in a strange, mocking tone:

'What has vengeance got to do with it? Love is also a great power, Zabulon.'

'The Inquisition has no further questions,' Witiezslav said quickly.

'Gentlemen, I think to continue with this scene ... would be unworthy of Others. The charge against Igor Teplov of violating the Treaty is dismissed. Alisa Donnikova can ... can go back now.'

Edgar seemed to be watching in a dream as Gesar got to his feet. The triumphant, victorious Gesar. With Zabulon hunched over on his bench ... the defeated Zabulon.

It was only when the faces of the Great Magicians suddenly trembled in surprise and confusion that he looked back at the centre of the hall.

Alisa Donnikova was disappearing. Her body was changing, sinking into the Twilight as a pale, insubstantial shadow. Lemesheva was crawling on all fours towards Zabulon's feet.

But Igor Teplov was also disappearing.

Withdrawing into the Twilight.

Edgar hadn't lied. This really was the first time he had seen a Light Magician dematerialise. Voluntarily. Without any struggle or protest or streams of power.

Just for one moment Igor Teplov, already transformed into an almost insubstantial shadow, turned to glance at his comrades. With a glance that looked guilty. But otherwise, he looked only at Alisa.

Then he disappeared.

The Twilight closed up. The air in the hall was icy; white, bristling hoarfrost clung to the walls like a shroud of mourning. The triumphant smile slowly returned to Zabulon's face. Gesar gazed at the empty circular grille with a weary, sad expression.

'Well?' Zabulon cried. 'Well? You see? Now where's your mentor? Where is he, the only one who was capable of *educating* the Messiah of the Light?'

He laughed and patted Lemesheva's head – she was standing on her knees in front of him. Then he turned to the Inquisition and said:

'Yes, it was a Day Watch operation. Within the limits of the Treaty. The exchange of two equal pieces – Alisa Donnikova for Igor Teplov. Do you have any more charges to bring against us?'

'The Inquisition has no charges to bring against you,' the vampire said slowly. He rubbed his face with his hand. 'In view of all the circumstances, the Inquisition will consider the question of the early restoration of Svetlana Nazarova's power. But that . . . will be later. Everyone . . . everyone may leave the hall.'

Svetlana was the first to rise from her seat. She walked up to Zabulon and stood for a second, looking into his face. Edgar suddenly realised with a sinking heart that the enchantress was going to strike the magician.

But all she did was say something to him. Then she turned away and walked out abruptly.

Edgar's legs felt stiff and awkward as he left his desk. He almost bumped into Gesar, who was musing sadly, engrossed in his own thoughts. Anton immediately came up to Gesar, pushing Edgar aside. He exclaimed:

'So what does this mean – Svetlana's daughter can be an Other, but not grow up to be the Messiah of the Light?'

Gesar nodded.

'Why?' Anton asked stupidly. 'Surely Svetlana herself . . .'

'Being a Great Enchantress and raising a Great Enchantress are two quite different things,' Gesar said wearily. 'Alas. I . . . so far I can't see anyone else to match Igor. I . . . I didn't know how much he loved that witch! I would have looked for some other way.'

'Whose daughter will it be?' Anton suddenly asked. 'Svetlana's and . . .'

'Whose? If you stop standing there like a fool, gawping at an old idiot, and go after your wife – it will be yours!'

Anton gave a feeble nod. And dashed out of the hall. Edgar also wanted to ask Gesar a couple of questions, but he caught the Light

One's glance and decided not to risk it. He turned away and stepped onto the narrow grey Inquisitors' wedge that jutted out between the black and white halves of the hall.

The Inquisitors were already pulling off their robes. One of them casually tossed his into Witiezslav's arms, opened a portal and disappeared. The others left the more usual way, through the door.

The vampire looked at Edgar and asked:

'Want to try it on?'

'I'm not sure the cut will suit me,' Edgar replied quietly.

'Who knows? But it's worth a try. Or are you intending to go back to Moscow?'

Edgar carefully took the crumpled grey material out of the vampire's hands. He asked awkwardly:

'I beg your pardon . . . but what was it that Svetlana said to Zabulon?'

'An Inquisitor has to have good hearing.' A crooked grin appeared on the vampire's face. 'Almost nothing at all. I'd call it a curse, but the Light Ones don't even know how to curse properly. She said: "May no one ever love you."'

Edgar nodded. He shrugged and said:

'He doesn't need anyone to, anyway.'

This book includes excerpts from songs by Vladimir Vysotsky, Yury Burkin, Kipelov, and the bands Aria, Voskresenie and Nautilus Pompilius.

Moscow – Nikolaev – Lazurnoe

June – October 1999

ALSO AVAILABLE IN WILLIAM HEINEMANN

# *The Twilight Watch*

## Sergei Lukyanenko

### THIRD BOOK IN THE NIGHT WATCH TRILOGY

It's high summer in Moscow. With wife Svetlana and daughter Nadya still away, spending the summer on a dacha not far from Moscow, Night Watch Agent Anton Gorodetsky is trying to enjoy his last day off. But when a call comes in from Gesar – his Boss and Night Watch head – requesting a private meeting, it quickly becomes clear he's going back to work early . . .

Gesar has received an anonymous note, stating that an Other has revealed the full truth about their kind to a human, and now intends to do the supposedly impossible: convert that human into an Other. Even more worryingly, the note has been sent to Zabulon head of the Day Watch, and to the Inquisition's offices in Berne – and only the very highest-level Others know the address . . .

'One of the most original and readable supernatural fictions in some time.' *Scotland on Sunday*

'JK Rowling, Russian style . . . [A] cracking read, owing more to Rowling or Philip Pullman than it does to the horror genre . . . Readable and addictive' *Daily Telegraph*

William Heinemann : London